STACY M. JONES

Miami Ripper

First edition

ISBN: 978-0-578-94322-0

This book was professionally typeset on Reedsy.
Find out more at reedsy.com

For Gladys - thanks for all the stories

Acknowledgement

Miami Ripper took a great deal of research as I knew nothing about the world of high-priced escorts and sugar baby relationships. I appreciate the women – Annie, Rachel and Laura – who were willing to speak to me so candidly, and to Gladys, the real Fanny Fontaine, who spent countless hours with me on the phone telling me stories and helping me get the story right.

Thank you also to the detectives, special agents, and forensics teams I've had the pleasure of working with through the years and the knowledge and expertise you have shared with me. Special thanks to 17 Studio Book Design for bringing my stories to life with amazing covers. Thank you to Dj Hendrickson for your insightful editing and Liza Wood for proofreading and revisions.

Thank you to my readers who enjoy these stories and were excited about this series as much as I was writing it. Your messages are a constant sense of encouragement.

CHAPTER 1

FBI Special Agent Kate Walsh pressed her foot down on the gas pedal of the cherry red BMW Z4 convertible and let her dark hair flow in the wind. She gripped the steering wheel with two hands and basked in the bright Miami sunshine. It was a drastic change from the wintery weather she left behind in Boston. She'd traded a winter coat for short sleeves and sunglasses. Had she not been in the middle of a criminal case, Kate would have also ditched her basic flats for sandals.

Normally, Kate hated driving. It was one of the only times in life her temper got the better of her. She spent most of the time amped up, stressed, and agitated. Most days, Kate would do just about anything to make her partner, Special Agent Declan James, drive.

At the airport, when the attendant at the rental place pushed up his glasses and informed them that they were out of the basic four-door sedans the FBI normally rented, Kate and Declan shared an annoyed look. Declan had pointed to the badge on his chest and told the guy they weren't leaving without a car. The attendant bent his head low and jammed his fingers into the keyboard then glanced up at the screen and mumbled to himself. He repeated the ritual three more times until he finally broke into a wide grin. He assured them he had the perfect car available to make up for the inconvenience.

When they had reached the parking lot and saw the car they would

1

be renting, Kate couldn't help but want to be behind the wheel. She had snatched the keys out of Declan's hand and slid into the driver's seat, giving him no time to protest.

It might be the only enjoyment she had for a while and she wasn't letting the opportunity pass. Kate and Declan had been called from Boston to Miami to help investigate a case that the newspapers were calling the Miami Ripper. A serial killer had killed eight women, all high-priced escorts in the Miami Beach area, over the last several months. Their bodies were found in mansions that were for sale. The owners had already moved, leaving each mansion professionally staged for buyers. The killer had empty homes where he could do whatever he pleased and so he did.

Like the furniture, the victims were found staged, sitting upright in bed with their backs against headboards and propped up by pillows. Their hearts had been cut from their bodies and had been placed in the bedroom – sometimes on a dresser or nightstand and once on a bookshelf.

In all of the cases, it was real estate agents who found the victims. It sent them screaming from the mansions horrified at the sight. The victims were found on weekends when real estate agents were prepping houses for showings. By all accounts, the real estate agents found the mansions locked with no signs of forced entry. As far as they or the local detectives assigned to the cases could tell, no one had forced their way in. No one understood how the killer had gained access.

The first case had garnered significant local media attention, but once the victim had been identified as a high-priced escort, the media attention dropped off. When the second victim was found and horrific details of the crime scenes revealed, the media started asking questions. It was the third victim that caused locals to start wondering if there was a serial killer in their community. While the local detectives did their best to investigate each case, by the fourth body, they knew a serial killer lurked among the rich and famous.

After the sixth victim, there had been a formal request to the FBI field office in Miami for help. When the local FBI agents got involved and looked over crime scene photos, they requested Kate. She and Declan were part of a specialized unit within the FBI. It was made of elite agents with specialized skills.

Kate's expertise was in old school FBI-style criminal profiling and interrogation. She relied on a mix of instinct, forensic linguistics, and criminal psychology. Declan's ability to read a crime scene remained unparalleled. He could spot a button out of place on a blouse in a closet from across the room. They had been paired up since they graduated from Quantico together.

There were times Kate would be farmed out to other government agencies and Declan would handle field work in Boston while he waited for her return. For the most part, the two bounced around the country consulting on challenging cases no one else could solve.

The Miami Ripper case was one of them.

As Kate pulled into the fast lane to go around a slower-moving SUV, Declan gave her a side-eyed look and grinned. "You're speeding."

"I know! It's great!" Kate giggled and tapped the gas pedal harder.

When Declan cleared his throat in protest, she eased off the gas and moved back into the slow lane. She admitted, "Probably not a great first impression if I get a speeding ticket."

"No one is going to give you a speeding ticket, but you are on an unfamiliar road and not the best driver. I'd like to arrive alive," he teased.

Kate ignored the insult about her driving, mostly because it was true, and clicked her tongue. "Unlike you, I don't flash my FBI badge to get out of trouble."

Declan laughed. "You never get in trouble."

"This is true." Kate pressed a few buttons on the car's GPS. Her exit was right down the road. They had taken I-95 from the airport and needed to turn on 195 to go over Biscayne Bay to N. Bay Road. They were meeting two detectives at the last murder scene. Kate and Declan wanted a walk-through of the scene and to get a feel for the place before they did anything else.

They were staying in Miami Beach at the Eden Roc Hotel. They had been surprised to have such luxury accommodations, but Martin Spade, the FBI supervisor in charge of their unit, had been adamant that they blend into the rich Miami scene. His only advice to them was to try not to look like FBI agents.

Kate and Declan had ditched their normal dull suits for upscale beach attire. Declan had on a pair of pressed tan Chinos and a sea-green linen shirt with the cuffs rolled up. Kate had opted for simple white linen pants and a blue shirt. It would have been reasonable that someone mistook them for a couple on vacation – except for the guns on their hips and badges on chains tucked into their shirts.

Kate took her eyes off the road and glanced at him. "Grab the file from the back and let me know the names of the detectives we are meeting."

Declan reached into the backseat and pulled out the manila file folder. He flipped it open and scanned down the first report. "Det. Ted Baer and Det. Isabel Navarro. They are both senior homicide detectives. Det. Navarro is Cuban-born and Det. Baer is from West Palm Beach. Navarro has been with the Miami-Dade police force for fifteen years and Baer close to twenty-five. They have a good homicide closure rate."

Kate liked that they had experience. "Either of them ever worked a serial homicide before?"

Declan flipped a few more pages. "Not that I can see here in what Spade sent us. They were smart enough to know to call the FBI. That's more than we can say for most local police departments."

That was true enough. Kate hated when Spade decided they should be involved in a case rather than being called in by a local police force. She looked over at Declan again. "Tell me about the last victim."

"Chloe Reed, twenty-eight. She was a graduate student at the University of Miami. From what Spade could find, she pulled in close to fifty grand a month. It doesn't look like she was working as an escort at the time of her murder though. She was involved with a rich older man."

"Are you sure that's what it says? Fifty grand a month?" Kate asked, her voice rising an octave. "Who makes fifty grand a month as an escort?"

Declan lowered his head to look at the paper a second time. "That's what it says. Miami Beach is filled with millionaires, many of them older and retired. Some of these women are raking in twenty-five grand for a two-day date. If an escort does that twice a month for different clients or the same, you have your fifty grand."

He closed the file and looked over at Kate. "You're not talking about your average sex worker, Kate. These girls are college-educated and are there for companionship as much as for sex. They probably have regular clients, too."

"What was Chloe getting her graduate degree in?"

"She was a pre-doctoral candidate in neurobiology."

Kate whistled. "Were all the other victims in a similar situation?"

"For the most part. There is one woman who was an attorney. According to the statement in the file from Det. Baer, the attorney was working as an escort to pay off her student loans."

Kate changed lanes and glanced at the GPS. Three more miles to go. "How did it work? Were all the women connected to the same madam or pimp?"

Declan snickered at her. "I don't think women like this have pimps."

Kate shrugged. "I haven't worked many cases with high-priced escorts. If we have serial killers targeting sex workers, it's typically been vulnerable women working on the streets or previously off Craigslist before they shut down those sections of the website. I'm going to need to get up to speed on how the killer is connecting with these victims."

Declan grumbled as he looked out the window. "Spade didn't have many details. It's good we are meeting the detectives first. I'm not sure if the killer is connecting with the victims through their profession or he's targeting them another way, but it's certainly part of their victim profile."

Kate turned onto N. Bay Road and her eyes shifted back and forth at the luxury surrounding them. No stranger to wealth, when Kate's parents were killed when she was still in college, they had left her a sizable estate including her brownstone in Boston that was worth millions. She didn't have to work at the FBI or anywhere for that matter. This was next-level wealth though.

Declan whistled long and loud. "You figure these men have to have money if they are dropping twenty-five grand on two nights with a woman. My first dates used to be going out for ice cream."

"Your dates weren't escorts." Kate paused. "I keep calling them escorts. Is that what they are called?"

"Call girls or escort I think is fine."

"I assume they are calling the killer the Miami Ripper because they are escorts and have had body parts removed like Jack the Ripper."

"I would assume so." Declan reached for his phone. He pulled up an article and flashed the screen to Kate even though she couldn't read it while driving. He read the headline and then a little of the article to her. "Just like Jack the Ripper, there is speculation that this killer might be a doctor given the surgical precision of how the victims' hearts have been cut out."

Kate turned off the main road into a driveway. Her stomach tensed the way it did whenever they were about to enter a crime scene. She clicked the intercom to be let into the grounds. A few seconds later, the wrought iron gates slid open.

"The victims were strangled, right? That was the cause of death in each homicide."

"That's what the file says. Why?" Declan asked.

"That's another similarity to Jack the Ripper. The neck. Jack the Ripper sliced their necks and this killer strangles, which some would say is more personal. Certainly takes more time."

Declan agreed. "This killer had all the time he needed. He wasn't in a rush."

CHAPTER 2

K ate parked the car next to a Miami-Dade Police Department cruiser. "Are the detectives with Miami-Dade or the local Miami Beach police?"

"Miami-Dade. The Miami Beach police haven't had more than ten homicides in a year going back several years. Most years, it was less than five," Declan explained, unbuckling his seat belt. "They formed a task force and it was decided, given the nature of the cases, that two senior Miami-Dade homicide detectives would take over."

Kate took one last look in the rearview mirror and swiped gloss across her lips and straightened the flyaway hairs that framed her face. She gathered her things and met Declan at the door.

Before they even had a chance to knock, a tall, tanned man pulled the door open. He extended his hand to Kate and then to Declan. "Agent Walsh. Agent James. I'm Det. Ted Baer, but please just call me Ted. We are going to be spending a good deal of time together so let's drop the formalities quickly."

"Agreed. Kate and Declan are fine," Declan said. "Ted, is Det. Isabel Navarro with you? We saw her name mentioned in our notes."

"Isa, which is what she goes by, is upstairs." Ted turned and led them into the mansion.

Kate couldn't help but look up. The home featured a two-story rotunda-style foyer with a massive, wide spiral staircase and a domed ceiling complete with a circular skylight. "How large is the home?"

Ted turned to Kate. "It's an 11,000-square-foot waterfront home with bay views and has six bedrooms and nine bathrooms. Nothing in the home was disturbed other than the master bedroom."

"Should we wear booties and gloves?" Declan asked, looking around for supplies. They had brought extras with them but had left them in the car.

Ted shook his head. "Crime scene techs have already been through and collected evidence. The real estate agent has cleaners coming in day after tomorrow to clean and resume her showings."

Kate shared the same disgusted look as Declan. "It's been barely two weeks since the murder."

"It's a twenty-three-million-dollar home. The owner doesn't care. He wants it back on the market now."

Kate simply nodded because she didn't know what else to say. Not only couldn't she understand selling the home that quickly after a brutal murder had occurred in it, but she also couldn't imagine someone would want to buy it. It seemed the detective had read the look on Kate's face.

"With the murder, it's only gone up in value." Ted frowned. "I don't get it, but then again I don't have the kind of money to buy a house like this so it's a different mentality, I guess."

Ted led them to the staircase and then climbed to the second floor. He turned to speak to them as he went. "We assume that the victim was alive when the killer brought her in. Maybe he played it off like this was his home. We aren't sure. There was no blood or disturbances anywhere else in the home other than the master bedroom and even that wasn't what we expected."

"What do you mean?" Declan asked, trailing behind Kate. She had noticed him taking in every nuance of the home. He always saw things others missed.

Ted pointed to a room at the end of the hall. "Just go in and see. I don't want to color your first impression with my opinion. The room hasn't been cleaned since the victim was found. The crime scene techs collected evidence but that's about it. It's exactly how we found it. We were on scene about thirty minutes after the real estate agent called 911."

The bedroom door was open and Kate stepped in followed by Declan. Det. Navarro stood at the far end of the room, looking out the window. She had the blinds pulled apart with her fingers and she held her gaze on something outside.

Kate walked over and stopped a few feet from her. "Det. Navarro, I'm FBI Special Agent Kate Walsh and this is Special Agent Declan James. Please, call us by our first names. Ted mentioned you like to be called Isa. Is that okay with you?"

The woman with long dark hair tied in a ponytail at the nape of her neck turned around. She blinked twice like she was surprised to see them standing there and then regained her composure quickly. She smiled and stepped toward Kate and shook her hand "Yes, that's fine for me. No one other than my mother called me Isabel."

"Isa it is then." Kate stepped back and took in the scene. The king-size bed had a plush gray headboard and two end tables next to it. The furniture was off-white and a chaise was positioned against a far wall. It had bright purple pillows on it. Kate imagined the bedding, before it had been taken in for processing, had probably reflected the feminine feel of the room.

A red stain had been left on the right side of the mattress. It was about the size of a basketball but not quite so uniformly shaped. Kate assumed it was the spot where the victim had been propped up. Directly across from the foot of the bed there was a dresser that had blood smears on the top. The heart had been placed there.

"She looked like she was staring at her heart from across the room,"

Isa said, following Kate's movements. "Sick if you ask me. What kind of creep does that?"

Kate had no answer, right now at least. She walked toward the bed for a closer look. Before reaching it, she stopped and retraced her steps with her eyes. She turned her head to Ted and then to Isa. "Where is all the blood evidence?"

Isa stood with her hands on her hips. "That's what we've asked ourselves at every crime scene."

Declan raised his eyebrows. "They all look as clean as this?"

"That's why we wanted to meet you here," Ted said, sweeping his hand in front of him in a gesture toward the state of the room. "This is exactly how we found the place. The only difference is the victim was sitting up against the headboard, with her arms propped up by pillows on each side. She had her dress on so you couldn't readily see the gaping hole in her chest, but there was blood stained on the front. She had bruising around her neck. The killer had even tucked her in. She sat there with the covers neatly pulled up to her waist. There was no blood on the floor or anywhere else around the room. Blood evidence was only found in two spots – there in the bed and on the dresser. The crime scene techs did a luminol test and there was nothing else."

"Do you suspect he killed her someplace else?" Kate asked.

Ted shook his head. "We think he killed her here. I just have no idea why there is no blood."

"Why here?" Declan asked. His expression told Kate he already knew the answer.

"If he had carried her in or dragged her, we assumed there'd be blood spatter in the foyer and up the stairs. The victim is close to five-foot-eight. While thin, she has an athletic build. Carrying that much dead weight would be a challenge for most men. The chance of leaving trace evidence would be great, and we found none."

Declan pointed toward the bed. "How much blood was on the sheets? By the stain on the mattress, it doesn't look like it was much. Not enough to account for her heart being removed."

Isa glanced over at him. "You're correct on that. The blood on the sheets was about what you're seeing on the mattress. It soaked right through."

Declan motioned for everyone to stand back as he assessed the space around them. This is what he did. It was almost as if he could see the scene unfolding in front of him. While Kate could tap into the killer's state of mind and motivation, Declan could see the actions of the killer based on the evidence at the scene.

Kate never pressured him while he did his thing. Sometimes it annoyed other FBI agents and local cops because they didn't understand his quiet focus. When Declan zeroed in on what made sense for a scene, he'd nod his head once as if accepting the information himself. Kate always waited for that moment, sometimes not even realizing she had been holding her breath.

After a few minutes, when the air in the room had grown tense from the silence, Declan gave the nod. "I believe the killer is bringing supplies in with him beforehand. He's meticulous about his work. I would assume he'd scope out the location first and then come in alone with plastic and his tools. Then he cleans up after himself."

Isa looked to Declan and then to Kate. "You got all that from a clean crime scene?"

Declan locked eyes with Kate. She knew the look. He wanted her to confirm she believed he was on the right track based on the psychological profile of the killer. She had told him over and over again, it wasn't magic. She wasn't a psychic. It didn't come together that easy for her as a crime scene did for him. This time, she didn't have a hard time agreeing with him.

The clean crime scene. The way the killer left the victim. The coldness of a home not currently lived in. It spoke to her.

Kate motioned with her hands as she spoke. "This is preliminary and based only on this crime scene so don't take this as gospel, but what Declan is saying fits the psychological profile of this killer. He seems fastidious so he's cleaning up after his mess. He also wants to take his time. What better way to do that than in an empty house with no threat that anyone will be along at night to disturb him. This isn't frenzied. It's not a thrill kill. He's measured and practiced."

Isa rubbed her chin. "You believe this happens at night then?"

Kate realized she thought that had been a fact. "I thought I had read in the file that these murders happen at night or at least in the evening."

"We believe so, based on the known whereabouts of the victim before the murder," Ted explained.

Kate wasn't sure if Isa had been testing her or genuinely wanted to know if she had an alternative theory. "Given when the bodies were found, I'd assume he'd kill when he had the most time with the victims. During the day, a real estate agent could easily bring buyers through. At night, he'd have the place to himself. Removing a victim's heart would take skill, planning, and considerable time, depending on how clean the wound was."

Kate looked to Isa to see if she'd provide more information. The woman said nothing.

Declan caught the exchange between them. "Is there anything else we need to know right now?" he asked, looking at Ted and Isa. Both shook their heads. "I think Kate and I will check into the hotel then and get a further read-in before we take the next steps."

Ted gestured toward the door, but Isa called them back. "I think we need to go to Blue Note this evening and scope out the place."

"Blue Note?" Kate asked.

"It was the last place four of the eight victims were seen alive. It has a bit of a sugar baby vibe to it. We believe some of the women are picking up their clients there."

"Sugar baby?" Kate asked. She couldn't place the term although she had heard it before.

Isa rolled her eyes. "Young women who date older men for money. Sex and company are exchanged."

"What time should we meet?"

"Nine should be good," Isa said, not looking at her. "I'm sure it might be difficult for you, but make sure you dress for the occasion."

CHAPTER 3

The Eden Roc Hotel was a luxury rarely afforded on an FBI criminal case. It made Kate suspicious about what Spade had in store for them. Unless Kate booked something on her own when they traveled, they were normally provided a basic hotel with the federal government rate. No frills. Certainly nothing like the lobby that they stood in now.

As Kate waited while Declan checked them in, her eyes shifted over the spacious lobby and hotel bar that was a feast for the senses. Eight floor-to-ceiling gold columns surrounded the circular bar. A chandelier of crystal drops too many to count hung above. The plush lobby furniture welcomed guests and invited them to sit for a while rather than rush to their rooms. The rest of the hotel had the same air of luxury.

Declan walked toward her and handed her the room key. "Spade sprung for one room. We have separate beds though."

"I should hope so." She laughed. "The last time we had to share a bed in that terrible motel in Montana you kicked me all night long."

Declan grinned. "I wanted to cuddle. You weren't having any of it. Revenge kicks."

They made their way to their room on the fifth floor and once inside started to unpack. They had just enough time to get ready for the evening, grab a bite for dinner, and meet Isa and Ted at nine. Declan

15

made quick work of pulling out clothes for the evening, but Kate stared at her suitcase trying to temper the rumble in her stomach.

She glanced up at Declan with her eyes squinted and worry lines making deep tracks across her forehead. "What do you think Isa meant by dress for the occasion?"

Declan raised his head from the pants he was ironing. "Sexy dress."

Kate grimaced. "I don't have a sexy dress. Since when do FBI agents have to wear sexy dresses?"

"Undercover. Trying not to stick out like a sore thumb." Declan set the iron down and walked over to Kate and peered down at the outfits she had on the bed. "None of this will do." He held out his hand. "Give me your credit card."

"For what?"

"Something appropriate to wear. There's a women's clothing shop downstairs. I'll find you the perfect dress." Kate shook her head but Declan insisted. "Katie, Miami Beach is more my scene than yours. Trust me for once."

Kate hesitated for a moment but then relented. She went to her purse and pulled out her credit card. "Don't choose something too outrageous. I still have to carry my gun."

Declan waved her card in the air as he left the room. "I know what I'm doing!"

Kate headed for the shower and tried not to think about what Declan was going to come back with. The hot water beating down on her calmed her nerves for a few minutes and the knots in her shoulders relaxed. She hated turning off the water but didn't want to be late. She stepped out of the shower and wrapped herself in a plush towel.

"Declan! Are you back?" she called from the bathroom.

There was no response so Kate dried herself and slipped on one of the hotel bathrobes. She stood in front of the mirror and ran a comb through her hair and applied her makeup. She called for him again and there was no response so she spent time styling her hair, trying to ignore the anxiety that ramped up inside her. Just when Kate thought she couldn't take the anticipation any longer, Declan called out to her.

Kate opened the bathroom door and saw the dress on the hanger before she saw him. The plum-colored dress had a low-cut V-shape neckline and on her would come to mid-thigh. She stared at it unsure how she was feeling.

He lowered the dress. "What do you think?"

She held her hand out pointing at it. "I can't wear that to a meeting with detectives about a serial homicide."

He thrust it toward her. "Yes, you can and you are. I sweet-talked the woman downstairs and got you the dress, shoes, and handbag all for under a thousand dollars." He handed her the other bag he had in his hand. "Hurry up so we can get some dinner."

Kate bit her lip and took the dress and the bag but didn't say a word to him. She closed the door in Declan's face. She hung the dress on the back of the door and stared at it for a few moments before she slipped off the robe and dressed.

By the time she slipped on the stilettos, confidence brewed in Kate like she hadn't felt in a while. She admired her figure in the full-length mirror. The dress was short and it showed off far too much of her muscular thigh. Her cleavage was high and pushed forward. It made her look like she had more on top than she had been blessed with but she wasn't going to complain. This was Miami Beach and she needed to blend into the South Beach scene. Kate slipped her cellphone, gun, and badge into the clutch.

Kate took one last look in the mirror and pulled the door open. She stepped out into the main part of the room holding her breath. She walked to where Declan could see her and held her arms out at her sides. "What do you think?"

He whistled and then smiled. "I don't think I can appropriately comment. It might ruin our friendship." He motioned with his head toward the door. "Let's go. I made a reservation for dinner downstairs at Nobu."

Kate raised her eyebrows. "We are living large on this trip."

"They owe us," Declan said with a wink. "Our goal tonight is to look like a normal couple out for the evening." He playfully roamed his eyes up and down Kate one more time. "I think we can manage it."

Declan put his hand on her back as they walked out of the room, down the hall, and to the elevator. Once downstairs, the restaurant seated them immediately. The service was more than they could have asked for.

Over dinner, Declan stopped eating long enough to raise his head. "I think I made a mistake with that dress. Our goal was to blend in, but you have every man turning their head."

"I know," Kate said, her cheeks flushing. "It's been a long time since I felt attention like this. Maybe we can use it to our advantage."

"Maybe, but I'm keeping you close." Declan looked around the restaurant and then leaned into the table. "Did you think Isa was a bit odd?"

"You noticed it, too. She made me uncomfortable but I can't explain why."

Declan finished the last bite of his sushi and then leaned back. "I thought maybe she was intimidated by you, but then I wasn't so sure. It was almost like she didn't trust that you'd be able to help. They requested us. I figured they'd be happy we were here."

"It could have been Ted who wanted us here and strong-armed Isa to agree. Maybe she feels like we are going to take the case away from them. You know local cops get territorial."

Declan shook his head. "There's something else going on with her. Let's try to figure it out tonight and get it out of the way. We don't want animosity brewing. It will distract from the case."

The server came over and Declan paid the check. He told Kate that Blue Note was on the same side of the street as their hotel and about three-quarters of a mile down the road. "Are you okay walking that far in those heels?"

Kate got up from the table and smoothed down her dress. "It's not my first time in heels, Declan. By the way, how did you know my dress and shoe size? You chose perfectly."

Declan winked at her. "We've worked together all these years. I know everything about you, Katie."

No one called her Katie except Declan and she had long ago stopped trying to fight him on it. As they left the restaurant, exited the hotel, and headed down the street, all eyes turned to look at Kate. Men smiled and even women appraised her with a smile. Declan was right. Instead of blending in, Kate stood out. The anxiety had long since left her and she walked with an added sway to her hips.

Ted and Isa were waiting for them on the sidewalk in front of Blue Note. Ted had dressed similarly to Declan in linen tan pants and a pastel buttoned shirt. Isa had on a dress to rival Kate's.

As Kate and Declan approached, Isa looked her up and down and tsked. "At least you dressed to fit in."

Kate stepped toward her. She knew Declan hadn't meant an all-out confrontation, but if that's what Isa wanted, that's what she'd get. Kate narrowed her eyes. "If you have a problem with me, I think we should get it out in the open. You're behaving strangely for a detective who called the FBI for assistance."

"I didn't call for you," Isa said. Ted tried to stop her from saying anything else, but she kept going. "We called for FBI agents who know what they are doing. Not a profiler into some pseudoscience bull who is going to wait in the wings and not get her hands dirty."

"Is that what you think I do?" Kate asked, her mouth dropping open in surprise.

"Isn't it?" Isa held her head high.

"I don't know what you've been told but my specialty is in interrogation. I have close to a ninety-five percent confession rate and that includes terrorists in the Middle East that the CIA couldn't crack. I don't sit in the office to do my work. I more than get my hands dirty, trust me."

Ted held his hand up to stop Kate. "I think what Isa was trying to say is we didn't expect the FBI to send us an academic."

Isa snorted. "What I said was the FBI is wasting our time sending us an elite academic snob."

Kate cocked her head to the side, not quite believing what she had heard. Local cops were notoriously angry when the FBI was called and worried their cases would be taken over by the feds. This was something else though. They thought Kate wasn't up for the job.

Declan had started to speak, but Kate interrupted him. "You asked for the best and that's what you're getting. You couldn't solve these cases on your own. You're up to eight victims now. You asked for help and the FBI sent their best. I'm not a pencil pusher academic. Since you don't think I'm up to the task, maybe you ought to go back to your office and take on an easier case and let Declan and I handle this."

Kate waited for a response but didn't get one. It was clear Ted had been stunned into silence. Isa raged red hot. Kate didn't care. She shoved her hair off her shoulder, popped a hip to the side, and shoved past them, strutting into the bar. As she opened the door, she heard Declan behind her.

"Making Kate angry never helps anyone. You know nothing about her or how hard she works. Kate could go head-to-head in the field with any agent from the FBI or the CIA. You should be grateful she even agreed to come down here and take the case. A week ago, she was ready to leave the FBI."

Ted started to speak, but Declan silenced him. "Don't bother. Before you come inside, I'd sort yourselves out. You need to do some damage control."

Kate smirked as she entered the bar. He always had her back.

CHAPTER 4

K ate had been in Blue Note less than ten minutes when an older man with gray hair and tan leathered skin approach. He had on a Jaeger-LeCoultre watch and a gold pinkie ring. He slid into the U-shaped booth without asking and smiled across the table, showing off a line of straight white teeth, most likely veneers or other dental enhancements.

"You're too pretty to be sitting alone," he said as a way of introduction.

Kate smiled shyly. "I'm waiting for some friends but it was nice of you to say hello."

"I'm a nice guy." The man relaxed back in the booth. "I haven't seen you in here before, and I make it a point to know all the girls."

"I'd hardly consider myself a girl," Kate said with a forced chuckle.

"A girl to me." His eyes lingered on Kate's cleavage for far too long. She would have been self-conscious, but the dress was having the effect she had hoped it would have. "Have your friends told you much about this place?"

"Enough." Kate had no idea what he was talking about, but she was starting to get an idea.

The man told her his name was Harris and then bragged about the money he had made through years of working in the finance industry. He held up his watch. "I bought this last weekend on a whim. Dropped close to thirty-thousand on it. You like nice things, don't you?"

"Of course, what girl doesn't. I can't afford such luxuries though. I'm in grad school."

Harris leered at her. "There are ways around that. Arrangements you can make."

Kate smiled broadly. "I guess my friends were right about this place. If I wanted to get into this special type of arrangement, what would it entail?"

"A special friendship – a win-win for both parties." Harris leaned over the table and reached across and took Kate's hand in his. He traced his thumb across her palm in a way that made her cringe inwardly. She didn't dare show him. "You won't ever have to worry about money again. You can have all the luxury your heart desires."

"What will it cost me?" Kate asked, licking her lips for effect.

Harris laughed. "Exactly that. I could use the companionship, conversation, and a little fun. That sounds like a fair trade-off, right?"

"It doesn't sound bad at all. I'll certainly consider it."

Harris pulled a card and pen from his pocket. He jotted something down on the back of the card and then slid it over to Kate. As he got up from the table, he gave her another smile. "If that monthly allowance isn't amenable to you, we can certainly find one that is. Give me a call."

As Harris left, Kate realized he didn't know her name. She hadn't offered it up and he never asked. He had flattered her and flirted with her and propositioned her and didn't once even ask her name. Kate reached for the card and then stared hard at the number he had written.

She was worth seventy-five thousand dollars a month. The thought sickened her as bile rose in her throat. Kate understood for the first time how easily young women could be tempted into the lifestyle.

"What are you looking at?" Declan asked, standing at the end of the

23

table.

"I'll tell you when you sit down." Kate looked past him toward the door. "Did they leave?"

He slid into the booth sitting where Harris had just been. "Don't know and don't care. I think we should call Spade and have him handle it. What they said wasn't right, Kate. You have nothing to prove."

Declan thought her feelings had been hurt. It was sweet of him but unnecessary. "I don't care about that. I care that this is unnecessary drama when we should be getting down to work. This guy could be in here. He could have been the man who offered to buy me for seventy-five thousand dollars a month." Kate handed him the business card.

Declan glanced down at the number and then flipped the card over. "Harris Smith," he said. "Sounds made up. You were only in here for a few minutes."

"He scurried over like a little rat as soon as I sat down. I was easy prey sitting by myself."

"Let me go get us drinks and then we can talk." Declan went to the bar. In these situations, he was good at ordering drinks that made it look like they were drinking alcohol when in fact they remained perfectly sober while those around them became more intoxicated.

If it were up to Kate, she'd order a Diet Coke and call it a day.

A few minutes later, Declan came back with some purple concoction with a flower perched on the rim of the glass. "Lavender lemonade for the lady and I've got a rum and coke minus the rum."

Kate took a sip and puckered. "Sour but good. If they can't play nicely then we need to call Spade and get the information we need another way."

"We'll get to that. Tell me about Harris." Declan took a sip of his drink and looked around the bar. "Distinct crowd in here. Old men and young women. I'm the odd duck out."

"That's why Ted and Isa wanted us to come here. They said it could be connected to the case." Kate took another sip of her drink and told Declan about her interaction with Harris. "He wasn't shy about it. He told me providing him company and conversation *and more* could be financially beneficial for me. Just like he would a lawyer, he'd keep me on a monthly retainer for services needed."

"Sick stuff. Are you okay?" He looked at her in the protective way he always did when he worried about her, which was often.

"I'm fine," she reassured him. Declan had been protective of her their entire friendship. Kate assumed it was because both of her parents were deceased, she had no siblings or husband, and was, for the most part, alone in the world other than him.

Before Declan could say anything else, Ted and Isa appeared next to the booth.

"I'm sorry for the misunderstanding," Ted said, looking at Kate. "As you can imagine, this case has been something of a shock to the community and has been hard to get a handle around. We asked for support and I think misunderstood your skillset at first. Declan got us up to speed. I hope we can work together going forward."

Kate had wanted to hear that from Isa, but she wasn't going to be afforded that. Isa's mouth was set in a firm line and she wouldn't make eye contact with Kate. She was sure the woman had been talked into coming into the bar to make amends.

Kate offered an olive branch even though there was no need. "I appreciate the dress recommendation. I definitely would have been out of place otherwise. Maybe you can tell us about this place and how it connects. We'd love to learn your take and understand the victim type a bit better." Kate moved over in the booth to allow Ted to sit. Isa sat next to Declan.

"What do you want to know?" Isa asked with a grunt. Ted shot her a look and she softened her tone. She rested her arms on the table. "We asked you to meet us here so you could get a feel for where some of the victims spent their time and picked up their clientele."

Kate wasn't sure she should tell them about Harris just yet. "I've worked cases involving prostitutes before but they were all sex workers on the street. That isn't what we are dealing with here."

Isa shook her head. "Far from it. Most of these women wouldn't even consider what they are doing as prostitution. They are selling their time, not their bodies. Most of the 'relationships' are based on more than sex. It's about companionship. Some of these men want a pretty young woman on their arm for exclusive events, some want intelligent conversation, and some want sex without the strings. All are willing to pay a price for it. It's a commodity like everything else. The women figure they are doing them a service, not too unlike dating, but are well compensated for it. The majority of the victims were highly intelligent women. This wasn't their only avenue to make money, but it sure paid a lot more than picking up a waitressing gig while they are in school. One woman, as you know, was a lawyer who was just starting in a small firm and she was paying off student debt."

"Besides in here, how are they meeting?" Declan asked, turning to look at Isa.

"There are a few ways. We were able to interview some of the victims' friends. We've found at least one person in each of the victim's lives who knew what they were doing. We are sure some of the women must have crossed paths with each other, but we don't have confirmation on that. They meet in a few different ways." Isa held up her hand and counted down on her fingers. "There are websites for this kind of relationship – sugar babies and sugar daddies. There is also a madam who has high-priced escorts, which two of the victims were doing, and then this bar."

Ted added, "There are also parties where they meet. There's a guy who hosts them."

Declan raised his eyebrows. "Like a pimp?"

"No. It's much more high-brow than that. From what we understand, he's merely bringing them all to the same place. The meetings between the men and the women are entirely up to them. The host doesn't broker anything. If two people meet, they determine what the relationship looks like for them."

"We don't think it's him though," Isa said with an edge in her voice.

"Why not?" Declan asked but neither Ted nor Isa responded.

"We haven't had a case like this," Kate said. "I want to get the terminology right. What's the difference between a paid escort and a sugar baby?"

Isa forced a smile. "A sugar baby has an ongoing relationship with the man for a monthly allowance for however long the relationship lasts. A paid escort is for a set time – a night or a weekend."

"What are the sugar baby relationships like?"

Isa leaned forward on the table. "Like a relationship for the most part, but they both know what they are getting into."

"I assume because these relationships are more than just an exchange of cash for sex that they are legal?" Declan asked.

Kate had wondered the same thing. She was envisioning some of the cases she had where sex trafficking was involved, but this seemed entirely different from how Isa described it and how Harris had approached her.

Ted nodded. "No one is selling sex technically. Now, the madam who has high-end escorts for the night or weekend or whatever, she's been busted several times. She has a stellar legal team though and the rich and powerful in her pocket. None of the charges stuck, and she's never served time. The local cops have stopped arresting her."

Kate took another sip of her drink. "Any idea where the killer is meeting these women?"

"Not a clue," Ted said with regret in his voice.

"I assume no suspect then?"

"Not a one, but we know he's out there hunting for his victim as we speak." Isa looked around the bar. "He could be in here right now hunting for his next victim and we'd never know."

Declan locked eyes with Kate. She hoped she hadn't just been propositioned by the killer.

CHAPTER 5

The next morning Kate met Declan in the lobby of the hotel. He had left to get the car from the valet. They were going to drive over to the medical examiner's office to hear about each case and the findings. They both wanted to speak to Dr. Mirza Bruce directly rather than rely solely on the files and information from Ted and Isa.

The evening before, they had been out well past midnight and Kate and Declan came back to the hotel and crashed. Exhaustion from the day had set in for both of them. Kate still wasn't sure how the working relationship with Ted and Isa would go. Ted seemed to be more on board. Isa, even if she faked it, would have to go along. Kate never did tell them about Harris. There didn't seem to be a point.

Declan drove to the medical examiner's office. He was more familiar with Miami than Kate and she had her fill with driving the day before. "Tired?" he asked, taking his eyes off the road long enough to glance at her.

"Stressed." Kate reached up and rubbed the line across her forehead that only appeared when she was worried, tired, or stressed. "Last night was eye-opening. Sounds like there is an entire culture from which the killer can choose his victims. I wouldn't even call it underground as it seems like it's happening in the open."

"That's what surprised me the most. I had heard of sugar daddies but had passed it off as a joke, some old guy dating a younger woman. I didn't consider it a lucrative career choice for women. I thought it happened by coincidence not something that was arranged at parties or on websites."

"I want to speak to the madam, too." Kate had asked Isa last night for the madam's name and she balked at providing it. Kate had to reiterate that her specialty was interrogation and that she wouldn't do anything to compromise the investigation. She was the FBI after all. It galled Kate that she had to fight for information that should have been readily provided.

If Isa didn't text her the information today, she'd be forced to call Spade to let him sort it out. Once Spade got involved, every avenue that needed to be opened would be. He held a lot of power with law enforcement across the country, and most importantly, in the federal government. A bit of an enigma, Spade was adored and feared. Kate didn't feel like pulling a power move like that though. Spade tended to use a sledgehammer when a regular hammer would do.

"I think we need to speak with the madam and interview some of the friends of the victims. The madam might have some good information. It might be a regular client of hers. I assume it's not someone having ongoing relationships with all of the victims. I'm more inclined to believe this is a one-time client of theirs or someone they met recently."

Declan changed lanes and pulled off an exit a moment later. "I agree with you on that. I'm not saying I don't think Ted and Isa did a good job, but I want you to have a chance to interview people like we are doing with Dr. Bruce."

"Agreed," Kate said, looking out the window. The office was on Bob Hope Drive and there was a college across from the medical examiner's building. It seemed too upbeat an area for the work they did.

Declan pulled into the parking lot and turned off the car. They gathered up their things and went into the building, discussing strategy for the meeting as they walked. Once inside, Declan flashed his badge and they were escorted upstairs to an office in the back of the building. The woman who had brought them upstairs opened the door and told them to take a seat.

While Kate sat, Declan went over to the wall that had lined rows of the doctor's diplomas and awards. "She's won several accolades for her work, Kate. I bet she's never had a customer complaint." He laughed at his joke.

"Just the one guy who wasn't dead, but he couldn't be too angry. I figured out he wasn't dead before I sawed into his skull."

Kate laughed that Declan had been caught. They both turned to the doorway and there stood Dr. Bruce. She was about five-four, full-figured, and had a commanding presence that dominated the room.

She got a look at Declan's face and offered a broad smile. "You're fine, Agent James. Lots of gallows humor here."

Kate stood and introduced herself. "Dr. Bruce, thanks for meeting us so quickly."

She shook Kate's hand then Declan's and sat on the edge of her desk. "Your reputation precedes you both. Outstanding work for the FBI. I was pleased to hear the Miami field office called you in." Kate must have made a face because Dr. Bruce picked it up right away. "Not getting too favorable of a welcome from Det. Isa Navarro, are you?"

"It's been a bit of a rocky start," Kate said, trying to be diplomatic.

"Don't worry about it. She's that way with everyone." Dr. Bruce clasped her hands in front of her. "Where do you want me to start?"

Declan sat down near Kate. "The first victim would be a good start and then go from there. It would be helpful to know if you immediately saw similarities or if there have been any major differences among the cases."

Dr. Bruce nodded. "I triggered alarm bells on the first murder. I knew there'd be more."

"Why is that?" Kate asked, intrigued already.

"You don't see cuts like I saw and then the removal of a heart with such surgical precision on a typical homicide case. I alerted law enforcement of that immediately, that this wouldn't be a one-time homicide." Dr. Bruce reached behind her and took a file off a stack of them. She flipped it open and read. "The first victim was twenty-eight-year-old Marci Kessler. She was found in the bedroom of a mansion that was for sale like the victims that followed. Her heart was placed nearby. Her toxicology was clear with no drugs or alcohol in her system. No sign of sexual assault, but I can't rule out protected consensual sex before her death. Her hyoid bone was broken and there were petechiae present from manual strangulation. Her ribs were also bruised. I'd guess the killer was sitting on her chest or pressing down with his body as he strangled her."

Kate asked, "She was killed before he started cutting her open?"

Dr. Bruce nodded. "If there is any saving grace in the case, that's all. All of the victims were deceased before he did that to them. There is one strange thing I found. No DNA or anything under her fingernails. Her hands were too clean like they had just been washed. There was also bruising around her wrists."

"From?" Declan asked.

"Restraints of some kind. I think it might be zip ties, you know the ones cops carry sometimes."

"Could it be sex play prior?"

"Can't say for sure. The bruising is enough that I'd imagine she was in the restraints when she was being strangled. Bruising on her arms also tells me her arms might have been behind her back as he was on top of her. She had little to no way to fight him off."

Declan looked at Kate and then raised his eyebrows. "Do you think this might be someone connected to law enforcement?"

Dr. Bruce gave a dismissive wave of her hand. "I think the flex cuffs are fairly accessible to the general population. I'm fairly comfortable saying that this killer has extensive medical knowledge and equipment. The cuts were made with a surgeon's instrument and the heart was removed much as you see in a transplant. This wasn't an amateur."

Kate had started to think the same when she saw the crime scene. Having it confirmed by Dr. Bruce was important to her. It would narrow down the suspect list.

Dr. Bruce went through each case for them and then Kate and Declan asked a series of questions. When they were done and had been brought up to speed on the forensics, Kate asked, "We have eight victims now and there doesn't seem to be a suspect or even a hint at a suspect. What are your thoughts on the killer?"

Dr. Bruce tossed down the last of the folders and sat for a moment in quiet contemplation. "I think you're looking for a surgeon. They tend to be a more meticulous breed in the medical community, and there does seem to be a controlled meticulousness about these murders, including how clean the crime scenes are. My understanding is that no real evidence has turned up in any of the crime scenes – not a hair or a trace of DNA left behind."

Declan shifted in his chair. "That's exactly the word I would have used. Meticulous. We looked at the scene of the last murder and there wasn't a drop of blood anywhere other than a small stain on the mattress. I speculated that the killer strangled and murdered the woman there and then removed her heart on plastic that he took with him when he left."

"That's not a bad guess. The bodies weren't moved around a lot after the incision. You can tell that from the look of the veins and arteries running near the heart and how clean the bodies are. I would venture to say he's cleaning them after the murders, too."

"Do you think there is any significance to the removal of the heart?" Kate asked.

"It might have been the killer's specialty in their medical practice and he's doing what he knows. I've also considered that it's less messy than disemboweling a victim like Jack the Ripper." Dr. Bruce motioned with her hand to her midsection. "A lot is going on here to start cutting into. It makes for messy work, especially under a time constraint. The chest cavity is a fairly compact region of the body."

Kate looked to Declan to see if he had more questions and when he didn't, she thanked Dr. Bruce for her time. "I hate to say it, but this killer will take more victims if we don't hurry up and find him."

"I agree with you completely."

Kate and Declan stood to go, but Dr. Bruce held her finger up to stop them. She went around her desk and pulled out a slip of paper. She walked to Kate and handed it to her. "This is the phone number and address for my niece, Lisha. She is a student at the University of Miami. Straight-A student and quiet or at least I thought. It turns out, she's in a relationship with an older man who has been paying her bills. I don't know all the ins and outs, but she's worried that she's among the population that's being targeted. She said she'd be willing to speak to the cops."

Kate thanked her for the tip. "We can keep this quiet if you'd like."

Dr. Bruce sighed. "Lisha's father passed away when she was young and she's paying for school herself. She's a good girl, Agent Walsh. I didn't want to hand this over to the local police for that reason. I don't want to ruin her reputation. I have confidence in your discretion and interview skills. She said she doesn't know anything about these murders, but I've spoken to enough family members that come through here to know sometimes people know things without really knowing them."

Dr. Bruce closed Kate's fingers around the note. "I wouldn't mind if you tried to talk some sense into her either. I tried to no avail."

Kate locked eyes with the doctor. "I'll speak to her confidentially. I'll also do my best to suggest what she's doing probably isn't the right path. No judgment but it's not safe for her, especially now."

"I would appreciate that." Dr. Bruce shook Kate's hand and then Declan's and walked them downstairs and back out to the front of the building. "Give me a call if you need anything else and let's hope we don't have to meet anytime soon."

CHAPTER 6

"What do you think of that?" Kate asked Declan as she got back into the car.

He shut the driver's side door and put his hands on the steering wheel. "The whole meeting or the fact that she handed over her niece's contact info?"

"Her niece. It had to have been a shock to find that out." Kate looked down at the slip of paper. "I want to call her now and see if we can meet with her. If she's willing to talk, she might be a wealth of information."

Declan started the car. "I assume we are not going to call Ted and Isa?"

Kate paused for a moment thinking she might but then thought better of it. "I don't think that's keeping this confidential, which is what we promised Dr. Bruce. I assumed if she wanted Ted or Isa to have the information, she would have given it to them herself."

"No argument from me." Declan glanced over at Kate. "I wanted to make sure we were on the same page. We did tell them we'd be over to their office later today to start going through the reports they have on each victim. Do you want me to cancel?"

"As much as I'd like to avoid Isa and take over the case on our own, we need them. Let's swing by Lisha's apartment. If she's home, we can speak to her. If not, we can leave her a message and head to the police station."

Declan agreed and Kate provided him the address, which he put into the GPS. It was only fifteen minutes from where they were. Kate felt more relaxed letting Declan drive and it allowed her to process what Dr. Bruce had told them. What she said about the killer probably being a surgeon made sense. Kate had noticed the killer's level of control throughout the crime scene. This was a man who took his time and planned carefully – from the location he chose to what he did with the victim and how he cleaned up the crime scene. He wouldn't be easy to catch. Kate had a feeling he had thought through everything, including an exit strategy.

"What are you so lost in thought about over there?" Declan asked, lowering the radio.

Kate stared straight ahead. "The killer is all about control. That much is obvious. I was thinking about whether he'd let us take him alive or kill himself when he felt like we were closing in."

"You don't think he'd want credit for his work the way most do?" Declan got on the interstate and kept with the flow of traffic, which was a good twenty miles over the speed limit.

"I think we'd have known that by now. If he wanted credit, he'd contact the police or reach out to the newspaper. He's not about the shock and awe of the kill. Look how he left the crime scene."

"There's a heart on the dresser. That's a bit of shock and awe – don't you think?"

"No. That has meaning to him. It's not a thrill kill though. I don't even know if it's sexual."

"Surgeons have big egos. Wouldn't he take pride in how long he evaded capture?"

Kate considered it because Declan wasn't wrong. Some surgeons she had met even had God-like complexes. "I think he's probably laughing at us right now and thinks he's going to get away with it forever. I'm sure he has an exit plan mapped out for himself."

"What do you think about victim selection?" Declan asked.

"He could have picked an easier target if he wanted to. If his goal was to go after sex workers, there are prostitutes on the street who might not have been reported missing. If he wanted to go after young women, there are certainly enough colleges around. He's choosing these specific women who are into the high-priced escort and sugar baby lifestyle for a reason. He is making sure the victims are found quickly. He could have dumped their bodies so they were never found. He chose mansions for sale and during a weekend, which are usually high traffic for real estate showings and open houses. He's making sure they are found soon after the murders. That also tells me he's not worried about getting caught."

There was something just on the edge of Kate's mind she was trying to bring into focus. Then it hit her all at once and she snapped her fingers. "The relationships these women are having are all about a monetary exchange. As Isa said they aren't about romance. These women don't have their hearts in them. He's choosing a setting that is an example of what these women want. These young women aren't in it for love so what do they need their hearts for? I think there's an element of this that's extremely personal to him."

Declan nodded along. "Like maybe he was burned by one of these relationships?"

"Maybe. I can't be sure, but I'm fairly certain I'm on the right track."

Declan pointed to a gated apartment community on the left-hand side of the road. "That's the address."

"There's a car there now getting ready to go through the gates. If you're quick you can slip in behind them." Kate didn't want to have to call ahead and give Lisha a chance to say no. She found it much easier just to show up and then call only if she wasn't home. The last thing Kate wanted was a gate ruining the element of surprise.

Declan hit the gas and made a quick left, pulling into the apartment community even though the oncoming car had to slow down to avoid hitting them. The other driver blew his horn and flipped them off.

"Look at us making friends," he teased as he pulled the car through the open gate. He drove them to building four and found a place to park.

"She's on the second floor. I believe, it's that staircase there." Kate pointed to the left side of the building. "Do you want to wait here and let me try first? She might be more willing to speak to just a woman."

"That's fine. I'll give Ted a call and make a plan for later today."

Kate got out of the car and walked toward the apartment building. The area in front of the building had been beautifully landscaped with bright flowers and greens. Kate had no idea how much the rent would be, but she assumed it cost a good deal. This wasn't the typical college apartment community. Kate climbed the steps, found apartment 422, and knocked on the door. A dog barked inside and a woman hushed him.

"Coming!" she yelled. A moment later, a petite, young woman with dark hair pulled back in a braid tugged open the door. "Sorry," she said flustered when she saw Kate. "I thought you were FedEx. Can I help you?"

Kate lifted the badge she wore on a chain around her neck. She first confirmed the young woman was Lisha. "I'm FBI Special Agent Kate Walsh. Your Aunt Mirza said you might be willing to speak to me."

Lisha frowned. "Aunt Mirza didn't exactly give me a choice, but you're here so I might as well." She opened the door wider and let Kate step inside.

The apartment had high ceilings and comfortable oversized furniture. After moving through the foyer, Lisha pointed to the sectional couch. "Have a seat. I can get you something to drink if you'd like."

Kate declined. "I don't want to take up any more time than I need to. My partner, Agent Declan James, is downstairs waiting for me. I figured it would be more comfortable if we spoke alone."

Lisha sat down on the end of the couch and tucked her legs under her. She positioned her body so she looked directly at Kate. "I appreciate that. As you can imagine, I've faced a good deal of judgment. I like to avoid it when I can. Aunt Mirza did an okay job of pretending not to judge, but I felt it anyway."

Kate smiled. "She's worried is all."

"I'm worried, too. That's why I told her. No one else in my family knows." Lisha looked down at her hands. "You have to understand. I'm not ashamed of the relationship. It's just not something I ever thought I'd do."

"How did you get into the relationship?"

Lisha's mouth drew in a firm line. It seemed painful for her to talk about. "A friend of mine. She brought me to a party and there were a lot of older men there. It seemed a bit odd and uncomfortable. I wanted to leave but my friend had driven so other than calling a rideshare, which I was set to do, I was stuck."

Lisha leaned back on the couch. "Some days, I'm angrier at my friend than others. There are days where I feel like she set me up and other times, I know what I got myself into. I just don't think I would have known anything about it all unless I had been introduced to it. I wasn't seeking it out." Lisha raised her head and looked Kate in the eyes. "Do you know what I mean?"

"I understand. I think that's how a lot of things start. We are introduced to it by someone we trust. I assume your friend was in a similar relationship?"

Lisha nodded. "I didn't know until that day though. I knew she was seeing someone with a good deal of money, but I figured it was some rich kid with a trust fund. I didn't know he was a sixty-year-old man. There's nearly a forty-year age difference between them. I didn't understand it then."

"You do now?" Kate asked with raised eyebrows.

A smile spread across Lisha's face. "I met John the night of that party and he's unlike anyone I've ever met before. He's intelligent and well-traveled. I don't want for anything. The relationship isn't like most people think. It's not all about sex. He enjoys my company and I enjoy his."

"You could find that with a man your age."

Lisha laughed. "College guys only care about getting drunk at frat parties and having a good time. They are never faithful and make promises they don't keep. At least with John, the rules are clear and I know what I'm doing with my time."

Kate hated bringing this up so she did it as gently as possible. "Of course, you're well compensated for your time too, correct?"

"I am, but it's not what it seems. I don't feel like a paid employee if that's what you're asking. At the start, John decided he'd pay my tuition and rent and utilities here. He didn't like me living with the three roommates I had before, and I could never afford a place like this on my own. He also gives me an allowance each month."

"What happens when you want out of the relationship?"

Lisha didn't seem to understand the question. She shook her head slightly. "What do you mean?"

"In a typical relationship, once it's over, the relationship ends. With your relationship, there is a good deal of money tied up in it. That seems to be the foundation of the relationship, at least at first. You're having the relationship for payment. The gifts he's given you and your rent, for instance – are you free to leave if you choose? What happens to your rent and lifestyle then?"

Lisha laughed. "I'm free to go anytime I choose. He's not holding me hostage. But I'll tell you what – there are girls into the glam of it all and blow through their allowances on fancy clothes and shoes. Others are paying off student debt, investing, and putting money in savings. If I end this relationship tomorrow, I'm in a financial situation that will carry me well into the future."

Kate didn't think it could be that easy. "Since these murders started, what have you heard within your community?"

"Many women are afraid. A few think they know who the killer is."

"Do you?" Kate asked, moving to the edge of her seat.

Lisha shrugged. "I've heard stories. We've all heard stories." She looked up at Kate. "I figured that's why you're here. You want to know who the killer is. I told my aunt but I'm not sure she believed me."

CHAPTER 7

Kate didn't want to hear this part alone. She convinced Lisha to let Declan join in the conversation. When Declan came up to the apartment and introductions were made, he sat down next to Kate.

Lisha got up and walked to the kitchen and came back with a glass of water. She stood this time looking down at them. "There is a man by the name of Andre Dale. He's got a mansion over on Star Island. It's more like a compound. There are three swimming pools, a tennis court and the home is massive. It's a Mediterranean mansion with close to twenty-thousand square feet of living space. He throws lavishly catered parties and invites young women for his rich retired friends. It's where many of the young women in this lifestyle have met their boyfriends. It's where I met John."

"This is the man you think is the killer?" Declan asked.

"It's what some of the girls have been saying. He's a charming guy, but he's hot-tempered. He likes things a certain way. He goes out of his way to get people what they want. Girls like certain drinks – they are on hand. The same with food and drugs."

Lisha toyed with her water glass. "There's a rule that we can't tell anyone about him or what goes on at his house. The parties are invitation only. You have to be invited by one of the girls already attending the parties. The same goes for the men. Andre has security all over the compound."

Declan looked over at Kate and then back to Lisha. "Why do you suspect him of being the killer? I'm not sure I understand."

"Andre is creepy." Lisha grimaced. "He knew things about me that no one else knew. I felt like he had investigated me before I arrived, which he could have done. My friend had to give him my name about a week before the party. He had plenty of time to dig into my life. He didn't just know where I went to school. He knew what courses I was taking, my grades, and even my class schedule, which even my friend didn't know."

"From what you describe, he's quite wealthy. How does Andre make his money?" Kate asked. She hadn't heard anything that sparked her interest yet. It made sense that Andre would want to know who was coming to his parties in advance and even check them out first. Kate was sure the last thing he'd want is a reporter or a cop, especially if there were drugs at his house.

"I don't know that. I've heard everything from banking to being a doctor. He's kind of an enigma."

"Does Andre ever get involved with any of the women?"

Lisha nodded, her eyes growing wide. "He has several young women who live on the compound with him. He's been known to 'try out a girl' before recommending her to his friends."

Kate narrowed her eyes. "Does that mean what I think it does?"

"It does, but it wasn't my experience. I met John about an hour into the party and he steered me away from Andre. By what John said, even a lot of the men think Andre is a bit odd."

Declan exhaled loudly. "A bit odd is a far cry from serial killer though. Have you ever seen any direct evidence that he'd be involved in these murders? Did you ever see him with one of the victims, for instance?"

"Chloe Reed, the last victim, was one of the young women who had been living with him off and on for a few years. The only time I was at his house, I met her briefly. Chloe and Andre seemed to have a contentious relationship. They argued that night and he grabbed her by the arm and scolded her for making a scene."

That certainly gave Kate pause, but it was a long stretch to being a serial killer. "What else do you know about Andre?"

"He's heavily connected from what I hear even with law enforcement. That's one of the reasons why a few of the women I know didn't want to come forward and accuse him."

Lisha set the water glass down and hugged her chest. "I got a weird vibe around him. I can't explain it better than that. He's friendly and charming, but it doesn't seem real. It seems like an act – like he's being who you want him to be. He's not someone I'd ever want to be alone with. When the murders started, he's the first person I thought of. I'm sure he's connected to more of the victims."

"How long before the murders had you met Andre?" Kate asked.

"A few months. John and I have been seeing each other for about six months." Lisha sat down and folded her arms across her chest.

Kate didn't want to press too hard in case she needed to come back for follow-up questions. "Do you think the friend that introduced you to Andre's party would be willing to speak with me? What about John?"

Lisha shook her head. "John wants nothing to do with this. He'd be angry with me for speaking to you about it. He reassured me that he will always protect me, but he said I'm better off not talking about it. He doesn't know who my aunt is. He doesn't know anything about my family at all. My friend won't speak to the cops. I asked her to, but she's afraid. We all are."

Kate stood and Declan followed her lead. She pulled a business card from her pocket and handed it to Lisha. "I appreciate you talking to me today. Don't hesitate to call me if you remember anything else. If you need anything or feel afraid, call me. Agent James and I will be in Miami for the foreseeable future trying to solve this case."

Lisha took the card and gave Kate a half-hearted smile. She walked them to the door and then closed it behind them. Kate and Declan didn't say anything until they were back in the car.

As Kate closed the car door, she said, "At least we have a name now of who is throwing the parties. I assumed if Isa was going to tell me I would have already heard from her. Did you speak with Ted?"

"He said to come by whenever we are ready." Declan started the car but didn't put it in drive. He sat there staring out the front window. "I don't get it, Kate. Why would a young woman like Lisha choose to have that kind of relationship? Many sex workers don't have options in life. They are selling themselves to put food on the table. These young women have options."

"I don't understand it either." Kate's energy level dropped and a sense of melancholy set in. It wasn't a choice she'd make in life. "At least, it sounds like John is good to her and Lisha told me she's saving money. I think for some of these girls, once they get a taste for this kind of lifestyle, it's hard to return to what they had before. That apartment is paid for. Lisha's college tuition is paid for and she earns a substantial allowance. She didn't tell me how much but it's enough she's putting money away."

"I don't know how they can live with themselves though."

"Don't be judgmental," Kate cautioned. "The men are just as bad as the women by paying for companionship."

Declan held his hands up in defense. "I think they are both sick."

"That's not going to help us solve this so get out all your judgment right now so we can press on with the case."

Declan smiled as he looked over at her. "I was sure you'd be the judgmental one, and I'd have to talk you down."

"Me too." Kate laughed. "Meeting Lisha changed things. I don't want to say it normalized it for me, but I can see how it happens. Older men also have a certain maturity and life experience. I can see why Lisha would be drawn to that in addition to the money."

Declan didn't say anything for a moment. When he did, he changed the subject. "We need to speak to Andre Dale and run a background check on him. Could be a promising lead."

"I had considered going undercover to get some intel on him first. Since he's going to run a background check on me before letting me come to a party, I don't know that we'll have the time to pull that off."

"I thought the same." Declan put the car in drive and made quick time over to the police station. On the way, they strategized how much they'd share with Ted and Isa or if they should still hold back. Even after parking and walking to the building, they hadn't come to a firm decision.

"Let's take the temperature for today. Isa might be better," Declan suggested as he held the door for Kate.

She shrugged not agreeing or disagreeing with him. If Kate were being honest, she'd rather not have to deal with Isa at all. "Let's take a look through the files first and then we can go from there."

The desk sergeant looked at their credentials and then gave them directions to find the homicide unit. They rode the elevator to the third floor and Ted met them in the hallway.

"I was just headed down to find you," he said, shaking Declan's hand and then Kate's. "Did you have a good meeting with Dr. Bruce? She's been an asset on this case."

"She's provided a wealth of information," Kate said. "With her information along with the crime scene details yesterday and our conversation last night, I believe I'll be able to create a working profile of the killer after we go through the victim files."

"That's great news." Ted smiled awkwardly and ran a hand down his face. "Mayor Harvey Littman is here and wants to meet you."

They didn't have time to play politics but Kate knew sometimes it was a part of the job. "Sure, we'd be happy to."

"That's good news, young lady, because I wasn't giving you an option."

The voice came from behind Kate and she turned to see a man of average height and build who had gone bald on the top. He had a combover that looked ridiculous and made part of his hair stand up like chicken feathers. Kate extended her hand. "FBI Special Agent Kate Walsh."

"You need to clean this mess up quickly," he said looking her up and down in a way that made her feel exposed under his gaze. His eyes landed on her breasts and he didn't look away.

Declan noticed it and stepped in front of Kate and introduced himself. He remained there shielding her body with his. "We can only do so much but it was good of you to stop by." Declan turned to Ted. "Do you have a place where we can start looking through that evidence?"

"I've arranged for you to have one of our conference rooms for as long as you need it."

"Thank you. We'll go there now." Declan angled his head back to look at the mayor. "We won't get anything accomplished if we stand around here socializing."

With that, the three of them walked off leaving Mayor Littman to stand there looking a bit dumbfounded at the exchange. Declan glanced down at Kate and his expression told her everything. He didn't get any better vibe from Mayor Littman than she had. Kate was starting to wonder if there was any man in Miami Beach that wasn't a letch.

Ted directed them to a room down a long narrow hallway. He opened a door and stepped out of the way so they could walk through. There were nearly twenty evidence boxes stacked against a wall.

"You'll find everything you need in those – there are statements from the victim's families, autopsy reports, reports from forensics at the crime scenes, photos, and more. If you have any questions, my office is the fourth one down on the right."

Ted got to the door and started to leave but turned back. "Kate, I hope that you're feeling more comfortable after we spoke last night. I believe you're critical to helping us catch this killer. I think we just got off on a bad foot."

Kate smiled. "No worries. When we're done here, the four of us should speak about the cases. I'm sure Declan and I will have questions."

"Absolutely," Ted said, his shoulders relaxing.

CHAPTER 8

K ate and Declan spent the next three hours scanning through files. The one thing that became clear quite quickly was that the victims were all a similar age. They ranged from twenty-five to twenty-eight. There were also no witnesses to the crimes and no connections found among the real estate agents and any of the victims. No one had confirmed that any of the victims knew each other, but Kate suspected that they must have.

Kate closed the folder in front of her. "There are no witnesses, at least none that have come forward. There's no active video surveillance either at the homes, which I find odd. I want to speak to a real estate agent and see if that's the norm or if the killer knows which homes to choose."

Declan sat back and stretched his arms over his head. "That's a good point. If he knows the video surveillance has been turned off or is non-existent then he has working knowledge of the crime scene ahead of time."

"He must have regardless. Don't you think?"

Declan thought about it for a moment. "I think we are looking at two different things though. Sure, he has a working knowledge of the layout of these mansions and that no one is currently occupying them. He could have made a phone call to find that out. For him to know there is no working surveillance on the property, he'd have to have a little more in-depth knowledge. I wonder if he's posing as a buyer and scoping out these properties ahead of time."

Kate hadn't considered that but it was a good idea. "It would mean that someone has had eyes on this killer. Do you think he's working with a real estate agent or calling the seller real estate agent and going on his own?"

"No idea. I don't even know how real estate down here works." Declan speculated, "It's kind of ingenious though. He shows up to see the house so of course his fingerprints would be found in there along with countless others. That's what I'm finding in the reports. There are too many prints all over the houses for forensics to do much with."

Kate had noticed that in each report, too. Fingerprint analysis wasn't going to get them anywhere. The crime scenes were too contaminated from that perspective. "With no DNA either, there isn't much to tie him to the crimes. Even if we catch someone, we are either going to have to rely on a confession or enough circumstantial evidence to make a case."

"There could be someone out there who saw or heard something," Declan countered.

"I wish they'd come forward then. We are quickly approaching another weekend, and he hasn't killed in a couple of weeks. Given his cooling-off period between the other murders, I wouldn't be surprised if this weekend there was another."

Declan raised his eyes to the ceiling. "Let's meet Ted and Isa and go over a few things including what we can do this weekend to get more eyes out there in the community. Maybe sit some cops on a few of the mansions that fit the crime scenes."

Kate thought that was probably the best idea and the most workable plan they had to date. "Do you want to let Ted know we're ready? I want to ask Lisha a quick question before we proceed."

Declan agreed and got up from the table. He left the conference room in search of Ted while Kate placed the call. Lisha answered quickly.

"Lisha, I don't mean to bother you again. I'm wondering if you're aware of any women in your circle who might be a real estate agent."

Lisha sucked in a breath. "Please don't tell me someone else is dead."

"Nothing like that," Kate reassured. "I have a few questions about real estate in Miami Beach. I thought if you know someone connected to both your lifestyle and real estate, they might be a good person for me to ask."

Lisha asked Kate to hold. The sounds of a drawer being opened and then slammed shut came through the phone. Lisha got back on the phone and gave Kate the woman's name and phone number. "Do you want me to tell her you're calling? I don't know her well but can give her a heads up if you'd like."

"I appreciate that, but I think it's probably best I call directly." Kate thanked her and hung up as Ted, Isa, and Declan walked into the room.

"Do you have questions about the cases?" Isa asked, sitting at the end of the table far away from Kate. There were no pleasantries and she didn't appear happy to be there.

"I think Declan and I are caught up. Between the meeting this morning with Dr. Bruce and reading through the reports, we have a good understanding of the cases." Kate paused and Isa stared at her. "We also got the name of the man who hosts the parties you mentioned last night. His name is Andre Dale and he lives—"

Isa interrupted. "We know Andre Dale and he's not the killer."

"Is he someone you interviewed?" Declan asked, sharing a look with Kate. He could tell her anger had started to bubble up again.

"There was no need to interview him. He's friends with the mayor," Isa said. "He's not involved."

Kate cleared her throat. "With all due respect, someone being friends with the mayor, who we just met, means very little to me.

Declan and I have arrested people of all walks of life for the most heinous crimes. We were told it was Andre Dale hosting the parties at his house on Star Island and that's what we believe. We will be interviewing him."

Isa pounded her fist on the table. "You'll do no such thing!"

Ted glanced at Isa at one end of the table and then to Kate at the other end. "It would be a delicate interview, Kate. Andre isn't just friendly with Mayor Littman, they are inseparable. He is a major contributor to the arts and has a good deal of power in the community."

Before Kate could say anything, Declan spoke up. There was a tinge of anger in his voice. "You're missing the point. Kate and I don't need your permission. We've been assigned to take over this case. Now, we can either work together or we can walk these files out of here and bring them to the FBI office in Miami and run the case ourselves."

He turned and looked right at Isa. "I don't care who Andre Dale is friends with or how much money he has. We have reason to believe he's setting up these arrangements with young women and older men. You're lucky I'm not considering him involved in sex trafficking."

Duly chastised, Ted conceded, "We will leave it in the FBI's hands then. I don't think it would bode well for us to take part in the interview."

Kate couldn't be happier with that decision. "I didn't see the name of the madam in your notes. I believe you said the first two victims worked for her. I want to interview her as well."

Isa sat back in her chair and folded her arms across her chest. She wasn't going to give Kate an inch. Isa could get territorial all she wanted. The FBI would simply come in and take over the case as they had done countless times before.

Ted seemed to have more sense. He grabbed a pen and notepad from the middle of the table and jotted down her name. He handed Kate the piece of paper. "It's not in the notes because she refused to speak with us. As soon as we made contact with her, she said she wouldn't speak without her lawyer present. When we tried to set up a meeting with her lawyer, no one returned the call. We don't have enough manpower to chase her down."

"Understood," Kate said and she meant it. It happened all the time in criminal cases. "Declan and I were talking about this upcoming weekend. Is there a chance we can get some surveillance on some of the local mansions that fit the crime scenes?"

"You don't think we already tried that?" Isa asked, scowling at Kate.

"Isa, I don't know what you've tried or haven't. It wasn't an insult. It was simply a question."

Ted expelled a breath. "We've tried it a few weekends and he still killed a woman and left her body. We don't have enough resources to be out there at every mansion that's for sale every weekend."

"How many properties are we talking about?" Declan asked.

"There were fifty or so that fit the last weekend we tried to set this up."

"All of them without surveillance in the home?"

A look of confusion came over Ted's face. "What do you mean?"

"The mansions where the killer is leaving the bodies don't have activated surveillance. Either it was never installed or it's been deactivated while the house is unoccupied," Declan explained. "That should narrow down the list considerably."

"Have you worked with any local real estate agents on gathering a list of these properties?" Kate asked.

Isa didn't say a word but the expression on her face said everything. They hadn't explored that avenue yet.

Even Ted shifted in his seat, looking uncomfortable. "We had been provided a list but not with that information specifically."

Kate pulled the slip of paper where she had written down the name of the woman Lisha had given her. "No worries. I have a contact here

I can call." She turned to Declan. "Let's go run down a few leads."

CHAPTER 9

Declan drove them straight to Fanny Fontaine's house on Ocean Drive. Kate had to look three times at the name to make sure she had read Ted's handwriting correctly. Fanny Fontaine. That seemed perfectly fitting for a madam. Kate wasn't sure if it was a real name or an alias the woman used. Fanny was well into her eighties and had been living in Miami Beach for more than fifty years doing exactly what she was doing today. She had built a lucrative business catering to the rich and famous.

Fanny's house sat on Pine Tree Drive north of the Eden Roc Hotel across Indian Creek. Kate did a quick search of the house on Zillow. Fanny lived in a six-thousand square foot home, valued at more than nine million dollars. It had a pool overlooking the water.

"The madam business must be going well for her. She has a deck overlooking Indian Creek with a pool and a dock for a boat," Kate explained, flipping through the photos in Zillow. "It looks like she bought the home three years ago based on the sales records."

"How do you plan to approach the interview since it sounds like she shut down Ted and Isa before they even got started?"

Kate gave him a sideways look. "I'm not going to approach this one. You are going to turn on the charm and flash your boyishly good looks in her direction. Like with most women, you'll be irresistible."

Declan's cheeks flushed. "You think I'm irresistible."

"I said to most women," Kate said, exaggerating the words. "I'm not most women. I can resist your charms all day and all night. If I go in there alone, she's not going to tell me anything. You're going to take the lead and see how far we get. Two of her girls have already been murdered. She must feel some responsibility."

Declan changed lanes. "You'd hope so, but I've found that those selling sex rarely feel remorse for anything."

"Pimps on the street, maybe," Kate countered. "Fanny must be offering something no one else is to make as much money as she has. She's going to want to protect that, and that's the side of her we need to appeal to."

"Got it." Declan pulled off Pine Tree Drive at the given address but was stopped by a closed gate. He opened the window and pushed the intercom button and waited. A woman answered and Declan explained who he was and that he needed to speak with Fanny Fontaine. The silence on the other end of the intercom made Kate cringe. They might be shot down before they even got started.

Just as Declan put the car in reverse to back out of the driveway, the gates slowly opened. He navigated through the gates before anyone changed their mind. He pulled up the brick driveway and to the front of the home where a heavyset woman, with dark hair and tanned skin, pointed to a spot on the side of the driveway. She wore a light blue and white caftan that went right to her ankles.

The woman had a commanding presence. Kate knew just by looking at her that she wasn't going to be easily intimidated. "Turn on the charm as heavy as you can."

Declan ran a hand through his messy hair. "I might be out of practice."

Kate opened the door, allowing Declan to get out first. She'd follow his lead this time.

Declan walked to the woman with an air of confidence and swagger

Kate only saw on rare occasions. He confirmed she was Fanny Fontaine and he extended his hand. "I'm FBI Special Agent Declan James. This is my partner Special Agent Kate Walsh. We've come a long way to speak with you."

Fanny didn't hold back her admiration for Declan's good looks. She eyed him up and down like he was a piece of the highest-grade meat at the butcher's. Kate saw no reason to protect him the way he had protected her when they encountered the mayor. Declan could handle himself.

Fanny put her hands on her plump hips. "I can tell by the accent you're not from around here. I'm assuming the northeast. Boston maybe."

Declan flashed a wide grin. "Exactly. South Boston to be exact."

Fanny relaxed her posture and laughed. "A rough and tumble Southie boy then. You're a long way from home."

"Can't complain about the weather upgrade though." Declan locked eyes with her. "Do you think you can spare some time to help us out? We hear you're the person to speak to – a woman in the know." He winked.

Kate could tell Fanny was eating it up. She nodded once and then escorted them into her home. They walked into the foyer, which featured a wide staircase with an intricately designed wrought iron banister and an ornate chandelier overhead. It was a straight shot through the foyer into a living room and then through sliding doors to the back patio. The patio had palm trees along the perimeter and a fantastic view of the blue water of Indian Creek. There was comfortable-looking patio furniture tastefully decorated around the pool and an outdoor bar and kitchen.

Fanny took a seat in the shade of a palm and explained she was having an afternoon drink and asked them if they'd like anything.

"I'd love a bourbon but can't drink on duty," Declan said. "Maybe some other time."

"Some other time indeed." Fanny relaxed into the lounge chair and grabbed the martini from the table next to her. "I'd ask what brings you here, but I assume it's the murders."

"It is," Declan confirmed, taking a chair next to her. Kate sat across the way, allowing their closeness to create a more intimate conversation. She'd be the observer here.

Fanny took a sip of her drink. Looking over the rim, she said, "You know, I already refused to speak to the Miami detectives on the case."

Declan crossed his legs at his ankles and relaxed into the chair. "I heard that but figured it was worth my time to try again."

"That female detective came in here threatening to send me to prison if I didn't talk. I kicked her out immediately and called my lawyer."

Declan nodded and offered a sympathetic smile. "That's not the approach we take. You're an ally for us and we aim to create an amicable exchange. There is no need for threats. We're sorry for your loss. We understand that two of the victims were women who worked for you."

Fanny hesitated for a moment. "I assume you know what I do."

Declan nodded. "I've heard mention, but that's between you and Miami Beach PD. You've been here a long time and I don't see that changing. I'm here because you want to protect your business and that won't happen if the women you employ don't feel safe. We are trying to catch this guy as quickly as possible."

"You assume the killer is a man?" She took another sip of her drink and lingered.

Declan pointed to Kate. "Agent Walsh is one of the most sought-after criminal profilers in the world. If she thinks the killer is a man, then it's a man."

Fanny turned and looked at Kate for the first time. She took her in. "You're pretty, Agent Walsh. You could be making a lot more money working for me and doing a lot less work."

Kate forced a smile. "Thank you. I like my work though."

"Too bad." Fanny shrugged. "You win some and lose some in this business. Why do you think the killer is a man?"

"Typically, in cases like this, the killer is a man. There's a good deal of force used in the strangulation."

"That means nothing to me. It doesn't take much to strangle someone."

Kate wasn't sure where Fanny was going with this. "Do you have reason to believe the killer is a woman?"

"No. I just don't want you to be shortsighted like the cops here."

"Certainly not," Kate assured. "We are open to any possibilities. Right now, we have been referencing the killer as a man, but if we find evidence to suggest the killer is a woman then we are open to it. Makes no difference to us as long as the killer is caught."

"I like that." Fanny took a deep breath. "I have a certain instinct about people and I trust you both. What would you like to know?"

Declan shifted his body to face her more directly. "We know that the first two victims were young women who worked for you. Do you suspect that one of your clients might be responsible?"

"No. Neither woman was working for me the night they were murdered. If they were out with someone, that was on their own and they should have known that was strictly forbidden. The reason I'm so successful is that I cater to repeat customers who are thoroughly vetted. I rarely take on a new client. When I do, the decision is not made lightly. I have men begging to be taken on as a client."

"Any new clients?" Declan asked.

"Not in the last year. My business brings me millions of dollars a year and my girls are well compensated. My top earner makes a half-million dollars a year. Just like I have clients begging for me to take them on, I have young women lining up for employment, but I'm select. Intelligence is highly valued. My clients aren't looking for a good time Sally. They want intelligent conversation and a respectful woman on their arm."

Fanny quieted for a moment as if choosing her words carefully. "This isn't for everyone, Agent James. I know many look down at the service I provide. I assure you though that the women who work for me are respected by my clients and respected by me. They feel safe and like they are part of a family. I've kicked clients out for not holding doors on dates. I don't put up with anything foolish. Both the clients and my girls know that. I'd rather lose business than develop a lax or bad reputation."

Declan asked a few more questions about the women who worked for her and it amounted to what they had suspected – well-educated, attractive, and sophisticated. "Do you have any idea who the killer might be?"

"I don't," Fanny said, fixing her caftan across her legs. "If I did, I certainly would have handed him over to law enforcement by now. This may surprise you, but I checked the alibi of each of my clients. I've probably done more work than the two detectives that were here. I have a private investigator who works for me that ran down every lead and alibi. I feel like I can safely tell you, it's not one of my clients. I have no idea who the girls were out with when they were murdered."

Declan looked to Kate to see if she had questions. She had a few. "Do you have any idea why the killer stopped choosing women who work for you after killing two?"

"I closed ranks quickly on the women employed by me. I paid them to stay home. I stopped all services until we checked the alibis of all my clients. Simply put – my girls were no longer accessible."

Since Fanny was being so forthcoming with information, Kate decided to get her opinion on a few other things. "What do you think about the men here in Miami Beach involved in what they call sugar daddy relationships?"

Fanny held up her glass. "Disgusting and despicable. I wouldn't be surprised at all if it was one of those old coots killing those girls."

Kate drew back in the chair. "I'm not sure I understand why you'd feel that way given your profession."

"It's because you don't understand the world." Fanny shifted in her seat to look at Kate more fully. "My girls sell their time and services for a price. It's an even exchange. Both parties come into the situation evenly. I know that's not the way all prostitution works. I'm not naïve, but that's the way it is for the women who work for me. The young women involved in relationships with those old men – it's anything but an even exchange."

"I'm not sure I understand," Declan admitted.

Fanny pointed and wriggled her finger at him. "You're a man through and through, Agent James. I can tell just by looking at you. Healthy libido, enjoys women, and even one of those rare men who truly respects women. If you hire an escort for the weekend, there is an expectation of what that weekend will entail. At least with my girls, you're both walking into it with your eyes open and it's consensual. All parties involved must show proof of health screenings and be free of sexually transmitted diseases and be drug-free. I drug test the young women who work for me once every two months and the same goes with my clients. I provide women a financial planner so they can make smart choices with their money. The women know my clients are thoroughly vetted – background checks and all. I don't mess around with anyone's safety. If one of the women wants to take time off, she takes time off. She doesn't want to see a client; she doesn't see him. It's that cut and dry with me."

Fanny continued more forcefully. "Now, with the sugar daddy relationships, it's a blank check to these young women who have never seen that kind of money in their lives. First off, many don't know what to do with it. They spend lavishly, develop drug habits, and get hooked on the lifestyle. Secondly, they have no protection. Once they are in the relationship, they are obligated. In exchange for the money being paid, those old men feel like they own those young women. Most of them I'd still consider girls."

"There isn't an even exchange," Kate said, feeling like she had more of an understanding now.

"Exactly." Fanny's face lit up and she spoke with her hands. "If a man is paying all of your bills including your rent and your education, do you feel like you can say no to something he asks of you? You have put your security and your future into his hands and eventually, he will abuse that power. That isn't something I'm speculating about. I've seen it firsthand. I have two women who work for me that got themselves out of those relationships. The women who work for me are paid well, but they decide what they do with their money and their bodies. The young women who have sugar daddies have very little control over anything."

Declan looked between Kate and Fanny. "They are at their mercy."

"Right, but what I do is illegal while all that is perfectly legal. Does that make sense to you?" Fanny didn't wait for Kate or Declan to answer. "It doesn't make a lick of sense to me at all. These murders are providing a tipping point here in Miami Beach that I'm surprised hasn't happened before."

Kate found herself agreeing with Fanny even though she was hard-pressed to think any prostitution was okay. However, on the legal issues Fanny raised, Kate agreed with her. "We've heard the name Andre Dale recently. Are you familiar with him?"

Fanny snorted. "Biggest offender of them all."

Declan raised his eyebrows. "Offender?"

"Oh, you don't know?" Fanny asked surprised. "Andre Dale has been accused of sexual assault on more than one occasion. The police don't take it seriously because he's best friends with the mayor. Golfing buddies. I've heard the mayor has been at Andre's little soirées."

It was almost like sitting in front of a huge chocolate cake. Kate wasn't sure where to stick her fork in first. "We'll get to what you know about the mayor in a moment, but how do you know Andre sexually assaulted women?"

"There was a young woman who worked for me for a few years. Then she was tempted by more money with Andre. He told her she could be making three times what I paid her and she never had to 'work'. He told her all she needed was a rich older boyfriend and she'd be set." Fanny shrugged. "It's an easy temptation when that is legal and this isn't. No one wants to be arrested for prostitution. That's a stigma you can't shake."

"What happened from there?" Kate asked although the picture was becoming clearer.

"She went to one of his parties and he sexually assaulted her in front of two other men. Testing the merchandise is what he joked about. I had taught her well though. She went right to the hospital and had an exam and called the police. There was DNA evidence. The nurse at the hospital who performed the exam believed her. Even the cop who came to take her statement believed her. Once it was handed over to a detective, that's when it all fell apart. Suddenly, the tables turned. Andre said she consented and it became he said, she said. With the testimony of the other men, both rich and powerful in their own right, the case was dropped. The woman spoke to a few other women who told her a similar tale. No one has ever been able to bring Andre down. He's untouchable in this town."

Declan shook his head in disgust. "Do you think Andre is capable of the crimes being committed?"

"I think all men are capable of great cruelty if it suits their agenda," Fanny said matter-of-factly.

Kate chose her words carefully. "The nature of this case requires a particular medical skillset."

Fanny's eyes opened wide. "What would that be?"

"The killer is removing the victim's hearts with medical precision. The medical examiner said that it would take the skills of a surgeon to do something like that so cleanly."

Fanny's hands came up to her chest to feel her heartbeat.

"The victims were already dead," Kate reassured. "They were strangled first. It was after they were dead that the killer cut out their hearts."

"I guess that is some solace. Andre is not and was never a surgeon to my knowledge." Fanny shifted her eyes to the side like she wanted to say more.

Kate caught the look. "Do you know someone who is a surgeon?"

Fanny didn't respond. Instead, she took a sip of her drink and looked away.

Kate didn't press the issue. "How has Andre made so much money?"

"I guess you haven't been around here enough to have heard," Fanny said, turning back to her. She sniffed dramatically once and tapped the side of her nose. "He has been running a cocaine empire since he first landed in Miami."

"The mayor doesn't mind that his best friend is flouting the law like that?" Declan asked.

"Who do you think his biggest client is?" Fanny responded with a chuckle. "You two are as green as green can be with the way things work here."

"How well do you know Harvey Littman?"

Fanny winked at him. "One of the girls who works for me knows him very well – intimately. He's a talker after the deed. She couldn't get him to shut up. It's proved useful."

That explained why Fanny was able to continue with her business free from the interference of law enforcement. Kate asked, "Is that how you know so much about Andre?"

"Honey, it's how I know so much about everything happening in Miami Beach." Fanny knocked back the rest of her drink. "Maybe you weren't listening, so I'll tell you again. The men who date the women who work for me aren't here just for the sex. They have wives who don't listen anymore. They crave someone to take care of them and pamper them for a few hours. Most of them can't shut up. I get stock tips and business advice. I know about mergers long before the press. I know who is going broke and who is winning big. I know whose wives are cheating and with whom. I know every down and dirty intimate detail of the most powerful in Miami Beach."

Declan reached out and touched her arm. "Aren't you worried about your safety? I'd think it would be dangerous to know as much as you do."

"Give me some credit, young man. Anything happens to me and those secrets will be for the world to know. Nobody crosses Fanny Fontaine." She glanced back to Kate. "That's why I'm sure the person who killed my girls wasn't a client. If they knew me, they'd never cross me. Andre has been trying to knock me out of business for years. Those relationships he's setting up. You can be sure he gets a cut of the money. A finder's fee he probably calls it. If I were you, he'd be number one on my suspect list."

"We don't want to take up any more of your time," Declan said, drawing her attention back to him. "We appreciate you speaking with us. Is there anything else you think we should know?"

Fanny stood and set her empty glass down on the table. She told them to wait right there. Kate and Declan sat quietly and waited. When she came back, she handed Kate a slip of paper. "Give Rosie a call. Tell her Fanny sent you. She was friends with the first two victims and can probably give you a wealth of information. She hasn't spoken to the cops either. I don't think they even know about her."

Kate stood and shook Fanny's hand. Declan did as well. She walked to the front of the house the way they had come in. Before they left, Declan asked, "I'm curious why you spoke to us and not the detectives?"

Fanny reached out and cupped his chin. "You remind me of a young man I once knew, and Agent Walsh has a trusting smile. Someone needs to find justice for those women and I believe you'll do it. Call me if you need anything else."

Kate left feeling a tinge of admiration for Fanny. It was a mixed emotion though that she wasn't quite sure what to do with.

CHAPTER 11

"Did you believe her?" Declan asked, as he pulled out of Fanny's driveway and accelerated into traffic. He turned his head slightly to look at Kate.

"Every word she said." Kate had no reason to believe that Fanny had lied to them. She had no reason to speak with them at all. She could have easily shut them out the way she had with Ted and Isa. "She's angry that powerful men are getting away with so much in this city."

"Why does she do what she does then?"

"She's in control in her world. Fanny sets the rules and the parameters. It sounds like the women who work for her do the same. As they say, prostitution is the world's oldest profession. Fanny is running her business her way and isn't letting anyone or anything stop her. I believe her when she says the women who work for her are there willingly."

Declan raised his eyebrows. "It sounds like you're condoning what she's doing."

Maybe Kate was and so what if she felt that way. "It sounds far better than the sugar daddy relationships. Fanny's right. Those women have little choice and control in their lives. They have handed it over to the men who have bought them."

"You don't think it works that way for the women who work for Fanny."

"If a criminal ever had morality and ethics, I think we just witnessed it." Kate stared out the window of the passenger seat. "I got the sense that Fanny would do anything to protect the women who work for her. I believe her and think we should follow up on the leads she gave us."

"Why the soft spot for her?"

Something about Fanny tugged on her heartstrings a little. There was no way for Kate to admit that to Declan though, so she ignored what he said. Kate pulled her phone from her pocket and clicked on the real estate agent's information and then pressed the call button. When Ava Crawford answered the phone, Kate explained who she was and that Lisha had provided her contact information.

"We'd like to speak with you right now, if possible." There was every reason for Ava to say no.

"I'd prefer not to meet you in my office, but I'm preparing a house for sale. How about we meet there? I'll be alone and we'll have privacy."

"Could you bring me a list of every mansion for sale in Miami Beach?"

Ava asked if there were any specific parameters Kate wanted. When Kate explained in more detail, Ava assured her she knew what real estate to include. Kate hung up and gave the address to Declan. "Even if Ted and Isa don't think what we are asking is possible, we need to check it out ourselves."

Declan pulled the car to the side of the road, waited until traffic cleared, and turned the car around to head back in the other direction. "I'm starting to think we need to interview everyone Ted and Isa already spoke to in case they missed something."

Kate had had the same feeling earlier in the day but worried about time constraints. "I think we need to at least hit the important witnesses like friends and family of the victims. We need to be gentle with Ted and Isa. While they have handled homicides, this one is a little out of the norm."

Declan smirked as he looked at her. "Are you giving me a lecture on playing politics so we don't anger anyone?"

"So you don't anger anyone. They already hate me," Kate reminded him. "One of us has to be able to get information from them."

"Usually, I'm the hated one. I'm happy to allow you to have that role this time." Declan changed lanes again. "Tell me about this woman we are meeting."

"She's a real estate agent who also happens to be in a sugar baby relationship. I figured we could kill two birds with one stone."

Declan weaved in and out of traffic like he had driven the roads all of his life. They arrived at the same time as an SUV. Declan waved the driver up the driveway and he pulled in after. The SUV parked and Declan pulled in right behind. Kate opened the door and got out, waiting for Declan before they walked up to the driver's side. They stepped back and let the young woman get out. Kate confirmed it was Ava.

"I was worried you'd beat me here." Ava handed Kate two pages. "Those are the homes that meet your specifications. What the MLS doesn't tell me is if the security systems are turned on or off. It only lists if there is a security system currently installed, so you're looking at twenty-five properties."

"What's the best way to find out if the security systems are currently engaged?"

Ava pulled a large black bag out of the back of the SUV. "You'd have to call the seller's agent and find out."

Kate glanced down at the list. All the homes listed were like the ones the killer had used before – large mansions, secluded from their neighbors, and unoccupied. "You were able to see that these homes were unoccupied?"

"Not from the MLS, but I ran it by one of the assistants in my office who knew that information. She is the go-to person for every home for sale in Miami Beach. I asked about the security systems, but that was the one thing she didn't know."

Kate held the paper. "Thanks for this. It's a big help."

Ava waved them inside. "Let me go get a few things set up. I have a showing in an hour so we have some time to talk."

Kate and Declan followed her into the home that had a similar look to Fanny's. They were in the same neighborhood and probably had the same builder. "I'm sure you're aware of the murders that have been happening," Kate said as they entered the kitchen.

Ava set her bag down on the floor and leaned against the counter. "I have and it has all of us worried about who could be next."

"We believe the killer is visiting the crime scenes before the night of the murders."

Ava's face paled. "Do you think he's going around looking at the houses pretending he might buy one? That would be easy to do. I have clients who call me all the time wanting to see houses. Some aren't even ready to buy. They are nosey, wanting to get a good look inside some of the mansions that are rarely for sale."

"We didn't want to frighten you," Kate said, understanding that was exactly what they had done. "We were hoping you'd be able to point us in the right direction to find out if anyone has a client that has seen the properties in question."

Ava rubbed at her clavicle with her fingertips. "You're not going to be able to find that out. We have so many people coming through these houses from all over the place. Sometimes we don't even see the buyers. Today, I'm seeing the buyer's representative. He's coming to ask some questions, take a video walk-through of the place, and will make a recommendation to his boss. During open houses, people show up without agents. It's not like we are checking identification. I can't see any good way to find out what you need."

Kate hadn't thought of all of that. "That's still good information to have."

Declan spoke up for the first time. "Have you had your suspicions of anyone since the murders started?"

Ava smiled shyly at him. "There's been talk about who it could be. I think everyone I've spoken to believes it's someone local."

"Why's that?" he asked.

"All the victims are local and so are the crime scenes. It makes sense he'd be local, too."

Kate couldn't argue with that logic. "We believe that the killer has some advanced medical knowledge." Kate explained how the victim's hearts were cut out.

Declan added, "There is a precision that can't be faked."

Ava frowned. "Do you have any idea how many doctors or former doctors are running around Miami Beach? It's like a medical retirement community. Just about every other client I see the wife or husband was in the medical field."

"Keep your eye out for surgeons," Kate advised.

"That narrows it down a little."

Kate glanced at Declan and he made an excuse to leave. When he was gone, Kate asked, "Ava, what do you know about Andre Dale?"

Ava bit her lip. "So, Lisha told you about that."

"That's why Agent James left. I thought you might be more comfortable speaking with me one-on-one."

"I'm not embarrassed by it." Ava shrugged. "At least, I'm not working as a paid escort. My boyfriend is good to me. I didn't graduate college and it's been hard to break into the real estate industry down here. I met Andre who introduced me to a friend of his. In addition to the financial help my boyfriend has provided, he's opened a lot of doors for me. Andre did as well."

"You do know that it's women like you that are the victims of these murders, right?"

Ava nodded and took an audible breath. "I feel safe because I'm not meeting anyone new. I see the man I'm involved with and that's it. It's my understanding that the victims were all on dates when this happened. I assumed those were first dates."

"Where did you hear that?"

"No one said it specifically. That's an assumption on my part." Ava fiddled with a paper in front of her on the counter. "It seems to me if the cops still have no suspect, then it's someone blending well into the Miami Beach community."

Kate patted Ava's shoulder. "If real estate doesn't work out for you, you might want to consider a career in law enforcement. You have some good insight."

"I don't think it's that complicated so that's why it surprises me he hasn't been caught yet. Hang around with Andre or at the Blue Note and you'll figure it out fast enough."

"What about websites? I heard some young women meet their boyfriends on websites that cater to older wealthy men."

"That might happen in other places but not here. All a young woman needs to do is be open, attractive enough, and she can meet a man just by stepping outside. The beaches are filled with them. Blue Note is filled with them. It's hook-up central."

Kate thought back to her own experience at the Blue Note. "Did you know any of the women who were murdered?"

Ava nodded and looked away. "I knew three of the women. That's why I figured it was first dates. The women I knew weren't exactly careful in who they went out with."

Kate asked a few more questions and Ava provided some details about her friends who had been murdered and their lifestyles. Kate didn't learn that much more than she had already known but it was good to hear the information firsthand.

"Do you think it could be Andre killing these women?"

Ava narrowed her gaze and she bit at the inside of her cheek. She stayed quiet for so long Kate started to wonder if she'd respond. When she locked eyes with Kate, she admitted, "I thought it might be him, but I can't be certain. Andre has access to all sorts of women and he gets angry when they step out of line. I've seen him have a violent temper, but I don't know that he'd go as far as to kill anyone. I also don't know what his background is." Ava turned back to her work and finished setting up sales sheets.

It was clear to Kate she was done talking. Kate left her card on the table. "Be safe and call me if you think of anything else, especially if you get any hits on properties that might fit the crime scenes."

CHAPTER 12

"All roads seem to lead to Andre Dale," Kate said as she met Declan outside. He leaned against the car, scrolling through his phone. "Did you hear me?" Kate asked again because Declan hadn't looked up.

"Yeah, Andre Dale," Declan said absently. He continued to stare down at his screen for a moment longer. Then he raised his head to look at her. "I asked for a background check on Andre Dale. I was just reading through the report. He's originally from Minnesota, where he has quite the rap sheet for domestic violence and three sexual assault allegations. He did a year in jail for one of the battery charges. He was a doctor – general practitioner but his medical license expired."

"Expired or revoked?"

"Expired. I didn't find anything that showed he had lost his medical license. He wasn't a surgeon though." Declan tapped Kate under the chin. "See, I wasn't out here goofing off."

"I didn't think you were goofing off," she lied. That's exactly what she thought he had been doing. "Let's get someone from the Miami field office to run down leads on these homes. Maybe they can get in touch with real estate agents and narrow the list for us before tomorrow night."

Declan stared at her as he tried not to smile.

"What?"

"I already did it. We need to drop off the list when we are done here."

"Okay," she conceded, her face turning red. "You're more on the ball than I gave you credit for today."

"Just today?" Declan asked as he pushed himself off the car and went around to the driver's side. "You see, Katie, I'm working on not being such a screw-up."

Kate opened the door and got in the passenger side. "You've never been a screw-up. You just get easily distracted."

He winked. "I'm one of the few men out there who can multitask."

Kate didn't say another word while Declan navigated the roads to reach the FBI field office in downtown Miami. Kate waited in the car while Declan took the list inside. She used the time to debate with herself about when might be a good time to visit Andre Dale. They didn't have a whole lot of evidence right now and he might lawyer up. There was one stop she wanted to make first – Rosie, the woman Fanny had mentioned to her.

Declan returned a few minutes later out of breath and flushed. "Took me forever to find the woman I had spoken to on the phone. She said she'd start on the list right after lunch." Declan patted his stomach. "Do we get to eat anytime soon?"

Kate checked the time on the console of the car. It was two and well past lunch. "Let's interview Rosie Fahey first."

"Who is that?"

"The woman Fanny Fontaine mentioned to us." Kate gave him the address on South Miami Avenue and he headed there, grumbling about how hungry he was.

Kate looked over at him like he was an impatient child. "I promise when we are done, you can eat."

Declan found the high-rise with ease and they pulled in front of the front door. The doorman directed them around back, but when

Declan flashed his badge, the man allowed them to keep the car in front. They walked into the building, past the concierge, and into the elevator. Kate hit the button for the tenth floor. When the elevator doors opened, they had to take an immediate right or left. Kate chose left and it was a good choice. The door to Rosie's apartment was dead ahead.

Kate rapped her knuckles against the door and then stepped back. A moment later, a curvaceous blond with her hair piled on top of her head opened the door. Kate flashed her badge, confirmed the woman was Rosie, and then introduced herself and Declan. "Fanny Fontaine gave us your information. She said you'd be willing to speak with us."

Rosie dramatically waved her hand and stepped out of the way so they could walk inside. "Whatever Fanny wants, she gets."

"Why is that?" Kate asked.

"I owe Fanny my life." Rosie pointed to the couch and told them to take a seat. She sat in a chair across from them. "I was headed down a dark path when Fanny met me. She let me live at her house and paid for me to go to college all out of the goodness of her heart. She didn't even want anything in return."

When Rosie saw the look on Kate's face, she added, "I know what you're thinking. She did all that so I'd work for her. Nothing could be further from the truth. I assume you're here because of what happened with Andre Dale. Because of that and the relationship I had gotten myself into that proved just as abusive, Fanny didn't want me to work for her. She made me go to counseling, and only after a year of therapy, she let me work for her. Even then she was hesitant. Weirdly, it was what I needed to take control back."

"Fanny told us about how she runs her business," Declan started, his voice tinged with the same skepticism that Kate felt. "I want you to know that what you tell us is confidential. You're safe to share the truth with us. What was it like working for Fanny?"

78

Rosie laughed, showing off a row of bright white teeth. "It's probably better than she let on. I know it seems unbelievable that women involved in sex work can be treated so well, but that's Fanny. It's the way she runs her business."

"Do you know how Fanny got into the business?" Kate asked, realizing now she had never asked Fanny that question.

"During the 1960s, she was living here and saw how men were treating women, particularly the escorts. You had all sorts of famous men down here at that time. It was a man's game and those girls weren't always willing. There was a lot of force and persuasion and the cops were even worse then. Arresting girls and then turning them back over to their pimps. Fanny watched it all go down. She didn't like it one bit. She figured prostitution wasn't going anywhere so she'd clean it up."

"She also became rich and powerful in the process," Declan said. He folded his arms over his chest and stared at Rosie.

She didn't intimidate easily and she locked eyes with him. "Fanny was already rich. She was a trust fund kid and then married some wealthy guy who died on her. She was loaded and bored." Rosie sat back in the chair and crossed her legs. "Fanny didn't need the money, but she wanted to help the girls. She flipped the game on its head and drove out all of her competitors. She set the rules about how escorts would be treated in Miami Beach. She always told us she might not be able to change the world, but the world around her would be better. I never took a job I didn't want to take. When I wanted to quit, Fanny helped me find this place. She never once asked me to pay her back for paying for college. The women who work for her aren't just her employees. They are her family."

Kate asked gently, "Fanny mentioned you knew Andre and said you might know a woman who was assaulted by him."

Rosie had a far-off look on her face. It wasn't pain but wasn't pleasant either. Rosie looked away as she spoke. "It was me Andre assaulted. Fanny didn't want to disclose my business to you but said I could tell you if I chose. It's a common story. I came here to Miami Beach hoping to find work, which didn't happen, and then a friend introduced me to Andre. He introduced me to his rich friends. I was hesitant to get into the lifestyle, but Andre convinced me. One night, when I was out with the man I was seeing, he took me to Andre's house. I didn't know why we were going there. He left me at the front door and drove off."

Rosie folded her arms over her chest, closing in on herself. "Andre was having a party, and at first, he tried to seduce me. When that didn't work, he forced me. Other people saw what happened. I fought him and got beat up in the process. When I finally had a chance to escape, I ran out to the street and called a girlfriend who came to get me. I went right to the hospital and made a police report. As I'm sure Fanny told you, Andre and his witnesses said it was consensual and denied any physical assault. They said the bruises must have happened after I left."

"That must have been difficult to deal with." Kate was skilled with these kinds of interviews but they never got easier. "Do you know other women this has happened to?"

"Five in total. Three never reported it to the police and the two others had the same experience I had." Rosie shook her head in disgust. "The system isn't fair."

Kate had handled her fair share of sex crimes cases with the FBI and it was rarely fair to the victim. There were few other crimes where the victim's behavior was in question as much as the suspected offender. No one ever asked a robbery victim why they'd wear a gold watch or carry a designer purse. No cop had ever accused a robbery victim of asking for it. There were reasons why sexual assault victims – both men and women – didn't come forward.

There wasn't much Kate could offer in defense. "Do you know if the other victims had similar incidents as you?"

"Each of the victims was at his home when it occurred. Some they were alone. Others there was a party going on." Rosie remained quiet for a moment longer. "Andre is rarely alone. He has a few staff that take care of the home for him and the grounds. He has at least two women living with him at any given time. How he keeps them all quiet is beyond me."

Declan leaned forward on the couch. "Do you think Andre could be the one killing these women?"

"No. Unless he's doing it for the sport of it, it's not Andre. He is outwardly violent and cruel. He doesn't need to kill these women; he is damaging them enough already. I'm not a psychologist, but Andre is narcissistic and sadistic. His anger is right at the surface. From what I read in the newspapers; it doesn't sound like Andre. He also rarely leaves his estate."

"You're the first person who has said that," Kate said.

"I, unfortunately, know him better than most. Andre is the easy answer and too obvious a suspect. He's probably excited by the idea that the FBI will question him." Rosie uncrossed her legs and rested her hands in her lap. "While I don't think it's Andre, I wouldn't be surprised if he knew who it was. He might even be supplying the killer with women."

CHAPTER 13

An hour later, Declan and Kate sat on a patio of a restaurant overlooking the beach. Declan popped a sweet potato fry in his mouth and looked out at the water. "Maybe after we wrap up the case, we can spend a couple of days relaxing."

Kate picked at her salad. "Do you think Spade is going to give us that? I'm supposed to be retiring or taking a break. I'm not even sure what I'm doing, but here I am. Besides, I'm starting to worry that we might not catch him."

"You don't think it's Andre?" Declan asked, his eyes locking with hers.

Kate shook her head. "I wish I could say it was him, but I don't know after talking to Rosie."

"What did she say that changes your mind?"

"Rosie said that he's sexually assaulting women with others in the house. He gets physically violent in front of people. He either can't control himself or he's enjoying showing his power in front of others. Neither sounds like the killer."

"I can't disagree with you there. Does that mean you're ready to interview him?"

"We have enough at this point." Kate took a bite of her salad, thinking about the best approach. When she finished chewing, she took a sip of sparkling water. "We need to pin down the last day of each of the victims' lives. We can start with Chloe, the last victim, and work backward. I didn't see much of a timeline in the police reports."

"Let me check with Ted and see if they started one. He didn't invite us into his office so who knows what he and Isa didn't share with us."

Kate jabbed her fork into the lettuce. "It's so much easier when the local cops coordinate with us."

"It's territorial, Kate. Don't expect too much." Declan finished the rest of the fries on his plate and then leaned back. "The sun feels good."

When the server came over, Declan handed her his credit card and took care of the bill. He caught sight of the look on Kate's face as he signed his name on the slip. "You look like you're plotting and planning a world takeover."

A smile spread across Kate's face. "Something like that."

"Should I worry?"

"Not yet. I'm thinking about how we can take Andre down in the process. I'd love to be able to leave Miami Beach having broken up his operation."

"That's way out of our scope and out of our jurisdiction."

Kate didn't care. She could make the counter-argument. "If Andre is bringing these women in and introducing them to their boyfriends and taking a finder's fee, that could easily be seen as sex trafficking or being a pimp at the very least."

"Don't get me wrong. I think he's scum, but it sounds like the women are willing participants. To prove sex trafficking, we'd have to prove the women are there against their will or being duped into these relationships. Everyone we spoke to said that they were there of their own free will."

She couldn't argue with Declan on that. What Andre did skirted the law in a way that left him free from accountability. Kate wasn't having it though. "Let's hope there's something on him. I'd give anything to break up his stranglehold in this community."

Declan and Kate left the restaurant ready to take on the rest of the day. As they walked to the car and then as he drove them to Andre's, Declan checked his phone every few minutes to see if the assistant at the FBI field office had messaged him. Kate was completely focused on the interview with Andre, but she glanced up at his incessant phone-checking.

"You think the best shot we have of catching him is at his next crime scene, right?"

"I don't know if it's the best shot, but it's worth attempting." Declan turned right onto Andre's street. "I don't want him to get anywhere near his next victim, but if we can't stop him from doing that, catching him at the scene is the next best option we have."

Kate couldn't disagree with that. "He's probably already picked out his next victim. I assume by how well planned the murders are, he'd done that in advance. I feel like there's a ticking clock hanging over our heads."

"There is." Declan navigated the narrow street and turned into the driveway. They were faced with a closed gate and another call box. "Let's hope we have the same luck as we did with Fanny."

Declan put the window down and stuck his hand out and hit the button. When a man answered, Declan explained who he was and the gates slid open.

Declan pulled up the driveway which was nearly a half-mile in length. The sides of the driveway were dotted with beautiful flowers and palm trees. The lush vegetation certainly was welcoming and put off the vibe of peace and serenity. Kate could see how women might be lulled into feelings of safety.

The road curved and the house came into view. An older man with a slight build stood waiting for them. He had a head of thick graying hair and was dressed in white linen pants and a blue linen shirt with the top three buttons undone.

"That's him," Declan said. "He doesn't look much different from the photo in his rap sheet. Older and with gray hair instead of dark brown but the same overall."

Andre stood there smiling as they pulled up. He seemed to relish the idea that the FBI was there to speak to him just as Rosie said he would. Declan parked and Kate opened the passenger door. She stepped out holding her badge up and introduced them.

Andre held his hand out. "I'm so glad you're here, Agent Walsh. I've heard the Miami-Dade PD called in the FBI. It's terrible what's happening. I can only hope you solve this quickly. Such beautiful young women being butchered." Andre shuddered for effect as his hand touched Kate's.

"Have you spoken to the local detectives yet – Det. Ted Baer and Det. Isa Navarro?"

"I told them I'd be available when they were ready, but I've not heard from them yet." Andre shrugged. "I wasn't sure how I could be of help. Given I knew each of the victims, I assumed they'd want to interview me anyway."

Declan came around the car and met them. "You knew all of the victims?"

"Yes," Andre said matter-of-factly like it wasn't a strange thing to admit. "Each one of those poor women had come to my home a time or two. If you're not aware, I throw fabulous parties that cater to women like them."

"What do you mean women like them?" Declan asked.

"Beautiful and looking for men to take care of them. I have fabulously wealthy friends who love dating young women and have the financial resources to provide."

Kate couldn't believe that Andre was so forthcoming with the information, but she suspected he was testing them to see their reaction. She also believed that he probably assumed they knew all about him and wasn't going to fall into their questioning quite so easily.

"We've heard about the parties," Declan said stiffly. "We weren't aware though that you knew any of the victims."

Andre squinted. "I don't know that I would say I knew them well. They were here in my home. They met some of the men I know. I can't recall how much interaction I've had with them outside of Chloe." Andre looked down at the ground and shook his head. "Poor sweet Chloe. She was such an intelligent young woman but so naïve."

Declan stood with his hands on his hips. "What does that mean?"

Kate touched Declan's back hoping that he'd loosen his posture. They didn't need to be confrontational quite yet. "Why don't we go inside and talk if that's okay, Andre. It's probably a little more comfortable than the driveway."

"Yes, of course. I'm sorry for not offering sooner. I have some fresh lemonade ready for us on the back veranda."

Kate stopped in her tracks. "How did you know that we'd be by?"

Andre hadn't meant to let that slip. He tried to recover so he looked over his shoulder to Kate and turned on the charm. "Excuse me, I meant I was about to have lemonade on the veranda and I'd be happy to share."

Kate offered a little smile. "Certainly. I was going to say how could you know. We didn't know until a little while ago we'd be stopping to speak with you." She turned to Declan and, by the look on his face, she could tell he had caught it, too. Someone had tipped Andre off that they would be by to speak with him about the case.

They followed Andre through the foyer and down a long corridor decorated with black and white photos of Miami Beach in its heyday. The photos showed images of Hollywood celebrities from the 1930s to the 1960s. There was even one of Winston Churchill and Elizabeth

Taylor. Historic properties like the Fontainebleau, a hotel that graced the property right next to the Eden Roc, were also featured. Andre's home furnishings were plush but understated with sleek lines and free of clutter.

Kate remained stone-faced not giving him the satisfaction that she was impressed with the place. She and Declan followed him out to the veranda. They took a seat under an awning around a built-in swimming pool. The back of the property overlooked the water surrounding Star Island.

Andre held his arms out wide. "As you can see, I have little reason to leave the place. I spend nearly all of my time here. I occasionally leave for dinner and drinks to socialize, but then I'm right back home. I've become a bit of a homebody." He looked over at Kate and smiled. "Most people come to me."

"I see," Kate said, giving a noncommittal nod. "As you know, we are here to talk about…"

"You want to know what I know given I was the last person to see Chloe alive," Andre said, letting the bomb drop as he sat down in the chair and crossed his legs. He stared at them both with a hint of a smile on his lips.

CHAPTER 14

Kate kept her eyes on him but offered no other expression. She wasn't going to give him the satisfaction of being shocked by the information. "I think that's a good place to start."

Andre's face fell slightly, but he recovered quickly. He wanted a reaction that neither Kate nor Declan gave him. "Well, anyway," he started. "Chloe came over for dinner that night. She was quite upset about the current state of her relationship and sought me out for some advice."

"Why was she upset?" Declan asked.

Andre picked up a glass and poured some lemonade from the pitcher. He rolled the ice around in the glass and then took a sip, smacking his lips for effect. "Chloe wanted to stop seeing the man she was involved with but knew if she did, the financial support she was receiving would go up in smoke. She wanted to figure out how to pay for her tuition and stop seeing him, which wasn't going to work."

Declan cleared his throat. "Why is that?"

Andre glanced over at Declan and laughed at him. "If the relationship ended, her boyfriend would stop paying her bills. She'd need to figure out a new way to pay for school."

"That seems to be a common theme with these relationships. The women become indebted to the men."

"Agent James, how is that any different than marriage? If a woman leaves her wealthy husband, her quality of life tends to go down unless she drags it out in court and steals his assets."

"Hardly stealing if they made a life together," Kate said. "Did Chloe give you any indication why she wanted out of the relationship?"

"He wanted her to do things she wasn't comfortable with." Andre bounced his eyebrows up and down. "You know, sexually."

"Like what?" Declan asked, his voice constrained.

"Her boyfriend wanted to watch her with other men and she wasn't into it." Andre waved his hand as if to dismiss it. "It happens. Sometimes you think a woman is more adventurous than she is. Chloe wasn't going to give in so moving on and giving up the money was her only option."

Kate raised her eyebrows. "Her boyfriend wouldn't accept her boundaries. Is that what you're saying?"

Andre held his hands up as he crossed his legs. "Agent Walsh, these men pay a premium to be with beautiful young women. They want what they want. If they aren't getting what they want, there are another twenty young women lined up who'd be willing to fulfill their desires. It's fairly cut and dry."

"How is it any different from prostitution?" Declan said and then added, "You know prostitution is still illegal, correct?"

Andre sighed loudly. "This isn't prostitution or anything like it. These young women aren't selling sex, but they are being compensated for their time and attention. It's like any relationship."

"That's debatable," Declan mumbled. "Chloe came here and met with you. What advice did you give her?"

"The advice isn't relevant. The bottom line was Chloe wasn't going to give in so she needed to end the relationship. She left here quite upset with few options in front of her."

"Where was she going when she left here?"

"I assumed home but she was murdered that night." Andre looked over at Kate, avoiding Declan's gaze. "I wish I could tell you more."

Declan cleared his throat. "How did she leave here?"

"She walked."

"Walked?" Declan asked. His disbelief was apparent. "How did she arrive?"

"An Uber or cab, I'm not sure." Andre took another sip of his drink. "I asked her if she'd like my driver to take her home and she refused. As I said, she was upset and not thinking straight. She took off on foot down the driveway. I never saw her again."

Kate pressed. "How do you know that you were the last person to see her alive?"

Andre pursed his lips together. "Figure of speech, I guess."

Kate knew it wasn't a figure of speech. He was playing a game with them. Kate let a smile linger on her lips. "You're lying to us, Andre. One way or the other, you're lying to us, and it's easy for me to tell."

"How's that?"

Kate shook her head. "Not something you need to worry about. I'd rather not get off on a bad footing with you. Once someone lies to me, there's very little reason for me to continue speaking with them."

"You're pretty, Agent Walsh. It's too bad you're an FBI agent. There are many more attractive careers for a woman like you. A woman who looks like you shouldn't have to work at all."

Declan inched forward in his seat and Kate reached her hand out to stop him. This was the hardest part about doing interviews with Declan. His first instinct was to protect her, and men like Andre loved to rile him up.

Kate wouldn't give him the satisfaction of a response. She pulled out her phone like she was checking for the time and was bored with the conversation. "I don't have a lot of time, Andre. Either you're able to help us or you're not. We have more important people to interview."

Andre snorted. "I doubt there is anyone more important to the case than I am."

"If that were true, the two detectives on the case would have been here a lot sooner. They told us not to bother interviewing you because you wouldn't know anything."

Andre squirmed in his seat. Kate knew she had him right where she wanted him. The last thing a narcissist wanted to hear was that they were irrelevant. "They just don't know what I know."

Kate motioned with her hand. "Then enlighten us, please, because right now this seems like a waste of my time."

Declan turned his head to look at Kate and she offered him a curt nod to let him know she was fine. He turned back to Andre. He caught on to what Kate was doing and pushed harder. "I don't think you know anything. I think you like to spend your time with pretty young women because you can't handle women like Agent Walsh – strong, attractive, no need for men like you. You're playing Little League because you can't handle the Majors."

Andre stood and pointed down at Declan. "Now, listen here, you don't know what you're talking about. I have women falling all over themselves to be with me. Even Chloe came on to me that night, but I wasn't having any of it. I turned her down."

They were closer to the truth now. Kate reached down and patted the gun on her hip. "You need to sit down, Andre. We won't speak to you all keyed up like that."

Andre pointed at Declan. "I want him out of here."

Kate stood. "Then I'll be going with him. I thought you had such important information to give us. I guess I was right that this is a waste of time. Agent James, let's go. We have that other interview to get to."

Declan stood and turned toward the house, leaving Andre to stand there and huff like a child about to have a tantrum.

"Wait!" Andre yelled and raked a hand through his hair. "We got a bit off track. I'm not lying. Chloe did leave here alive that night. I misspoke. I can't be the last person to have seen her alive because she was with the killer after all. Believe me, I didn't kill her."

Kate turned slowly back to face him. "I believe that you didn't kill her."

Andre narrowed his eyes. "You do?" he asked surprised.

"Yes. I'm not here because you're a suspect. I'm here because I thought you might be able to provide valuable information to help us catch this killer." Kate placed her hands on her hips. "You're lying to me though and playing games. I don't have time for either. You admitted to knowing all of the murder victims and that you have parties where young women meet rich older men because you suspected we already knew that. You also admitted to seeing Chloe the night of her murder to shock us. You thought it was better to admit that up front like you have nothing to hide, which tells me that you do have something to hide. I don't believe being the killer is your secret though."

Andre smiled broadly and clapped his hands together. "Bravo, Agent Walsh, bravo. You are spectacular. I had heard about you before you arrived and I didn't think there was any way you could live up to the hype. Agent James," he said motioning with his hand, "is all brawn like I suspected, but you are magnificent."

Kate reached into her pocket and pulled out her business card and handed it to him. "We're done talking today. You let me know when you want to stop being so arrogant and obnoxious. If I think it's worth my time to speak to you, I'll be back. If not, I have more important people to speak with."

Kate turned and rested her hand on Declan's back nudging him forward.

"Don't leave!" Andre called after them.

Kate didn't even turn around. "Don't even look at him," she whispered to Declan.

"I need to get out of here before I hit him, Kate."

"That's exactly why we are leaving. I'm pretty close to knocking his teeth out. He needs to learn who is in control here, and it's not him. Not now and not ever."

"Agent Walsh, come back here!" Andre yelled, scurrying after them as they walked into and through the house. "You are not going to be able to solve this case without me. I demand that you turn around and speak to me. I pay your salary with my taxes. Turn around now or I'm calling your boss!"

Declan and Kate kept their pace to Andre's front door. As Declan held the front door for her, he laughed. "Spade will love this guy. He doesn't know what he's getting himself into."

Kate wanted to laugh but she had to maintain her stoic demeanor. Andre followed after them ranting and raving for them to come back. She ignored him and shut the car door without even glancing in his direction.

As they pulled out of the driveway, Kate checked the side mirror and saw that Andre stood at the front of his house, kicking the ground in front of him. He couldn't believe that he had lost control of the interview.

CHAPTER 15

"That was intense," Declan said as they got out onto the main road. "I'm going back to the police department because I want to give Ted and Isa a piece of my mind for alerting Andre that we'd be interviewing him."

"You caught that?" Kate asked, looking at her phone.

Declan pounded the steering wheel with his fist. "Of course I caught that. He was prepared for us. He had time to plan what he was going to say."

"We have no idea if it was Ted and Isa."

"Who else would it be?"

"I don't know, but you need to calm down." Kate sent off a quick text message to Spade, alerting him that the FBI might be getting a call. Given Andre's narcissism, he'd do everything he could to get them removed from the case. When that didn't work, he'd try again to smooth talk Kate. She dropped her phone in her lap and tightened her ponytail. "I thought you were going to leap out of your chair and punch Andre for what he said."

Declan gave her a sideways look. "I thought about it. I know you want me to stay calm and not defend you, but I'm not going to sit there and let some creep talk to you like that."

"I knew he was going to talk to me like that." Kate appreciated his need to protect her. It didn't get the job done though. "Sometimes I need them to behave like that so I can show them who is in charge. We have different approaches is all."

Declan chuckled. "You wanted to play mental chess and I wanted to break things – like his nose."

"That's one way to look at it." Kate's phone chimed. It was a text response from Spade letting her know that he'd handle everything on their end. He surprised her with something else, too. She read the message again and set the phone down. "Spade said he's already spoken to the mayor and the chief of police. They are demanding we leave Miami Beach. They want us off the case."

"Why?"

"Spade said that Isa called the mayor to make a formal complaint. The mayor went to bat for her with the chief and then there was a call to Spade."

Declan navigated over to the slow lane. "Are we leaving?"

Kate shook her head. "Not a chance."

"Isa went over her boss's head and went right to the mayor?"

"I can't imagine that went over too well." Kate thought about how strange that was. Law enforcement was a lot like the military in its structure. People didn't just go over their boss's head without repercussions. "I would assume that Isa has a relationship with the mayor that extends beyond work. She bypassed several layers of supervision to get to the mayor. I can't imagine the chief is happy with her."

"She must really want us gone."

Kate considered. "Or she thought that no one would be the wiser. I wonder how many other times she's gone directly to the mayor to get what she wants?"

Declan looked over at Kate. "We need to address this."

"We don't have a choice." The last thing Kate wanted was more drama. There was a good deal of ground to cover and a killer still lurking for his next victim. The last thing they needed was petty squabbles with the local cops.

Declan pulled into the police station parking lot and found a spot near the door. Before either of them could get out of the car, Ted and Isa had approached and stood next to the driver's side. Kate didn't want a confrontation right now, but it appeared they were getting just that. Ted's mouth was set in a firm line and Isa looked like she had received a thorough dressing down.

Kate opened the car door and put her feet to the pavement. She said hello to them both. "Is everything okay?"

"No," Ted said pushing Isa forward. "We had a situation while you were gone. You're going to need to decide if Isa remains on the case."

It was clear Declan wasn't in the mood to pull any punches. He got out of the car and slammed it shut. "I vote off the case considering you called the mayor who now that I think about it is probably the one who tipped off Andre that we were going to interview him."

Ted bore his eyes into Isa. "You told the mayor they were interviewing Andre?"

Isa stood with her hands on her hips, unflinching. "That's why I called Uncle Harvey. I wanted to avoid upsetting Andre Dale. You know that isn't going to be good for anyone."

"Uncle?" Declan asked with a tone of annoyance. He looked back at Kate who shrugged.

"He's my aunt's ex-husband. He's my uncle by marriage."

Kate walked around the car and stepped toward them. "You could have jeopardized the case." Isa started to argue and Kate held up her hand to stop her. "I don't want to hear it. I've given you more respect than you have earned. You compromised the investigation and you're causing stress where there doesn't need to be any."

Declan was equally frustrated. "The FBI gets a bad rap for coming into a local community and taking over a case. Kate and I work hard to be inclusive because this is your community. You should know it better than we do. Everyone works better when it's a collaborative investigation. Not only did you go behind our backs and outside of your chain of command, but you also provided information that compromised the investigation. The fact that you're the mayor's niece is a major conflict of interest in this case. I can't trust you. You're gone."

Kate didn't want to, but she'd have to deliver the final blow. "Isa, I'm sorry, but you can't work this case. For all of the reasons that Declan said, but mainly because I can't trust you. We have to be able to have trust with the detectives we work with. I have to know without question that the detectives we are working with are willing to follow the evidence no matter where it leads."

If looks could have killed, Kate would be dead. Isa didn't say a word, she turned around and headed back to the police department. Isa got close to the door and stopped like she was about to turn around but she never did. She took a few steps and then threw open the door and disappeared inside.

"Ted, we're sorry," Declan started to say but the detective cut him off.

"Please, don't. I'm the one who owes you both an apology. I've spent a good deal of time managing Isa on this case since we decided to call in the FBI. She got territorial and angry that we were calling in the feds and then flipped out completely when the FBI Miami field office said we needed to call in the both of you. Your work was all they could talk about, and Isa got jealous or insecure. I don't know, exactly. She's been difficult ever since. I had no idea she'd go right to the mayor though. I wanted to question Andre at the start when his name kept coming up, but Isa wouldn't hear of it. I was going to do it myself but then decided calling in the FBI would be better."

Ted paused and looked up at the police station building. "My office has a door so let's go up and continue our discussion. I hope that we can continue to work together. I need you both on this case."

Declan slapped the man on his back. "We need you too, Ted. Don't worry about Isa. It will all get sorted. Hopefully, with her off the case, things will run a little more smoothly."

Declan and Kate followed Ted into the building, and up to his office. They didn't see Isa anywhere. Ted closed the door and pointed to a table at the side of the room. "Take a seat and we can discuss what you've found out so far."

While Kate hadn't trusted Isa, she did trust Ted. He was a stand-up detective who had simply been in over his head with the murders and with managing Isa. She told Ted about the interview with Andre and how difficult he was.

"Even with him alerted ahead of time about the interview, I have him where I want him. I don't believe he killed any of the women, but I get the feeling he knows a lot more than he's telling us."

"Regardless of that," Declan added, "we heard from a woman who Andre sexually assaulted. I believe her story and that there are more women like her out there. She said she went to the hospital so an evidence kit should have been done. Do you know why those cases didn't go forward?"

"Andre believes, and rightly so, that he's untouchable in this community. Having an in with the mayor gives him power over the police department, and he gets away with everything. I'm glad, Kate, that you don't think he's the killer."

Declan pushed his chair back from the table and bounced his knee. "Kate said earlier that we need to bring down Andre before we leave Miami Beach. I thought she was crazy at first, but now, I'm all in."

Ted smirked. "Then you might as well buy some property and put in a change of address. Andre is untouchable." Ted looked right at Kate. "Will there be repercussions for you from the interview?"

Kate shook her head. "He threatened to call my boss, but I gave Martin Spade the heads up. Spade will go to bat for us. We'd all probably enjoy listening to a call between them."

"Good," Ted said, "I don't want any more trouble for you here. So, what's next?"

"We have a few questions about the last victim," Declan said, glancing around the room. "Do you have a board or anything in here where you kept a visual timeline of the murders?"

Ted pointed toward the door. "I put it in the conference room you were in this morning. I figured we'd need more space to talk."

"Let me ask you this first. Can you give us an overview of Chloe's last night leading up to the murder?"

Ted explained Chloe spent the early part of the day at a salon getting her hair and nails done. Then she went with a friend to lunch and disclosed she had a date with a new guy later that evening.

Ted folded his hands on the table. "The friend didn't get a name or anything. My understanding is Chloe had broken up with her previous boyfriend and was having some issues. After lunch, we know Chloe went to her residence and then left around six that evening. We saw her on security footage getting into a cab and leaving. She was dropped off on Star Island, but the cab driver said Chloe made him pull over to the side of the road. They weren't in front of a house or anything so we don't know what she was doing. That's the last known sighting of her."

"We can fill in part of the gap," Declan said. "She was with Andre."

CHAPTER 16

"Andre Dale?" Ted asked, confusion in his voice. "I thought Kate said he wasn't the killer."

"He's not, but he admitted that Chloe came to his place to ask for advice. I don't think that's what she was doing there," Kate explained evenly. "I believe Andre summoned her there because she was having issues with her boyfriend. He wanted her to have sex with other men and she wasn't into it. They broke up. According to Andre, Chloe was worried about how this would impact her financially so the fact that she might have had a date lined up for later that night isn't surprising."

"How long was she there?" Ted asked, shifting in his seat. The man looked uncomfortable like he knew it was information he should have had sooner.

Kate explained how combative Andre was in the interview. "Andre stonewalled us. He said Chloe got angry with him and left on foot. He said he watched her walk down the driveway and she was gone. She could have called another rideshare."

"No," Ted said emphatically. "We searched through records for the whole night. Only six drivers were covering Miami Beach that night. We have her being dropped off on Star Island but never picked back up. We checked the cab company too and her cellphone records don't show any calls made after she left her apartment."

Declan swiveled in his seat to face Kate. "Then Andre is lying or the killer was watching her."

"It could be both." Kate paused for a moment thinking. "When we pressed Andre on the information, he started playing games. He wants to remain in control. He admitted knowing each of the victims and seeing Chloe the night she was murdered. He told us this before the interview with him even started. We know now he had been tipped off, but he didn't seem concerned that we knew that. Most innocent people would be terrified of what it meant. He had no problems or concerns with it at all."

Ted slumped forward resting his arms on his desk. "That sounds like him. I don't know what we're supposed to do with that though."

"I know you're concerned about repercussions for going after Andre, so don't go after him. Let Declan and I handle that. If Andre thinks he's untouchable, he hasn't been up against the FBI. I'm trained to deal with men like Andre."

Ted nodded and offered a relieved smile. "Do you think Andre knows the killer?"

"I do," Kate admitted. "I'm not sure if Andre knows the killer and is protecting him or if it's someone in his circle and he's not aware that this person is the killer."

"Do you have a feeling either way?"

Kate shook her head. "I'm going to let the evidence lead me."

Declan's phone chimed and all eyes turned to him while he read the message. He pointed down at the phone. "That's my contact at the Miami FBI field office. She was able to search for properties that had the alarm systems currently disabled or non-existent. She's come up with a list of twelve properties."

Ted raised his eyes to him. "I don't understand."

Declan set his phone on the table. "We were able to get a list of properties that matched the other crime scene locations. We had quite a long list at first, but an assistant at the FBI field office was able to contact the real estate agents who are selling each of the homes and figure out which had the security systems currently disabled."

"Do you think we can get the resources to watch twelve properties this weekend?" Kate asked.

Ted rubbed at the back of his neck. "I can probably call in a few units but not enough to cover all twelve."

Declan sent a text and then looked up at them. "I asked if there were any resources that we could borrow from the field office. I'm sure we can get a few agents willing to help this weekend."

"We have no idea if he's going to kill someone this weekend," Ted said, looking at Declan like he thought it was a waste of time.

Kate didn't disagree. It could be a complete waste of resources but so was sitting there all weekend waiting for another victim's body to be identified. "At this point, I don't think we have much of an option but to give it a try."

"I agree," Declan said, reading the text that just came in. "We have four agents who are willing to help us. We can cover a few houses this weekend. If it doesn't pan out, it will be a lost weekend. At the very least, maybe the killer will see the police presence and know that we are watching."

Ted narrowed his gaze. "Won't that just make him change up his routine?"

Kate crossed her legs and rested her arms on the table. She leaned in to talk to Ted. "If we disrupt the killer's routine, then he has to change how he's doing things and that's when he will start to make mistakes."

"We're throwing him off his game, so to speak," Declan added.

"I guess it is worth a shot then." Ted looked between them and then stood. "Let's head into the conference room and I'll walk you through the timeline we know to date."

Kate and Declan shared a look, encouraged they were making progress. They followed Ted to the conference room and took a seat. He turned two large white boards around so the information could be read.

Ted walked to the far end of the first board and pointed to a photo of a young dark-haired woman with big dark brown eyes. Kate knew from the file that Marci was twenty-eight, but the young woman didn't look any older than her early twenties.

"The first victim found was Marci Kessler," Ted said, pointing to a crime scene photo of the front of the home. "The home is listed for eighteen million. Marci was found on a Sunday morning when the real estate agent went to prepare the place for a showing. The potential buyer had not arrived yet. Her heart was found on a nearby dresser. Other than blood below the body and on the dresser, the crime scene was clear."

Kate tapped a pen on a pad of paper in front of her. "We know those details. What have you learned about Marci's movements up until that point? Any family or friends give interviews with anything relevant?"

"Marci lived alone in a condo in South Beach off Ocean Drive. She didn't tell her friends much about her lifestyle. A few people knew she had been a high-priced escort and worked for Fanny Fontaine, but they didn't know much else. She is originally from Orlando and her family knew nothing about her life. They assumed she was here going to school, which she was."

"She graduated or drop out?" Declan asked.

"She got her master's in psychology and was preparing to start a doctorate program." Ted let out a frustrated breath. "She was working for Fanny to put herself through school. My understanding is that she was not out on a scheduled date that evening."

"We spoke to Fanny who was forthcoming with information." Kate watched as Ted's eyes grew wide. "She sounded as eager as we are to catch this killer. She confirmed that neither of the victims who worked for her was out on official dates that evening."

Ted looked down at Kate, clearly impressed. "I'm surprised she spoke to you. Fanny Fontaine is as untouchable as Andre Dale. She outright refused to speak to Isa and me, and there wasn't a thing we could do about it. What else did she have to say?"

"Andre supplies the mayor with coke," Declan said.

Ted sucked in a breath and held it, staring at them. His face grew red and it was obvious he was having trouble controlling his anger. "I had no idea."

"That's part of the reason why Isa needed to be off this case," Kate confirmed. "We have no idea who it will impact as we dive in deeper."

Ted rubbed his brow, his anger and annoyance still hanging in. "As you know I'm a Miami-Dade PD detective, not Miami Beach PD, so there was a lot we had to learn and locals wouldn't share much. The relationship between the mayor and Andre has been a minefield from the start."

"I don't think it's something we can worry about right now." Kate didn't want them to get sidetracked. "Go on with Marci's last few hours. I want to get a feel for what these victims were doing and who they were talking to before the murders."

It took Ted another minute to calm himself down. Any detective would be angry – out of their normal jurisdiction and walking through a minefield. Ted stepped back near the board. "We can trace each victim until about seven the night they were killed. The early part of their days was all routine. Marci spent Saturday morning at a local coffee shop with friends. After, she went to the beach and then to the gym in her building. She was back home by mid-afternoon and shopped for clothes online and then nothing. We heard she had a date but no one had the details. Her cellphone didn't show any unusual numbers. We weren't able to pick her up on surveillance video either.

We can confirm from building security, she left just after seven in the evening, stepped outside of her building, and got into a black four-door Mercedes with tinted windows. We have no confirmation on a driver and no one got the tag number. It's a common car around here so nothing was picked up on street surveillance either."

Declan asked, "Do any of the potential suspects have that kind of car?"

"We don't have any suspects."

"Did you check Andre Dale?"

Ted shook his head, casting his eyes to the floor.

CHAPTER 17

K ate and Declan sat at a table on the deck of the Eden Roc outdoor bar and grill. The dinner rush had come and gone. The few people out there were sipping drinks and relaxing on the deck enjoying the warm ocean breeze. Kate couldn't see the water, but she could hear the waves crashing on the shore below. They had grabbed a table far from other people so they could talk without being overheard.

They didn't gain much information from the meeting with Ted. Mostly, what became apparent was what hadn't been done. Family and friends of the victims had been spoken to and those were statements they had read earlier in the file. Not a lot of leg work was put into tracing the last days and hours of the victims.

After the meeting, Declan ran a search for what cars belonged to Andre. A black Mercedes was not listed. He had a white Land Rover and a blue BMW registered to him in the state of Florida. Nothing else came back registered to him in the state or any other.

Kate sipped her water. "We have no idea how the killer is targeting the victims. We think it's through their relationships with these older men but we don't know. This could be something distracting us from what's really going on. Could they all be going to the same shop where he sees them? Could they be seeing the same doctor? The possibilities are endless right now."

Declan eyed her. "You're working yourself up into a frustrated state when it's not needed." He nudged Marci's file on the table. Ted had handed some over so they could review further.

"How much do you think Fanny knew about Marci's life outside of work?"

Declan raised his eyebrows. "Are you thinking about speaking to her again?"

"We didn't go into that interview focused on the victims. I wanted more general information from her. To be honest, I didn't think she was going to speak to us at all."

"I didn't think she'd speak to us either based on what Isa and Ted had said. We can speak to her again."

Kate picked at the shrimp pasta in front of her. She speared a piece with her fork and then popped it into her mouth. She set her fork down and stared at him. "Can I tell you something?"

Declan leaned into the table and bobbed his eyebrows. "Anything but make it juicy. I'm bored."

Kate tipped her head back and laughed. "You're crazy. It's not anything personal. It's about the case. Initially, I thought the relationships the women were having might be the cause of the murders. The men are too old to fit the profile."

"What do you mean?"

"Think about it. That guy Harris, who hit on me last night, is well into his sixties. Andre is the same. If I didn't know anything about the relationships the victims were having and went into the case blind, I'd profile a much younger suspect."

Declan pulled back. "You hardly ever second guess yourself."

"I prejudged these women. I got sidetracked by their profession and the scandalous nature of it. We don't even really know if it's a factor yet."

Declan sipped his soda. "I wouldn't be so hard on yourself, Katie.

We walked into this with the local detectives pointing in that direction so that's where we went. What are you thinking now?" He saw Kate's hesitancy. "Katie, it's you and me. No one else is here. It's a working profile that's all – open to change."

Kate relaxed into the chair and threw out thoughts. "Medical training but that's a given. He's local to this area and knows it well. He also blends well enough that he's not causing alarm with the victims or anyone else."

"Makes sense so far."

Kate closed her eyes and tried to picture him in her mind. "He's probably in his forties to early fifties. He's strong and has a good physique. He's someone no one is looking for right now."

Declan didn't disagree with her. "How do you think he's getting the victims?"

"He's meeting them somehow. He might be paying for sex but he's not raising suspicion. He is someone flying under the radar."

"You don't think there's a connection to Andre?"

"I think there is, but I'm not sure how yet. I haven't changed my mind about that."

Both Kate and Declan leaned back when the waiter came over to remove their plates. He asked them if they'd like anything else, and they both ordered more to drink. The young man looked on the verge of saying something but held back.

Declan looked up at him. "Is there something you need?"

The young man set their plates back on the table and brushed his hands down the front of his apron. "I heard you're with the FBI."

"We are," Declan confirmed.

The young man looked over his shoulder to the left and then to the right. He bent down toward Declan. "I might know something about one of those women who were murdered."

Declan raised his head to him. "What do you know?"

108

The young man bit his lip. "You need to talk to the bartender over there. The first woman who was murdered. I can't remember her name. She used to come to this bar nearly every night. I thought for a while that she was his girlfriend, but he told us it wasn't like that. I don't know how she knew him, but they were friendly."

"Is there a reason you think that might be important?" Kate asked, not sure why it was relevant. People went to bars all the time.

"He's been known to, you know...make deals with men in the hotel." The young man blushed and turned away from Kate.

"For sex?" Declan asked and he nodded. "Is there anything else you think we should know?"

"One time, she was down on the beach with a guy and she came running back up here after like an hour. She was screaming and yelling and Eric told her she better knock it off. She left though and appeared afraid."

"How long ago was this?"

"About a week before she died."

Kate knew her expression would be hard to read. She wasn't surprised, but she also wasn't sure that this had any bearing on the case. She thanked the young man and promised they'd follow up. He left the table looking relieved.

"What do you think?" Declan asked once the waiter was out of earshot.

"The bartender knew Marci so that might help us. I'm not sure otherwise." Kate checked her watch. It was close to ten when the outdoor bar closed down. She looked over Declan's shoulder and noted that most of the customers had left already. There was only one couple at a table far from the bar. "Let's go talk to him now."

Both Kate and Declan stood from the table. They had changed clothes after the meeting with Ted so neither looked like an FBI agent. Kate had her badge in the pocket of her skirt and Declan had his on his chain under his shirt. He pulled his out and flashed it at the bartender who was stacking glasses behind the bar.

"Can I help you?" the bartender asked.

Declan introduced himself. "We're looking into the murders that have happened in Miami Beach."

"Right, I heard something about that," he said, not making eye contact. He turned his back and continued stacking glasses.

Declan tapped on the bar to get his attention. "Take a minute and speak to us. I'm sure your boss will approve."

Eric glanced toward the back of the hotel. "I have about five minutes. What do you need?"

Declan sat down at the bar. "We have reason to believe that you knew the first victim, Marci Kessler. It's our understanding that you were finding her men to have sex with, presumably for money."

Eric dropped the towel he had been holding and his mouth parted. "No, man, you've got that wrong. This isn't that kind of hotel. That isn't something I would do."

"Did you know Marci Kessler?" Kate asked, believing what he told them. Eric had an expression of shock that wasn't faked.

"I knew her, yeah. She and I dated for about six months. Then I found out how she made her money and I couldn't handle it. We stayed friends though."

"It took you six months to figure it out?" Declan asked with a hint of skepticism in his voice.

"We had a casual relationship at first. It was nothing serious. I didn't ask what she did with her time."

"What did she say she did for work?" Kate asked.

Eric leaned back and crossed his arms over his chest. "She was in school. When I asked how she could afford to live in Miami Beach, she told me her parents had money."

"How did you find out the truth?"

Eric looked down at the ground and his face fell. "I saw her out one night at a restaurant in downtown Miami. It was like three days after we decided to be exclusive. I didn't say anything to her then, but it was obvious she was involved with the guy. They were all over each other. When I confronted her about it later, she told me the truth."

"How did you react?"

"I was angry. I can't lie about that. I yelled and we argued. I told her she had to stop or we were going to break up." Eric shrugged. "She chose the money over me."

"That must have made you angry," Declan said. "It gave you a reason to hurt her for sure."

"No, it's not like that," Eric explained, his anger rising. "As I said, we ended up friends. She made her choice and I made mine. I moved on."

"Who was the man she was with on the beach?"

Eric's eyes shifted. "You heard about that?"

Both Kate and Declan looked at him but didn't say a word. There was nothing to say.

"Listen," Eric said, his tone serious. He stood upright and locked eyes with Declan. "I didn't hook her up with anyone. She begged me to introduce her to a wealthy guy who visits the hotel a lot. She said she had seen him and was attracted to him. She promised it wasn't for work. I made an introduction and told her not to do anything stupid or embarrassing."

"That's not the way it turned out?" Declan asked.

"No, man, it wasn't." Eric pointed down toward the beach. "She went on a walk with him after I introduced them and she asked him for money. She solicited him. He called here at the bar furious with me, wanting to know why I was setting him up with a hooker. He told me he said no and she stormed off. I had someone cover for me. When I found her, I yelled at her and I kept yelling at her. I told her to go back to him and fix it. When she refused, I kicked her out and told her never to come back."

"What happened the next time you saw her?"

Eric ran a hand through his hair. "I never saw her again. She was murdered about a week later."

Kate believed him. His body language and inflection in his voice all rang true. "Do you think this man had anything to do with her murder?"

Eric shook his head. "No. Definitely not. He's from California and was here on business. He wasn't even here when the murders happened."

CHAPTER 18

Eric had reluctantly given Kate the man's name and contact information. Mick Stratford was thirty-eight and lived in Los Angeles. He was a well-known agent for A-list Hollywood celebrities. At the very least, even if Mick didn't know anything that could help them, Kate wanted to confirm Eric's story.

"You believe Eric?" Declan yelled from the bathroom.

"I don't have any reason not to trust him."

Declan popped his head out of the bathroom door. "Are you calling Mick to confirm?"

"I was going to do that now."

"I'll leave you to it then." Declan closed the bathroom door, and a moment later the shower turned on creating a background hum in the room.

Kate sat on the edge of the bed dangling her bare feet over the side. She reached for the Post-It where Eric had written Mick's cellphone number.

The man answered quickly and then was stunned into silence when Kate introduced herself.

"I knew the woman only briefly, Agent Walsh. I left town the morning after meeting her." Mick asked someone to quiet down and then got back on the phone. "I'm sorry. I'm on location and it's noisy here. I saw on the news about the murders. I don't know how I

113

can be of help to you though."

"How did you meet her?"

"I was not a client of hers if that's what you're insinuating."

"Not at all. All I want to know is how you met."

"The bartender at the hotel. I'm in Miami quite a lot and love staying at the Eden Roc. Eric always hooks me up. He said he knew a nice girl that I might like." Mick chuckled. "You'd think I date a lot given my line of work, but I work constantly. There's been little time for anything else. I was up for meeting a nice girl."

Kate pressed further. "What happened when you went out?"

"We met at the hotel bar and had dinner. Marci seemed nice so I suggested a walk on the beach after dinner. The sun was setting and I figured it would be a nice way to end the date." Mick's voice constricted. "We got about five minutes into the walk and she started pawing at me. I wasn't going to say no so I kissed her. We sat down on the sand and were making out when she stopped. She pulled back and told me that it would cost me ten thousand dollars for the weekend. I didn't even know what to say. I was furious."

Kate remained quiet even though he had paused. She wanted him to continue speaking, but when he didn't, she nudged him. "What happened next?"

"I said no. I've never paid for sex in my life, and I wasn't starting then. I live in LA. I can get laid at the snap of a finger, but that's not what I'm interested in at my age. I told Marci no and she flipped out. She started screaming and yelling and told me she was going to tell people that I paid for it anyway. She said she'd go to a tabloid so I might as well just pay her to keep quiet then."

"I assume that made you angrier."

"Angry doesn't cut it. I was livid, but I refused no matter what she said. I have a great public relations firm on retainer. If I had to mitigate any damage, that's what I would do. When I told her that,

Marci slapped me and then took off. I thought Eric had set the whole thing up so I called him at the bar and yelled at him. He assured me that wasn't what he was doing. He said he'd handle it."

Mick asked the people in the background to quiet down again, which Kate appreciated. It was hard to hear him.

When he got back on the phone, he raised his voice. "I got up to the bar in enough time to hear Eric tell her to make things right with me, but she took off. He apologized to me profusely. He was worried I'd get him fired. I assured him I wouldn't say anything and I went back to my room. That was the end of that."

The story checked out. It was exactly what Eric had told them. She had no reason to believe the two had spoken to get their stories straight. "Did you ever see or speak to Marci again?"

"No. I had a flight at eight the next morning. I was back here in Los Angeles when I saw the news about her murder. Do you have any idea what happened?"

"It's part of a larger case. We believe there is a serial killer targeting women like Marci."

"Do you think it's because of something like what Marci did to me?"

"I don't know," Kate said almost absently. She hadn't thought about that before. Maybe the killer was choosing his victims from women who had solicited him. There was a chance he had thought the women were interested and when he found out they weren't, he targeted them. The murders were not spontaneous though. They were planned.

"Hello. Are you there?" Mick said when Kate got quiet. "Do you need anything else?"

Kate stared down at the floor trying to think of anything else she might want to know. "Did you see anyone following Marci? Did she mention any men who had been bothering her?"

"She didn't say anything about other men," Mick said quickly but then grew quiet. "That's not true. When we were having dinner, she got annoyed about a guy sitting a few tables over from us. She said that it was someone she knew who wouldn't take the hint. When I asked her what she meant, she said it was a guy who had asked her out a few times, but she wasn't interested."

Kate's ears perked up at that. "Did Marci give you his name or any information about him?"

"Not really. She said he was a local guy but she wasn't interested."

"Did you see him?"

"The guy was sitting behind me. I turned around for a second and took a look. He was well-dressed, probably early forties, and had blond hair. He looked like he worked out. Nothing distinctive about him otherwise."

Kate got up from the bed and went to the desk. She grabbed a pen and a small pad of hotel stationery. "How tall would you say?"

"I'm a little over six foot and he looked like he could be about the same. Hard to tell though because he was sitting."

Kate asked a few more questions, jotted down more notes, and then thanked Mick for the information. She assured him that she'd try to keep him out of the case if possible. Mick didn't seem to mind. He even joked that the whole thing would make for a good movie if the killer was caught.

As Kate hung up, Declan came out of the bathroom wearing only a pair of boxers, and towel drying his hair. He shook himself like a dog. "Did you find out anything?"

Kate slumped in a recliner in the corner of the room. "Eric told us the truth. Mick confirmed it. He also said that at dinner that night, Marci saw a man who had been stalking her." Kate paused and shook her head. "Maybe not stalking, but he had been persistent in trying to date her. Marci wasn't interested."

Declan pinched the bridge of his nose. "I don't get it. If she's soliciting strangers and getting turned down, why not go after easy money?"

"Maybe he wanted a relationship and not to pay her. I don't know though."

Declan threw the towel on a nearby chair and flopped down on the bed. "I probably left you enough hot water. You should get some rest. You look tired."

Kate didn't say anything. She rested her head back and stared up at the ceiling.

"You're doing that thing with your eyes that causes the wrinkle in your forehead to show up. Relax, Kate. You're no good to anyone without sleep."

Kate reached her hand up to her forehead and rubbed at the line Declan mentioned. "You don't have to point out my flaws."

Declan laughed. "It's not a flaw. It's adorable." He walked over to her and reached out his hand. He pulled her out of the chair. "You'll feel better after a shower and a good night's rest."

Kate headed for the bathroom and mindlessly went through her evening routine. A few minutes into a hot shower, it hit her how right Declan had been. Kate yawned and struggled to keep her eyes open. She finished the shower and her nightly routine. By the time she walked out of the bathroom, Declan had the lights off and television on. She slipped into her bed and was fast asleep before she even settled in.

The call came at two in the morning. Kate's cellphone rang on the table next to her bed. She reached and slapped at the tabletop until she had her phone in her hand. She looked at the screen before her head was even off the pillow. Declan sat up and turned on the light. Kate blinked her eyes to adjust to the brightness and answered the call.

"Agent Walsh, this is Fanny Fontaine," the woman said nearly breathless. "You need to come to my home right now. One of my girls was attacked. She believes it was the killer. She's here now and willing to speak to you." The call ended before Kate could ask any questions.

CHAPTER 19

"Are you okay to drive?" Kate asked Declan as they navigated their way to Fanny's house. He kept rubbing his right eye and Kate feared he wasn't seeing well.

"Fine," he grunted and then yawned. "It's just itchy. We only got like three hours of sleep. I'll be fine by the time we get there. What did Fanny say again?"

"One of the women who works for her..." Kate stopped herself midsentence. "She said one of her girls so I assumed that she meant one of the women who work for her was attacked. She believed he might be the killer?"

"Did she know him? Was it one of the men she'd been out with?"

"I don't know, Declan. She didn't say any more than that." Kate had wanted to know more before they tore out of their hotel room into the night, but Fanny had hung up and then didn't answer when Kate had tried to call her back.

"Why didn't she call the police or go to the hospital?"

"I don't know," Kate said frustrated, not with Declan but the situation.

"Sorry," he said absently, refocusing on the road. "I know you don't know. I'm saying aloud what's in my head. I don't expect you to have an answer."

"It's all things I want to know, too." Kate reached down and patted the gun on her hip. It wasn't that she didn't trust Fanny. She didn't know the woman well enough to trust or not trust. They were going out in the middle of the night to meet someone without any backup while a serial killer was on the loose.

Declan and Kate had debated calling in Ted for backup but figured it would be better to let the man sleep because they all had a surveillance shift later that night.

Declan pulled into Fanny's driveway, bypassing the gate that had been left open. "That's weird," he remarked as they passed. "If there is someone on the loose who attacked me, I think I'd want to ensure as much security as possible."

Kate had also thought it odd. "She knows we aren't far. Fanny said she had security in her home so maybe they aren't alone or worried about it here."

Declan kept driving and pulled right up to the house as they had before. "You armed?"

"Of course. I texted Spade too and told him we got called out to Fanny's house. Are you worried?"

"Not really. But then that's usually exactly when I should be." Declan flashed her a sleepy grin.

They got out of the car assessing the environment as they approached the house. There were lights on but all seemed quiet. Declan knocked on the door and then tried the door and found it locked.

A moment later, a tall man in jeans and a polo shirt answered the door. His chest and biceps stressed the fabric of the shirt. A patchwork of veins ran down both arms. Anabolic steroid use would do that to a man. Kate assumed this must be the security Fanny had mentioned. He closed the door behind them and took them down a long corridor to a room at the end of the hall. He didn't speak but pointed to the closed door.

Kate knocked once and then pushed the door open. A young woman with streaked mascara sat at the end of a queen-sized bed. Fanny reclined in a chaise in a corner of the room. She seemed relaxed and far too calm.

Kate waited for Declan who was right behind her and then they introduced themselves to the young woman who said her name was Paris Winter. Kate assumed it was an alias.

"What happened?" Kate asked as she stepped closer and looked over the woman for signs of trauma. Other than a scratch across the woman's neck, Kate didn't see any visible injuries.

Paris didn't raise her head. She kept her eyes focused on the floor. "I took a date Fanny didn't know about. When we got back to his place, he attacked me."

Declan stepped toward her. "Attacked you how?"

Paris reached her hand up to her neck to the scratch. "He offered me something to drink and when I turned my back to look out at the water, he wrapped his hands around my neck. He tried to strangle me."

Declan squatted down to assess the scratch more closely. It was about four inches in length and ran from the front of her throat to the right side of her neck. "How did the scratch happen?"

"When I tried to get his hands off me."

"How did you get away?" he asked.

"When I couldn't get him to loosen his grip, I elbowed him and he let go. I punched him and then kicked him."

Declan glanced back at Kate and she understood his question. "Where did you learn to fight like that?" Not many women would have had the presence of mind to do that.

"Me, Agent Walsh," Fanny said, finally speaking. "All of my girls go through a self-defense course. I can only do so much on the front end to make sure they are safe. They must be able to defend themselves if something goes wrong."

Declan stood fully upright with his hands on his hips and glared down at her. "I thought you didn't send them out with men you haven't fully vetted. You gave us a whole speech about how all of your clients are safe and would never harm one of the women. What happened to that?"

"I don't like your tone, Agent James," Fanny said, pushing herself up off the chaise and standing. She was so short she only came up to Declan's chest, but she was still an imposing figure. "This wasn't one of my clients. Paris, against all advice and breaking her employment contract, sought someone out on her own." Fanny looked back at the young woman. "And look at what that got her."

She turned back to Declan. "Even though I'll probably fire her, Paris still came running to me when she was in trouble. Everything I told you was true. I don't own these girls though, Agent James. I don't have the time nor the inclination to babysit them. If they choose to moonlight, then they put themselves at risk."

Kate wanted to defuse the situation between Fanny and Declan. She stepped around them both to Paris. "Is that what happened? You were moonlighting and met someone on your own?"

Paris sniffled and nodded. "I thought for one night it couldn't hurt. Fanny didn't have any work for me, and I was bored sitting at home. I figured one night couldn't hurt."

"See how wrong you were?" Fanny scolded.

Kate caught Declan's eye and motioned with her head for him to take Fanny out of the room. She didn't care if they duked it out in another room or outside. Kate needed information without interruption.

When they were gone, Kate sat down on the edge of the chaise Fanny had been sitting on. She clasped her hands and rested them on her knees. "Tell me what happened tonight, Paris."

Paris brushed strands of her honey blonde hair out of her eyes. "As I said, I was at home and bored. I tried calling friends but no one was around. I went to a hotel bar. No action so I left and went to the Blue Note. I was there maybe twenty minutes when I met a guy. He told me his name was Lenny. He didn't tell me his last name and I didn't ask. He knew right away why I was there. He made me an offer for the night and I took it. We stayed at Blue Note talking and having drinks for about an hour before he told me he wanted to leave. He said he lived right down the road and had a condo overlooking the ocean. I felt safe with him."

Paris shook her head, fighting back tears. "I didn't have any reason to believe he'd hurt me."

Kate got his address and made a note file in her phone. "Tell me what happened once you got to his place."

"He kissed me in the hallway near his door and then he unlocked the door and let us in. He flipped on the lights and took me right to the window to see the ocean. It was hard to see at night but you could hear the waves. It was peaceful, serene even. That's when he asked me if I wanted anything to drink. I turned back to look out the window. I saw him through the glass coming up behind me. I figured he'd kiss me or have his hands on me. I never thought he was going to strangle me until he was doing it."

Kate believed Paris so far. "You said you fought him off. Then what happened?"

"After he fell to the ground, I took off out the front door and kept on running. I took the stairs down instead of the elevator. I figured if Lenny followed me, he'd go to the elevator. The concierge at the front desk asked me what was wrong as I ran past, but I didn't stop long enough to tell him. I wanted to get out of there. I ran until I was in a crowd of people and then called Fanny. Two of her men came to pick me up and brought me here. After I told her the story, she called you."

"Why did you think Lenny is the killer?"

Paris raised her head to look at Kate and they locked eyes. "I had heard the killer was choking women. That's what Fanny told us. When I got back here and told her, she said it might be the killer. Do you think it was?"

"I don't know," Kate said honestly. It did sound like the killer's method of operation but too sloppy to be him. "What does Lenny do for work?"

"I think he's retired from finance. He rambled on about his stock portfolio at one point."

"How old was Lenny?"

"I don't know," Paris said, wiping tears from her eyes. "Maybe in his sixties."

Kate asked a few more questions, but Paris wasn't able to tell her much more. "Do you want to make a police report about what happened?"

Paris shook her head. "No. I know Fanny isn't going to like that answer, but then I'd have to tell the cops what I was doing. I don't want to get in trouble."

"They won't arrest you," Kate assured but Paris still said no. This was the number one reason why when prostitutes were attacked or raped, they didn't come forward. Nine times out of ten, the reports aren't taken seriously and the judgment the women faced wasn't worth it. Kate asked one more time and Paris said no again so Kate gave her a business card and she left.

Kate found Fanny and Declan sitting in the living room chatting like old friends.

"Do you think it's the guy, Agent Walsh?" Fanny asked as Kate entered the room.

"I can't say for sure, but it doesn't sound like it. I'm not sure of that guy's intent but Paris doesn't want to make a police report."

Fanny narrowed her eyes at Kate. "So, you're going to do nothing about it?"

"I didn't say that. Declan and I will interview him and see what we can find out. That's the best we can do right now in the middle of the night." Kate stifled a yawn and resisted the urge to lay down on Fanny's couch.

CHAPTER 20

The next morning at nine Kate and Declan stood outside of Lenny's condo door. They had considered visiting the night before but given Paris didn't want to make a police report, they figured talking to him in the morning might get them further.

Kate knocked once and then twice, harder than the first time. "Lenny," she called out.

After she had already grown impatient, an older man with sparse white hair opened the door. He knotted the belt on his robe as he pulled the door open. "I'm Lenny. Don't be shouting out here so early. What do you want?"

They both flashed their badges. Declan explained, "We need to talk about what happened here last night with Paris."

He fiddled with the tie on his robe. "I don't know what you're talking about. I was here alone all evening."

"Not what the bartender at the Blue Note told us," Declan fibbed. They hadn't talked to anyone at Blue Note, but it was an easy lie to tell.

Lenny tilted his head to one side and then to the other probably trying to decide how much they knew. He must have believed Declan because he stepped back into his condo and motioned with his hand for them to enter. "Take a seat in the living room and let me get dressed."

The living room was a straight shot from the doorway and exactly as Paris had described. There was a leather sofa and chair and a floor-to-ceiling window overlooking the ocean. Kate understood now why it had been easy for Paris to get away. It couldn't have been more than fifty feet from the window to the front door.

"No." Declan stepped in front of Lenny blocking his way. "Let's sit down in the living room and talk now. You're fine the way you're dressed." There was always a concern a suspect or witness might go get a weapon.

"Um, well..." Lenny said looking around. He must have thought better of it because he sat down on the couch and didn't argue. "What do you want to know?"

Kate and Declan each sat in chairs facing the couch. There was a table between them. They had decided beforehand they'd get straight to the point. They had called the concierge that morning and gotten the man's full name. They ran him in the system and he had no priors.

Declan took the lead. "We spoke to Paris last night and she said you tried to strangle her with your hands."

Lenny squinted. "Even if that happened, and I'm not admitting it did, wouldn't that be the local police? How is this an FBI matter?"

"Just tell us what happened last night."

Lenny shook his head. "No. You tell me first."

Declan raised his voice. "We are investigating the murders that have been happening to escorts in the city. You tried to strangle a woman like the killer has been doing."

Lenny let out a shriek that made both Declan and Kate jump in their seats. "That isn't me! I swear I have never killed anyone. Oh my." He clutched at his chest and heaved forward. "I've never. I've hired escorts, but I've never killed anyone. I had my hands around her neck as foreplay. I swear to you I thought she'd like it a little rough. Then she freaked out. I didn't mean to hurt her."

"Calm down," Kate commanded more loudly than she had meant to. "Tell us what happened."

Lenny gasped for breath and clutched at his chest. Kate couldn't tell if he was being real or faking it. The last thing she needed was for him to have a heart attack.

Declan leaned forward in the chair. "You need to relax."

Lenny calmed himself down and then recounted nearly the same story as Paris. The only difference was Lenny explained that while at Blue Note, Paris had mentioned that she liked being strangled. Lenny was doing it for her.

He held his hand up like a Boy Scout. "I would have never done it otherwise. I've never done something like that before, but figured she'd might as well enjoy herself, too."

Paris had left out a critical piece of the story if it were true. Kate believed Lenny though. The man seemed terrified of getting into trouble. "What happened when Paris left?"

"She nearly broke my nose and she kicked me in the balls. I sat down on the couch and cried like a child."

Declan raised his eyebrows. "You didn't go after her at all?"

Lenny locked eyes with Declan. "You ever been kicked in the balls? You ain't running nowhere."

Declan ignored the commentary. "You weren't concerned she might go to the police?"

"Not really." Lenny looked between them and shook his head. "I can't believe you think I'm that killer. I'd never do something like that." He pulled the robe around him tighter and his face went from shock to indignant.

Kate didn't care about how annoyed he seemed. "Do you know anything about the murders?"

"Just what's been in the newspapers. A few of us have spoken about it."

"Yeah," Declan said, standing. He stretched his legs and stared down at the man. "What's the talk of the town?"

Lenny raised his eyes to Declan. "It's none of us. That's all I can tell you."

"Us? Who?"

"None of us guys who frequent the Blue Note. There's some rumor going around that it's one of us retired guys who is doing this to those young women. I can tell you it's not us. You're barking up the wrong tree."

"What about Andre Dale?" Kate asked.

"I don't know anything about him." Lenny snapped his fingers. "You should be looking for a guy like the one watching us last night."

"What guy?"

"There was a guy in Blue Note last night watching us."

Kate assessed him to see if he seemed to be telling the truth. "Tell me about him."

Lenny repositioned himself on the couch. "I was already there when Paris arrived. I was sitting in a side booth chatting with two buddies of mine. We saw the guy come in. He's been in there before trying to talk to girls but most haven't been interested. Paris talked to him for a few minutes and then gave him the brushoff. He went farther down the bar and ordered a drink and then stood there and watched her. She didn't pay him any attention, and that's when I walked over to her."

"What did he look like?"

Lenny described a man similar in appearance to the man Mick described seeing at the Eden Roc bar. They were of a similar height, weight, overall appearance, and same stare. Lenny didn't know the man's name and had explained that no one spoke to him much at Blue Note.

"Is there any particular night he goes into Blue Note?"

Lenny shook his head. "There doesn't seem to be any rhyme or reason to his showing up there. He doesn't talk to anyone but the women."

"You said some of the women seemed to know him. I would assume then they'd know his name."

"I guess," Lenny said. "Why don't you ask Paris? As I said, it seemed like she knew him." He tugged at his robe again. "Are we done? I need to get dressed."

"You good?" Declan asked Kate.

She told him she was and they headed for the door. Declan turned before they left. "You might want to keep your hands to yourself before someone decides to go to the police."

Lenny didn't say another word but nudged them out with his hand and closed and locked the door behind them.

As they walked down the hall to the elevator, Declan turned to her. "Where to now, boss?"

"We have a list of people, friends and family of the victims, we need to interview today. I want to go back and speak to Paris though." Kate reached out and hit the button for the elevator. "Are you feeling a bit scammed by all this?"

"It's a bit he said, she said. Who do you believe?"

Kate hitched her thumb over her shoulder. "Lenny back there doesn't seem like the type to strangle a woman. I think Paris told him she liked it rough and he stupidly tried what she said. He's not our killer. I also don't think he was trying to kill her. Paris handled it and won't press charges so what have we got? Hopefully, he'll remember that feeling in his balls before he tries it again."

Declan stifled a smile. "I had the same thought. I wanted you to say it first. If I said it, you'd think I was a misogynist."

Kate rolled her eyes. "Don't you men ever slow down when it comes to sex? These older guys are way too much for me."

"Kate, one of the highest rates of sexually transmitted diseases is in senior living."

Kate scrunched up her face. "Don't tell me such things."

Declan laughed at her. "It's true though."

Kate didn't want to think about senior living sex. "I want the name of this mystery guy. He sounds like the same guy that Mick mentioned to me."

"Let's go then."

An hour later after making several phone calls to track Paris down, they found her walking out of a tanning salon. She got to the sidewalk and saw Kate and Declan leaning against their car. She slowly walked toward them, raising the sunglasses off her eyes to her head. "Is there something more you need?"

Kate stepped toward her. "We spoke to Lenny and he mentioned a man who spoke to you at Blue Note before he came over to you. Do you know who I'm talking about?"

"Did you arrest him?"

"No. He disputes your version of events." Kate looked back at Declan but his face remained passive. He wasn't going to take this on. She turned back to Paris. "He said you told him you liked it rough. He was doing what you asked." The only response was a half-hearted shrug that Kate didn't know how to take. She repeated her question about the guy from Blue Note.

Paris smacked her gum and cocked her head to the side like she was thinking about the night before. At first, she started to shake her head like she didn't know but then she stopped. Her voice raised an octave almost to a squeak. "Do you mean Zack Nash?"

"Who is Zack Nash?" Kate asked, folding her arms across her chest. Without the tears from the night before Paris didn't seem vulnerable. There was also something about her Kate didn't trust.

"He's a guy who hangs out at Blue Note. I've seen him a few times, but I'm not interested in him."

"I didn't know interest factored into your line of work."

"You don't understand, Agent Walsh. He doesn't want to pay me. He's asking me out to lunch and dinner for real – like he wants to be my boyfriend or something." Paris scoffed and giggled. "I'm sure he doesn't make nearly enough money to be my boyfriend."

"That doesn't interest you then?" Declan asked, a tinge of annoyance in his voice. "You wouldn't date him because he doesn't have enough money?"

"Don't be mad, Agent James," Paris cooed. She sauntered over to him and ran a hand down his chest and his stomach. He caught her hand in his before she went below his belt. "Sometimes I make exceptions if they are handsome enough. You're certainly handsome enough."

Declan dropped her hand and looked right into her eyes. "Not even if you were paying me."

Paris pouted and stepped back. "Anyway, what does Zack have to do with all of this? He's harmless. Annoying but harmless."

"Nothing you need to concern yourself with." Kate stepped back toward the car.

Paris smirked at her. "Are you upset because I got your boyfriend all hot and bothered?"

This was a different woman than Kate had witnessed the night before. She looked over at Declan and he was anything but hot and bothered. His back was stiff and he had that keyed-up anger like he was about to lose it.

Kate reached out and touched his arm. "Let's go interview a witness who won't waste our time."

Declan stared Paris down for a few more seconds and then turned and got into the car, slamming the door behind him.

CHAPTER 21

About a mile down the road, Kate looked over at him. "Are you okay?"

Declan's hands tensed on the steering wheel. "I don't like this case."

"That doesn't sound like you." If there was anyone who rolled with the punches, it was Declan. He usually went rogue at least once a case, which is why no one else in the FBI wanted to work with him. He had been tame so far in Miami.

"I can't tell who the good guys are." Declan turned his head slightly to look at her. "I don't like or trust Paris. You saw the way I spoke to Fanny last night. I don't trust her either. I didn't trust Isa, and Ted is in over his head. I feel like it's you and me alone on this case."

Kate patted his thigh. "Isn't it always you and me on a case? Besides, you liked Dr. Bruce."

Declan laughed. "Okay, I liked Dr. Bruce. She seemed to have it together."

"I thought you liked Ted."

Declan shrugged. "There is so much he missed and he didn't stand up to Isa right away."

"Cut him some slack. This isn't an easy case for anyone. You wouldn't stand up to me right away either."

"That's because I'm afraid of you," Declan said, watching the road and trying to keep a straight face. "Where to now?"

Kate gave him directions to the witness they would speak to next. When they had gone through the file of witness statements that Ted had given them, Kate had made a list of people, and the plan now was to go through that list one by one and see if they could gather any more information than what had been told to Ted and Isa. It would be an arduous task, but it had to be done.

They worked together throughout the day going down the list, stopping at people's homes and even offices. Declan and Kate had both taken turns asking questions and trying to understand the victims' lives a little better, focusing specifically on the last week each of them had been alive.

Kate had made a point of asking what people knew about Andre Dale and Zack Nash. It seemed the victims had kept quiet about their lives. Family and friends knew very little. In the end, Declan and Kate hadn't been able to gather much more information than what had been in the files.

Feeling defeated, they drove back to the hotel to get dinner and then prepare for the long night of surveillance ahead. They ate dinner in near silence. When Kate looked down at her empty plate, she wasn't even sure she had tasted her food. Eating had been a mechanical process that evening, more of a chore to be accomplished than something they had enjoyed.

Once back in their room, Kate finished getting ready while Declan made calls to the FBI field office and Ted's team about the location of their surveillance assignments. Surveillance was another of Declan's specialties. He could handle the logistics of the most complex cases with ease. It tripped Kate up to coordinate timing and locations and then remain on top of it throughout the night. Declan had gladly taken point, and Kate was more than happy to hand over the reins.

They left the hotel at close to seven that evening and set out to the surveillance location on Star Island. Kate had driven so Declan could finalize phone calls. He also had his iPad in case they'd need to search for information.

Kate wanted to pull up some database searches on Zack Nash. She didn't have a feeling one way or the other about the guy, but more information was needed. She didn't even know if he connected to any of the victims. He sounded like the man Mick had seen, but until they had a solid photo of Zack, confirmation was out of reach.

Kate pulled to a stop outside of the home and cut the car lights. She let the engine idle for a few minutes until Declan confirmed they were in the best position to see the home and then she hit the button to shut off the car. The home had a decent amount of tree cover. Palms lined both sides of the driveway and the front of the home had been professionally landscaped.

Kate had a good view of the front door and would be able to tell if any lights came on in the front of the home on either floor. "Do you think he's going to pull up into the driveway and walk in the front door?"

Declan kept his eyes focused on the home. He had binoculars up to his eyes and the strap around his neck. He watched for a few more moments and then rested them on his chest. "I don't know what he's doing. I chose homes tonight that didn't have a front gate. Two of the crime scenes had closed locked gates, but the rest didn't. I figure he's probably choosing houses that are more accessible."

That made sense to Kate. They still didn't know exactly how he was getting into the homes. None of the mansions had been broken into. The assumption was the killer found a way in when he visited the home before the night of the murder.

A few cars came and went past them, but none stopped. There was a row of mansions that dotted the road but were hidden from view given the lush vegetation on each property. Palms swayed from the slight night breeze, but the stillness of the evening unnerved Kate. Used to the hustle and bustle of Boston, this seemed remote.

"Not much going on here for a Saturday night," Kate remarked, glancing out the driver's side window at a passing car. They had put the top up on the car to give them more coverage. To anyone driving by, they'd look like a couple parked on the side of the road. They had alerted the Miami Beach police ahead of time in case anyone saw them and called the cops. Kate couldn't imagine many cars parked on the road for any length of time. There was a chance the killer would see them and divert his activities.

None of the cars that passed fit the killer and a single woman victim, and none slowed near the home as if considering pulling in the driveway. Kate remained focused on the home as Declan checked in with the others. So far, all was quiet.

At ten till midnight, a light flickered toward the back of the home and Kate wondered if she were seeing things. She sat up straighter and leaned into the steering wheel, her eyes focused on the spot. "Was that a light?" she asked Declan, pointing to the right side of the home.

"Where?" he asked, bringing the binoculars to his eyes.

"Around back on the right side. I think it's coming from the yard."

Declan shifted his head slightly. "It is a light. I can't tell what it's coming from though. Almost looks like it could be from a flashlight. I'm not seeing anyone though so I'm not sure." He set the binoculars down and turned to Kate. "Let's go check it out."

Kate patted the gun on her hip as she did before she approached any scene. She knew it was there, but it was habit at this point. Declan took the lead and she followed in the rear, keeping an eye on his back and scanning to the left and right covering them both.

All at once, Declan took off in a run. Kate did her best to keep up with him, her soles crunching on the gravel of the driveway. Declan cut across the lawn and kept running. He turned only once, "I saw someone," was the only direction he gave her.

Kate's footing slipped slightly as her shoes sank into the soft grass. She assumed the lawn had been watered recently because with each step she sank in a little deeper. She moved faster and caught up with Declan as he turned the corner from the side of the house to the back.

He stopped abruptly and pointed his gun into the darkness. "FBI! Don't move! Put your hands up!"

It took Kate more time for her eyes to adjust to the darkness to see what Declan had already noticed. A man, with a flashlight in his hand, stood at a back window peering into the house. Hearing Declan's words, the man turned and faced them. He jerked his hands straight up over his head bringing the flashlight with him.

"Please don't shoot. I live next door," the man said, his words coming out rushed. His face had contorted in fear. "I thought I saw someone back here and I came over to see what it was."

As they were focused on the man, the roar of a boat engine rang out in the distance and all of them turned toward the water.

The man pointed. "See, I told you there was someone back here!"

Declan took off in the direction of the dock and water, leaving Kate to stand there with the neighbor.

"What's your name?"

"Kevin Callahan. I live next door." The man wobbled. "Can I put my hands down?"

"Not yet," Kate said, advancing on him. She held the gun in one hand and patted him down with the other. The only thing he had was an industrial yellow flashlight, one so big it could have been used as a weapon. He didn't have anything else on him, barely even clothing. He had on boxers, a white tee-shirt, and was barefoot.

She motioned for him to put his hands down. "What did you see that brought you out here?"

Kevin expelled a breath and relaxed. He turned and pointed next door. In the darkness, Kate couldn't see the house. "I was upstairs in the back bedroom and I saw the light first. I stood at the back window and listened. That's when I heard two voices – one man and one woman. I know no one is supposed to be over here. The owners moved out months ago. I figured someone was trying to break in."

"Did you call 911?"

Kevin rubbed his forehead. "That probably would have been smart, but no, I didn't. I figured by the time the cops got here, they'd have robbed the place and been gone. I grabbed my flashlight and headed over. I wanted to scare them off, which I did."

"Did you see them?" Kate strained to find Declan, but he had been absorbed into the darkness.

"No," Kevin said cursing. "I wish I had."

"Did you hear what the people were talking about?"

Kevin started to speak but stopped and thought for a moment. "It's weird now that I'm thinking about it. The guy said something like he forgot to leave lights on and he was sorry it was so dark. She laughed and told him it was spooky. He told her to hold on and they'd be in the house in a moment. That's the last I heard because I took off downstairs and out here." Kevin looked at Kate. "What's the FBI doing out here?"

"Working on a case."

"Those murders that have been happening?"

Kate nodded once. "We were out front."

Kevin shook his head and tsked at her. "The waterway would be the easiest for someone to sneak in and out of the properties."

Kate locked eyes with him. "What do you mean?"

"You didn't notice?"

"What?" Kate asked, not sure what he was trying to say.

"I thought the FBI was supposed to be smart." When Kate didn't respond, he went on. "I noticed after the last murder that all the crime scenes had houses with water access. Every single one of them had a boat dock on the water. The killer could have easily come the back way and had all the time in the world to break into the house and kill the woman."

Kate hadn't realized that before. They had been solely focused on the other elements of the homes. She had no idea if what Kevin told her was accurate or not. She'd check as soon as she could. It could be the first major break in the case.

Kate looked down at his bare feet. "Is that what you thought about when you came over here tonight? That you were confronting a killer?"

Kevin let out a nervous laugh. "Heck no. If I had thought the killer was over here, I would have made sure my door was locked and called the cops. I figured it was a couple of kids out for a good time or someone breaking in to steal what's left in the house."

"You're lucky you didn't get hurt. There's no telling what this killer would have done if you confronted him."

"You think it was him?"

"I don't know." Kate looked toward the water and anxiety amped up. Declan should have been back by now. She turned to Kevin. "Go back to your house. We'll be over if we have questions."

Kevin walked back into the darkness. He had turned his flashlight on and she watched the light bounce off the ground and then the trees along his path. She walked the rest of the distance to the water and relief washed over her when she saw Declan standing on the dock. He had his phone up to his ear and he barked orders about getting cops in the water to search.

Kate walked out onto the dock and met Declan as he hung up the phone. He cursed and shoved his phone in his pocket. "I don't think they are going to be able to get a unit into the water fast enough to find them."

Kate looked out into the water but couldn't see much. "Did you see anything?"

"White boat. I think it had a blue stripe down the side. I don't know boats enough to tell the make and model." Declan bit his lip. "Do you think we just let him slip through our fingers?"

"Based on what the neighbor said, I'm fairly certain that was him."

CHAPTER 22

The next morning Kate and Declan were scheduled to meet with Ted in the conference room at the police station. None of the others on surveillance the night before had heard a peep. After Kate and Declan had walked up from the dock and got back in the car, Declan called Ted to explain what happened in detail. It was decided they'd meet Sunday morning to take a look at all the crime scenes again to see what else they might have missed. They also sent a crime scene unit to the house that morning to see if there was any trace evidence left behind that they missed in the dark.

Declan insisted on stopping at a little shop near the hotel. While Kate lingered at the counter, Declan ordered each of them a steaming hot coffee and a bag of Boston crème donuts. Kate eyed him, wondering who was eating an entire dozen donuts.

Declan had simply smirked. "We're cops. We eat donuts."

"That's a bad stereotype," Kate said, trying to remember the last time she had allowed herself such a treat. It had been so long she couldn't remember.

"Sometimes it becomes a stereotype because it's true." Declan paid the woman behind the counter, picked up the carrier with all three coffees, handed the bag of donuts to Kate, and they walked to their car.

When they arrived at the police station, Ted had pulled the murder boards around and had file folders opened all over the table. Ted's back was turned to the door when they entered and he seemed so lost in thought he didn't acknowledge their arrival.

Declan cleared his throat. "Looks like you started without us."

Ted turned around with a dry erase marker in his hand. "I couldn't sleep last night after we finished the surveillance shift. I've been here for about two hours. Not that I'm very far along."

Declan pulled a cup from the carrier and handed it to Ted. "I grabbed a dozen donuts, too."

Ted took a sip of coffee and gave an appreciative moan. "This is so much better than what we have here." He dug into the donut bag.

Kate took a seat near the window and looked down at the file in front of her. It was Chloe's, the last victim's file. "What have you figured out so far?"

"The neighbor." Ted paused as if thinking. "I think you said his name was Kevin. He was correct. I went over each case again and each of the homes has a boat dock and water access. I don't know how we missed it before."

"It's so common around here, I don't know that I would have caught on earlier either," Declan said, sitting down and taking a sip of his coffee. "It's a little like saying there are palm trees and a well-landscaped lawn at each crime scene. Don't beat yourself up about it."

"Maybe," Ted said, shaking his head. His face showed the anger and disgust he felt.

Declan handed Kate her coffee and shoved the bag of donuts toward her. It slid across the table, moving folders in its path. "Eat. It's going to be a long day." He held up his cup and winked at her. "We are going to fuel it with caffeine and sugar."

Kate knew he was trying to lighten the mood with her. She had tossed and turned most of the night and hadn't gotten a good night's sleep. She felt miles behind the killer. Kate reached into the bag and pulled out a sticky donut. Her finger dipped into the chocolate glaze at the top. She pulled off a piece and popped it into her mouth, savoring the sweet taste.

"Told you it was good," Declan said before turning his attention back to Ted. "What about looking at boating licenses in the area?"

"Not going to do much. Nearly everyone has a license. We also don't know that it's someone living right here in Miami Beach. Their boating license could be out of Orlando or Jacksonville. You're talking about a state primarily surrounded by water. That's a massive number of people."

Kate had suspected that. "It sounds like while now we know the killer is arriving at the crime scenes by water access, that won't help us catch him."

"I'd say that's a fair statement," Ted said. "It's another piece of the puzzle. It does answer the question about how he's going unnoticed by the neighbors. We got lucky last night with the next-door neighbor noticing. We've spoken to the neighbors at each of the scenes and no one has seen or heard a thing."

Kate assumed no one heard or saw anything because the houses were spaced apart and had a good deal of vegetation between them. An entry from the water would make it that much more likely the killer could slip in and out unnoticed. "We should at least have some extra water patrols tonight."

"Already taken care of," Ted assured. He turned to the board and stared. "We will have three units out tonight and every weekend until he's caught."

Declan sipped his coffee. "It makes a certain kind of sense he comes in by boat. He could have the plastic tarp in there and even the medical tools he's using after the women are strangled and no one would even question it. He could tell the women that he needs to bring the items in from the boat and I don't think anyone would be suspicious."

Kate rubbed her forehead in frustration. "It makes for easier cleanup, too. He can drop bloody clothing and the tarp in the water. Depending on how far he goes out into the ocean, chances are no one would ever find it."

Ted clicked the marker top off as if to jot down a note. "Should I try to see if we can get some teams to search Biscayne Bay? All of the murders have happened connected to the bay side rather than the Atlantic Ocean."

Kate glanced up at the board. "Is that true? They are all on the bay side?"

Ted went to the board and walked them through the locations of each murder. He pointed to the property photos as he went down the line. Two had happened on N. Bay Road on Miami Beach with their backyards connecting to the bay. The rest were on the islands in the bay including Star Island, Palm Island, and San Marino Island.

Ted pointed to the last photo. "It's far busier on the Atlantic side and not many one-family dwellings. That's something we've known from the start, but we had no idea the killer used the water for transport."

Declan turned to Kate. "What do you think about searching the bay?"

Kate had no idea. She knew nothing about tides or the current of the water. She raised her eyes to meet Ted's and admitted her lack of knowledge. "If there's a possibility that we could find some evidence, then go for it. Otherwise, I don't want to waste anyone's time when there are probably easier avenues to focus on right now."

"Let me make some calls." Ted left Declan and Kate sitting there alone.

Declan pulled another donut out of the bag and took a bite. "Does this fact change your profile at all?"

"Not really. I still think we are dealing with someone younger rather than older. He's planned carefully and chosen the less risky avenue into these homes. It might indicate that he's not a risk-taker. He's calculated in what he does. That much is for sure."

Declan tapped at his head and finished chewing. "I like what you said about risk because I was thinking about something while you were speaking. The killer chose high-priced escorts at first and then changed his victim selection. He might have figured out how strict Fanny is and realized how she was always looking out for them. Maybe he moved on to other women because they were less risky for him."

"That's possible," Kate said. "If he wanted the lowest risk, he would have chosen prostitutes working the streets in downtown Miami. There's something about these particular women he's chosen though. I think he's making calculated risks to meet his objective."

"His objective being killing women who are exchanging sex for money?"

"Not just that," Kate said with frustration in her voice. She was having a hard time articulating what she meant. "There's something about the women who are living the good life, making all of this money, and leading better lifestyles than they would have had exchanging sex for money."

"Like they don't deserve what they have?"

"In a sense, yes," Kate said, not even sure she had hit on it correctly.

Before Declan could respond, Ted stood in the doorway of the conference room looking ashen. He sucked in short breaths of air and clutched at his chest. Kate worried he might be having a heart attack. She jumped from her chair and went to him. Declan was right behind her.

"Ted, are you okay?" Kate asked, reaching for his wrist to check his pulse.

He swallowed hard. "There's been another body found. Ava Crawford called 911 from a home she's showing this morning on

Hibiscus Island. They just alerted me."

Tears formed in his eyes and Kate knew there had to be more. Another victim certainly was heartbreaking, but it wasn't unexpected.

"Ted, what is it? What's going on?"

Ted dragged a hand down his face. His voice broke. "It's Isa Navarro."

Kate recoiled. "I don't...I don't understand. Are you sure?" was all she could get out.

"It was a uniformed officer on the scene who recognized her."

"Let's go there now." Declan put his hand on Kate's back. He guided her into the hall. "Are you okay?"

Kate pulled herself out of the initial shock. "I'm fine. We have a job to do." She turned back to Ted, who didn't seem to be focused on anything. She reached out and touched his arm. "Ted, do you want to stay here?"

"No, I'm fine," he said, brushing her off. "I need to see her for myself." Ted moved into the hallway with Kate and Declan and started to follow them down the hall.

Kate and Declan got to the elevators and realized Ted wasn't right behind them as they had assumed. Kate turned back in enough time to see Ted's face fall again.

He held up his phone. "I thought maybe if I called her and she answered, we'd know right now it isn't her. She didn't answer though."

Kate wasn't sure what to say because if it had been her partner, she'd be a puddle on the floor.

CHAPTER 23

Kate and Declan crossed from Palm Island to Hibiscus Island and then were stopped at a guard stand. The island was both gated and guarded. Declan flashed his badge and was given entrance. Ted had decided to take his car to the scene and was a few minutes behind them.

Losing a colleague affected people differently. Kate turned her head to Declan. Even as much as he annoyed her sometimes, Kate would be utterly lost without him.

Declan shifted his eyes to her as he parked the car behind a row of police cruisers. "You're thinking about losing me, aren't you?"

"Stop reading my mind." Kate turned away and stared out the window at the Mediterranean-style mansion. Ava leaned on the back of a police cruiser. Her makeup had streaked down her face and she was being comforted by a police officer who spoke to her with his head bent. Kate would have to interview her, but she wanted to see the crime scene first.

Declan reached over and squeezed Kate's hand. "I told you before, you're not getting rid of me that easily."

"I feel a sense of responsibility for Isa. Don't you?" Kate's voice cracked as she spoke. She wasn't going to cry, but the emotion built up in her.

Declan looked out the front windshield toward the mansion and the uniformed officers milling around. "Whatever brought Isa to this place wasn't something we did. We made the right decision to remove her from the investigation. Don't take on something that's not your own. It serves no one. Guilt won't bring her back."

Declan had been accused before of being cold and callous. In reality, he was probably the healthiest among them. He had a good perspective especially when it came to work and what control was in his hands and what wasn't. Kate didn't agree or disagree with him. She reached down and gripped the metal handle of the door and opened it. Her feet hit the pavers that made up the driveway. She adjusted her clothing as she looked around. Kate didn't see the medical examiner's van or the crime scene unit. Ted hadn't arrived yet. Kate and Declan were the first senior investigators on the scene.

Kate caught up with Declan who was headed toward a group of uniformed officers. He flashed his badge and one cop directed him to an area with gloves and booties for their shoes. Kate heard the cop mention that this crime scene was a bit different. She caught the word *messy* and winced.

Kate and Declan put booties over their shoes and pulled on gloves. When they were ready, a young officer escorted them into the home. The foyer had high ceilings with white walls and wooden beams running across the top. The beams carried into an open adjacent living room that had simple clean furnishings and the uncluttered feel of a home not being lived in.

As Kate and Declan glanced around the area, the officer pointed. "It's upstairs. Second door on your left."

He didn't follow them up the stairs. The house had an eerie quiet feel and Kate's stomach tightened with each step. She held onto the black iron railing and followed behind Declan. He reached the landing and when he moved to the left, that's when Kate spotted the bloodied handprint on the wall at the top of the stairs. It would be marked with a crime scene marker and photographed when the crime scene investigators arrived. She stepped over a gold tube of bright pink lipstick and a hairbrush. Kate didn't see a purse or wallet but the signs of struggle were evident. The door to the room had been partially closed. Kate wasn't sure if the officer first on scene had left it that way or simply returned the door to how he had found it.

Kate held back and let Declan go first into the room. He'd be seeing the crime scene nearly undisturbed, which would be a first in this series of murders. As Kate stepped into the room, her eyes darted from the bed to the furnishings and then to the floor. The *mess*, as the cop downstairs had said, was everywhere. This was unlike all the other crime scenes in nearly every way.

Kate didn't allow herself to look at Isa too closely, propped up in bed like the other victims. She focused instead on the blood on the walls, the floor, and the furniture. There was no way that it was only Isa's blood. There was too much.

Declan pulled back the covers from Isa's lap and looked down at her bare legs. He pulled the V-neck of her dress to the side to reveal her chest. "She has too many stab wounds to count, but he never took out her heart." He craned his neck to look back at Kate. "Why is that?"

Kate didn't know right now. She couldn't even think straight as she assessed the scene. Isa's hands were bloodied and raw. Every nail had been broken and her hands were covered in blood. "The killer's DNA must be here this time. She threw him off his pattern."

"Is there a chance she wasn't his intended victim?" Declan asked, standing upright next to the body.

Kate had thought of that. Isa wasn't an escort and wasn't in a relationship with an older man, that they knew of anyway. "You're thinking that because she doesn't fit the victim type, right?"

"In nearly every way, Kate. She is at least ten years older than the other victims."

"She doesn't look like it though." Kate stepped toward the body and looked over the scene. "She could easily be mistaken for her mid-twenties."

"Fine, I'll give you that," Declan said. "Isa has been working on this case. If we believe the guy we scared off the other house last night was the killer, then how did she end up here? You'd think at some point her suspicions might have been raised. It doesn't make any sense to me."

It didn't make any sense to Kate either. She knew Declan's rising anger wasn't directed toward her. He was as frustrated as she was by the murder. "There is no tarp. Did he bring in his bag with the medical tools or stab her with something already in the home?"

"Good point." Declan began searching the room alongside Kate. They grid searched the room going over every inch of it. Isa had one high heel on and the other Kate found under the bed. She snapped a photo of it along with a few others of the scene. The crime scene unit would do the same, but she didn't want to wait for them.

The trail of blood on the floor led to an adjoining bathroom. The light had been turned off, which forced Kate to feel along the wall for the switch. When she turned the light on, she stepped back. The black and white subway tiles had been marred with blood. There were blood droplets on the white marble countertop and the silver handles of the sink.

As Kate leaned over the white bowl of the sink, that's when she saw it lying there on top of the drain. The yellow and black screwdriver had been washed clean. There wasn't a visible drop of blood anywhere on it. She'd need the forensics team and Dr. Bruce to confirm, but Kate was sure this was the murder weapon. She left it there for the crime scene techs to bag and tag.

As Kate popped her head out of the bathroom door to tell Declan she found the murder weapon, it occurred to her how clean the downstairs had been. There was no way the killer would get out of the home without leaving a trail of blood.

She told Declan about the screwdriver. "There has to be a back staircase from upstairs. There's blood in the hallway but none leading down the front steps. He didn't get out of here without leaving a mess along the way."

Declan agreed and stepped out into the hallway with Kate right behind him. It was the third door he tried that brought him to a staircase that led to the downstairs. Kate followed Declan down the steps the killer had recently traveled. The killer had done his best to clean up, but droplets of blood outlined his movements down the stairs, through the kitchen, and out the back door.

In the back of the home, there was a large canopy and an outdoor kitchen. An eight-person table had chairs neatly lined around it. The patio led to a built-in pool and, at the farthest edge of the lawn, pavers created a path down to the dock.

"Let's leave the outside for the crime scene techs." Declan turned and they were about to go back upstairs but an officer called Kate's name.

"We're in the kitchen," she yelled back and they waited.

As he approached, he pointed toward the front of the house. "You need to come with me. The crime scene unit is here. Dr. Bruce and her team arrived, too." The officer started to say something else but stopped, staring at Kate with a blank expression on his face.

"Are you okay?"

"There's a woman out front who looks like the dead woman upstairs."

Declan and Kate shared a look of confusion and followed him to the front of the house, stopping briefly to pull off their gloves and booties. They dropped them in a bin near the door.

As they stepped outside, he stopped and spoke over his shoulder.

151

"The media is being kept at bay down the road, but they can still film up here with their cameras. You probably want to go around the side of the house to speak to this woman. We've shielded her from the media for now, but we won't be able to do that for long."

Kate didn't understand what the young officer meant until she walked to the police cruiser where a woman was sitting in the passenger seat. Two officers stood in front of the door blocking Kate's way. She asked them to move and then reached down and pulled the passenger side door open.

Kate looked at the woman and then back up to find Declan standing in the front of the house speaking to Dr. Bruce. She waved them both over. When they stood flanking her on each side, Kate pointed. "You're not going to believe this."

The three of them stood there at the passenger side door looking at a woman who looked exactly like Isa.

CHAPTER 24

"I'm not Isa if that's what you're thinking," the young woman said. She tried to stand but Kate gently pushed her back. "Let me out of here so I can find my sister. Her cellphone is here. I did the find your phone thing and it came up here. Where is she?"

Dr. Bruce looked to Kate. "I'm going in the house. I'll leave this in your capable hands."

Kate motioned for the woman to step out of the police car. She put her hand on the woman's back and guided her to the side of the house as the officer had suggested. Only after they were out of sight from the media that lined the road in front of the home and the other officers still milling around the front, Kate introduced her and Declan. "You said Isa is your sister. What's your name?"

The woman brushed her dark hair off her shoulders. Kate could see now that this woman's hair was much longer than Isa's. "I'm Elise. What's going on here?"

Declan narrowed his gaze on her. "You said you tracked Isa's phone here. Why were you looking for her?"

Elise bit her lip and shook her head. "I don't have to tell you anything. I know my rights."

Kate stepped closer to Elise and put her hands on the woman's shoulders to brace her. "I'm sorry to tell you but your sister has been murdered. She's in the house. That's why we are all here."

Elise's dark eyes grew wider and then filled with tears. A hand shot to her mouth and she crumpled under Kate's hands. She slid right to the ground and sobbed.

Kate motioned with her head toward the front of the house. She wanted Declan to go help the crime scene unit. "Tell Ted about Elise when he arrives. It was a shock for us. He may know Isa had a twin, but he should be warned before he sees her."

"He should have been here by now." Declan walked toward the front of the house.

Kate waited while Elise cried in long screaming sobs. There wasn't much for Kate to do except wait. She had made many death notifications and each person behaved differently. There was nothing to do but wait for the person to get through the initial emotion so she could ask some questions and gain more information. Kate spoke soothing words to try to ease the woman's pain. Even at that, she knew nothing she said mattered.

Finally, when Elise was drained of all emotion, she raised her head to look at Kate. "This is all my fault. I got my sister killed. It should be me in that house."

Kate reached her hand down to take Elise's and helped the woman to her feet. "Let's find a place to sit and talk." Kate guided her to a table and chairs in the far part of the yard away from the house. She sat Elise down in a chair and then took the one across the table.

"I know this isn't easy, but if you want to catch the person who did this, you need to tell me what you know."

Elise wiped the tears from her eyes. "Agent Walsh, my sister was at my apartment last night. She was devastated that she'd been kicked off the murder investigation. She understood why it happened, but it broke her nonetheless. We had gone to bed, but at a little after midnight, I got a call to meet a client."

"Client?" Kate asked with raised eyebrows.

"Yes, a client." Elise held her chin high and she never broke eye contact with Kate. "I used to work for Fanny Fontaine. Then I had a client who wanted more of an exclusive relationship so I stopped working for Fanny. He and I were quite happy for a few years. Then, as with many of those types of relationships, I aged out."

"Aged out?"

"That's the side of those relationships no one talks about." Elise held her hands out to her sides. "I'm nearing forty. You look at my face and see someone who might pass for their twenties. My body doesn't lie though. There's cellulite, and my breasts are starting to sag. I don't have the energy I did in my early twenties. I don't have the tolerance I had in my twenties. I'm no longer a naïve young girl prostituting herself. No one wants a wise old whore." Elise chuckled to herself.

Kate had never heard someone speak with such candor. "Does that mean you went back to taking clients?"

Elise nodded. "What choice did I have? I have a business degree but no experience. A full-time entry-level job wasn't going to keep me in the lifestyle I've become accustomed to. Fanny didn't want me back because when I left her the first time, I burned bridges. You only get one chance with Fanny. She doesn't play around. I have a website. That's how clients find me now. In the right circles, people know me. One client refers another and so forth."

"Is it unusual to get a call so late?" Kate wasn't sure how all of it worked.

"It is. He's a newer client. That's the only reason I called him back. I had seen him before so I figured he was awake and wanted some company. He pays and tips well – too well. I've thought from time to time that he wanted a relationship with me. He never came right out and asked, but he knew that wasn't what I was interested in."

Elise took a deep breath and fought back tears. "It was a business decision. I weighed the risk of alienating a new client and figured it would be better to go. Isa woke up as I was getting ready to leave."

Kate raised her eyebrows. "I assume she stopped you from going?"

"Not at first. She was used to my work." Elise looked away for a moment then fixed her eyes back on Kate. "Isa hated my work, especially because she was a cop and a good one. She hated the life for me. I can't tell you the number of times she tried to talk me out of it over the years. Isa was happy settling for being broke when she went through the police academy and then working her way up. She was satisfied with a used car and Target jeans. She never cared so much about money. Isa wanted to make a difference. I cared about money. We grew up poor and I didn't want anything about that life."

Elise looked away. "When I saw a chance for a different life, I took it. Then I got hooked on the money and glamour and lifestyle. I couldn't give it up." Elise chuckled softly and turned back to Kate. "If there's anything that Fanny Fontaine does wrong, it's that she makes us feel too empowered for what we are doing. The rest of the world isn't like working for her. Girls make that mistake, thinking the grass is greener someplace else. They have no idea until they experience it."

Kate didn't want to talk about Fanny. "Let's get back to last night."

"Right," Elise said, crossing her legs and sitting back. "Isa asked me about the guy I was going to meet. I told her he recently moved from downtown Miami to a house on Sunset Island. His house cost him like ten million dollars and is immaculate. I've never seen a single man live in such a clean environment. I'm not talking tidy. Everything in the home was white and pristine. I teased him a few times that he must have obsessive-compulsive disorder. He laughed and told me surgeons have to be precise."

A knot formed in Kate's stomach. She knew why Isa would take an interest. "He was a surgeon?"

Elise nodded. "A big-time surgeon in Los Angeles he said. He went to college in Miami but had lived in Los Angeles for a long while. He said there came a point he had to leave."

"Why did he have to leave?" Kate asked hitting on the words *had to*.

"I don't know. He never said."

"Are you sure he said *had to*?"

"Yes. I thought it was weird too, but he wouldn't tell me so I dropped it."

A picture was forming in Kate's mind of the events of the previous night. "I take it Isa convinced you to let her meet the guy?"

Tears formed in Elise's eyes. She didn't wipe them away this time. "She told me she worried about my safety with all these murders and that he sounded like he might be the killer. I told her there was no way that was true. I had met the guy before and he was probably one of the nicest men I'd ever met. He was sweet and respectful to me. He never once gave me a reason to suspect him."

"Isa wasn't convinced?"

Elise shook her head. "Not in the least. She wouldn't let me leave the house. She asked me if he knew I was a twin and I said no. If you met my sister, you know she walked around with a chip on her shoulder. I figured that was because she was protecting me all the time. Her back was always up about it."

Kate understood Isa a little bit better now. "Did Fanny know that your sister was a cop?"

"Did she ever," Elise said, drawing out each word. "When I first went to work for Fanny, Isa blew a gasket. She threatened to arrest Fanny, but she couldn't do anything. Isa was Miami-Dade Police Department and Fanny was in Miami Beach Police jurisdiction. Isa even went to our uncle who has gone on to be the mayor. She had so many screaming arguments with Fanny that eventually Isa was kicked off the property and wasn't allowed back. Fanny gave her more chances than I would have."

Kate had momentarily forgotten that Elise would also be related to the mayor of Miami Beach. "Does your uncle know what you do?"

"He didn't at first, but then I got to know Andre who is my uncle's best friend."

"Does Andre have anything to do with how you meet clients now?"

"No." Elise had regret in her voice Kate didn't understand. "If he did, I'd be in a much better financial situation. Andre knows everyone. As I said, I've aged out of his crowd."

There was so much Kate wanted to know, but she needed to stick to the topic at hand. "Did your client have a boat by chance?"

"Yes, we met up once on it and he drove us around Biscayne Bay. The four times I met him, we had sex on his boat. It's where he liked it. He used to joke that he liked the risk of getting caught."

That certainly fit with the profile Kate had. "How did you prepare Isa to meet your client?"

"It was easy. As you can see, we look identical. Isa asked me questions about what we had talked about before and how I acted with him. The only difference about us is our haircut, but there's no reason I couldn't have cut mine off. I did her hair and makeup and gave her a dress."

Kate thought back to the crime scene and didn't recall seeing Isa's gun or badge. She asked Elise about it.

"No, she left both at home." She started to break down again and this time didn't stop herself. "If Isa had her gun, she'd probably still be alive."

"I want to ask you one last question and then I'll give you some time to yourself." Kate waited until Elise raised her head and looked at her. "What is your client's name and address?"

"Peter Lyons." Elise pulled her phone from her pocket and read Kate the address on Sunset Island.

CHAPTER 25

Kate left Elise seated in the backyard with an officer standing guard nearby. She told Elise that it would not be safe to release her at that time. In truth, Kate had no idea what they were going to do with her. The killer, who Kate at that moment assumed was Peter Lyons, may or may not have any idea that he had killed a detective rather than the escort he had hired for the evening. Kate had no idea what Isa might have told him.

Kate made her way across the front yard, past a throng of crime scene investigators and uniformed cops, and walked into the house. She found Declan and Ted standing in the living room deep in conversation.

"I have a name and address of a potential perpetrator. He fits the profile," she said, interrupting them.

"You found out what happened?" Declan asked, stepping back and allowing Kate to enter into their circle.

Kate explained the events of the evening before and how it came to be that Isa was on a date with Elise's client. She focused her attention on Ted. "Did you know about Isa's sister?"

"I knew she had a sister, but I had no idea they were twins. I didn't know Elise was an escort. Isa never mentioned it, probably too embarrassed. Had I known, it would have been a conflict of interest in this case. Isa was eager to work on the case though, probably more than any of us. I had thought it was because it was going to be one of those cases that could make or break a career. Isa wanted to advance."

"She paid for it with her life," Kate said sadly. "She took a huge risk last night. She wanted to protect her sister, but she could have begged her to stay home. Instead, she left her badge and gun at home and went out to meet someone she probably suspected was the killer. I can't even imagine what went through her mind. I have no idea how she thought she'd take him down." Kate's face warmed and she was sure it was red. The anger in her voice became more apparent with each word. Even Declan stared at her with his eyes big and mouth slightly agape.

He reached his hand out and touched her arm. "Kate, calm down. Isa protected her sister and her actions likely will result in us catching this guy."

"I know. I know." Kate brushed his hand off. Maybe she was being irrationally angry. Guilt might have been getting the best of her. If Isa had still been on the case, she might have called Ted or Kate and Declan to go with her.

Kate tucked her dark hair behind her ears. "We need to get a search warrant for this address and get a SWAT team to come with us. There is no telling what Isa said to him. He might know he killed a cop or he might be sitting there thinking he's gotten away with another murder. We need to be prepared for anything."

Ted nodded in agreement. "What about Elise? What do we do with her now?"

Kate turned to Declan. "Could you call the FBI field office? We need to get working on a search warrant, two agents to escort Elise to a safe house, and call for SWAT. We need to keep her out of the eye of the media for now at least. Once we get over to the suspect's house, we can determine the best course of action for Elise long-term."

Declan stepped away to make the calls while Kate asked Ted if he was okay. This was the first she had seen him since he had tried to call Isa back at the police station. "You disappeared on us. I was worried about you."

Ted expelled a breath. "I went to Isa's house to double-check before coming over here. It was locked and I couldn't get in but no one was there. I was desperate for it not to be her. I thought if I could find her, then it wouldn't be true. I couldn't face the scene upstairs."

Kate glanced toward the stairs. "Have you gone up there?"

"I did and wish I hadn't. We have a job to do and I can't let personal feelings get in the way." Ted lowered his head and looked at the ground. "I'll never forgive myself that my last interaction with her was so awful. I was angry with her for what she did. I should have tried to reach out to see if she was okay."

Kate knew nothing she said would make a difference. "I'm a mix of emotions, too. I'm angry at the whole situation. I'm angry that Isa sacrificed herself when she didn't have to. She still could have called us."

Ted grimaced. "I know. When you told me what happened, all I could think about was that if we hadn't had that argument earlier in the day, she would have called me."

Kate patted his arm. "All we can do is look forward. Second-guessing ourselves won't do much for Isa or any of us right now." She said the words, but she didn't put much stock in them. It was something that was much easier said than done.

Declan joined them. "I have a warrant in the works and two agents on their way to escort Elise to a safe house. We should get over to that address. SWAT is headed there now."

Kate nodded and turned to Ted. "Let's hold off on death notification for now, especially given Isa's connection to the mayor. We need to see how this plays out. If the killer knows he killed a cop instead of his intended target, he's going to run. Does Isa have any other family locally?"

"She has a brother and an aunt. Both of her parents are deceased. I don't know of any other siblings. I made an identification upstairs so we won't need them to come to the medical examiner's office. I agree though we need to hold this back for now. Do you need me to go to the suspect's house with you?"

Declan reached out and patted Ted on the back. "We have it covered. A SWAT team with the FBI's Critical Incident Response Group is meeting us in twenty minutes. Kate and I need to get going, but I need to know where I can bring the suspect in for questioning? I can use the FBI Miami field office interrogation room if needed."

Ted glanced out toward the crowd of onlookers and the media that lined the road just beyond the closed gate and uniformed officers standing guard. "The FBI office is probably more secure than the Miami Beach police department or even my office downtown. That's what the media will be expecting."

"Good call." Declan shook Ted's hand. "I'll be in touch as soon as we have him in custody."

Kate gave Ted a sympathetic look. "If you need anything, even just to talk, give me a call. I don't know when I'll be done interrogating him, but as soon as I can call you back, I will."

Declan and Kate walked to the car and pulled gear from the trunk they had left there after they picked up the rental at the airport. They each donned a bulletproof vest and checked their guns to ensure they were fully loaded and ready to go. They also grabbed walkie-talkies and turned them to the local frequency. It's how they'd communicate with SWAT. It was a ritual they had gone through together countless times.

As he pulled the driver's door shut, Declan eyed Kate. "Do you think Peter Lyons is going to be at the house?"

"No."

"I don't think so either." Declan started the car. "I wanted to give Ted a little hope though."

"Me too." Kate stared out the window at Ted who was on his phone, his face tense. He reached up and rubbed his forehead twice. Kate had noticed over the last few days he did that when he felt stressed or was upset. "I assume we'll get to the house, and it will be empty. We'll have to go through it for evidence and then get down to the hard work of trying to locate him."

"I called Spade after I called the FBI office."

Kate glanced over at him. "What did he say? Is he going to want us to stay on this if Lyons has taken off?"

"Spade said we are staying down here for the foreseeable future. He doesn't think this guy went far." Declan saw the look on Kate's face and laughed nervously. "Don't shoot the messenger. I don't know why Spade thinks that and I couldn't debate him about it. Let's go see if Lyons is there and we can play it by ear. Are you in that big of a hurry to get back to Boston?"

"Not particularly." Kate stared out the window as Declan drove. At a time like this, she'd normally be amped up ready for a confrontation with a suspect. Her heartrate should be climbing and the sweat moistening her palms the way they did right before any life-or-death situation she faced.

Kate did a quick read on her emotional response and found herself lacking. It was because she didn't believe that Peter Lyons would be at the house or even still in Miami Beach, no matter what her boss, Spade, seemed to think.

Kate chewed on her lower lip as she watched Declan's hands tense and relax on the steering wheel. She was about to tell him to relax but her phone chimed. She dug in her pocket and pulled it out. She read a text from Spade letting her know that the search warrant of the house had come through. They were not able to get an arrest warrant yet. It didn't surprise Kate. They didn't have any DNA evidence back yet and the only witness, Elise, never saw Isa with Peter. It had been conjecture on their part that Peter was a suspect.

"We got the search warrant," Kate said, letting the phone rest on her leg. "You told SWAT that they are there only to back us up, right? I don't want them storming in. If Peter is there and we can get him to come with us for questioning, then I want to take him in that way. I don't want him to immediately lawyer up."

As Declan changed lanes to go around a slow car and then accelerated, he confirmed he had told SWAT exactly that. "They will stay out of sight until we give the signal. I don't want to spook this guy any more than you do."

Declan had pulled far away from any cars and rode in the left lane for the next three miles. When they crossed the bridge onto the island, he checked the GPS. "We are less than a mile away now. I pulled up a map and the house is barely visible from the road. The back faces the bay and a high gate and thick palms surround it."

"Where is SWAT?"

"In position, Kate." Declan looked over at her. "They know what they are doing. They are trained like the SWAT from our field office in Boston. Trust them to do their job."

Kate should be accustomed to working with new FBI teams since she was farmed out to different FBI field offices and even other government agencies so often. She had no idea why she was asking such silly questions. Kate chalked it up to nerves and told Declan as much.

A moment later, she spotted the number on the black mailbox that sat atop a white pole at the edge of the driveway. Declan turned his blinker on and stopped in the middle of the road as oncoming traffic passed. He turned into the driveway, which sloped down. As soon as they bridged the crest, Kate saw that the gate was open.

Declan inched the car forward, going slowly. The palms and vegetation on the sides of the driveway were so thick an ambush couldn't be ruled out.

"Do we continue?" he asked, giving Kate a sideways glance.

Kate turned her head to the left and the right, scanning the vegetation around them. Like many of the homes in Miami Beach, the grounds were immaculately landscaped. It was lusher than Kate had seen, thicker and more foliage. The house was completely shielded from view. "Continue," she said. They'd have to take the risk.

Declan inched the car forward, going slower than Kate had ever seen him drive. While she couldn't see his foot on the gas pedal, she could only imagine how lightly his foot applied pressure. Once the driveway widened, the house came into view.

The two-story Dutch-West Indies-style home sat before them. The brown front door with large panes of glass was flanked by massive hurricane shutters. The shutters were not pushed back flush with the home but rather jutted out creating walls on each side of the door. Narrow long windows with blue shutters sat on each side of the grand entrance, giving the home its only bright pop of color. Across the second floor, a veranda ran from one end to the other.

Declan pulled behind a lone golf cart parked askew near the front entrance. A golf towel had fallen out and landed near the front left tire. It appeared as if someone had been in a hurry.

"You ready?" Declan asked with his hand on the door.

Kate swallowed hard, her throat suddenly dry. She nodded once, and it was only as she reached for the doorhandle that her chest constricted and her heart began to beat faster.

CHAPTER 26

Declan pounded on the door and called out for Peter Lyons. He waited and did it again a few seconds later. He stepped back from the door and went to one side window and peered in. "Nothing. No movement inside."

"Peter Lyons!" Kate called this time. "This is the FBI. We have a warrant to search your home."

They were met with silence. With the sheer size of the door and thickness of the wood, they'd need SWAT's battering ram to get into the home. Declan reached out and turned the knob, shoving the door open.

"That's not a good sign," he said. As Declan called for SWAT, a rustle of palms and shrubs revealed a heavy SWAT presence as agents stepped out from shielded view.

Declan gave the agents his operational assessment and the supervisor concurred. "Give the place a walkthrough and we'll pull up the rear."

With their shields and higher-powered weapons, the five SWAT agents made their way into the home. Kate knew these weren't the only SWAT with them, there were others including a long-range sniper nearby.

Declan had Kate's back and she went in before him. She stopped short when she caught sight of the blood streaks across the hardwood floors. "We have blood, Declan. Two o'clock," she pointed to the floor. The trail led to the staircase and then disappeared.

They followed SWAT through the downstairs rooms and cleared each room with efficiency before moving to the next. Nothing seemed out of place, and Kate didn't find any more blood. Elise's words echoed in her head about how Peter liked everything a certain way. *Pristine* is the word she had used. That certainly described the scene in front of them. The kitchen didn't have a crumb on the counter or a dish in the sink. Except for the blood, there was nothing out of place on the first floor.

SWAT gave the all-clear signal and motioned for them to follow as they formed a strategic line with their backs to the wall of the staircase. They moved up the stairs in a single-file line with their guns pointed toward the second floor. Declan pulled up the rear with Kate wedged between SWAT and him.

Kate's heart thumped in her chest now and her stomach growled, not from hunger but fear. It did that sometimes in the field – like a tornado siren wailing to let those around know it was time to take shelter. Kate had no shelter to take though. She focused on the mechanics of her body and pushed the fear out of her mind. She wasn't sure where the feeling came from but she knew they weren't alone in the home. The reality of what they'd face at the top of the stairs made her suck in a breath.

Her feet hit the second-floor landing and she followed in line to the right. SWAT started the process of clearing each room in a line down the hall. Each room had the smell of faint stale air like it had been closed up for a long while. The only room that appeared to have any life was the master bedroom and even that was empty except for the oversized furniture that made Kate feel like she had entered into a king's bedchamber. The four-poster bed sat square against the back wall. A Moroccan red comforter had been pulled tightly up to the headboard and throw pillows had been neatly arranged.

It wouldn't have surprised Kate if someone measured the pillows with a tape measure and found them all placed equally distant from each other. No toiletries or men's cologne sat atop the dresser. A simple black watch box sat in the middle with its lid down, beckoning Kate to open it.

SWAT pulled open a door that led into a walk-in closet bigger than some bedrooms in Kate's brownstone. She marveled at the neatly lined, pressed shirts all facing the same direction and on blue hangers. Shoes had been placed in cubby shelves that went from ceiling to floor. A small glider step ladder had been pushed to the back of the closet. Kate considered herself a neat freak and this was a bit much even for her.

The closet connected to a bathroom. Kate strained for another word than pristine but that's what it was. The white tile floor, white marble countertop, and white walls appeared as if they were brand new. Kate couldn't imagine anyone living in the space and keeping it this clean. The owner didn't even keep toiletries on the counter. A bar of soap and a bottle of shampoo in the shower were the only hints the home was occupied.

SWAT backed out and Kate and Declan followed. She knew he'd have much to say about the condition of the room, but this wasn't the time for comparing notes. Their safety remained at risk until the entire house had been cleared.

SWAT spoke to each other with hand signals, a language of their own. Kate followed some of it and then simply fell back in line and followed through the bedroom and out into the hall. There was one last room at the end of the long narrow corridor that wrapped like a U-shape.

The door had been left slightly ajar and SWAT nudged it open as they filed in. Kate saw the man's feet first, one flip flop on and one bare, lying by the side of a four-poster bed similar to the one that had been in the master. His legs were wrapped in tan linen. Kate assumed the man's shirt had been white but blood stained the garment from top to bottom and side to side. Only specks of white peaked out at the edges of the collar and the hem.

The man's face had been badly beaten. Fresh purple bruises covered one-half of his face. The swelling made him nearly unrecognizable. For a moment, Kate wondered if this was Peter Lyons. She checked the photo she had of Peter on her cellphone and the man's nose and facial structures were different. Peter's nose narrowed to a point and his cheekbones defined thin cheeks. This man's face was fuller, rounder even, giving him the appearance of a double chin.

Given the amount of blood, Kate assumed the man was dead. When a SWAT officer bent down and checked for a pulse, he sprang up fast and asked for them to call an ambulance. The SWAT officer bent down again and checked the man over. He had what appeared to be a single gunshot to the abdomen. There was nothing for them to do for him except hope he didn't bleed out before an ambulance arrived.

They cleared the rest of the room as quickly as possible as Declan made the call to emergency services. Kate made fast work of searching the room for the man's identity. Most of the dresser drawers were empty. In a top drawer of the nightstand next to the bed, she found a black leather wallet tossed in among undershirts and boxers. Kate opened the wallet and found a Florida driver's license with the name Davis Lyons, forty-eight, and an address in Orlando. She didn't know if this was the suspect's brother or some other relative. The photo matched the man on the floor.

Kate bent down next to him and reached for his hand. It was cold to the touch. "Davis, I'm FBI Agent Kate Walsh. We are getting you help. Just hang on and an ambulance will be here soon."

The man didn't stir although his chest rose and fell with each shallow breath. She repeated her words, hoping that he could hear her and know that help would be there soon.

The SWAT officer in charge asked Declan and Kate if they were fine to go have a look around and do another sweep of the place.

Declan cleared them to go. He stood over Kate and watched her hold the man's hand and speak to him softly. "What do you think?"

Kate kept the man's limp hand in hers and angled her body to look up at him. "I don't know, Declan. This could be Peter's brother or another relative. I assume there was some kind of struggle. I don't see a gun around so I think we can rule out self-inflicted."

Declan couldn't seem to stand still. He walked to the edge of the bedroom threshold and stuck his head into the hall. He said something Kate couldn't hear and then walked back to her. "That ambulance is taking too long."

"You only called a few minutes ago. Give it time," Kate assured him but she felt the same. Davis might be their only witness, and she needed him alive. She felt cold for thinking in those terms. He might be a father or uncle or brother, but in those moments when life and death hung in the balance, Kate couldn't focus on the humanity because it was too hard to bear. She had to keep focused on the mission at hand.

The time dragged on until an ambulance siren wailed in the background. "See, I told you," she said looking up again, but Declan was gone. She was left alone in the room. Kate focused her attention on the injured man. "Davis, you're going to be okay. You have to pull through and tell us what happened to you. We are looking for Peter. I'm hoping you can help us find him."

At the mention of the suspect's name, Davis's face tightened and his eye lids fluttered slightly. "Did he do this to you?" In response, the man's hand moved in hers. Kate couldn't call it a squeeze because he didn't have that much strength. It was communication though and she'd take it. It confirmed for Kate that he was conscious enough to hear her. Davis never opened his eyes.

"Did Peter shoot you?" Pressure on Kate's hand confirmed. "It's okay. You're going to be okay." Kate wanted more time but knew by his shallow breathing that if she didn't get up and let the paramedics do their job, he wouldn't pull through. As soon as Kate heard the voices downstairs and heavy-booted feet coming up the staircase, she leaned down. "I'll see you soon, Davis. The paramedics are here. You're going to be okay. I'll be by the hospital later to check on you."

Kate released his hand and pushed herself up from the floor. As soon as the paramedics arrived in the room, she stepped out of their way and explained his condition. "He's somewhat conscious. He was able to respond to me by moving his hand."

The two paramedics got Davis on a stretcher and began working on him as Kate stepped into the hall. Declan was halfway up the stairs when he spotted her.

"SWAT wants us outside right now. They found the killer's trophy room. I called Ted and the crime scene techs. We are going to be here a while."

CHAPTER 27

After Kate watched the ambulance go, she walked to the backyard and stood on the lawn outside of the small rectangular building. To an outside observer, the building could have been a guest house, a pool house, or even an office. A simple sky-blue door sat in the middle with windows on each side. The interior blinds had been drawn so it was impossible to see inside from Kate's vantage point.

"The outdoor space wasn't visible from the main house," the SWAT officer explained. He stood on the edge of the lawn and looked down at her as he spoke. She had no idea how tall he was, but Kate guessed about six-five. "It was only once we got out here that we realized beyond the twelve-foot-high hedge was this guest house or whatever you want to call it."

"You went inside?"

"Agent James did too." He pointed to the door. "It was unlocked so we went in and then stepped right back out. It's nothing like the house. There are women's clothes strewn all over the floor and a collage of newspaper articles on the wall. Next to that, it looks like surveillance photos of women. On a credenza right across from the door and under the collage is a basket with women's jewelry."

Kate tried not to make any judgments before she saw it firsthand. She waited for Declan to get off the phone. She wanted to ask him his impressions of what he'd seen. She wanted to go inside, but the last thing Kate wanted to do was contaminate the crime scene any more than they probably had already.

With the area cleared, the SWAT agent was free to go. He said goodbye and turned to leave but didn't get far. He spun back around and looked down at Kate. "Agent Walsh, this guy is sick. I've been following the case since it started and, if there's anything I can do to help you bring this guy in dead or alive, it would be my pleasure."

"I'll let you know. We appreciate your help today." He nodded once and left with the rest of his team. Kate stood looking at the door willing herself to have patience.

After ending his call, Declan sidled up to her. "The crime scene unit wants us to wait. They want to photograph everything before we start looking through it. They should be here in less than ten minutes."

Kate kept her eyes focused on the door. It wasn't the answer she wanted to hear but knew it was the right one. "This guy is in the wind now. What's the plan? Should we blast his photo all over or start a quieter search?"

Declan jabbed his finger toward the blue door. "Once I get in there and sort out what evidence we have, I'll know more."

"Did you send out a BOLO at least, especially because we are close enough to two airports? He could get on a flight and disappear forever."

"Already called in. If he hasn't left already, there will be eyes out for him. I told them to detain him quietly for questioning."

Kate checked her watch. "Where are they, Declan? I don't have any more time to waste. Did you ask anyone back at the field office to help us with research on Peter Lyons? We need all the information we can get."

Declan knew her well enough by now to anticipate what she'd ask. "I'm on it," he assured. "Within the hour, we should have the major highlights from work to finances to personal life. I asked for everything they can find, including any social media information."

"Good. Good." Kate heard his words and responded in kind, but she was focused on what was behind the door. "What did you see when you went in? You said it was enough to call the crime scene unit, but what specifically did you see?"

"It's a mess in there. Too much to know what we are dealing with." Declan grew as frustrated as Kate waiting for the crime scene techs. Kate had asked them to hold back for their safety in case there was a firefight with SWAT. Still, though, they should have been there already.

As Declan pulled out his cellphone, he said, "I'm going to call again." He never got a chance to make the call though as a crime scene tech walked into the backyard.

"Sorry," he muttered, putting his bag on the ground. "There was an accident on the road into the island."

Kate's heart thumped in her chest. They had just sent Davis Lyons in that direction in an ambulance. "What happened?"

The man shrugged. "I don't know. Someone said something about a guy jumping into the bay from the bridge. Looked like paramedics were already on the scene."

"Declan…" Kate said his name, but she didn't finish her thought or wait for him to respond. The feeling grew in the pit of her stomach and then spread to every nerve in her body. She turned and ran toward the front of the house, leaving them staring after her.

"Kate!" Declan called after her as he followed.

Kate didn't have time to turn around and tell him what was running through her mind. She had to get to the scene of the accident. That was the only thing that mattered to her. She pushed past a throng of crime scene investigators heading toward the back of the house, carrying in their equipment. A few said hello to her, but Kate couldn't respond. She remained singularly focused.

Kate got to the car and pulled hard on the door handle. Locked. She cursed and patted down her side pockets and then the back. She didn't have the keys. Kate looked up at the sky and cursed again.

Keys jingled behind her. "I have them, Kate. Where are you going?"

Kate motioned with her hand. "Get in and I'll explain on the way."

Declan hit the button to unlock the door and Kate ran to the passenger side and slid in. "Let's go," she called to Declan who remained standing at the driver's side with a look on his face that didn't match her urgency. "We don't have time. Get in the car!" Kate punctuated each word for emphasis.

Declan shook his head and got in. "Where to?"

"The accident. The crime scene investigator said that there was an accident that delayed them. Davis communicated with me by moving his hand. I need to find out more information – as much as I can while he's still alive. I can't let him bleed out stuck in traffic, Declan. Get me close enough and I'll run the rest of the way."

Declan started the car and pulled down the driveway. "Kate, the ambulance is probably at the hospital already. You're not going to be able to reach them. We should be back with the crime scene investigators."

"Just get me there. He said paramedics were already on the scene." Kate slapped at the dashboard. "I know it's them. They aren't there for the accident. They are stuck, and he's going to die right there before we even get a chance to question him."

Kate knew Declan had never seen her this frazzled. She always kept her calm demeanor. Some said she was too calm. It had allowed her to keep her head in every situation no matter how harrowing. This time, Kate wasn't even sure why this had her so keyed up. Declan was right. She had no idea if it was the ambulance that Davis was in. Call it a gut feeling or women's intuition, she didn't care – she just knew she needed to get to him.

Declan drove them as far as he could. He came to a screeching halt behind a minivan. The driver of which stood next to the open door on his tiptoes trying to see above the traffic. Declan glanced over at Kate. "I told you we weren't going to get far."

Kate didn't care. She had meant it when she said she'd run the rest of the way. She shrugged off her suit jacket and shoved open her car door and got out. She turned and ducked her head back in the car. "Go back. Stay. Doesn't matter to me. I'll contact you when I can." Then she took off in a sprint.

The sun beat down on Kate's face and she wished she had thought to grab sunglasses. She squinted and tried to shield her eyes with her hand, but it threw her off balance as she ran. Sunglasses probably wouldn't do any good even if she had them. They'd probably slip off her face from the sheen of perspiration caused by the exertion of the run and the Florida heat.

Kate ran up the middle of the road, her feet keeping to the double yellow line. Cars on her right were at a standstill and there was no oncoming traffic on her left. Whatever accident had happened, it had deadlocked the road. Twice now a car in the right lane inched out of line and pulled into the middle of the road to turn around and head back.

Kate wasn't sure how long she had run. The arches of her feet, encased in simple flats, ached from the constant pounding on the pavement and she was forced to slow her pace. She was almost there though. She spotted the barricade in the road and two uniformed cops standing in front of it. Kate sucked in her breath and jogged to the accident site. She pulled up short when she arrived.

Kate had expected to see smashed vehicles and paramedics tending to injuries. Instead, there was one lone ambulance parked askew at the side of the road with its back doors flung open and no movement inside. There were no paramedics in sight and no one injured lying in the road. For a moment, hope surged through her that the ambulance carrying Davis had made it through the traffic to the hospital, but she wasn't sure if that was the case.

"What happened here?" Kate reached for the chain that held her badge and pulled it out of the top of her shirt where it had fallen during her run. She showed them her credentials and introduced herself, but her eyes remained fixed on the ambulance that sat just beyond the barricade. "I heard there was an accident and I need to see the patient in that ambulance."

"You're going to have to take a swim if that's your plan," the officer grunted. "Your patient attacked a paramedic and jumped over the side."

CHAPTER 28

"What are you talking about?" Kate asked, not sure she had heard him correctly. "He's a witness in a case I'm working. He was a gunshot victim and barely conscious. I need to see him immediately." Her voice raised to such an octave that the uniformed cops shared a look of concern and then moved the barricade so Kate could walk through.

She jogged up to the ambulance but there was no one in the back. The stretcher had been turned over on its side. Bloodied gauze bandages were strewn all over the floor and an IV bag's contents formed a significant puddle. Kate left the side of the ambulance and came around to the front.

There she found the two paramedics who had been at the house attending to Davis. One of them held a bloodied gauze pad against his eye as a single streak of blood ran down his face. He spoke to a cop who stood across from him jotting down his words in a notepad.

Kate flashed her badge to the cop. "What happened here? Where is the patient?"

The paramedic with the bloodied face introduced himself as Trevor. "I was in the back with him. We had set up an IV and I was looking him over trying to stop the blood. It didn't make sense though. I couldn't figure out where the blood had come from. It looked to me like he had stopped bleeding and his vitals were improving."

Kate remembered back to how they found Davis in the bedroom. "That can't be," she said, shaking her head. "He was near death when you left the house."

"Right. I know." Trevor moved the gauze pad and revealed a gash above his eye. "I yelled up to Bryan that it didn't seem like he'd been wounded when all of a sudden he attacked me. He ripped the IV out of his arm and threw himself on me. Bryan pulled over immediately, but I couldn't move fast enough. He hit me with something sharp in his hand. I have no idea what he cut me with. Then he shoved open the back doors while we were still moving and jumped out."

Bryan pointed over the side guardrail. "He leaped over the side before I could get out and come around to the back. He hit the water with force and went under. I don't think he survived, but I'm not sure. He never resurfaced. I called it in immediately."

Kate could barely register a thought. She went to the side of the road and peered down into the blue water. The current was strong and she had no idea the distance from the bridge to the water, but it was probably survivable. Sunset Island wasn't far from mainland Miami Beach. It sat in Biscayne Bay across from the Miami Beach Golf Club. In theory, a strong swimmer could get from the mainland to Sunset Island via the small body of water between them.

Turning back to the paramedics, Kate asked hopefully, "Did he say anything?"

Trevor shook his head. "Nothing. He didn't even say anything when he attacked me." He pulled the gauze pad away from his eye and then looked at Kate. There was a long gash that went across his brow down to the side of his eye. He'd need medical care.

"Go on. I'll follow up if I need anything else." She motioned to the local cop. "Let's get traffic back moving again. We'll need to get a boat on that water to search."

Kate stood by the side and looked down into the water again. She couldn't make heads or tails of why Davis would jump. As she stared into the water, something the paramedic said struck her as odd. She turned quickly.

"Trevor," she called as he climbed into the passenger's seat of the ambulance. Kate ran up to the door. "Did you say that you couldn't find a wound? He had what looked like a gunshot wound to his abdomen."

"It looked that way at first," Trevor said with frustration in his voice. "Once we got him in the ambulance, I tried to treat the wound so I wiped his belly with antiseptic wipes to clear the area. I wanted to see where the blood was coming from, but there was no wound. I couldn't find any injury at all. I think he faked it."

"All that blood," Kate said to herself. She couldn't make sense of it no matter how hard she tried. Davis had been wounded. She saw it with her own eyes. He was barely breathing. She watched as his chest rose and fell ever so slightly. Kate didn't think there was any way he could have faked that. She told Trevor to go and she'd be in touch if she had more questions. The cut above his eye was bleeding more now and there was no reason to detain him.

Her cellphone buzzed against her thigh. She pulled it out of her pocket and looked at the screen. She held it up to her ear as she stared off across the bridge. "I'm here, Declan, and he's gone."

"He died?"

"No, gone. He attacked a paramedic and jumped over the side of the guardrail and concrete barrier. He's in the bay."

Her words were met with silence on the other end of the phone. Declan's heavy breathing came out in short puffs. "A supervisor with the crime scene unit called me. They want us back at the house. They said there are things there we need to see."

"I'll be right there."

"We'll figure it out, Kate. We always do."

Before Kate walked back to the car, she called Ted and explained what had happened. He said he'd get cops in the water immediately to search. Ted also pushed Kate about making a statement to the media. She assured him that as soon as she figured anything out, she would. If she were put in front of a camera right now, Kate had no idea how to explain the events that had transpired that day.

Twenty minutes later after turning around in traffic that had only started to move again, Kate and Declan got out of the car and walked around the side of the house to the backyard. She explained to him what the paramedic said one more time. It still didn't make sense to her so she understood Declan's confusion and couldn't answer any of his questions. She simply didn't know.

Jessica, the crime scene investigative supervisor, motioned them toward the back of the main house. She stood where the grass met the patio. "See those red drops right there?"

Kate and Declan both lowered their heads to look on the ground. There was a cluster of red dots on the blades of grass that trailed onto the patio. "What is it?" Kate asked.

"Fake blood."

Kate's head snapped up. "What?"

"We found a few droplets on the grass and patio. We followed the trail." Jessica pointed from the small house to the back door of the main house. "Follow me."

They followed Jessica to the backdoor and opened it. Kate stepped inside thinking they'd be entering into the kitchen, but instead, it was a small utility room with a washer and dryer, a row of hooks for hanging jackets, and a set of stairs that went to the second floor. The drops of blood continued on the tile floor.

"Did SWAT search back here?" Kate asked Declan.

"They came in here when we were in the kitchen."

Kate assumed they had but she hadn't been back this far in the house and had no idea it was even there. Little yellow tags like small sticky notes marked the floor where each drop of fake blood had been located. They followed Jessica up the stairs to a back corridor with a door dead ahead.

Jessica opened the door and they stepped into a bathroom Kate hadn't been in before. There were larger splashes and pools of fake blood on the floor and countertops.

"You ready for this?" Jessica said, flashing a grin as she opened a second door in the bathroom at the far end. She stepped out of the way so Kate and Declan could walk past.

Kate could barely believe her eyes. She looked around the room taking in the scene in front of her. She stood in the bedroom where they had found Davis. All at once, recognition of what had happened took hold. "He faked his injury," she whispered.

Kate walked around to the other side of the bed where they had found Davis on the floor and pointed at the large pools of blood that remained. "There was blood on the floor downstairs when we first walked in, too. Is it all fake?"

"Yes, ma'am. Every last drop of it. If you think this is crazy, wait until I show you what we found out back." She motioned for them to follow her.

Declan and Kate shared a look and went back down the stairs and out the way they had come in. They followed Jessica across the back lawn as crime scene investigators parted to let them pass. Before they entered the small house, Jessica handed them each a pair of gloves.

When Kate and Declan were ready, Jessica entered the small building and began pointing out items. "You have a basket of women's clothing plus all the clothes found on the floor. We bagged and tagged most of that already. You have some women's jewelry over on the shelf. What you probably can't take your eyes off is the collage he's created with photos and newspaper clippings. Some of it looks like it was printed from online news sources about the case."

Kate and Declan walked right up to the collage and scanned over the images. Some of them were photos taken with a telephoto lens. Most of the women weren't facing the camera and seemed oblivious that a photo was being taken. Some photos were taken at large gatherings with many people around, but the object of the photographer's desire couldn't be denied. He had zoomed in on women's legs, breasts, hands, and faces. There were more photos than Kate could count that were just women's mouths parted slightly, some smiling as if caught in mid-conversation.

"He'd be an amazing photographer if this wasn't so creepy," Declan said, echoing something Kate had thought but hadn't said aloud. "He's watching them, stalking them. Do you see any of the victims here?"

Kate's eyes roamed over the photos until she landed on one. "Right here." She pointed at a photo at the top of the collage. The woman had a short purple dress and high heels. She stood in a crowd with four men around her. "That's Marci Kessler, the first victim."

"Isn't that Chloe Reed?" Declan asked pointing to a photo in the lower right-hand corner.

Kate leaned down to get a closer look. "That's the last victim, Chloe. I'm sure there are others too."

Jessica cleared her throat behind them. "You'll have more time to look at the collage, but I need to show you something else." She grinned again, unable to hide her excitement. "The most interesting thing is behind that door."

Kate followed with her eyes to where Jessica pointed. There was a door at the far end of the large open room. It was painted blue like the front door and had a crystal doorknob. Jessica walked to it with Kate and Declan right behind her.

As she opened the door and stepped through, she moved so they could enter. "This room is a treasure-trove of information. I don't

183

know who you're dealing with here, but he's a master of disguise."

Kate wasn't sure where to look first. In front of her was a floor-to-ceiling mirror that ran the length of the wall. A vanity positioned in front of the mirror had more makeup than Kate had ever seen in her life. There was a row of hairpieces in plastic bags, flesh-colored prosthetics, and five contact lens cases.

"What is all of this?" Declan asked, his eyes darting around the room. He stepped closer to the vanity and stared down at the tabletop to inspect it all. Next to all the makeup and supplies were a series of selfies probably taken with a phone. In each one, the man looked slightly different – varying eye color, change in hair style and color, and drastic changes in the shape of the cheekbones and nose. The lips were the giveaway. They were the same thin pink line in each photo.

Kate looked over the photos and then stopped dead on one. She reached for it and picked it up, bringing it slowly closer to her face until it was right in front of her eyes. Davis. She had held the killer's hand and didn't even realize it. She let out a string of curses that made Jessica step back and Declan look at her wide-eyed and impressed.

CHAPTER 29

onday morning Kate and Declan sat in the small conference room at the Miami-Dade Police Department with Ted, Jessica, and Dr. Bruce. They had called the meeting to go over all of the evidence that had been collected the day before both at Peter Lyons' home and the murder scene.

After Kate realized that Davis and Peter were the same man, the case blew wide open. Declan called the FBI Miami field office for an update on the background information he had requested the day prior and Kate called Ted. Resources from the Miami Beach and Miami-Dade police departments, the Florida Department of Law Enforcement, and the FBI were called in to begin a search.

Once they got a handle on what they were dealing with, Kate had made a statement to the media and gave them several photos of Peter Lyons. The biggest issue they had was the multiple identities that Peter could take on and how easily he could change his appearance. The man Paris knew as Zach Nash was Peter Lyons in disguise. Kate assumed that was the same man who had been spying on Marci at the Eden Roc the night she had her date with Mick. They had found documentation for six other identities, all with photos that looked like different people.

A tip line had been set up so that people could call in with any information they might know about Peter Lyons or one of his identities. So far, other than what they knew about Zach Nash, nothing had come into the tip line of any significance.

Kate had called the meeting because they all needed to be on the same page as quickly as possible, even if they were all still half-asleep. She had no idea how Jessica was even still awake. She had arrived at the conference room after working all night in the lab. She set a large file and a cup of coffee down on the table and slouched in a chair at the end of the table. Her hair, unlike at the crime scene the other day, was down around her shoulders. Kate hadn't noticed it yesterday, but Jessica had blue strands of hair in the back and bottom of her blonde locks and a nose piercing. It made her look far younger than her years. Kate had been told Jessica was the best crime scene investigator Miami-Dade had, and so far, she had proven as such.

Jessica started the meeting by first discussing all of the evidence found at Peter Lyons' house. It wasn't a surprise to Kate and Declan because they had seen the majority of it the day before. DNA, blood, and fingerprints were taken, but there were no hits in the criminal databases. It was not a match to the evidence found at the Isa Navarro crime scene and for that, they were stumped.

Isa's murder was the only crime scene where they had physical evidence. Right now, they couldn't tie Peter Lyons to that or any of the other murders – there were no witnesses and no physical evidence. An arrest warrant had been issued for Peter Lyons based solely on circumstantial evidence and his attack on the paramedic. Kate hoped her work as a skilled interrogator could get him to confess – if they ever found him.

When Jessica was done going over the evidence and the lack thereof, Kate took a sip of her coffee and looked at each one of them, except for Declan who sat to her right. Kate stumbled over her words, not sure how to express what she wanted to say. Finally, she admitted, "Isa's death is a loss for all of us. I feel responsible but she sacrificed herself. If she had not switched places with her sister, we wouldn't be here right now." Kate took a breath and sniffed back tears.

Ted reached for Kate's hand on the table and rested his hand on top of hers. "We know what you're trying to say. It's a hard loss, but at least something good came of it. It wasn't as senseless as it first seemed."

All Kate could do was nod in agreement. The emotion caught in the back of her throat. She jutted her chin toward Dr. Bruce, sat across the table. "We appreciate how quickly you were able to do Isa's autopsy. I know that toxicology will take a while to come back, but anything you can tell us now will help."

Dr. Bruce pulled a medical file from an oversized purse that hung on the back of her chair. She placed the file on the table and flipped it open. She read her notes as she explained the findings. "Isa was not strangled like the other victims. There was bruising around her neck like he attempted strangulation, but I believe she was able to fight him off. The other victims had handcuff marks around their wrists. Isa did not. I don't believe the killer was able to carry out his normal ritual. The bruising on her body happened before death and there was significant DNA evidence collected from under her fingernails. That also isn't a match to Peter Lyons but we have no match right now, which as we've said doesn't make sense."

Declan interrupted. "We ran Peter's DNA against the database and right now haven't come back with anything. Let's hope his murders here are his only ones."

Dr. Bruce agreed. She went on to explain more about the bruising, which was on Isa's chest, face, hands, and legs. She raised her eyes to Kate. "As you saw, Isa was stabbed twenty-one times. It was a puncture wound to the heart that killed her. The killer did not attempt to remove her heart. I believe based on the blood spatter that he must have been covered in blood himself – both his own and Isa's. Isa was not to my knowledge sexually assaulted."

There wasn't a sound in the room as everyone sat stone-faced absorbing the information. Finally, after the silence grew uncomfortable, Ted asked, "Based on the evidence you saw on Isa's body, are you able to give a sequence of events?"

Kate knew that was hard for any medical examiner. She understood the question and it was information she'd like to have herself.

Dr. Bruce shifted in her seat to face Ted. "This is merely speculation on my part based on the pattern of injuries. You shouldn't take this as fact because no one was there. The only two people who know what went on in that room were Isa and the killer."

Dr. Bruce lifted her hands to her neck with her fingers together pressed against her throat. "There is fingerprint bruising on Isa's neck where I believe he came up and attempted to strangle her from behind. The middle and ring fingers left the most bruising so I believe he was lifting as he did this, indicating the killer probably had some height compared to her."

Kate raised her hand to interrupt. "That would be correct. If it was Peter Lyons, he's about five-eleven and Isa was five-seven."

"Just under five-seven from the measurements we took," Dr. Bruce corrected. She continued with her hands on her neck. "I believe that Isa might have even been close to losing consciousness, but she fought back. That's when she sustained much of the bruising over the rest of her body. At some point, one of them got ahold of a screwdriver, and either he took it away from Isa or he's the one that had it. There are some shallow stab wounds on her arms and thighs like she was fighting him as it happened. At some point, he made the fatal blow to the chest."

Kate hated imagining Isa's last moments alive, but the insight helped her understand how he moved and planned. Isa's death wasn't like the others, but she imagined Peter suggesting the handcuffs to the other victims – sex play possibly, given the victims' line of work. Once they were cuffed and on the bed, they'd be completely under his control.

It was like Declan could read her mind. "The other victims were prone on the bed when they were strangled, correct?"

"Yes." Dr. Bruce closed Isa's file. "There was different pattern bruising in the other cases. It's a much different situation. If we didn't know she was out with Peter Lyons, I might never even have connected the cases."

Declan turned to Kate. "Does it give you any insight?"

Kate wasn't sure how to break it down for them. She clicked her tongue and sat back in the chair folding her hands in her lap. "We know the killer, Peter Lyons I assume at this point, is a controlled, well-planned killer. If we look at the evidence we've found so far, he's expended a lot of time and effort into fooling people with his different identities, stalking his victims, and planning each of the murders. When we look at Isa's murder though, it's frenzied. I don't think that's just because she fought back. I think it's because she threw him off his game and he couldn't recover control. Once things were out of order, he went right in for the kill by strangling her from behind. Something either tipped him off or set him off for him to begin strangling her like that."

"What do you think that was?" Ted asked.

"I think whatever he normally says and does to get the victims into handcuffs didn't work for him and he lost it. He probably tried it once or twice. When he couldn't convince Isa, control her basically, he panicked. He decided he needed to kill her right then only Isa fought back."

Kate thought about the scene unfolding in her head and then back to Davis lying on the floor. "The blood on Davis yesterday was faked. I don't know if the bruising around his head and face was real or fake. It could have been bruising that Isa caused fighting back. I think Peter

189

scrambled and grabbed whatever he could to stab her."

Declan asked, "Do you think Peter had the screwdriver with him?"

"I would assume so because why would a screwdriver be in that bedroom randomly. We know he carries some sort of bag with him for his handcuffs and medical scalpel when he cuts out their hearts. We have no real way of knowing what else he has with him."

Declan stared down at the table and asked what they were all thinking. "How do we account for the lack of Peter's DNA and the unknown match?"

"I don't know. Maybe there is someone else present with Peter at the crime scene."

Declan shook his head like he was trying to knock something loose. "Are we sure the killer is Peter?"

Kate started to speak but no words came out. "If not, then why this big elaborate game? What about his trophy room? We'll figure out the DNA issue. It could be a part of his game." Kate turned to Ted. "No sign of him in the water?"

They had sent police dive teams to search the area of the bay where Peter went into the water. Kate hadn't heard anything yet but assumed if Peter's body had been found, they would have heard by now.

Ted shook his head. "Nothing so far. His boat is missing. There is a VanDutch sport yacht registered to Lyons. He also has a larger yacht at the marina that has a full crew. That is still there and we have a surveillance team on it."

"Can he get far in his sport yacht?" Dr. Bruce asked, admitting she didn't know much about boating.

Ted shifted in his chair, hesitating in his response. "He could easily get away from Miami and go up the coast or out to the Florida Keys. I don't think he'd attempt any open water distances to Bermuda or the Bahamas. He'd probably take the larger yacht for that. If he's desperate enough though, who knows what he'd do."

Jessica chimed in from the end of the table. "He jumped off a bridge into the bay. I think we can assume he's capable of anything."

Kate didn't disagree. "At this point, I assume Peter planned to jump and knew exactly what he was doing."

Ted's face drew back in surprise. "You think Peter Lyons is still alive? I'd think after going into the water like that we might consider he killed himself."

All eyes turned to Kate. Pressure to get it right hung over her, but she had no more answers than they had. She told them as much as she watched their faces fall. "Peter Lyons was a planner. Even if he didn't think we'd get to him as quickly as we did, he was right there on the floor with his hand in mine and he fooled me. He's fooled everyone with disguises and who knows what else."

Kate took a breath. She hated admitting her stupidity at that moment. "I'm not easily fooled. He had a plan and he executed it. I think we'd be wise to work from the idea that Peter Lyons got away. I know we have eyes on his banking info and credit card. Unless he's operating in cash or has other assets we aren't aware of, he's not getting far. We need to go back to work, following up on every lead and getting in contact with everyone who knew him. The real work begins now to confirm everything we can about him and bring him to justice."

"That's if he's not dead," Ted echoed and everyone agreed. He stretched his arms over his head and looked around the table. "All right, Declan, tell us what the FBI found out about Peter Lyons. Who is this guy who is capable of murder, leaving someone else's DNA at the scene, and jumping off a bridge to escape?"

CHAPTER 30

Declan stood from the table and went to the side of the room where extra chairs had been lined up against the wall. He grabbed his bag and brought it to the table, tossing it down on top. One by one, he pulled out files that the FBI Miami field office had given him earlier that morning.

Before the meeting at Ted's office, Kate and Declan had met with the local FBI agents and gathered the information about Peter Lyons that they had pulled together. Kate read some of his background that morning. She was relieved that her profile hadn't been that far off.

If Peter was still alive, knowing she had an understanding of his personality type might make it easier to find him. Of course, her profile evolved the more she learned – like that he was a master of disguise and he could lie with ease to law enforcement.

Once the four thick file folders were out of the bag and stacked on the table, Declan pulled the bag off the table and tossed it back on the chair. He flipped open the first folder and read a few notes and then explained what had been found.

"Peter Lyons is forty-eight. The driver's license for Davis Lyons was correct on the birth year but not the birthdate. He was born in Orlando and grew up there. He went to the University of Miami and stayed there from undergraduate through medical school. Lyons then went to California where he did two surgical residencies and then lived in the Los Angeles area until about a year ago."

Dr. Bruce, who had been taking notes, looked up at Declan. "What brought him back here?"

Declan picked up another folder and handed it to her. "Multiple lawsuits for malpractice. Peter Lyons was a highly sought-after and skilled plastic surgeon, catering to high-net-worth clients in Los Angeles, Beverly Hills, and Malibu. He had two clinics set up and close to twenty staff. He made hundreds of millions of dollars a year. Peter's work got sloppy over the last three. Reports indicate he had a significant cocaine addiction."

Dr. Bruce picked up the file and skimmed through it. She explained some of the surgical jargon that was in the report and then detailed three of the civil lawsuits that had been brought against him. Thanks to one of the most high-profile attorneys in Los Angeles, Peter had won each of his lawsuits. No one, it seemed, knew about the cocaine addiction or was willing to talk about it on the record.

"How do we know for sure Peter had an addiction?" Jessica asked, leaning back in her chair and kicking her legs up on the chair next to her.

Declan turned in her direction. "A nurse who worked in his clinic. Peter fended off the lawsuits and people kept going to him for work. The warning signs were there, but he was so well-known and admired, people figured Peter was still the best plastic surgeon in town. The nurse claims that Peter paid off a few of his patients not to sue him when mistakes were made. The real toll of his addiction wasn't known. He quietly went to rehab toward the end but most of the damage was done at that point. The Medical Board of California received enough complaints that they launched an investigation and revoked his medical license."

Dr. Bruce tapped the file. "Looks like he tried and failed to get his medical license in New York and here in Florida. I don't think, given the lawsuits and the statements his staff made to the Medical Board in California, that any state would license him to practice again."

It was clear Dr. Bruce had sat long enough. She pushed her chair back from the table and stood with the file in her hands as she paced the side of the table. "Looks like he did both a cardiothoracic surgical residency and then later a plastic surgery residency. That's unusual but not unheard of. I think from reading his medical school information, I can surmise that plastic surgery was a secondary path for him. I'm not sure why he changed from the cardio path. It's possible he figured that he'd make more money and have more freedom starting a plastic surgery clinic. It seems like L.A. would be the place to do that. I can see why he got off the cardio path."

"Agent Walsh," Jessica interrupted. "They say that serial killers have stressors that set them off killing. Do you think losing his medical license could be that?"

Kate wished she had a better answer, but she had no idea. It certainly could be a stressor. Losing a medical license though gave no hint as to why he chose the victims he did or why he chose the methods of his murders.

She explained that to Jessica. "Peter was in Miami Beach for at least a year before he started killing that we know of. If it was his medical license, then there was a delay. We need to explore his background more and interview people who knew him."

Jessica seemed satisfied with the answer because she didn't press further. She drank more of her coffee and closed her eyes as she listened to Dr. Bruce.

"We won't get Peter's records from the rehab because of HIPPA laws and confidentiality, but it seems the nurse included information about Peter's addiction and a stint in rehab in her statement to the medical board." Dr. Bruce moved the report closer to her face and read. "She said that Peter came back from a month in rehab and to her knowledge never used cocaine or other substances again. He seemed genuinely remorseful about what he had done to his patients while under the influence. It was too late though. Word had gotten out that Peter went to rehab and about the patients he had paid off. He was in the process of cleaning up his reputation when the medical board revoked his license. The nurse said that Peter seemed to know it was coming and accepted their decision."

Declan, who had remained standing, folded his arms across his chest. "I find it hard to believe that he was fine losing his license after all of his hard work. Did the nurse say what Peter's plans were then?"

"The nurse said he was resigned with what had happened, but he did appeal and fight the decision," Dr. Bruce said evenly. "I don't think it was that he was fine with the decision, but he had to know that he was taking risks. People have had their medical licenses revoked for less. Peter didn't win the appeal, but by that point, the nurse was long gone. She had quit the practice and went to work for another doctor."

Ted poured himself a cup of water from a pitcher on the table. He took a sip. "Is there any point in the timeline we lose track of him?"

Kate reached for one of the files she had glanced through earlier. "There's not much known about his movements when he's back here in Miami. With his medical license gone and no way to make money, Peter ends up focused on his investments. We saw from financial documents that he was day trading a lot more frequently. He was good at making money this way. I don't believe that Peter ever took a job again. He certainly had enough money tucked away to last a lifetime. The sale of his home in Los Angeles more than covered his house in Miami. It probably helped pay for one of the boats. Financially, he was set."

Ted motioned with his hand as he spoke. "I'm hearing a lot about his work and finances, but I want to know about his personal life. What was the man doing with his spare time? He's forty-eight. Was he ever married or have kids? Girlfriends?" Ted paused and threw up his hands. "Boyfriends, maybe? What's his deal?"

Declan shifted his body to speak directly to him. "Not married and no children that we know of. I assume he was heterosexual."

Dr. Bruce asked, "How are you assuming that?"

"Elise said that he had hired her for sex and that he had also tried to pursue a relationship with her."

"We need to find out more about his personal life." Kate gestured to the files in front of them. "Ted's right. We know a lot about his finances and his work but not anything personal. We have no idea about his friends or who he is connected to within the community. This is work we have to do now, particularly to make any headway on a search for him. We need to start interviewing people Peter knows."

Jessica sat up in the chair and dropped her feet to the ground. "If you don't need anything from me, I want to go upstairs and start going through more evidence. I know Peter Lyons hasn't come up as having a criminal past in any of the databases, but I want to focus on what I do best and see if I can find a needle in a haystack that might help. I want to explore more of the DNA from the crime scene, too."

Kate told her to go ahead and let Dr. Bruce know she could go back to her office as well. They were about as caught up as they were going to get. Ted offered to go to Peter's neighbors and see what information he could gather. Kate thanked them all as they filed out of the room.

When they were gone, Declan sat back down at the table with her. He leaned back and rubbed a hand down his face and then reached over and squeezed her shoulder. "You're beating yourself up. It's written all over your face. You need to stop being so hard on yourself."

Kate shifted her eyes to him. He could see through her façade like he always did. "I've messed up this whole case, Declan. Of course, I'm being hard on myself. First, I get the profile wrong and then we kick Isa off the case, which gets her killed. Worst still, I held the killer's hand and didn't even realize it. I should have quit the FBI when I wanted to and not let Spade talk me into staying. I've lost my touch."

Declan offered her a sympathetic smile. "Katie, my girl, you are one of the smartest people I've ever known. I was in that room with you and didn't know Davis was Peter Lyons. There was no way any of us could. SWAT cleared the house with us."

"How did it happen?" Kate asked, trying to keep the edge of annoyance with herself out of her voice. "I want to know how Peter got from the backyard up to that bedroom without us having any clue. He must have known that we were coming for him. Why didn't he just take off? Why the big charade?"

They had discussed this at length the night before. The truth was they didn't know and probably would never know how it happened unless Peter told them. Declan didn't have much to offer her. "Go back to basics."

Kate pinched the bridge of her nose. "What do you mean?"

"Your training." Declan pointed at her, driving home his point. "Go back to basics. Why would an offender like Peter stick around and fool the cops?"

"I don't know."

"Yes, you do." Declan inched forward in the chair and got right in her face. "You're wallowing in self-pity for things you think are mistakes when we both know you did what you had to do. Now, stop being intellectually lazy and tell me why this creep stuck around to fool us because we both know he had enough time to get out of Dodge between the murder and us showing up at his place."

Kate groaned and dug her palms into her eyes. Declan did this to her sometimes. He pushed and challenged her more so than anyone else. He didn't know the answer to his question and wasn't being rhetorical. If Declan could pop open her skull like a can of Pringles and dig around in her brain for the information, he would have done

197

it.

Kate closed her eyes and considered his question. *Why would Peter take the risk to stick around and fool them when he could have left and gotten away?*

Kate sat there quietly for a minute more and then it hit her. She turned to Declan to find him sitting there smiling at her. It unnerved her the way he knew her so well. "Peter Lyons wants us to think he's dead. The only way to do that was to ensure that we were a part of his fake suicide. He knew we'd go to his house and find all the disguises and different identification cards. He set us up. I said earlier that I believed he had planned that jump. He's alive, Declan. I'm sure of it."

Declan pulled her delicate hand away from her face. "Let's go get him. Think of how good it's going to feel once you get him across the interrogation table."

CHAPTER 31

They started with the only known person who had spent time one on one with Peter Lyons – Elise Navarro. Kate and Declan went to the high-rise hotel in Fort Lauderdale where the FBI had put her for safekeeping. Elise wasn't happy to be locked away but had gone willingly to the hotel the night before because she was afraid that Peter would come after her. Kate had considered calling Elise to let her know they were on their way to speak to her but thought better of it. She liked the element of surprise because it made for better, more honest interviews.

Kate and Declan showed their badges to the FBI agent at the door and then knocked. Elise answered wearing a black pair of leggings and a tee-shirt. Her face had been scrubbed of makeup and her hair sat in a bun at the top of her head. To Kate, she looked even younger than the day before.

"Is there news?" she asked, moving to let them in.

"No." Kate walked across the room to the small lounge area. It had a couch, chair, and television. Declan followed and they both sat on the couch, not waiting for an invitation.

Kate looked over at her. "We need to ask you a few questions."

"I don't think I can go through this again." Elise stood at the doorway seeming hesitant to join them. By the look on her face, it was obvious Elise was dealing with immense guilt and fear.

Kate offered words of encouragement until Elise took one tentative step after another toward them. Once she sat in the chair, Kate got started. "You told us that you had gone out with Peter Lyons before, which is why you were willing to meet up with him so late. We need to know everything you know about him."

"I told you everything." Elise sat back and crossed her arms over her chest and pulled her legs up under her. "I don't know what more I can say."

Kate knew there had to be more. They had barely even scratched the surface. "When did you first meet him and how?"

Elise took a deep breath. "It had to be about six months ago. He was referred to me by another client."

Kate did the math. That was before the murders started. "What was that client's name?"

Elise shifted her eyes away. "I can't give you that."

"You have to," Kate said with an edge of anger in her voice. They had no time to play games. "We both know the work you do is illegal. No one is looking to arrest you or the men. This is about bringing your sister's killer to justice."

Elise chewed at her bottom lip. "Andre Dale," she said, still not meeting Kate's eyes.

Kate inched forward on the couch. "Andre Dale is your client? Why? He has access to all the women he wants. You told me you had aged out of his circle."

Elise raised her head and looked past them. "Andre doesn't get women as easily as he'd like people to think he does." Elise shrugged like she knew how bad he was but didn't care. "I'm sure you know he's been accused of assaulting a few women. No one wants to go to his parties anymore. He keeps girls around the house to make it look good, but they aren't involved with him."

"I don't understand that," Kate said, itching for details.

Elise motioned with her hand. "The women who live with him are paid to be there – like props. I know them personally and not one of them is intimately involved with Andre. He wants to keep his playboy reputation. The only way to do that is to keep women around. I'm not afraid of him if that's what you're going to ask me next."

"Why not?" Declan pressed.

"He's best friends with my uncle, the mayor. I knew Andre wouldn't hurt me. He values his friendship with my uncle too much. When Andre heard that I had left Fanny and then I was dumped by the guy I was seeing, Andre asked me what I was going to do. I told him I'd go out on my own."

"Did Andre help you with that?"

"Not with the business, Agent James. He offered to be my first client. Then he referred me to others."

Kate knew there was a lie in there somewhere. "You told me yesterday that you had a website and that's how clients found you. Now, you're telling us you got your clients from Andre. Which is it?"

Elise blew out a frustrated breath. "Both. I do have a website. Andre refers me to clients but not the men who come to his parties. They want younger women. He knows other men. Andre prefers me to meet only those he refers though."

"Did he take a cut of your profits?" Declan asked the question Kate had been thinking.

"If you're asking me if Andre Dale was my pimp – the answer is a definitive no. No such arrangement occurred. My uncle has no idea about my line of work. It would be terrible for him if it comes out. Andre wanted me to be safe, but he also wanted me to be discreet. He figured if he referred me to men he knew both would be accomplished. Up until that night, I never felt unsafe. I had no problems at all."

Elise leaned forward. "It was also one of the reasons I was willing to meet Peter Lyons so late. I trusted him because Andre introduced

201

me and told me that Peter was a good guy. I didn't want to get into this yesterday because I knew you'd judge me."

"No judgment. Let's back up," Kate said, redirecting the conversation. "Tell me about the first time you met Peter Lyons."

Elise looked at Kate wide-eyed and let out a nervous chuckle. "How graphic do you expect me to get?"

"I don't care about the sex, for now. What was he like when you met him? What did he tell you about himself?" Kate turned slightly and nudged Declan's thigh with the back of her hand, and she hoped he understood her look. She might need to know about the sex and it would probably be good if he stepped out of the room and let them talk. Declan nodded once in understanding.

Elise messed with strands of hair that had come loose from the bun. "We met for dinner at a downtown Miami restaurant. I knew he lived on Sunset Island. He had already told me that. He told me that he wanted to take me to a place that he frequents so we went there. I always meet a date in public first, especially when it's the first date."

"You met at the restaurant then?"

Elise nodded. "Even though Peter was friends with Andre, I still wanted to meet him first in public. I can usually get a sense of people. I took a cab to the restaurant and he was already seated at the table. He had already ordered us an appetizer and wine. I had figured that I'd get there early and watch for him, but he beat me to it. That was one of the first things I noticed about Peter's personality – always controlled and in charge, always prepared. He was never late, never distracted, or off his game."

"Is that different from other clients?"

"It's a mixed bag. Some men can't wait to get to the sex so having to meet me for dinner or out in public, they are jumpy and anxious and want to rush things. Other men are nervous." Elise smiled. "There was one guy who was so nervous, he bumped into the waiter and then knocked our drinks over on the table. Half the dinner was on his shirt. He's a young guy though, and I wasn't even sure why he hired me. He could have easily gotten a girlfriend."

That brought up a question Declan had asked Kate earlier. She hadn't known the answer though. "Why did Peter Lyons hire you? He was only forty-eight and a good-looking guy. I wouldn't think he'd need to pay for sex."

"I asked him the same question over dinner. He told me that he didn't want to have any commitments and that having a girlfriend would take up too much time and give him too many responsibilities. He was happy with the occasional intimacy even if he had to pay for it."

Elise put her feet back on the floor and looked right at them. "Men pay for sex for various reasons. Many of my clients are older and think they can't have a sexual relationship otherwise. Some, like Peter, don't want the complication of a relationship or messiness of casual sex with women who could become attached to them. Others still are cheating on their wives. There are various reasons, no one better than the other."

Kate remembered something that Elise had said the day before. "You told me yesterday that Peter wanted to have more of a relationship with you but that you turned him down."

"That was later," Elise corrected her. "At first, Peter was full steam ahead on no commitment and just sex. In fact, at the end of our date, he said he'd call me if he ever wanted to see me again. He didn't call for a month. The second time we went out, he had softened up a bit. He was different. Calmer and less rigid. It was after that date, he texted me a few times and asked me if I had ever dated a client. I told him no that I don't do that. He told me he was going to make me change my mind. He started calling me, and normally, that would have bothered me. Peter was sweet though. He didn't pressure me or anything. I figured he was just lonely."

"In all of these conversations, what did you learn about him?" Kate asked.

Elise stared at Kate as if she wasn't sure where to start. "Peter told me he was an only child and that his father was gone a lot and his mother had left the family. He was raised with considerable wealth. He told me about college and starting a plastic surgery medical practice in Los Angeles. He didn't go into detail about his life out there. When I asked why he returned to Miami, he said it was a place where he had his last good memories. I figured whatever happened out in L.A. he wanted to put behind him. I asked him what he did for work now, and he said he was retired and had more than enough money to live the rest of his life comfortably."

Elise paused and rolled her eyes up toward the ceiling. "I'm not sure what else to say. He didn't tell me about friends or if he'd been married or anything too personal. We mostly talked about my life, books, television shows, and that kind of thing. It was never a heavy conversation."

Elise got up from the chair and then leaned against it. She looked down at Kate. "I'm not a therapist, but some men will indeed tell an escort anything. They use them like therapists. It wasn't like that with Peter. It felt more like getting to know a guy who is closed off emotionally. If you're going to ask me if I saw any signs that he could be a serial killer – no, absolutely not."

Kate hated to ask Elise the question, but she had to. She hadn't gotten much from the interview she didn't already know. "I can have Agent James leave if you're more comfortable, but I need to know what sex was like with Peter."

Elise raised her perfectly shaped brows. "That's where it was a little weird. Agent James can stay if he wants. I'm not embarrassed."

"Weird, how?"

"Peter wanted to handcuff my hands behind my back. He also asked if he could strangle me during sex. That's not the usual request."

This was what Kate assumed she'd hear. "Did you allow him to do this?"

Elise shook her head. "Absolutely not. I told him I wasn't into anything like that."

"What was his response?"

"He seemed flustered at first, like because I'm an escort that I should just do what he wanted, but if I'm not into something, I'm not doing it. I don't care how much they pay me." Elise shrugged. "I did compromise with Peter though. I told him I'd keep my hands behind my back and we could have sex like that. It was uncomfortable but not terrible. He did reach for my neck more than once. When he did that, I'd move my hands and shove him away. I finally told him he'd have to decide which was more important to him – me acting like I was restrained or choking me because if he tried to strangle me again, I wouldn't pretend to be restrained."

"Was Peter okay with that?"

Elise met Kate's eyes. "He didn't have a choice. I thought it was why he didn't call me right away after our first night together. I figured he found another escort who was willing. Then he called and we had sex the same way, but he never reached for my neck again. I thought he was good with it."

"You mentioned before you had sex in his boat. Did he do the same then?"

Elise confirmed. "It was like a habit or ritual. Do you know how people do the same thing the same way every time they do a particular thing? That's how it was with him. No variation."

"Did Peter do anything else sexually that you thought was strange?" Declan asked.

She shifted her weight from one foot to the other and smirked down at him. "I don't know what kind of weird stuff you're into, Agent James, but don't you think that was enough?"

Red rose in Declan's cheeks and he cleared his throat. He looked to Kate. "I think we're good here. We can go."

CHAPTER 32

Declan started the car, pressed his foot to the gas, and pulled out of the parking lot into traffic faster than anyone should. They made it only a few yards and he was forced to slam on the brakes at a traffic light. He relaxed his hands on the steering wheel and looked over at Kate. "She probably thinks I'm some kind of pervert."

"Oh, so that's what's wrong with you." Kate stifled a laugh. She knew based on his bad driving all was not well with him. "Since when does talking about sex bother you? Does it matter what she thinks of you?"

"It matters to me." Declan groaned. "She's probably going to tell her friends that some pervy FBI agent didn't think handcuffing and choking was strange enough."

Kate smiled over at him and patted his leg. "I can call and tell her that you're as vanilla as they come."

Declan rolled his eyes. "That's worse, and I didn't say that."

Kate had heard enough about his exploits while they were at the FBI academy that she could have written a book on Declan's sex life. It was tame though in comparison to what they heard today. "It's not strange—" Kate started to say.

"I think it's strange," Declan said, cutting her off. "Tell me you're not secretly into handcuffing and choking. I won't be able to look at you the same way ever again. I'll have to pretend you're still a virgin just to make it through the day."

Kate sat closed-lip for a moment eyeing him and making Declan squirm. Finally, when she didn't think he could take it a second longer, she laughed. "I'm not into it. I'm just saying that I wouldn't classify it as strange for everyone. Some people could be into that without it causing an issue."

Declan hit the gas as the light turned green. "You think it was an issue for Peter?"

"Clearly," Kate said, dragging out the word. "The very acts he used as part of the murders were sexual fantasy for him. What he did with Elise was in the lead up to the murders. I'm curious now if he murdered the women who allowed him to handcuff them."

"Is there a reason he didn't kill Elise right away?"

Kate watched the traffic go by. "I wondered that. I can only assume that something triggered him later and he started killing." Kate ran through a list of other similar murders she had seen, trying to pinpoint cases she had encountered before. One, in particular, she had studied in grad school jumped out to her.

"I think we need to consider that Elise was not the first escort he hired. This is probably something he's been doing for a while. It may be the only way he can achieve an erection and complete the act. It's possible he accidentally killed an escort during sex and then got a taste for murder."

"That's sound logic. How does removing the heart come into play?"

"I have no idea. We are a step closer to understanding him than we were before though." Kate checked her phone but no one had called or texted her. She was surprised she hadn't heard from Spade. "Where are we going now?"

"Andre Dale, of course." Declan checked the side mirror and then moved into the left turning lane. "He's friends with Peter so I figured you'd want to interview him again. Andre needs to cooperate or we can tell him we will be bringing him in as an accessory."

Kate wrinkled up her forehead in a question. "Do you think Andre is an accessory? He admitted he was the last person to see Chloe and that she had someone come pick her up. It could have been Peter. If they were as close as Elise made it out to be, it's possible. We know that Andre was sending clients to Elise. There's no reason to think he wasn't doing that with other women."

"It's possible," Declan said absently as he checked the GPS for Andre's address. When he refocused his attention on the road, he added, "I never thought Andre was innocent in all of this. I could see him supplying women to Peter. The question is if Andre had any idea what Peter was doing. Even if you know your friends well, you don't know everything."

"That's certainly true." Kate stared out the window as they drove toward Andre Dale's house. There was a light breeze in the air that made the palms bend gently. Kate wasn't sure she could ever live somewhere so hot and it wasn't even summer.

Kate dreaded having to interview Andre again. He wouldn't cooperate with them. That much was obvious the last time they were there. This time, Kate needed information from him and he'd have all the control. "We need to go into Andre's like we already have evidence on him. That's the only way we are going to get him to talk. I have to put him on the defensive."

Declan glanced over at her, a hint of skepticism on his face. "What if he lawyers up? We won't be able to interview him again."

"Chance we have to take," Kate said resigned with her decision. It was the only chance she saw for breaking Andre's tough demeanor. She'd have to fake her way through it because she had no evidence to back it up.

Declan pulled up to the closed gate and before he could put his hand out to click the button on the intercom, the gate glided open so they could enter. "Guess he was expecting us."

Kate grew quiet because the simple act of opening the gate threw her off her game. If Andre was expecting them, it meant he was prepared. Declan continued talking, but Kate wasn't paying attention to what he was saying.

As Declan pulled the car to the front of the house, Andre made an appearance. There was a smile spread across his face and he waved as if he were excited to see old friends.

"What do you make of that?" Declan unhooked his seatbelt and shut off the car. Kate didn't respond, she barely registered what he had asked.

"Kate," Declan said more insistent this time. "Why does he look so happy to see us?"

Kate looked past the smile and relaxed demeanor to the man's eyes and his hands. It was in the pupils of his eyes she saw fear and a tremble of his hand. "He's faking it, Declan. He's worried about what we know. He's had to have seen a news report already that we are after Peter Lyons. He knew eventually we'd connect it to him." Kate reached for the door handle and then turned back to him. "Remember, no one knows it was Isa Navarro who was murdered. We've let the community believe it was Elise."

"It's not my first day, Kate. Not a rookie anymore," he said dryly, but then the corners of his lips turned up. "Thanks for the reminder."

Kate had known that with everything going on that it was an easy bit of information to overlook. They had kept Isa's name out of the media along with other details that made her murder different from the others. They could only assume that Peter had figured it out, but in case he hadn't, it was an element of surprise they wanted to keep close to the vest. Allowing people to think that Elise had been murdered allowed Kate to test who might know the truth. It also kept

Elise safe for now. Even the women's uncle, the mayor, hadn't been told the truth. The Miami-Dade Police Department had balked at the idea, but the FBI pulled rank and shut them down.

Kate pushed open her car door and put her feet to the pavement. She mimicked Andre's good mood. "I'm so glad you are okay speaking to us again. You always seem to know when we'll be by."

Andre reached for both of Kate's hands and she slipped her hands into his for a moment. She resisted when he tried to pull her in for a kiss on the cheek. He made her skin crawl and this wasn't a social call. His face changed only slightly when she rebuffed him. "Andre, let's go inside and chat for a few minutes if you have the time."

"Sure, let's go out back like we did the other day." Kate and Declan followed Andre through the house to the backyard. Unlike the first time they were there, Andre didn't have drinks prepared for them. He motioned with his hand for them to sit down and then sat in the chair across from them. "How can I help you, Agent Walsh?"

Kate didn't waste any time. "I'm sure you've heard by now there was another murder."

"Yes." He nodded his head once and frowned. "I saw the tragic news on the television. I also believe that you now have a suspect."

"We do," Kate said without saying more. She watched his face and waited for him to say something else.

Andre pointed to his chest. "I have an alibi for the time of the murder if that's what you're here about. If you have a suspect, I'm not sure why you're here interviewing me. I'm not involved."

"Aren't you?" Kate asked, leaning her arms on the table.

He frowned again. "I don't understand."

"I think you do."

Silence hung between them and Declan shifted in his seat. This kind of interview style always made him a bit uncomfortable and Kate knew that. He'd rather go at a suspect hard and bully them into a response. If there was anyone who was "bad cop" in the partnership it was him. It was often hard for him to sit still and let the silence hang the way it needed.

Kate was fine with silence. She locked eyes with Andre and stayed perfectly still watching his face contort like he wasn't sure what she wanted him to say. That was the point. She didn't want him to say anything other than the truth. Declan took an audible breath. Kate resisted the urge to drive her fist into his thigh to remind him to keep quiet. He held steady though as the seconds ticked by.

Finally, Andre threw his hands up. "I'm not sure what you want me to say."

"The truth, Andre. We don't like wasting time." Kate leaned back. "If I were you, I'd go into this conversation knowing that we already know the truth, but we'd like you to confirm a few things for us. This way, you don't make me angry by lying. Nothing good will come of that today."

Andre's eyes shifted to Declan like he might save him or help him out of the situation.

Declan kept steady eye contact with him. "Andre, the thing about Agent Walsh is she's incredibly patient until she's not. I've known her for most of our adult lives and when her temper blows, you better watch out."

Kate tapped on the table. "Let me make this easier for you, Andre. Tell us how you know the victim and how you know our main suspect, Peter Lyons."

"I don't."

Kate held up her finger. "Lie one. Try again."

Andre straightened his back. "I think you should go while I call my lawyer."

"That's fine," Kate said and stood. "We'll be back with a search warrant and an arrest warrant. I can't imagine what that will do to your reputation with your neighbors. To help you along, we might give the press a call so they can be here when we serve them. You better put on a good shirt. A perp walk on this case will make national news."

A bead of sweat formed on Andre's forehead as he looked up at her. "Sit down," he said resigned. "I know Elise from her uncle, Mayor Harvey Littman. He was married to Elise's mother's sister."

"How else do you know her?" Declan asked and then stopped himself from saying more.

"I assume you know what Elise did for work. I tried to talk her out of it. I knew she had worked for Fanny for a while and then had a long-term relationship. She went on her own after that. It wasn't good for Harvey. If the press found out, it would create quite a scandal."

Kate smirked. "Is that why you hired her and then sent clients her way?"

Andre lowered his head but raised his eyes in a look akin to a puppy being scolded. "You know about that?"

Kate jabbed her finger down on the table. "I told you, Andre, I know it all. We need you to confirm a few things. You can answer us here or we can bring you into the FBI office, which probably wouldn't do much for your reputation or the mayor's."

"Yes," he said, his face finally registering some remorse. "I paid Elise for sex and introduced her to clients, one of them being Peter Lyons. I had nothing to do with her murder though. You have to believe that."

Declan's phone chimed and he pulled it from his pocket. He glanced down at the screen, clicked around with his finger, and then excused himself from the table. "Important information has come in about the case," he said to Kate as he walked off.

"Tell me, Andre, how do you know Peter Lyons?"

"I met him at a charity event about two months after he moved to Miami Beach. We got to know each other fairly well. I wouldn't

213

consider him a friend but someone I see from time to time at events."

"He ever been to one of your parties?"

"No," Andre said, his tone serious. "He wasn't a social guy like that. The events I saw him at were charity events – one for the local children's hospital, one for an arts program, and a handful of others. He's a quiet guy and somewhat closed off. At these events, he mostly stood off by himself. There have been rumors about him since he moved here that he lost his medical license in Los Angeles. People had questions and Peter never struck me as someone who wanted to answer them."

Kate pulled out her phone and clicked through photos until she found the one she wanted. She turned the screen so Andre could see. "What version of Peter do you know?"

"Version?" Andre asked as he leaned down and looked at the photo. "Who is that?"

"That's Peter Lyons." Kate flicked to the next photo and the one after that. These had all been on the news and shouldn't have been a surprise to Andre. "He was a master of disguise. We found several driver's licenses..." Kate never got to finish her statement. Out of the corner of her eye, she saw Declan charging back to the table.

"Where is he?" Declan picked Andre up by the front of the shirt and got right in his face.

Andre kicked his legs, trying to plant his feet on the ground. "Where is who? Let me go!"

Declan dropped his hand from the front of Andre's shirt but didn't step back. "Peter Lyons called you several times before the murder and then five times after up until about an hour ago."

Andre sucked in a sharp breath but didn't say a word. His eyes darted between Declan and Kate, knowing he'd been caught.

CHAPTER 33

Kate found herself in a position she never liked, trying to catch up to the evolving information. "Did you speak to Peter Lyons recently, Andre?" She remained seated and resisted the urge to pull Declan back. It might be good if Andre had fear in him, and Declan could certainly deliver. His South Boston temper went unrivaled, especially when he was in a fight for justice.

Andre shook from his head right down to his feet. It was like watching someone have their own earthquake. Declan grabbed at the front of his shirt again. He'd never get rough with him, but the threat needed to remain.

"I'm not playing games with you. When was the last time you spoke to Peter Lyons?"

Andre made eye contact with Kate. "Get your goon off me or I'm calling my lawyer."

"Answer the question, Andre, or you might as well call your lawyer and you can enjoy your perp walk because we are bringing you in."

With Kate not coming to his rescue, Andre held his hands up and pushed Declan back. "I'll tell you if you let go."

Declan loosened his grip but didn't pull back. "Go on."

Andre looked at the back of the house, still stalling for time. "He called me earlier today as you said, but I don't know where he is or what he's doing."

215

"He's alive then?" Declan asked.

Andre locked eyes with Declan. "Of course he's alive. Did you think he wasn't?"

"He attacked a paramedic and jumped off a bridge into the water. Yes, there was some thought he might have died." Declan stepped away from Andre and sent a quick text.

"Sit back down, Andre. Let's continue our conversation." Kate raised her hand with her elbow positioned on the table and made the sign for inch with her thumb and index finger. "Why don't you try the truth this time because you are this close to going to prison as an accessory."

Andre adjusted his clothing and smoothed down his pants and sat. He crossed his arms and shifted his eyes down. "I swear I don't know where he is."

Kate didn't believe him, but she wasn't going to press that issue right now. "What do you know? Did you know last night that he killed Elise?"

"I didn't at first." Andre dropped his head to his hands. "Peter called me because he knew that I had been in contact with you. He said that he had accidentally killed a woman and he worried that the police would think he was the serial killer that everyone was searching for. Peter told me that he had to plan an escape to prove he was innocent."

Andre offered a pleading look. "He didn't tell me what the plan was. I figured it out while watching the news. Everything I told you about him was true. I don't know him very well. He told me later the woman he killed was Elise and that he called me because he knows I have pull with the mayor. I don't know what he thought I could do, but he assumed I'd be able to help him."

"Are you helping him?" Kate asked.

Andre shook his head. "I told him to turn himself in and explain what happened."

Declan slammed his hand down on the table. "That's a ten-minute call, Andre. We have a record of five calls, most ranging close to twenty minutes each. Where is he?"

When Andre hesitated, Kate stood and pulled plastic zip tie cuffs from her pants pocket where she had put them earlier. She waved them in front of him. "Let's go then. You're obstructing justice at a minimum, but we have enough to get you for accessory to serial homicide." She turned to Declan. "Call our media department and let them know we have a perp walk coming."

Andre refused to move even as Declan stood. "Please, Andre, give me a reason to use force. Nothing would make me happier."

A drop of sweat beaded on Andre's forehead and trickled across his cheek and down his chin to his lap. He gulped and his Adam's apple bobbed. "I don't want to go to prison."

"Then tell me what you know and I'll see what we can do." Kate had no idea what he was going to say so she couldn't make him any promises. She stood over him with her hands on her hips, the plastic of the zip tie sticking out from her side.

"What I said was true. Peter told me he killed Elise and didn't want to get in trouble. I told him I couldn't help him. I was horrified by what he told me. I was going to call the police, but he kept calling me. I figured because I didn't call you immediately that you'd think I had something to do with it if I called after speaking to him at length. The conversations evolved though and he admitted that he's killed other women in the past." Andre rubbed his forehead and closed his eyes. "I asked him if it was the murders here and he said no. He was adamant about that. He said he was being framed. I don't know what to believe."

Kate zeroed in on him. "What were the murders in the past he mentioned?"

"He wouldn't tell me."

"Where is he now?"

Andre's head snapped up. "I have no idea. I swear to you on that. As I said, he never told me how he escaped but said that he left his passport at the house and then realized when it was too late that he couldn't use his credit cards to get out of town because you'd figure it out. He wanted cash."

"Did you give him cash?" Declan pressed, still standing over him.

"No, of course not. I was terrified for my life." Andre's voice had risen to the level of a screech. "He asked me for money after he admitted killing people. How am I supposed to feel? What if he came here and I gave him cash and he killed me to keep his secret? There was no way I was going to risk that."

Kate raised her voice. "You didn't think it was important to call us with that information?"

"I didn't want to be involved in any of this!" Andre's face grew red and his breathing became uneven.

"You're in it now up to your eyeballs." Declan looked to Kate but she wasn't sure what she wanted to ask next. She motioned with her hand for him to go on. He bore back down on Andre. "If you don't know where Peter is, then do you have any idea where he wanted to go?"

"Costa Rica. Peter said he has a place there. With no passport and no money, he's not going to get far. As far as I know, he's still in Miami."

"What about his boat?"

"I'm sure that's what he used to get away. He didn't tell me that, but it's an assumption on my part. He said you got to the house sooner than he thought you would so he wasn't fully prepared. That's why he left without his passport and cash." Andre looked up and pointed at Kate. "You messed up his plan."

"How did he survive the jump off the bridge?" Declan asked.

Andre laughed aloud. "Do you know anything about him? He was a championship swimmer in high school and college. Other people have jumped off that bridge before and lived. He had done it too. I don't know how far he swam to his boat, but I'm sure he had it close."

At least Peter was still in Miami and stuck for the time being. There was so much more Kate needed to know. "What other resources does Peter have here in Miami? Are there other people he can go to for money?"

"I don't know, Agent Walsh. I was serious before when I said Peter is a quiet guy. He lived here, socializing some, but people don't know him. He's elusive. I never would have thought he was a killer. If I had known, I never would have introduced him to women. Do you believe he's the one who killed the other women here? Peter was adamant it wasn't him."

"You said that Chloe was here the night she was murdered, but that she left and you didn't know where she was going. Is that true?"

Andre shifted his eyes in the way he did when he was about to lie. Kate cautioned him again about the importance of the truth. "Peter picked up Chloe here by boat," he said, resigned. "I convinced her to go out with him one more time. She had gone with him before. I called Peter after they found her body and he told me that she left his house when she got a call. He told me that she cut their date short to go back to the boyfriend that she had broken up with. I believed him."

"Stay right there," Kate said, motioning to Declan to follow her. They walked toward the house, and when they were out of earshot, Kate asked, "What do you want to do about him?"

Declan glanced back at Andre sitting at the table. His head was down and he stared at his lap. Declan turned back to Kate and leaned in. "I bluffed back there. We don't have any record of Peter using his cellphone."

"What?" Kate asked, her voice loud enough that Andre looked over at them. Declan had never done something like that to her. She wasn't sure whether to be angry or impressed.

Declan held his finger up to her mouth. "Shush. That was Jessica who texted me. She said they can't get anything from Peter's cellphone. They think he probably shut it off and threw it in the water. There's no signal and hasn't been since he went off the bridge. Andre just confirmed though that Peter has a working cellphone he's calling from. He also confirmed he's been in recent contact."

Kate rubbed her fingers across her forehead. A tension headache had formed. "Why would you risk it?"

"He was lying and we both knew it. Jessica's text allowed me to bluff like something big came in. It worked." Declan stood there with a grin that went ear to ear. He was proud of himself.

Kate didn't have the heart to scold him for going rogue on her. "What do we do now?"

"We should bring an agent over here to keep an eye on him. We can wire his phone and get Andre to help us bring Peter in. The alternative is we bring Andre in for being an accessory after the fact. I think we should use him though."

"You think we can get an arrest to stick? The evidence is fairly thin." Kate had her doubts. No one would fault Andre for not recognizing his friend was a serial killer.

"He's done nothing for hours with information that Peter killed someone. I think we can get it to stick, but you and I both know, we want Peter. If Andre helps, I'm sure the state attorney will go easy on him."

Kate looked over at Andre and considered her options. She didn't see anything else on the table. She turned back to Declan. "Watch your wording with him. We haven't spoken to anyone in the Miami-Dade Office of the State Attorney. We don't make promises we can't keep."

Declan walked back over to the table and sat down with so much force the chair scraped back on the concrete. "You've got two options,

Andre. You either help us to bring Peter in or you can go to jail today. It's up to you."

Andre turned to look at Kate, but the expression on her face only reinforced what Declan said. "How can I help you?"

"We wire your phone for audio and you call Peter and tell him you're willing to meet."

Andre began to shake again. "I don't want to meet him. He'll kill me."

"We'll send an FBI agent over here to keep you safe," Kate reassured. "We'll be here with you while you make the call and during the time you meet. We want to bring Peter in alive."

"I don't want to go to prison." Andre dropped his head in his hands and sucked in deep breaths like he was about to hyperventilate.

"Calm down, Andre," Declan said. "You might redeem your soul a bit helping us. I doubt it though. You're a terrible human being."

CHAPTER 34

After an FBI Agent arrived with the equipment to record a call on Andre's cellphone, Declan set it up and skimmed through Andre's recent calls for the number that Peter had called from. He confirmed the number with Andre and then jotted it down.

Because Declan had bluffed, they hadn't known Peter's new phone number. Andre had never asked Declan how they had obtained the information about the calls, which Kate was thankful for because they had no answer. It was a risk she still couldn't believe Declan had taken.

Andre's hand shook when he placed the call, but he still went through with it. Peter didn't answer and they had made no progress. Kate and Declan waited about twenty minutes to see if Peter would call back, but when he didn't, they left and the other FBI agent remained. Kate promised Andre they'd be back and could be reached by phone at any time.

They still had other leads to run down. While Declan hoped it would be easy to use Andre to track Peter, Kate didn't think it would go as planned. She didn't trust Andre at all.

Kate had two people she needed to speak to right away. Ava Crawford and Fanny Fontaine. First, though, they needed information from the Miami FBI field office about known locations that Peter Lyons frequented and any other contacts he might have in the area.

After leaving Andre's house, Declan drove to a small café down the road and pulled into the parking lot. Kate ran into the café and ordered coffee and snacks while Declan made the calls. By the time she handed him the coffee cup through the driver's side window, the calls were done and Declan was ready to tell her what he had discovered.

He took a sip of coffee and pulled a muffin from the bag. "Jessica is going to call the cellphone provider and see if we can ping the location. I assume that isn't staying in one spot though. He's organized, but not organized enough to escape. If he figured out that we'd track him through his credit cards, he's smart enough to know we can track him through his phone."

"True," Kate said, taking a sip of coffee and savoring the taste of the dark roast. "Peter doesn't know that we have his new number. It's most likely a burner phone anyway. What else did you find out?"

Declan leaned his head back against the headrest and stared up at the ceiling. They had closed the top of the car because the mid-day sun was too much. "This guy is a ghost. Peter stuck close to home and his boat. He's not a member of any associations they can find. He isn't paying dues to a country club. They didn't find much of anything."

"Has he kept in contact with old colleagues?"

Declan shook his head. "I had two agents follow up with people who had worked with him in Los Angeles. No one has seen or heard from him since he left. Peter has no siblings or known relatives that we can find. The guy was living mostly off the grid in the social sense."

"Andre said that Peter attended charity events. He must have been involved with someone, somewhere."

"Nothing we can confirm." Declan sat forward and sipped more of his coffee. "Andre said Peter told him he wasn't the killer. He said he worried he was being framed. Do you think there's any truth to that?"

Kate nearly spit out her coffee. "I believe Peter denied being the killer, sure. But no, I do not believe Peter is being framed. Peter Lyons is the killer we are after. I'd bet my whole career on that."

"His method of operation isn't the same, Kate. Nothing is the same between those first set of murders and the last. Doesn't that bother you?"

It bothered Kate more than she let on. The fact that Peter would have forgotten his passport and cash bothered her, too. She couldn't make it make sense.

"I'll admit, it's given me pause," she said with hesitancy in her voice. "We know from the murder scenes, this killer is highly organized. Peter's escape was highly-staged and organized. Forgetting his passport and credit cards is sloppy and disorganized. The way he killed Isa is sloppy and disorganized. The evidence he left in his house is sloppy and disorganized. We are dealing with someone who has a plan and when that goes off without a hitch, he is organized. If one thing is derailed or goes off-plan, it's chaos. He has low adaptability, which means he should be easier to catch now."

Declan gave her a sideways glance. "You don't think there's something off about this last murder scene? You think he got spooked and it all went to crap? Can it be that simple?"

Kate raised her hands in surrender. There was no point arguing about it. "We need more information about Peter from people who know him to see if this is a pattern. Do you have the number for the nurse who worked with him?"

"In a file," Declan said absently as he scrolled through his phone. He turned the phone toward Kate. "Clara Tipton. An agent talked to her this morning. She said she was willing to help with anything we need." He gave the number to Kate who added it to her contacts as they spoke.

"I want to speak with her directly about Peter's behavior before and after the drugs. I want to know what changed and what stayed the same. We are missing a big part of his personality." Kate finished the rest of her coffee and muffin. "Let's go see Ava now."

They had called Ava earlier and scheduled a time to speak with her. She was at a house preparing it for a showing as she had been the previous time. Kate felt horrible that she had been the one to find Isa's body but was encouraged to hear Ava had jumped back into work so soon.

A few minutes later, they arrived at the home and pulled up right behind Ava's car. She was bent over the trunk trying to lift something out. Kate couldn't see exactly what she was doing, but a leg from what looked like a real estate sign crested the top of the trunk and dropped back down again. Ava seemed to be fighting a losing battle with it. Declan put the car in park and got out to help her. Kate was right behind him.

"Usually, my partner is here to help me," Ava said, thanking Declan. "I couldn't get him to come to the house today. His girlfriend is a real estate agent, too, and she refused to go to her showing alone."

"Are you okay here alone?" Declan asked, turning his head to look up at the two-story empty mansion. The place showed no sign of life.

Ava brushed the strands of hair out of her face. "No choice. I have a job to do."

"What about your boyfriend? You said he's helping you financially."

"Sure, he's helping some, Agent James. I can't rely on him forever though. I'm trying to build a business here." Ava grabbed the signs Declan had pulled from her car and carried one over to the front of the house. She kicked the legs out and positioned it to showcase the times of the open house to all those that visited. She carried the other sign to the end of the driveway.

When she walked back to them, Ava grabbed her bag from inside the car and motioned toward the house. "I don't have a lot of time but will answer what questions I can. I already told the Miami-Dade detective everything I know."

Kate followed right behind her and held the door for Declan. "I want to understand what you saw when you first went into the house."

Ava walked through the foyer and into the kitchen. She dropped her bag on the counter and stood there with her hands on her hips. "The downstairs was normal. I was in the house for probably twenty minutes without realizing anything was wrong. I didn't suspect anything until I went toward the stairs. The first thing I noticed was the metallic smell. I know now that was blood. I didn't know it then or I wouldn't have walked up the stairs."

"How far up did you go?" Declan leaned against the center island as he spoke.

"All the way. I didn't see any blood until I got to the top of the stairs. I don't know why, but I went into the room." Ava squinted her eyes as if recalling the horror and shook her head. "The image of her in the bed won't leave me. I didn't see anything on her other than the blood. There was blood, so much blood, everywhere in that room. I ran out as fast as I could and called 911."

Ava's story was the same as her 911 call and statement to the police. Kate had read both reports. "Did you see anyone other than the victim?"

"No." Ava groaned. "Please tell me the killer wasn't in the house while I was there."

"Routine question, Ava. I'm sorry for frightening you." Kate asked a few more questions and Ava's responses were the same as she had given before. When they were done talking, Kate showed her a photo of Peter Lyons. "Do you know this man?"

Ava took Kate's phone and looked down at it. "This is the guy in the news, right? The one you think killed that woman?" She locked eyes with Kate who confirmed he was the killer. She handed the phone back to Kate. "I don't know him, but he looks familiar to me."

"He is a master of disguise. Take a look at some of these other

226

photos." Kate held the phone out so Ava could see and scrolled through five photos. When she got to the last one, Ava asked her to go back a photo. "Does he look familiar?"

Ava bent down and stared hard. "I know I've seen him before at a party at Andre's house."

Kate looked at the photo and was surprised to see it wasn't a photo of Peter as Elise had known him. It made her question Andre's honesty because he said he never knew Peter to wear disguises. Kate pointed. "Are you sure this is the man you saw at Andre's?"

Ava nodded. "I'm positive. I spoke to him but don't remember his name. He's shown up at one of my open houses, too. I didn't speak to him though. He toured the home like everyone else and grabbed an information sheet."

All at once, it hit Kate why Peter had easily visited the homes before the murders and no one had been the wiser – he had been in disguise. Kate asked a few more routine questions and then thanked her for her time.

As Ava walked them to the front door, she paused at the threshold. "Do you think this is the guy who killed all those women? Are we safe now?"

Kate reached out and touched her shoulder. "He hasn't been caught yet, but it's him. If you see him or have any interaction with him, call us right away."

Ava assured them she would, and Kate and Declan left. The closer Kate got to the car a sinking feeling spread in her gut. "I wish Ava had known more," Kate said, getting into the passenger seat.

"What were we hoping for?"

"I don't know. I had hoped Ava would have been able to tell us something about Peter Lyons." Kate pulled on her seatbelt and worried that they weren't making progress. "He's out there, Declan. He could kill again for all we know."

Declan turned his head sharply to look at her. His mouth agape. "You can't possibly think he'd try that now. The whole city is looking for him."

"Given how the last murder went, he might not have scratched his itch."

Declan cursed under his breath. "Let's hope that's not the case. Let's go back to the hotel and strategize some more. You can call the nurse and I can follow up on some other leads."

Kate nodded but her thoughts were far away, trying to fight off the feeling that the killer would strike again soon.

CHAPTER 35

O nce back at the hotel, Kate remained in the room to call Clara Tipton, the nurse who had worked with Peter Lyons. Declan said that he'd be down at the hotel bar and to meet him there when she was done. Kate sat on the bed and slipped off her shoes. She rubbed the sole of her left foot, hoping to dull the cramp that had been there since earlier that morning. More than anything, she wanted to lay back on the bed and close her eyes to nap. With a killer on the loose, there was no way she'd allow herself that luxury.

Before Declan had left the room, he had checked in with the FBI agent keeping an eye on Andre. Peter never called back so there wasn't much going on there. Declan said he had other leads to follow, but didn't give her the details and she hadn't asked.

Kate pushed herself off the bed and went to the desk. She pulled a pen and notepad from the holder and pulled up Clara's number. It rang only twice before a woman with a sweet melodic voice answered. Kate asked for Clara and the woman confirmed it was she.

"I appreciate you taking my call," Kate said after introducing herself.

"I'd do anything to help. When the FBI first called me and told me that Dr. Lyons might be a suspect in the murders, I vowed to do anything to help. He caused so much destruction here in Los Angeles, I feel bad that he's terrorizing another community."

Kate pulled the phone back from her ear, overcome by surprise. She hadn't been expecting such extreme language used to describe Peter's time in Los Angeles. She didn't want to lead Clara or infer anything though. "Can you tell me what you mean by terrorize?"

Clara snorted into the phone. "Agent Walsh, if you've seen the lawsuit documents it doesn't detail half the issues we had. Dr. Lyons terrorized his female patients. There's no other word to describe it."

"What does that mean though?" Kate asked again.

"Dr. Lyons," Clara started and then let out a laugh. "I don't even know why I'm still calling him that. Force of habit, I guess. He's no longer a doctor as you know. Peter was a phenomenal doctor when we met early on. I was his primary nurse from the moment he opened his practice. I was the first person he hired. He was one of the most organized, precise plastic surgeons I'd ever met. The office was spotless and his paperwork and records beyond compare. Peter took his time with his patients – he was caring and attentive. His assessments on patients were unlike any doctor I'd ever seen. You get some plastic surgeons who want to throw the kitchen sink of treatments at patients, even when they don't need it. That wasn't Peter, at first. He only did the work that was necessary to help the patient. He even talked some patients out of more extreme work they wanted to do. There were several he referred to psychologists before performing procedures to make sure they wanted them. It wasn't a fix for self-esteem he'd tell them all the time."

The person Clara described sounded like someone who could have pulled off the first series of murders. "Something changed then?"

"Everything changed when he started taking drugs." Clara clicked her tongue. "It was like night and day. Peter became erratic, downright disorganized, and a slob. Early on, he'd flip out if there was a wrinkle in his shirt. When he was using cocaine, it looked like he pulled his clothes from the floor."

"Do you know when Peter started doing drugs?"

"Umm…" Clara paused and counted back years. "It was three years before he lost his practice completely. We had about two years of dealing with it at the practice. At first, we didn't know what was going on with him. We knew he had a recent break-up and we assumed it was the result of that. You know how men can be when they get their hearts broken. It gradually became worse. He'd miss appointments. His work in the operating room became sloppy and mistakes were made. I saw him doing lines of coke in his office once and that's when I put a stop to it all. Lawsuits were pending and I told him he had to go get clean or he'd lose everything."

Clara sighed loudly. "As you know, it was too late to save him."

Kate wanted to ask about Peter's relationship but that could wait. "During the time you knew him, did Peter ever seem violent to you?"

"Physically violent, not really except for one odd incident." Clara hedged and Kate prodded her. Finally, she admitted, "During the time Peter was using cocaine, there were a few instances where he sexually harassed a patient. Peter was inappropriate and made advances. He's a good-looking guy and a doctor. Some women didn't mind and took him up on the offers he made. I didn't like it one bit. Other women were offended and never came back. I don't think they ever lodged a complaint though."

"Anything else?" Kate sensed there was more.

"Well…" Clara cleared her throat and dropped her voice lower. "There was one time when Peter was doing a woman's Botox. She was in the chair, tipped back and he was beside her. He slipped his hand across her neck and it was like something changed. He gripped her tightly and started to strangle her. It was like the man I knew was gone. I ripped his hand off her and Peter snapped back into his body. I can't explain it better than that, but it was almost like he didn't know what he was doing."

"Was that the only time that happened?"

"Yes," she assured. "It frightened me so I watched him closely. I thought about going to the police then, but Peter had been so shaken up by what he had done that I didn't think he'd ever do it again. It was out of character for him, even on drugs."

They spoke for a few more minutes about Peter's change in personality on and off drugs and the incidences that led to the lawsuits, which were all mistakes during procedures. Kate even asked her if Peter was known to wear disguises. Clara laughed at the idea and told her that Peter didn't have a creative bone in his body, that she knew of anyway.

Kate saved the most important for last. "You mentioned that Peter had a break-up. Do you know much about that?"

"Peter kept his relationships private. I only know of one woman he was seeing during the entire time I worked for him. Her name was Emily Shaw and she lived here in Los Angeles. I only met her once. Beautiful woman and intelligent. I believe she was a doctor as well, but I don't know her specialty. Peter took the break-up hard. That was around the time he spiraled out of control."

"Do you know why they broke up?"

"No. Only that Emily ended it."

Kate asked a few more questions and found out that Emily possibly worked at the Ronald Reagan UCLA Medical Center. Kate could hopefully hunt down her contact information. She only had one last question for Clara.

"Do you think Peter is capable of these murders?"

"If you had asked me that when I first met Peter, I would have said absolutely not. Now, I just don't know. What I saw scared me. If you believe it's Peter, I can't tell you that it's not."

Kate hung up from Clara and tossed her cellphone on the desk. She leaned back in the chair and realized she had clenched her fist for most of the call. She opened her left hand and flexed her stiff fingers.

The information Clara provided hadn't been surprising. She didn't think his nurse would know that much about his personal life anyway. The fact that Clara didn't think Peter was creative enough to wear disguises did catch her a bit off guard. It might have been something he adopted after living in Miami Beach and was a necessity to pull off the murders.

Kate got up from her chair, checked her reflection in the mirror, and realized her mascara had run under her right eye. She swiped her index finger across it, clearing the black mark, and went into the bathroom to freshen up.

A few minutes later, Kate returned to the desk feeling slightly more pulled together. She had brushed her hair and twisted it up in a ponytail and put some powder on her face to dull the shine. Looking better always made her feel better and ready to tackle the world. She double-checked the paper where she had written Emily Shaw's name and then called the medical center and asked for Dr. Emily Shaw. Kate was surprised when she was put on hold and then transferred to a cardiac floor.

A nurse, probably sitting at the main desk on the floor, answered and Kate introduced herself. The nurse informed Kate she had no idea where Dr. Shaw was at the moment, but she'd do her best to track her down. She tried to get Kate to leave a callback number, but Kate wouldn't be persuaded. She'd wait on hold as long as she needed to. There wasn't time to waste. The nurse, seeming put out that Kate would wait, told her she'd try to page Dr. Shaw but couldn't promise the doctor would take her call. She huffed as she placed Kate on hold.

Faster than Kate anticipated Dr. Shaw was on the line, a little out of breath. "Dr. Shaw," Kate said and introduced herself again. "I don't know if you have time to speak, but this is time-sensitive."

"I know all about that, Agent Walsh. My whole day is time-sensitive. I have a few minutes for you. Please call me Emily." While Emily sounded younger than Kate imagined the woman was, her voice was clear, strong, and confident.

"I want to understand your relationship with Peter Lyons. I understand that you were seeing him for some time."

"For three years and two months." There was a tinge of regret in her voice. "I always blamed myself for what happened to Peter when I ended the relationship."

"If you don't mind me asking, why did you break up?"

Emily sighed. "It was several things. Peter had a rough childhood growing up. He was not close to his parents. His mother left the family when Peter was two. He had a series of truly horrible step-mothers and it caused him to be insecure and needy with women. He was exceptional professionally, but he was a bit of a train wreck. I got tired of taking care of him when he didn't seem to want to improve on his own. I had suggested therapy several times, but he wasn't interested. It broke my heart to end it with him, but as they say, I couldn't go down with the ship."

"Did Peter ever meet his biological mother?"

"He said something about meeting her when he was going to college in Miami, but I don't know anything about her."

"Does Peter's mother live in Miami?" Kate asked, not able to hide the surprise in her voice.

"I don't know if she's still there. She was when Peter went to the University of Miami. He never spoke much about her. I asked a few times and he shut down the conversation, so I didn't press the issue."

Kate explained why she was asking so many questions about Peter as gently as she could. She mentioned how Peter handcuffed the victims and strangled them. "Did Peter ever show any tendency for violence when you were with him, particularly during sex?"

"Never," Emily said in a tone that convinced Kate she was sincere. "I would have left him immediately. He was insecure. I'd constantly have to reassure him that I was still interested and that I wanted to be with him. He'd get jealous over nothing and sulk. It was, at times, like dating a college-aged boy. I needed something different in my life."

"Does it surprise you that Peter is our main suspect in these murders?"

Emily was quiet for several moments. She breathed heavily with short puffs of air into the phone. "I'm not sure, Agent Walsh. It's hard for me to imagine Peter like that. At the same time, I know how destructive he became after we broke up. That kind of person might be capable of anything."

That was probably the fairest statement Kate had ever heard from someone. She asked about the disguises and Emily assured Kate Peter had never done that when they were together. Emily couldn't even make sense of it from the Peter she once knew.

Kate only had one question left. "I can't overlook the fact that you're a cardiologist and Peter is cutting out these women's hearts. Was he ever interested in your work to that extent?"

"He did some cardiac work early on but it didn't stick for him. He had more of an interest in plastic surgery. We talked colleague to colleague, but nothing in-depth. We all receive the basics in medical school though, Agent Walsh. Peter was an exceptional plastic surgeon." Emily paused and then stressed the point again. "When I say exceptional, that's probably not even a strong enough word. He was the best I'd ever seen. Peter didn't just treat people who wanted to look better, he helped patients who had deformities and breast cancer survivors. If Peter wanted to cut out a woman's heart, it wouldn't be hard for him to do that with the same kind of precision. I don't think that act has anything to do with me though."

"Why do you say that?"

"There was only one thing Peter ever said to me about his mother in the entire time we were together." Emily paused again and then spoke quietly into the phone. "Peter said he never knew how a mother or any woman could be so heartless. I think that relationship is probably the catalyst for these murders more than anything."

Kate hung up with Emily and remained at the desk, staring at her reflection in the mirror. She'd never encountered a serial killer who didn't have a screwed-up past – some more so than others. A deep sadness overcame her and she fought the tears that had started to form. Not many were as lucky to have the parents Kate had even if she lost them when she was only in college. She gave herself a half-hearted smile in the mirror and then got up from the desk to go find Declan.

CHAPTER 36

Kate stood at the back of the elevator as she rode to the lobby of the Eden Roc Hotel. A couple had gotten on the elevator a floor below her and were now holding hands snuggled into one another in front of her. When the elevator stopped and the doors opened on the lobby floor, they were locked in a passionate embrace. They hadn't realized the doors had glided open and Kate stood behind them wondering how she could sneak past.

Kate coughed and the woman turned, her face reddening. The woman held the man's hand tightly and explained they were on their honeymoon as if that excused the public display of affection. They stepped out of the elevator hand in hand. Kate smiled and congratulated them while she fought off the hollow feeling inside. She couldn't imagine a day when she'd be the other half of a couple. She wasn't even sure that was what she wanted for her life.

As Kate stepped off the elevator, the circular bar across the lobby caught her attention. Several people were sitting around it during the middle of the day. There were couples with their bodies turned toward each other, legs entangled, who sat sipping cocktails. Single patrons watched a television that was affixed at the center pillar behind the bar. The lobby was otherwise quiet at that hour.

Kate turned to her left to go to the side door that led to the hotel bar outside. As she did, a man at the far end of the bar caught her eye.

Kate stopped and slowly angled her body for a better look. There was something about his profile and the shape of his nose that struck her as familiar. Kate couldn't place where she had seen him before.

Kate walked toward the bar, crossing the middle section of the lobby. She kept her eyes on the man as she sidestepped couches and a chair. He hadn't turned since she began watching him so she kept her eyes on his profile, trying her hardest to place him.

Kate made it close to twenty feet from the bar when the man turned slightly and more of his face came into view. He noticed her staring at him and slowly swiveled on the barstool until he faced her. His hands rested in his lap and his legs dangled below him, the tip of his right shoe perched on the metal footrest. A smile started to spread across his face, but then recognition took hold. He inched forward as if wanting to get off the stool and then made a back-and-forth rocking motion seeming unsure what to do.

Kate scanned over the features on his face and she still couldn't place him. It wasn't until her gaze landed on his thin lips that she knew. She lowered her eyes to his hands and she confirmed her suspicion. It was the same man whose hand she held while she prayed that he wouldn't die – Peter Lyons.

Kate reached for her gun and pulled the weapon from her holster. She wasn't fast enough though because Peter shoved off the barstool and slammed into her, knocking her off her feet. She lost her footing and fell back against a side table, hitting her elbow with a sickening crack. Pain shot down her arm to her wrist. She yelled out in pain and closed her eyes instinctively. She forced herself upright and opened her eyes as Peter took off running toward the entrance of the hotel.

She grunted as she fought the pain in her arm as she stood. Kate jumped clear across the top of an ottoman and ran for the lobby door. She had no time to call for backup. No time to call for Declan. Peter slammed into a man coming into the hotel but he made it out the door before she got to the front desk.

"Call the police!" Kate yelled as she skidded past them. She kept in pursuit and sidestepped the older man as he struggled to his feet. Kate had no time to help him.

She yanked open the door and sunlight blazed across her face. She shielded her eyes with her hand as she searched the street in front of her. Cabs lined the roadway, but Peter wasn't in any of them. Kate turned to the left and scanned the crowd of people on the sidewalk, but Peter wasn't there either. She spun around to her right in time to catch him running, weaving in and out of people. He cut sharply to the right toward another hotel.

Kate gripped the gun in her right hand and launched herself into an all-out sprint. She got to where Peter turned and realized it wasn't a hotel but a narrow wooden walkway that dead-ended at the beach. Thick palms dotted the path and flowers encroached as weeds slapped against her legs as she ran. Peter glanced over his shoulder and saw her gaining on him. He reached the end of the walkway and cut to the left out of sight. Kate groaned as her lungs burned with hot sea air.

Kate got to the end and cut left as Peter had. She could see him far up the beach moving in and out of sunbathers, kicking up sand behind him as he ran. Kate ran in pursuit but her feet sunk into the sand and she lost traction. Peter was much more adept at running on the beach than she was. Kate pushed herself forward but then yelled out in frustration and stopped. She had lost him in the crowd of people.

Kate let out a string of curses as she dropped her hands to her knees, sucking in deep breaths of air and coughing from the sand and salt. Her hair had come undone from her ponytail and wet strands stuck to her forehead and cheeks.

As soon as she caught her breath, she called Declan. His phone rang and rang and a moment later, she explained to his voicemail what had happened. Kate made her way across the beach back to the Eden

Roc, passing sunbathers who glanced up at her as she passed. She wasn't dressed in beach attire and still had her gun in one hand and her phone in the other. She holstered the gun when she caught the look of a mother reaching for her child as she passed.

Kate kicked the sand as she trudged back to the hotel. She reached the narrow concrete walkway that led from the beach to the hotel bar and leaned her hand against the waist-high retaining wall. She slipped off one sneaker and then the other to rid them of sand. As Kate bent down to pull her socks off, Declan called her name. Kate glanced up as he walked toward her.

Declan looked down at her bare feet and sneakers thrown to the side. "Odd time to go for a stroll."

Kate straightened up. "I'm not going for a stroll. I saw Peter Lyons sitting at the bar in the Eden Roc lobby. I didn't know it was him at first, but as I got closer, we recognized each other. He knocked me over and I ran after in pursuit."

As Kate stood there explaining, the adrenalin that had been surging through her ebbed, and the pain in her right arm shot through her like she was being stabbed. She winced in pain and reached out to cradle it. "I cracked my elbow on a table when Peter shoved me. Is it starting to bruise?"

Declan moved around her and whistled when he saw it. "You've got a nasty cut that's bleeding quite a bit. You're going to need to get that x-rayed. Looks like you did some damage."

Kate rolled her eyes, annoyed. "We don't have time for this."

"You can't walk around bleeding like that." Declan walked away from her, leaving her standing there holding her arm across her body. Kate couldn't focus with the pain. When Declan returned, Ted followed right behind him. Declan handed her a towel for her arm, which she took and applied to the cut.

"I heard what happened," Ted said, taking a look at her arm. "The hotel called as you requested and we got a police unit out there. Do you know which way he went?"

Kate pointed down the beach. "He's probably long gone by now. I couldn't keep up with him running in the sand, and I didn't have a clear shot with so many people around. He got away from me again."

Tears from the pain and humiliation welled up in her eyes, but there was no way Kate was going to cry in front of Ted. She swallowed hard and turned her head to look at the ocean.

"Kate." Ted reached out and touched her shoulder. "Don't be so hard on yourself. We've had cops searching all over the place for him and you got closer than anyone. He took you by surprise and you had no backup. We'll get him."

Kate had never felt so ineffectual in her job. Her own mistakes were costing them precious time and putting lives at risk.

"Kate isn't great at being human," Declan said to her back and she tried not to smile. It was something he said often when she was being too hard on herself. He laughed. "I, on the other hand, am all too human. I make mistakes all the time. I'm emotional and hot-headed. I lose my temper. I go rogue and off-script. Kate though, barely human. When moments of humanity, like bleeding all over the sidewalk, happen, she gets a touch of what it feels like to be like the rest of us and she hates it."

Kate lowered her head and looked down around her. Declan was right. She was bleeding all over the ground. She looked at the towel that had been on her arm. It too was soaked through with blood. "Ted, I spoke to Peter's ex and his nurse. Peter's biological mother is here in Miami. I don't know her name or where she lives, but can you pull his birth certificate in Orlando and get her name and then find her address? I think it's important we speak to her."

"You think she's letting him stay with her?" Ted asked.

"I doubt it. Peter's ex, Emily, said that he didn't have much of a relationship with her. He'd said more than once that he didn't understand how she could be so heartless. There's a chance his relationship with his mother is fueling his killing spree."

"I'm on it." Ted walked back up toward the hotel and left Declan and Kate standing there.

"Come on, Katie. Let's go get you bandaged up." Declan reached his arm around her like she was suddenly a frail injured patient who couldn't walk on her own. She'd let him get away with it for now.

CHAPTER 37

T he trip to the emergency room took two hours Kate and Declan didn't have to waste. It was a good thing they went because Kate needed ten stitches and had a bad sprain. The emergency room doctor had fitted her with a sling, wrote her a prescription for pain medication Kate probably wouldn't get filled, and sent them on their way.

Declan insisted they stop to eat so Kate could take a break and they could catch up on the case.

As they sat down at a table on a restaurant patio far away from other patrons, Declan said, "At least that's not your right arm. You can still shoot if you need to."

Kate hadn't even thought of that. "It's not broken. I can probably ditch the sling by tomorrow. I'll need to find something I can eat with one hand."

Declan winked at her. "I'll feed you if you need me to."

With her head lowered, Kate raised her eyes to him. "You'd love that, wouldn't you? You'd like nothing better than having to take care of me like a child. It would even the playing field."

Declan clutched his heart in mock injury. "You hurt me. I'm only looking out for you."

The server came back and they ordered. Declan got the biggest burger on the menu while Kate opted for a salad with grilled shrimp.

As they sat there waiting for their food, Kate filled him in on her calls to Clara and Emily. She detailed both conversations in depth.

"In the end, I didn't learn that much more than we already knew, but it was good to speak to two women who knew Peter, at least for a time in his life. It sounds like his life went off the rails when Emily broke up with him. He had issues before, but based on what Emily said, it sounded like he imploded after the breakup."

"Breakups are never easy." Declan sat back and raised his head to the sky.

"Are you speaking from personal experience?" Kate had been there when Declan's soon-to-be-ex had him served with divorce papers shortly before they left for Miami.

Declan shifted in his chair. "I'm not planning to go on a murderous spree if that's what you're asking."

Kate knew the tone he used meant he didn't want to talk about it. She wouldn't pressure him. "What did you find out?"

Declan took a sip of his water. "Not much more than you. I spoke to a few of the police units who were searching for Peter, but they weren't having any luck." He motioned with his hand. "He was sitting right at the lobby bar in plain sight of everyone. Was he in disguise?"

"He was and that's why it took me a moment to recognize him. His hair was reddish-brown and he had a mustache. Peter wasn't using one of the known disguises that we saw either. He's staying somewhere he has access to makeup and supplies."

"We haven't found his boat," Declan reminded her as the server dropped off their food. They both dug in and let the conversation quiet until they finished. Declan moaned as he ate and claimed it was the best burger he'd ever had.

Kate laughed at his enthusiasm while she chopped at her salad with her fork. It was impossible to cut the bigger pieces of lettuce so she did her best not to make a mess. "Have we heard anything from the agent staying with Andre?"

"Nothing. They haven't heard from Peter all day." Declan wiped his mouth with his napkin and finished off the rest of his food. When he was done, he stacked his knife and fork across his plate.

"Do you think Peter knows we went to speak to Andre?"

"If he saw us there, he might suspect. But why was he at our hotel? Why risk getting caught like that?"

Kate had wondered the same. "It's possible he didn't know we were staying there. I should have checked the desk to see if he was a registered guest."

"It was the first thing Ted did when he arrived. They have no record of him and the bartender said he was paying in cash."

"Seems like he might have enough money to get around but not enough to get out of Miami."

"I suggested to Ted that the Miami Beach police start searching all the empty homes that are for sale. It seems to me if Peter was willing to break in to commit murder, he might use one of them as a house while he's hiding out."

A renewed sense of optimism bubbled up inside. Kate hadn't considered this, but it was a great idea. "I've been debating whether we should go on television and give another statement about seeing Peter in Miami Beach. My only concern is if we corner him too much, he might strike out. You know what happens to a caged rat."

Declan ran a finger up his water glass, tracing a trail of condensation. He shrugged. "I'll let you decide that. I don't know what will spook him or not. Have you figured out why Peter seems to have dueling personality traits?"

"Emily and Clara said that the Peter they knew before the drugs was organized as we saw in the first murders. Clara said that his personality changed drastically after the drugs." Kate relaxed back in the chair and adjusted the sling against her chest. "I've been considering whether Peter might be taking drugs again."

Declan cocked his head to one side and raised an eyebrow. "Could Peter have committed the first murders high? It seems like he'd need a clear head for that. Dr. Bruce said the way he cut out the heart had surgical precision."

"I wasn't talking about those murders, but rather Isa's."

"So, he decides to start doing drugs again and tries one more kill?"

Kate squinted. "Yeah, that doesn't make much sense. I'm stuck trying to figure out why her murder is different."

"I thought you decided it was because he figured out that she was a cop."

"I had thought that but then Andre still thought it was Elise who had been murdered. If he had figured it out, don't you think Peter would have told him?"

Declan motioned palms up like he wasn't sure. "I think we shouldn't trust anything Andre has to say."

"You're not wrong there. There's something that isn't adding up for me. Let's stick a pin in it and come back to it." Kate took a sip of her water, stalling for time. She set down her glass and condensation pooled under it. "I think we should give a statement to the media. It will force his hand. We need to close ranks on him and let him know he's surrounded. The only option he has is to surrender because he isn't going to get far from Miami Beach. The airports and ports are being monitored. He can't get access to his yacht. His bank accounts and credit cards are being monitored and he doesn't know enough people to get cash. The police have his plate numbers so he's not going to get far on the road, especially with no money. Surrender at this point is his only option."

"He could kill himself." Declan waved to the server who had stepped out onto the patio to bring another table their food. He made a motion with his hand like he was signing the bill and she nodded in understanding.

Kate wasn't sure if Peter would choose that option. "If he was going to kill himself, he would have already done it. He tried to fake his death and now he knows that we know he's alive. I don't know if he'll do it for real."

Kate's phone rang in her pocket, and she tried to reach for it with her right hand but it was across her body on her left side. She squirmed, trying to reach for it while Declan watched her.

He tried not to break a smile as he stood and came around the table and stood over her. "We're about to get friendlier than we have in a long time."

Kate looked away from him as he reached into her pocket, gave her a little pinch through her clothing, and pulled out her phone. She turned back to see him looking at the screen. "Who called?"

"Dr. Bruce." Declan clicked a button and then put the call on the table on speakerphone. "We're at lunch outside and there are other patrons around. Kate injured her arm so she's having a little trouble managing."

Kate glared at him. She could have taken the call with her right hand. "I'm here, Dr. Bruce. Is this something we can talk about now or do you need us to call you back?"

"We're fine, Kate," she reassured. Paper shuffled through the line and Dr. Bruce told Kate she hoped her injury healed quickly. She had heard from Ted what had happened. "I'll be quick about this. I got some results back from Isa's autopsy. When I swabbed her body, I came back with three different DNA blood types. One of them is Isa but the other two are unknown."

Kate shook her head, trying to make sense of it. She leaned into the table as best she could. "What does that mean?"

"It means," Dr. Bruce coughed quietly, "that there might have been two people with Isa at the crime scene. There might have been contamination from someone on the scene or it might mean there was more than one killer. There is Isa's DNA and a good deal of the killer's blood and then a tiny sample that doesn't match either. Jessica should go back over the evidence and watch carefully for this third sample."

"Are you able to do any type of matching to tell if it's male or female?"

"No, I can't do much with it at all. The sample is so small, I'm lucky we found it at all."

Kate thanked Dr. Bruce and assured her they'd follow up with Jessica. Kate's lips parted. "I can't believe this, Declan. A third person is exactly why this murder scene is so different from the others."

"Slow down," he cautioned. "Dr. Bruce said it could be contamination from someone in the room. We don't know anything yet."

Kate heard what he said, but she couldn't get her thoughts to move on from what Dr. Bruce said. Another person involved in the murder could be the reason this murder appeared so different. She didn't know what it meant though. Was someone helping Peter or did someone interrupt the murder? She had no idea, but if it was true, it would break the possibilities wide open.

CHAPTER 38

Kate and Declan waited until they were back in the car to place the call to Jessica. The crime scene investigator's excitement over the possibilities could hardly be contained through the phone. Jessica assured them that she hadn't found any evidence so far to back up what Dr. Bruce had found, but she had a considerable amount of evidence to still go through.

They ended the call and Declan started the car. "Where to, my lady?" he asked with a horrible British accent and a cheeky grin. It didn't matter what accent Declan tried, his thick South Boston always snuck through.

"I thought we'd go have another chat with Fanny Fontaine. I'd love to know if she knew Peter Lyons or one of his aliases and her impressions of him."

Declan backed out of the parking spot and turned onto the main road. At this point, they didn't need GPS because they had traversed the streets so many times. Kate had committed addresses to memory and she wasn't even driving. The area wasn't that big. It was akin to being in the Back Bay of Boston. The only difference was the vast waterways where Peter could hide his boat.

They were about two blocks from Fanny's house when Kate's phone rang. She lowered her head to see who it was and then pushed the talk button. "Ted, did you find something about Peter's mother?"

"Not yet, but there's something you both need to see." His voice had a tightness in it that indicated whatever he found wasn't good.

"Where do you need us?"

"Isa's apartment. Since the murder took place elsewhere, we hadn't sent a unit to go through her house. Her sister, Elise, is the next of kin. On a hunch, I had asked her for permission to go through Isa's things." Ted blew out a breath. "I can't even explain what we found."

Kate had several questions, but given Ted's no-nonsense tone she let it drop. She'd see what he was talking about soon enough. Ted gave them the address and Declan pulled the car over and turned around to head back toward Miami.

Isa lived on a quiet street in the North Beach area of the city. She had a small well-kept bungalow painted blue with white shutters. Someone had recently cut the front lawn and the flowers that had been planted at the base of the front porch were well-kept. Isa's bungalow was one among a row of them that dotted the street on both sides. Isa had a palm tree in the front yard with a colorful garden of flowers around the base. Kate hadn't taken Isa for someone with a green thumb.

Declan pulled the car into the driveway and parked behind Ted. As soon as Declan cut the engine, Ted waved to them from the front door.

When Ted got a look at Kate's sling, he tsked. "You okay? Looks like you got banged up pretty good."

She patted the sling with her good hand. "No break so it should heal quickly," she said and then changed the subject. "What did you find?"

Ted wiped his brow with his hand. "I can't even find the words to tell you. Come on in." He held the door open and they followed him into the home. Ted guided them through a living room that had newer furniture and then they walked down a narrow hall.

They passed by three rooms – a master bedroom, a guest room, and a full bathroom. It was the fourth door at the end of the hall that Ted opened. He walked into the room and went to the far wall. There in front of them was a murder board, much like they had at the police station. Isa had made her own with notes, photos, and lines connecting people.

Ted pointed to the corner on the floor. "Isa had copies of every single file we had. Plus, she's done background research on several other people." Ted turned to look at them with his eyes wide. "Isa identified Peter Lyons about a month ago. It looks like she did some significant background research on him and followed him on more than one occasion."

Kate didn't know where to look first. Isa had several photos of him on the board including two with him in disguise. Isa noted: *Flare for the dramatic. Changes his appearance when he hires prostitutes in downtown Miami. Changes again when in Miami Beach at social events. Changes again when he looks at homes in Miami Beach with real estate agents. Took me two weeks to see the real Peter Lyons.*

"Look, Kate," Ted said an air of excitement in his voice. "He's connected to everyone. There are photos of him with two of the victims, with Andre Dale, and even with Fanny Fontaine." Ted bent down to a box of files and photos and pulled out four black and white shots. He handed them to Kate. "It's the mayor with Peter Lyons. Isa knew this man was connected to her uncle."

Kate looked at each photo, going over every detail. In the first two photos, Andre and Peter sat at a table in a restaurant smiling and talking. In the next two photos, Peter and Harvey were on a golf course. Kate could tell from the photo that the two men were friends rather than casual acquaintances. The way the men stood near each other and the way in which their bodies leaned into the other as they spoke gave it away. They were relaxed and animated as they spoke.

In the last photo, Andre, Harvey, and Peter were in the backyard at what looked to be Andre's house. There were other people around – older men and young beautiful women. In the photo, the three of them stood talking, their heads bowed down as if sharing a secret. There was a clear comradery among them.

Kate wasn't sure how Isa had obtained the last photo. She tried to picture Andre's backyard and where Isa would have had to be standing to get the shot. It was likely that Isa was in a boat in the waterway behind Andre's house.

Kate handed the photos to Declan to review and then turned to Ted. "Are there any notes that Isa wrote about how she came to suspect Peter?"

"I didn't go through everything in the box, but I didn't find anything out here in the open." Ted motioned toward the board. "She has several suspects listed though. She suspected Peter but he wasn't the only one. Fanny Fontaine is on the board. I don't know how Isa could think an old woman could murder those young women like that."

"She has men who work for her. Fanny could have one of them do it," Declan said, not taking his eyes off the photos.

Ted shook his head. "I don't understand what this world is coming to. What do you want to do with this information, Kate?" He checked his watch.

"If you have someplace you need to be, Declan and I can stay and go through everything. I think it's worth a look. Who knows…maybe Isa has some information that can help us find Peter."

Ted shifted his weight and seemed to hesitate about letting them stay in the house alone. "I didn't tell Elise that you'd be here."

Declan raised his head to look at Ted. "She's in FBI custody. I'm sure she'll be fine with it."

"I can give her a call," Kate offered, hoping some diplomacy might ease Ted's concern.

"I'm sure it's fine. I'm probably just worried for nothing." Ted handed Kate a key from his pocket. "Lock up when you're done."

When Ted left and Kate heard the front door close, she let her shoulders drop and her eyes drift around the room. "I get tense around Ted, but I'm not sure why."

"He has a good deal of nervous energy. That's probably what you're picking up." Declan left the room and headed into the hallway. "I'm going to check out the rest of the place," he called over his shoulder as he left.

Kate remained where she was. While she was curious, there was a part of her that didn't like the idea of rummaging around Isa's home. It was an odd feeling for an FBI agent whose life was spent digging into other people's lives and psyches. Kate glanced down at the box and hesitated. She wasn't sure how she was going to maneuver going through files with one hand. She spotted a simple wooden straight-back chair in the corner. It looked like something that would be at a desk in grade school. With her good hand, Kate pulled it over to the box and sat down. She nudged the box with her foot and cradled her arm against her as she bent down to grab the first file.

She held the file in one hand and put it across her lap. The file had a man's name Kate didn't recognize. She opened and read Isa's notes. The man was a frequent client of Fanny Fontaine and had been for years. Kate skimmed through the notes Isa had written detailing the man's whereabouts on the nights of the murders. By the third murder, he seemed to have a solid alibi and Isa checked him off her list.

Kate reached for another file and realized Isa had a distinct process. She'd suspect someone – although there were no notes as to why she suspected them – and then she'd investigate thoroughly, detailing everything she could about them. Isa even included if the man was a client of Fanny's or obtained women from Andre. She noted their current relationships, net worth, and current activities. It looked like she'd try to match up their activities to dates of the murders and most had solid alibis. After an alibi was identified for some of the murders, Isa abandoned that suspect and moved on to the next.

Kate read the notes and guilt washed over her. Isa was a good detective and it was clear how much Isa wanted to solve the case. Kate kept going through the files and then stopped when she opened the file on Harvey Littman.

Isa had investigated her uncle. Kate's mouth opened slightly as she read the investigative notes. A moment later, she exhaled loudly, realizing she had been holding her breath. Isa hadn't gone easy on her uncle. She didn't give him a pass because he was family. No, it seemed Isa worked even harder.

It went far beyond the murder investigation. Isa connected the dots on a drug trafficking ring that went from Miami to New York and out to California and Washington State. In Isa's scribbly handwriting, she had created a chart with Andre's name at the top and right under it, Harvey. From there, it branched like a family tree with multiple limbs – each identifying a network of individuals in a particular city and state.

Kate flipped through the file, absorbing as much information as she could. At the end of the file was a stack of black and white photos, each time-stamped. She turned the pile upside down and then grabbed the last photo, turning it over. It was dated more than two years ago. This work had to have predated the Miami Ripper murders by about eighteen months. She was so consumed with looking through each image that she didn't hear Declan at the door.

"Kate," Declan said with an edge of frustration in his voice. She snapped her head up and looked at him, confused by his anger. "I've been calling you. Didn't you hear me?"

"No..." she started to say and wanted to tell him about what she had found, but he cut her off.

Declan held a familiar FBI folder in his hand. "It seems Isa Navarro failed out of the FBI Academy ten years ago."

CHAPTER 39

"She was trying to prove herself," Kate said quietly, almost to herself.

"What do you mean?" Declan asked, entering the room. He walked over to where Kate sat and stuck his hand out to give her the folder he had found.

She looked down at the mess of papers perched precariously on her lap and then inched her slinged-arm forward. Kate scrunched up her face as she looked up at him. "Just read me what it says."

"Oh right," he chuckled. Declan leaned against a nearby desk and read Isa's FBI Academy assessment aloud. It detailed that Isa was strong academically, one of the best in her class, but that she had an attitude problem. She constantly argued with her superiors and her classmates. Isa always knew best, except for when she didn't. Twice she put her classmates in danger when running through simulation exercises to mimic real-world scenarios that agents face. She failed hostage negotiation completely. In the end, her FBI instructors asked her to leave the program. It noted that Isa was irate and vowed to prove they were wrong.

Declan closed the file and tossed it behind him on the desk. "It's sad because it seems like she would have made a great agent if she had been willing to admit she didn't know everything. I was bad in the academy. I went rogue all the time, but I listened to my superiors."

Declan smirked. "I was just so much more advanced than the others, they couldn't understand my genius."

Kate would have laughed but there was truth in his statement. Declan had excelled in their class and he did have better instincts than most. Kate pointed at the papers. "Isa was going after her uncle and Andre by herself. We need to check with the DEA to see if they have any of this information."

"I have a local contact. I'll call them after I review what Isa found."

Kate pulled out the piece of paper where Isa had created the drug trafficking chart. "I have no idea how she tracked down so many people or even how accurate the information is that she found, but it's clear how much work she put into it."

Declan took the paper and lowered his head to read it. Within seconds, he was slack-jawed and wide-eyed. "Can this be real?"

"I have no idea. We need to keep this between us right now until we get a meeting with the DEA. It's not that I don't trust Ted. It's just going to be better if we bring it to the DEA one-on-one. Where did you find Isa's FBI folder?"

"It was in her bedroom safe." When he saw Kate's shocked expression, he held his hands up in defense. "It was open. You think I can crack a safe that quickly?"

"No, but we don't have permission to go through Isa's things. You should put it back."

Declan shrugged and grabbed the file. He got to the door, but Kate called after him. "Did you find anything else of interest?"

He leaned against the doorjamb looking at her, trying to hold back a grin. "You scold me for snooping and now you want to know what I found."

"You already snooped. I might as well know if you found anything."

Declan shook the folder. "This is all."

When Declan returned to the room after returning the folder to

257

Isa's safe, Kate handed him some of the folders she hadn't had a chance to read through yet. "Andre's file is in there. Do you remember how adamant Isa was that Andre wasn't involved in the murders?"

Declan nodded. "I thought it was odd at the time."

"I wonder if she didn't want us investigating him or her uncle because she thought we might uncover the drug operation. It seems she wanted the win and to prove to the FBI she could be a good agent. If we found out about it, Isa wouldn't have been the one to bring them down."

Declan pulled out the desk chair and took the stack from Kate. "I don't understand how Isa thought she'd bring them down on her own. Even if she took the information to the DEA, they'd have a whole team on it. That was Isa's biggest problem. This line of work is a team effort."

Kate nodded but didn't add more. Isa wasn't there to defend herself and there was no point speaking ill of the dead. Kate pulled Peter Lyon's folder from the pile and flipped it open. At this point, Kate wasn't all that surprised to see Isa had uncovered most of the information about Peter that they now had. She noted it was Elise who tipped her off to Peter in the first place.

Kate read aloud from the report, garnering Declan's attention. She detailed how Elise noted Peter wouldn't take her to his home at first. They had stayed primarily on the boat. Then when Elise insisted that she didn't want to be on the boat, that it made her nauseated, he had gone to an empty home, claiming it was a friend's house. Peter's strange behavior was enough that Elise told Isa about it.

Kate frowned. "Elise never said anything about this to me. She told me she trusted Peter."

Declan didn't know either. "Maybe she felt guilt over it. If she knew she didn't trust him and was going out with him anyway and Isa took her place, then she probably has guilt."

Kate furrowed her brow but didn't say anything. She focused her attention on the report and Declan did the same. They sat like that for the next thirty minutes until Declan slapped a folder shut with a clap that made Kate jump in her seat. She had been so engrossed in what she had been reading, the noise jolted her to the present.

"I've read enough," Declan said. "I'm calling my contact at the DEA. I'm sure if this information is accurate at least a few of these names will be familiar to them." Declan stood and took the file with him as he left the room to make the call.

Kate wasn't sure why he left but assumed it was so she could continue to read in quiet. She scanned more information about Peter Lyons and his background, double-checking Isa hadn't found something they had missed. Given how the case had been going, Kate wouldn't have been surprised. Isa had even uncovered the lawsuits in California. Kate didn't see any notes about calls to anyone like Clara or Emily, but the amount she had uncovered was impressive.

Kate was just about to close the file when a note on the last page caught her attention. There at the bottom of the page in small scribbled black ink was the name Nancy Blackwell – Peter's mother. There was a smaller note next to it with an address and phone number.

Kate arranged the files back in the box, keeping Peter's file out to take with them. She arranged things as they had found them and shoved the box back into the corner and went in search of Declan. She found him standing in the living room holding the phone to his ear, reading off a list of names that were on Isa's chart.

Kate stood there quietly while he finished the call. She shifted the sling closer to her body and winced. Pain crept from her elbow down to her wrist. The doctor had told her to take the day off and get ahead of the pain with the medication he had given her, but she didn't have time for that. Kate had faced worse injuries in the field and would power through like she normally did.

Declan finished the call and his whole demeanor seemed lighter. The tension had left his shoulders and his back relaxed. "I spoke to a DEA agent and Andre has been on their radar. Not to the extent of the information that Isa found, but they will explore it. They also are aware of several of the names on Isa's list. They had no idea about Mayor Harvey Littman. It looks like what Isa uncovered was legit at least in part for right now. They wanted to speak to Isa directly and I had to explain that she had been murdered."

"What will they do now?"

"We need to drop this off to them and they will run with it."

"Did you tell them that Andre is currently with an FBI agent and critical to our investigation?" Kate worried what would happen if the DEA swooped in now.

Declan reached out his hand and rested it on her shoulder. "Have a little faith in me. I took care of that. They will start looking into the information. They like to build a case before they bring anyone in."

Kate raised the file. "Isa found Peter's mother. There is an address and phone number. I say we go right now."

Declan pulled Kate into him until she was resting against him. He looked down into her eyes. "I can tell you're not feeling well. How about you go back to the hotel and I'll check in with Peter's mother?"

Kate shook her head. "I need to be there."

"Katie," he said drawing out her name.

"Don't Katie me." She put her hand against his chest and shoved him back. Kate walked to the door and reached for the doorknob. Without turning around, she said, "I promise if I don't feel better after we visit Peter's mother, I'll go back to the hotel, pop a pain pill, and call it a night."

Declan walked toward her until he stood right behind her. "You're as stubborn as I am," he said, reaching around her to open the door.

Kate chuckled. "This isn't news to you."

"How far away does Peter's mother live?"

"Not sure." Kate handed him the folder. "I don't have anything more than a street address. I assumed it was here in Miami."

Declan flipped it open and looked at the address. He typed it into his phone. "It's only about twenty minutes away. I wonder if Isa visited her."

"I doubt it. She kept fairly detailed notes and there was nothing in there about her speaking to Nancy."

They left Isa's house, making sure to lock the door behind them. Kate glanced back at the house and sighed loudly. She wore her grief over her parents' death like a shawl, sometimes it would be firmly on her shoulders weighing her down and making her keenly aware of the swelling emotion. Other days, she had shrugged free of it and life felt a little lighter and brighter. Today, it was like the shawl had wrapped itself around her entire body and was trying to bind and constrict her. The grief was heavy and burdensome, compounded by Isa's senseless loss.

She wouldn't dare face Declan because he'd assume her expression was all about the pain radiating in her arm. Kate laid her head back and closed her eyes. "Let's hurry and get this over with."

Declan started to ask her a question about her arm but must have thought better of it because he stopped speaking and turned on the engine. Soon they were moving, and Kate allowed herself a few moments rest.

When they pulled to a stop, Declan shook her arm gently. "You awake?"

Kate opened her eyes and turned her head to look at him. "Of course I'm awake," she lied. She had fallen asleep if only for a few minutes. "What is that the older ladies say...I was just resting my eyes."

The corners of Declan's eyes crinkled. "You're too young to rest your eyes, but I'll allow it today." He hitched his jaw toward a white one-story house with a sparse yard and a driveway that looked like it was in desperate need of repair. An older model Toyota sat in the driveway.

"It looks like she might be home," Kate said, reaching for the door. Declan unholstered his gun and Kate looked back at him sharply. "You think that's necessary?"

"I do, Kate. Peter could be hiding out here. I know his ex-girlfriend said they hadn't been in much contact, but you never know what's transpired since."

"True enough." The last thing Kate wanted to do was scare the woman by showing up at her house with guns drawn. It was the sensible thing to do though.

Kate stepped out of the car and waited for Declan to come around to her side. Together, they walked up the driveway. He continued to the door while Kate peered into the Toyota's passenger side window. A cup from a local fast-food restaurant sat in the cup holder, but other than that, there wasn't anything in the car Kate could see. It looked like Nancy had kept it clean and free of clutter.

With his gun held low near his right leg, Declan knocked on the door with his left. "Kate," he yelled as the door nudged open from the force of his knock. He jumped back from the door and called her name again.

"What?" she asked from the driveway. He didn't answer and didn't need to. As soon as Kate got to the edge of the small concrete front porch, the smell knocked her back. Something, or rather someone, was dead inside.

CHAPTER 40

K ate's eyes watered and she fought the instinct to cover her nose and mouth with her hand. "Let's get this over with and then call in a crime scene unit."

Declan gulped air and moved swiftly to the door. "FBI," he called as he shoved the door open. He stepped inside and Kate followed. Wetness slipped down her cheek, and she used the back of her good hand to wipe it away. The motion, with the gun in her hand, was awkward, but she had little choice.

The living room had a couch and chair and television stand. There was a large floor-to-ceiling bookshelf in the corner that was crowded with books. Kate wasn't sure how it stood upright and didn't topple over. From the living room, it was a clear shot to the kitchen. There was stale food on the counter and dishes piled in the sink. They still hadn't found the source of the smell.

Declan cut right down a long narrow hallway. They didn't have to look far. In the first bedroom, a woman lay sprawled in a nightgown covered in blood. Her corpse had turned gray and was bloated from decomp.

With the overwhelming smell, it was impossible to stay in the room for longer than a moment. Kate gagged and dry heaved, fighting off the feeling of being sick. "I can't stay in here," she said as she backed out of the room.

Declan had made it in farther, far more used to crime scenes like this than Kate. His eyes were fixed on a photo by the bedside table. Kate couldn't make out the image from where she stood. She gagged again and headed for the door. "I'll call the crime scene unit."

Kate did a quick check of the other rooms to ensure they were clear and then she got out of the house as quickly as possible. Once she got to the front lawn, she moved far away from the front door and then bent over gagging. She sucked in fresh breaths of air and willed her stomach to settle.

Once she calmed herself down, she holstered her gun and reached for her cellphone. She called Dr. Bruce at the medical examiner's office and then that Miami-Dade Police Department. She finished her call just as Declan came out of the home, holding a framed photo in his hand.

His face had paled and he sucked in quick breaths of air. "Who is that?" he asked, pointing.

Kate took the gold-plated eight-by-ten photo frame from him and lowered her head to look at the photo. Two women stood side by side on a pier with the ocean in the background. Kate was sure one of the women was probably Nancy, but the other woman looked vaguely familiar. Both of the women had long, straight dark hair parted down the middle. They wore simple blouses, skirts, and sandals. If Kate had to guess by how they were dressed, the photo was taken probably in the seventies.

"I'm not sure," she said still staring at the photo.

"Fanny Fontaine." Declan said her name in one breath.

Kate gasped and shook her head. "You've got to be kidding me?" She looked down at the photo again and Declan pointed to Fanny. Kate scanned over the young woman's face and starting with the bridge of her nose up into her eyes and forehead, the image became clearer to her. The hairline was the same, too. Kate lowered her eyes again and only now recognized the woman's half-smile and rounded soft jawline. She was looking at a photo of Fanny from at least forty years ago.

Once Kate recognized her, she couldn't unsee it and wondered how she didn't recognize her at first.

"What do you think this means?" Declan asked, garnering Kate's attention.

"I don't know, but the only way we are going to find out is to speak to Fanny." She handed the framed photo back to him. "Did you happened to see how Nancy was killed?"

Declan raised his eyebrows. "I don't think at this point we can assume it's Nancy. It probably is but the body is in rough condition. We are going to need to make a positive identification first." He shook his head. "I grabbed the photo and left."

Kate wished now she had stayed in there longer. "I couldn't breathe in there. I should have just toughed it out."

"No reason to." Declan confirmed Kate had made the calls to the crime scene unit and the medical examiner. He reassured her, "They have the gear to go in there like that. Let them handle it. We'll get the information we need soon enough."

Kate nodded but didn't like admitting defeat. They waited there together on the front lawn until Dr. Bruce and her team arrived. No neighbors had come out of their homes to ask what they were doing or to see what was going on. They wouldn't start interviewing the neighbors as they had no jurisdiction. This would be the case of a Miami-Dade homicide detective unless it was determined that it was related to the case.

As Dr. Bruce stood at the back of the medical examiner van getting her things together, Jessica and her team from the Miami-Dade crime scene investigation unit pulled up along the sidewalk. She waved to Kate and got out of the van.

Jessica nodded toward Kate's sling and wished her a speedy recovery. "I heard you were first on the scene. What have I got in store for me?"

Declan rocked on the balls of his feet. "Woman in her bed. I'd guess maybe in her late sixties or early seventies. The body is in bad condition so hard to tell. Full rigor has come and gone. Her skin is greenish-gray. I'd say she's probably been dead three to five days, but Dr. Bruce would know better."

Jessica's mouth was set in a firm line and she nodded taking in the information. "How much damage did you two do to my scene?"

It was a good-natured ribbing that Kate and Declan were used to. Crime scene techs hated when detectives trampled over the crime scene before they arrived on site. Kate smiled. "Nothing too bad. The smell was apparent before we went in. We did a basic sweep of the home and then found her in the bedroom. We didn't touch anything other than that photo," Kate said, pointing to the photo in Declan's hand.

Declan went to hand it to Jessica, but she rolled her eyes at him. "Not without gloves on first, which is what you two should have had before you touched it."

Declan laughed. "Our prints are on file. Simple elimination. Besides, it's who is in the photo that's important."

Jessica leaned in. "Who is that?"

"Fanny Fontaine. Peter Lyon's mother and Fanny Fontaine were friends at one point."

"The plot thickens," she teased and saluted them as she moved past them toward the house. Jessica shouted instructions to her two colleagues as they got themselves ready to enter the home.

Kate and Declan walked to the car and waved to Dr. Bruce as they went. "Give us a call when you know anything," Declan shouted.

"Go back to the hotel and rest, Kate. Doctor's orders!" Dr. Bruce struggled into her jumpsuit and pulled on a hairnet so her hair

266

wouldn't mix with that at the crime scene.

Kate waved with her good hand, ignoring the directive, and opened the passenger side door.

Declan had heard though. "Am I taking you back? You promised you'd rest after we spoke to Peter's mother." He pulled open the car door, staring over at her, but the grin that turned up at the corners of his lips indicated his words were teasing. He knew as well as Dr. Bruce did that Kate wasn't going to rest.

Traffic was light that afternoon and Declan navigated them back to Miami Beach in record time. He pulled the car into Fanny's driveway and hit the intercom button for the gate. A moment later, it glided open without anyone asking who was there. Declan inched the car through the gate and up to the house.

"Do we have any plan for this interview?" he asked as he parked.

Kate thought about the question for a moment. They needed to be on the same page. She turned to him. "The only thing that's important to me is that we don't disclose that Nancy is dead. I want to find out as much as possible and see if she tells us the truth. I plan to go in and ask if she knows Peter and then if she knows his mother. I don't want to lead her unless we need to. Then, if she's not forthcoming, we'll have to press her harder."

Declan opened his door and chuckled. "I'm going to do the strong, silent, sexy FBI agent routine that comes so naturally to me."

"You do that," Kate said dryly as she got out of the car. She leaned her back against the car as she looked at Fanny's house. Her mouth felt like cotton and she needed a glass of water. Kate had no idea how she'd get through the interview without it. She wiped her good hand down her pants and noted that her palms were sweaty. There was no real reason for the nervousness that had crept up on her.

Kate shook the feeling and noticed that Declan was watching her. "I'm fine," she reassured, walking with him to the front door. Before they could knock, one of Fanny's bodyguards opened the door and let them in.

They had seen him there briefly the last time they were at the home. He pointed toward the backyard where they had met Fanny before. Kate thanked them and he responded with a single nod and then disappeared.

They found Fanny reclined on a chaise lounge under the shade of a palm tree. She had a long bright pink caftan on and a wide-brimmed white hat. Large sunglasses shielded her eyes and Kate couldn't tell if they were opened or closed.

"Fanny," Declan said as they approached. They stood at the foot of the chaise and waited for her to respond.

After a few uncomfortable moments of silence, in which Kate wondered if the woman had fallen asleep, Fanny lifted the sunglasses from her face and waved them to the side. "You're standing in my sun. I don't like it beating at the top of my head, but I'm trying to soak up as much Vitamin D as possible."

Kate was glad Fanny hadn't said she was trying to get a tan because other than her wrists, ankles, and feet, she was fully covered. "We need to speak with you about Peter Lyons."

The corners of Fanny's lips turned up in a smile. "I wondered when you two were going to get around to connecting me to him. Took you long enough."

"You know him then?" Declan asked, giving Kate a look.

"Oh, sugar." She waved her hand at him dismissively. "Me and his momma go way back. We're practically like sisters. Pull up some chairs and get comfortable."

CHAPTER 41

"What happened to you?" Fanny asked Kate as Declan brought a chair over for her. "Your partner rough you up?" She winked at Declan. "You're too respectful to hit a woman."

"You're right about that," Declan said, taking a seat.

Kate inched her slinged-arm forward. "Peter Lyons shoved me, and I hit my elbow on a table."

"Peter did that to you?" Fanny asked, her voice raised an octave.

Kate nodded. "What can you tell me about him?"

Fanny locked eyes with Kate and then with Declan. "I've heard his name mentioned on the news lately connected to those murders. I have a hard time believing that was Peter."

Kate pinned her gaze on her. "Why is it so hard to believe?"

Fanny clicked her tongue. "He was shy and sweet when I knew him. Peter was always a sensitive kid. I just can't reconcile the kid I knew with the butcher who did that to those poor women."

"With all due respect," Declan started, clasping his hands in front of him, "boys grow up and sometimes become sinister men who do evil things. I've seen it far too many times."

"I'm sure. I'm sure," Fanny said, conceding the point. Her face didn't reflect her words though. She offered a condescending smile but didn't press the issue. "What is it that you want to know?"

There was a lot to ask, but Kate needed to get the immediate important question out of the way first. "When was the last time you saw him?"

Fanny shook her head. "It was a few months back but only once. I had heard from his mother that he was back here in Miami Beach, but they had a strained relationship." She waved them off like it was old news. "I haven't seen him recently. I heard on the news he's on the run. I have no idea where he might be."

"We understand Peter didn't know too many people here. Is there a chance he will reach out to you for help?"

Fanny wagged her finger at Kate. "As much as I don't think he killed those women, I wouldn't harbor him here if that's what you're thinking. Peter and I never got on too well on account of how poorly he treated his mother."

Kate leaned toward Fanny. "We understand that his mother left the family when Peter was quite young. You said the relationship was strained. Why was that?"

Fanny looked at Kate in disgust. "It's not Nancy's fault if that's what you're insinuating. There was domestic violence between Nancy and Peter's father. When she couldn't take it anymore, she left. He had money and came from a wealthy family. It would have taken whatever money she had to fight him in court, so she left and let Peter be raised by his father. He had never hurt the boy that Nancy saw so she wasn't concerned for his safety. Had Nancy stayed though, she'd be dead today. That man would have killed her."

"Did Nancy tell you about the domestic violence or did you see evidence of that?"

Fanny glared at Kate, her eyes daggers of anger. "Cold hard evidence. Don't mistake me for a fool who can be easily duped by a sad story, Agent Walsh. Nancy and I met here in Miami Beach right after she left Peter's father. She got a job in a hotel bar right away. She was handy behind the bar and poured a good martini. Nancy had a charm about her, so she made good enough money to afford a place to live and cover her basic expenses. I had drinks at the bar often, and we became fast friends. The first night I saw her, she had remnants of bruising on her face. I asked her what had happened. She wouldn't say then, but I knew the look. Then Peter's father showed up there one weekend to make sure that Nancy wasn't going to try to get the boy back. He beat her pretty good and she came to me."

Kate winced at the thought of it. "Did she go to the police?"

Fanny shook her head. "You didn't go to the cops for domestic violence in the 1970s, Agent Walsh. I don't think they even had laws on the books back then. A husband could beat his wife. Sure, it was frowned upon but nothing more. No, she came to me and my husband took care of it. I don't know the details, but after that, Nancy came to live with us for a long time to get back on her feet."

"Did she work for you?" Declan asked what Kate had been thinking.

"No. I wasn't doing that work then when my husband was alive." Fanny had a look on her face as if remembering years ago. "When I started, Nancy wasn't interested. I offered to make her a partner, but that wasn't anything she was interested in doing."

"What did Nancy do for work?" Kate asked.

Fanny tapped at her head. "She was a smart, tough woman. She worked at that bar and put herself through school. Nancy became a lawyer in record time. You know what she did with that degree?" She didn't wait for a response. "Nancy went and worked for legal aid, helping women just like her have legal representation when they couldn't afford it. I swear she made more in tips working at that hotel bar, but it was honest work. Nancy couldn't have been happier. She retired two years ago."

"What about her relationship with Peter?"

"Well, what do you think happened?"

Kate could imagine, but she needed to hear it from Fanny. She kept her eyes on the woman until she started telling the story again.

Fanny closed her eyes. "The father poisoned Peter against his mother. He told him his mother didn't love him and that she left the family. He called her all sorts of names. Said Nancy was out whoring around in Miami and was worthless. Nancy tried several times to set Peter straight, but he wouldn't hear of it. Peter was downright mean to his mother at times. He was here for college and Nancy hoped with enough time, the relationship could be repaired. It wasn't. I don't even know what her interactions with him have been like since he came back. It hurt Nancy too much to talk about it."

Kate expelled a breath and adjusted her sling. "Do you know if Peter was ever violent toward Nancy?"

Fanny opened her eyes and looked at Kate. "Never that I'm aware of. If Peter was and I found out about it, it would have been the last thing he ever did. I'm not saying I would have killed him because I don't like to get my hands dirty. I'll just say that it would be the last time anyone saw Peter Lyons alive."

Kate believed her and the look of admiration on Declan's face said that he did as well.

"Have you seen Nancy recently?" Declan asked.

"We went to lunch last week. We get together every other week or so for lunch or shopping. Just spending time together." Declan glanced down at Kate and Fanny caught the look. "Is there something going on?"

Kate didn't think there was much the woman missed. "We are sorry to tell you this—"

Kate didn't get a chance to finish her sentence because Fanny interrupted her. "Nancy's dead, right? That's what you've come to tell me."

"We suspect it was Peter."

Fanny looked away. "Peter's father is long since dead. Nancy led a low-risk life. It makes sense why you'd think it was him." Fanny wiped a tear from her face. "I'd ask what happened, but I don't want to know. I don't think I could bear knowing what Nancy went through at the end. When did it happen?"

"We're not sure." Kate pointed between herself and Declan. "We found her body right before we came here. The medical examiner and crime scene investigators are there now. We found a photo of you and Nancy as young women, probably soon after you met."

Fanny smiled as if remembering something special. "Nancy kept a photo of us from a party on the beach. The last time I was at her place it was in a frame by her bed." Fanny sniffed and looked down at her hands. "We always were the best of friends."

Kate gave Fanny a moment to grieve and then pull herself together. "We need to find Peter Lyons. We believe he's responsible for all of these murders."

Fanny raised her head. "I heard he killed Elise Navarro. She was one of my girls before her sister got involved."

"You didn't tell me that when we were here the first time."

"I've never outed any of my girls, Agent Walsh. I'm not about to start now."

"Did you know Elise and Isa well?"

"Elise only worked for me for a short time. She was an ambitious girl but willing to take too many risks to make a quick buck. As you know, that's not the kind of operation I run." Fanny chuckled. "To think I had the mayor's niece working for me as an escort. That must have stirred quite the family scandal."

Kate thought back to Isa's work on the drug trafficking network. "Do you have any information about cocaine trafficking in Miami Beach?"

Fanny watched her carefully for a moment. Kate could tell she was trying to read her expression so she kept it neutral. "Are you asking me if Elise was involved in drug trafficking or had a cocaine habit?"

"Did she?"

"Elise was never into drugs that I was aware of while she worked for me. I don't know much about her life after. Her sister was a bull though so I can't imagine that would have flown with her." Fanny pursed her lips. "In general, I know there are large amounts of drugs trafficked into and out of Miami Beach and Andre Dale seems to be at the center of it."

"Would it surprise you if I told you Harvey Littman was involved?"

"Not at all. He's glued to Andre's hip." She threw her hands up and the sleeves of her caftan flapped against her arms. "I don't know anything about it though."

They weren't there about the drugs, so Kate let it drop. "Do you have any idea where Peter might have gone?"

"I'd tell you if I knew." Fanny scooted forward on the chaise and put her feet to the ground. She pointed her finger between Declan and Kate. "I'll tell you this right now. You better hope you find him first because if I do, there won't be anything left of him for you to prosecute."

Declan held his hand up in a motion to stop her. "You can't say things like that, Fanny. You can't make those threats. Leave Peter to us and justice will be served."

Fanny tipped her head back and hooted toward the sky. "You can't guarantee me anything. You better find him," she warned again. "I'll give you a head start, but if you don't, then you can come back here and arrest me."

Declan blew out a breath and turned to look at Kate. She didn't say a word because at that point if Fanny could find Peter, she could have him. It was completely unethical to even think such a thing and she'd never say the words aloud. Peter Lyons had officially frustrated Kate beyond any suspect she'd ever been after. Much to Declan's dismay, Kate didn't address Fanny on the issue.

"Thanks for your time," Kate said, standing. "We'll be in touch if we need anything else."

"Good luck," Fanny mumbled as they left. They made it inside the home when Fanny could be heard yelling for her bodyguards.

Declan stopped to listen at the doorway. "She's sending them after Peter, Kate," he called to her back.

"We can't seem to find him." *Let them do their worst* is what Kate thought but didn't say.

Declan moved quickly to catch up to her at the front door. He reached for her shoulder. "You're leaving like this? What about what Fanny is doing? She is planning to go after Peter."

Kate tilted her head to look up at him. "Then we better find him first."

CHAPTER 42

The sunset over the horizon turned the sky a bright shade of pink. Palms swayed and rustled in the warm Florida breeze. The hotels with their bright neon signs didn't reflect the current mood or what Miami Beach had come to symbolize for Kate. Forever it would be known as a city where wealthy men paid young women for sex both legally and in relationships that skirted the law. The underbelly of the city had been exposed and it would never seem the same to her again.

There wasn't a lot left for Kate and Declan to do at the moment, so he drove them back to the hotel. Declan pulled up to the valet and tossed the attendant the keys as he ran around the car to open Kate's door and help her out. She allowed him to take her good hand and pull her to her feet. Declan held out his arm so Kate could take it and they walked into the hotel like a happily married couple who had been out for the evening.

Kate turned her head to look at the bar and nothing seemed disturbed. It was like the incident earlier that day had already been tucked away as some old Eden Roc history – *Remember when that FBI agent spotted the serial killer drinking at the bar. He knew he'd been made so he knocked her to the ground before she chased him.* Someone at the hotel would tell that story years from now. Kate only hoped the ending would be that they caught the serial killer and brought him to justice.

Declan jabbed the elevator button with his finger and then tugged on the back of Kate's shirt.

She turned from looking at the bar and raised her eyes to him. "What?"

"Are you okay? You have that morose vibe you get about you sometimes."

The elevator doors slid open and Kate and Declan stepped inside. He hit the button for their floor. Kate sighed and her shoulders slumped. "I was thinking about how the hotel looks the same – it was all just back to normal. That happens a lot with crime. People are horrifically murdered and the crime scene gets cleaned up like nothing ever happened. Most people go through life never even realizing they might be standing on the spot someone was murdered or where there was a tragic accident. People die off and the memory fades."

Declan shifted his eyes to her. "That's heavy, Kate. Don't you think it's better that it happens like that? If we all had to walk around with that kind of heaviness on our shoulders, it wouldn't make for a happy life."

Kate thought about that for a moment. She normally would have agreed with him and chided herself for being silly. The energy that hung over her though wasn't letting her shake off the mood so easily. She caught his look, but she didn't have anything to say. Kate stood there looking at her reflection in the elevator doors, trying to choke back the tears that threatened to fall. As soon as Declan's hand touched her shoulder and his fingertips grazed her neck, she broke down and he pulled her into him.

Her slinged arm cradled between their bodies created the only barrier. Kate took a breath and then sobbed into his chest. He held one protective arm around her back and patted the back of her head with his other hand.

"It's okay, Katie," Declan whispered. "We are going to find Peter Lyons and it will all be over. Your arm will heal and all will be okay. I promise."

Kate knew that was a promise he could keep. The tears kept coming and she didn't stop even when the elevator stopped its ascent and she heard the elevator doors open. Declan nudged her forward toward the door and she let herself be lead. She turned slightly to see an older couple standing on the threshold of the elevator door watching them.

"Long day and too much sun," Declan said, guiding Kate out of the elevator.

The older woman smiled and nodded her head. It was clear she knew Kate was having a hard day but was kind enough to pretend she believed Declan. "Hope you feel better, sweetie," was the only thing she said as they walked by.

Kate tried to hold back the tears until she was tucked safely inside the hotel room, but halfway down the hallway, she came to a realization and the tears started up again. "I can't even take a shower or wash my hair," she sobbed.

Declan pulled her a little closer. "I already thought of that."

She angled her eyes toward him. "What do you mean?"

"You'll see." He walked Kate down the hall and then slipped the keycard into the lock. He held the door open for her and they walked into the room together. There on the hutch that held the television was a black garbage bag and some thick gray electrical tape.

Declan stood there with a broad smile across his face. "You can take off the sling and put the bag over your arm and we can tape it up so it doesn't get wet."

Kate reached her hand out and brushed her fingers over the garbage bag. "When did you think of this?"

"Earlier today, so I called the hotel and made sure it was here for when we got back."

It was a small gesture but meant so much to Kate that the tears welled up in her eyes again. No one ever took care of her – except Declan. She hugged him, wrapping her good arm around him. "You think of everything."

"This has been a rough case for you. I told you it will get better."

Kate stepped away from him. "I don't think I can wash my hair with only one hand."

"I'll do it for you," he said, kicking off his shoes and pulling out his shirttails from his pants.

Kate wiped her cheeks with the back of her hand and sniffed back a giggle. "I know I'm desperate, but I'm not taking a shower with you. I don't think our friendship should cross that line."

Declan reached for the top button of his shirt and undid button by button. "It's not like we haven't seen each other naked. You're being modest for no reason."

Kate wasn't sure if he was being serious. His tone certainly indicated he was, but the way the corners of his lips turned up hinted at something a little more mischievous. "I don't remember the last time we saw each other naked, but I assume it was either in the line of work or a drunken night in the academy."

Declan pulled off his shirt and reached for the hem of his undershirt and pulled it clear over his head, leaving him in tan slacks and nothing else. He reached for the button on his pants as Kate's eyes grew wide.

"Come on," he urged. "I want to order room service so let's get naked soapy time out of the way."

She pointed. "Don't you dare take off your pants."

That's exactly what Declan did. He unbuttoned them and made a dramatic display of unzipping and sliding them down past his boxer briefs. He kicked out of them and then threw them on the bed. "You're too modest, kid. Let's go wash your hair." With that, Declan turned and walked toward the bathroom in just his underwear.

Kate stood there not sure what to do. Her hair desperately needed to be washed and there was no way for her to do it. She reached for the button on her shirt but hesitated. "Declan!" she called to him and he popped his head out from the bathroom. "I'm not taking a shower with you!"

Declan couldn't contain his laughter anymore. "Of course you're not. Keep your bra and undies on and we'll get you in there well enough to get your hair washed. Then I'll leave and you can strip down and shower in peace." He hitched his strong jaw toward the garbage bag. "Bring the stuff so we can fix up your arm."

Relief washed over her and she reached for the garbage bag and tape. As she walked toward the bathroom, Kate realized she was smiling. Declan had a good plan, but more than that, he had teased her to the point that she had forgotten all about the heavy morose energy that had consumed her only minutes before.

Kate entered the bathroom to see Declan standing by the edge of the walk-in shower. He had pulled her shampoo and conditioner out and had turned on the water to get it warm. He eyed her. "Fair warning. I've done a lot of things before to women in the shower but never washed their hair."

Kate couldn't help but let out a laugh. "I'm so glad we're friends and that I never slept with you when we were younger." She turned so Declan could loosen the clasp on the sling and they got down to work.

Nearly ninety minutes later, they were both showered, had put on their pajamas, and were sitting in their separate beds with trays of food in front of them. The television had been turned to an old rerun of one of Kate's favorite nineties sitcoms. Kate had splurged and instead of her usual healthy salad or grilled chicken or fish, she opted for what Declan ordered for himself – a BBQ mushroom bacon cheeseburger, fries, and a root beer.

Kate turned slightly to look at Declan. "Do you feel guilty for sitting here and enjoying dinner while Peter Lyons is still out there?"

Declan popped a fry into his mouth. "Not at all. There's nothing we can do right now. Miami-Dade and Miami Beach cops are searching for him. There are officers from the sheriff's office out there, too. Not much more we can do right now. We might as well get some rest because I'm sure tomorrow is going to be another long day. Ted texted me while you were finishing up in the shower and said he was calling it a night, too. They switched agents with Andre Dale for the night and still no word from Peter. We need to eat, relax, and get a good night's sleep."

Kate didn't disagree with him, but the weight of the case still bore down on her. "How long do you think Spade will want us down here if we can't find Peter?"

"We'll find him, Kate. I can feel it in my bones." Declan paused and finished up the last bite of his burger. He wiped his mouth with a napkin. "If we don't, I give Spade a week before he's got us going someplace else. When they find Peter, he'll drag us back here. That's what he does."

It was one of the reasons why Kate's work for the FBI was so draining. She rarely had a chance to get comfortable in one spot before she was being sent off to another. It was good she had no ticking biological clock or desire to get married. A normal FBI agent in a field office could probably make it work but not the specialized unit they were in.

Kate tried not to think long-term about anything. She had to face the present circumstances and press on. They finished their dinner, cleaned up their room, and then got ready for bed. Declan swore he wasn't tired, but soon after dimming the lights and lowering the volume on the television, Kate heard his soft snores from across the room. She adjusted her pillow and then laid her head down, feeling grateful for him being nearby.

CHAPTER 43

The next morning, Kate met Declan on the patio near the swimming pool for breakfast. Declan had gotten up early and said he was going for a run on the beach. While he was gone, Kate had gotten out of bed and prepared herself for the day. She even managed a one-handed ponytail, a feat she wasn't sure she'd ever be able to pull off again.

By the time Declan came back, Kate had been on her laptop searching for more background information on Peter. Even when Declan had finished getting ready for the day and stood at the door complaining about how starving he was and that he needed food, Kate had remained focused on her laptop. She promised she'd be down to breakfast soon. It had been wasted time though because Kate's search turned up nothing.

"Have you ordered?" Kate asked, sitting down across the table from him. There were empty tables and chairs around and only one couple on the patio sitting closer to the bar area. Kate checked her watch. It was nearing ten and she assumed she had missed the breakfast rush.

"Coffee, bacon, and eggs and got you the same." Declan hadn't raised his head from his phone yet. "I got the autopsy report back for Nancy from Dr. Bruce this morning. She said she fast-tracked it for us."

The server brought over their coffee and Kate helped herself to the cream and sugar. "Does the report say anything surprising?"

Declan set his phone down and locked eyes with her for the first time that day. His eyes drifted up to her ponytail and he smiled in acknowledgment that she had done it herself. He tapped on his phone. "Nancy died of a gunshot wound to the gut. She bled out. Terrible way to die. I don't understand how any son could do that to his mother. If you're that deranged that you're going to kill your own mother, take a headshot at least. Don't make her suffer."

"You're thinking like someone who wouldn't kill their mother." Kate took a sip of her coffee and sat back. "Peter hasn't shot any of the other victims. He has no guns registered to him. I double-checked that this morning. There weren't any guns or ammunition found in a search of his home either."

"Maybe he didn't use a registered gun," Declan offered, taking a sip of his coffee. "Is it unusual for a serial killer to change up how they kill?"

Kate gestured with her hand. "This was Peter's mother. I would expect the murder to look different. I haven't heard anything about Peter owning or using guns though. No one we have spoken with said he liked guns or went to the gun range. The difference is not surprising, but a little odd. How long had she been deceased?"

"Roughly four days. Dr. Bruce said the shot was made at fairly close range. She was surprised we didn't see more signs of a struggle at the house."

Kate thought back to the crime scene. "We found her in bed. Maybe Peter came in and shot her in the middle of the night."

"Are you saying Peter came into the room, stood over his mother, and shot her while she was lying in bed completely defenseless?"

"It didn't have to be like that. He could have gone into the room and startled her. What if she woke up and got out of bed to confront him? Maybe he pointed the gun at her stomach and pulled the trigger."

Declan shuttered. "That's cold, Kate."

"We've seen worse," she said evenly. "Anything back on DNA found at the crime scene?"

Declan shook his head. "I don't think we know much of anything right now. Jessica hasn't called us with any update about the scene. Peter makes logical sense as the number one suspect. It was probably him."

The server brought over their identical meals and placed them down. Declan's eyes lit up like a man who finally had food after being starved for days. Kate was still full from the night before. The burger had sat like a rock in her stomach all night. If her arm was better, she would have joined Declan on his run.

The two ate in near silence and as they were finishing, Kate spotted Ted out of the corner of her eye. She set down her fork and waved her hand high so he'd see them. "Ted's here," she said to Declan and then finished off her eggs. As Ted approached, she told him to pull up a chair.

"What's going on, Ted?" Declan asked, popping his last piece of bacon in his mouth.

Ted slapped a folder down on the table. "Jessica had some interesting findings at Nancy's house."

Declan pushed his empty plate back and pulled the report in front of him. He flipped it open and peered down. "We were discussing that case this morning. What did she find?"

"There was an errant shell casing under the bed with a print on it. There were also two bullets lodged in the wall, indicating someone had taken aim and missed. We have a neighbor who saw someone fleeing from the home around the time of the murder." Ted sat back and shifted his eyes between them. His leg bounced under the table enough that it rattled the tabletop.

"You want to guess who it was?" The excitement in Ted's voice couldn't be contained.

"I'm guessing it's not Peter if it's got you this hyped up," Kate said, raising her eyebrows and glancing at Declan who seemed just as perplexed as she was.

"Mayor Harvey Littman." Ted slapped his hand down on the table, rattling the plates and glassware.

Kate reached for her water glass to steady it. "I don't understand. Miami Beach's mayor killed Peter's mother?"

"It appears so. That's where the evidence points."

Declan turned his head to look at Kate and then back at Ted. He seemed as confused as Kate. "Why would Harvey Littman kill her? How does he even know her?"

"All questions that need answers," Ted said. He turned to Kate. "We're bringing Mayor Littman in for an interview. I talked to the chief and he's open to you interviewing if you'd like since it might be connected to the murders."

Kate's mouth fell open slightly. "You think this murder is connected to the others?"

"I just meant since it's Peter's mother, you have reason to be involved."

Declan gave her a knowing look across the table and Kate remembered the other bit of information they had recently learned about Mayor Littman – he was directly involved in the drug smuggling ring. "Sure, Ted. I'd be happy to do the interview."

"Perfect." Ted grabbed the file off the table and offered it to Kate. She declined since he had told her the important bits already. "You can look at it right before the interview if you want. I'll call you when we are bringing him in. I don't want to make him sweat too much or he might lawyer up."

Kate nodded. She'd be surprised if he didn't lawyer up immediately. "We'll head to your office as soon as we are done here. Any word from any of the officers searching for Peter?"

"Not a peep. He's probably gone underground for now. Since you spotted him yesterday there hasn't been a sighting reported." With that news, Ted headed back into the hotel and left.

Declan called for the bill and paid it. As he stood from the table, he asked, "Is there anything you want to do before going to the police station?"

"I want to go back to the room and do some research on Mayor Harvey Littman."

Declan agreed it was a good idea. "I don't feel like I know enough about this guy to interview him. He's all over this case – accused of drug trafficking with Andre Dale, his niece the cop was murdered, and now tied to the murder scene. We should have been looking at him all along."

Kate walked with Declan into the hotel and back up to their room. She mulled over what he had said about looking at Harvey sooner. The reality was, though, he was never connected directly to the case until now. Once they were heading down the long corridor to their room, Kate reassured him. "We had no reason to suspect him. He was a murder victim's uncle."

"You're right." Declan unlocked the door and smiled down at her. "See, now it's your turn to tell me I'm being too hard on us."

Kate sat down at the desk and fired up her laptop. While she researched, Declan made calls to the field office to request assistance on federal searches on Littman to see what they could find. From what Kate read, Littman had a fairly clean record, which made sense given his position in local government.

During the time he ran for mayor, Littman's political opponent would have spent time doing opposition research, so if there was anything bad to come out about him, it would have already happened. That told Kate he was a man who kept his secrets well-buried.

Harvey Littman had never been arrested. He had a clean record, a good credit score, and wasn't involved in any bad financial dealings that she could find. His assets matched his income and there were no red flags. If he was earning money from the drug trade, Littman had done a good job of laundering it. Kate didn't even see his name connected to any questionable businesses so he had covered his tracks well.

When she exhausted her search, Kate closed her laptop and spun the chair around to face Declan. "They find anything?"

"He's clean, Kate. Squeaky clean. Not even a parking ticket." Declan bit at the inside of his cheek making it look hollow.

"That's what I found, too. What's bothering you?"

"Do you think Littman would be the kind of guy to pull the trigger himself? I'd think he'd have too much to risk."

"You never know what people will do in anger." Kate stood and grabbed her bag. "It does bother me that he's never been in any trouble before. If he's involved in the drug trade that means he's good at laundering his money and covering his tracks. Why then would he have left such a messy crime scene? He had to have known the cops would find out."

Declan reached for the door. "Maybe he figured we'd see it was Peter's mother and tie it to the rest of the murders and not look at it too hard."

"I thought of that, but Peter wasn't on our radar four nights ago when the murder happened."

Declan cocked his head to the side. "You're right. I guess all we can do is see what he tells us."

Kate and Declan left the hotel and in the car on the way to the police station, his cellphone rang. He answered on the car's Bluetooth so they both could hear. Ted had called to say that Littman had agreed to speak with them and that he didn't even ask what it was about. Littman made Ted promise to tell them that he was more than happy to help the FBI.

As they hung up, Kate said, "I don't care why he thinks he's coming in as long as he's there."

They rode the rest of the way in silence, but as Declan pulled into the Miami-Dade PD parking lot, Kate's cellphone rang. She looked at the number and recognized it. It was Fanny Fontaine. Kate stared down at the phone as it rang and debated sending it to voicemail. She had no idea what Fanny could want, but Kate didn't have time right before the interview. She debated too long because the phone stopped ringing.

"Fanny will leave a voicemail if it's important," Kate assured Declan as they exited the car. Within seconds though the phone rang again and again Kate let it go to voicemail. As they walked toward the front of the police station, Kate's phone rang for the third time.

"Get it, Kate, or your phone is going to ring through the entire interview."

Kate grumbled to herself but answered it. As she did, she said to Declan, "Go ahead without me. I'll be up in a minute."

CHAPTER 44

Drops of sweat beaded down Kate's back and her face flushed. She pushed open the glass doors and entered the police station. She flashed her badge at the officer sitting at the front desk and was given a floor and office number where she should go.

Kate moved quickly through the first-floor brushing past cops who were milling about. She caught the elevator door before it closed and stepped inside with five other police department personnel. "Fifth floor," she said to the cop closest to the buttons.

Kate breathed in and out slowly, trying her best to control her breathing while she ran over the words Fanny Fontaine had said to her. Kate tried to make sense of them the best she could. Right now, all she needed was to find Declan and talk it through with him. Often, just the act of explaining to him and debating out the evidence gave her a clearer picture.

The elevator doors opened and Kate had to tip her head back to see the row of numbers above the door to see if she was at her floor. The button indicating the fifth floor lit up red and she stepped out of the elevator just as the doors started to close. She turned to the right, the only way to go, and stopped. Kate stood at the intersection of a long, narrow, well-lit corridor empty of people but filled with rows of doors that were all shut. Kate walked to the right and looked at the number on the outside of the door and realized she had gone the wrong direction. She turned, heading back to the left.

Kate wished she could reach up under her shirt and wipe the sweat from her back. It pooled at her lower back making her shirt stick to her. She squirmed to the left and right trying to shake the feeling. When she reached the door where Declan should be, she knocked once and then turned the doorknob and entered.

Both Declan and Ted were sitting at a small rectangular table looking through a two-way mirror. Mayor Harvey Littman sat in another room staring forward at what would look like a regular mirror to him. He assessed his reflection as he sat there. His mouth set in a firm line, what was left of his dark hair had been slicked back, and glasses perched high on his nose. He was the picture of calm.

"We have a problem," Kate announced, turning to Declan.

Declan looked at her with his eyebrows raised. "What's going on?"

"Fanny Fontaine said that Ava Crawford is missing. One of the women who work for her is good friends with Ava and she hasn't been able to reach her all day, which is unusual. The woman told Fanny and then called the real estate office and no one has heard from Ava since she left a house showing last night. They have been concerned but hadn't called the police. Fanny decided it would be best to call me directly."

Ted inched forward like he was about to stand. "Do you want me to send a detective over to speak to Fanny and the witnesses she has?"

"That would be great, but she already told me she's only willing to speak to Declan or me. I need to interview Littman." She locked eyes with Declan. "You mind going? I think you should bring a Miami-Dade officer or two with you as backup just in case."

"I'm on it," Declan said, standing. Ted got up too and said he'd radio a police unit to meet him at Fanny's house. As Declan walked by Kate, he squeezed her shoulder. "You got this. Keep your head focused on

Littman and I'll take care of Ava. We'll find her, Kate."

Alive. That was the word that Kate wanted him to finish that sentence with, but she knew he couldn't because it might not be true. "I'll call you as soon as I know anything. Assure Fanny we will do everything we can to find Ava."

Declan nodded and left the room with Ted. Kate used the time until Ted returned to watch Littman through the mirror. He sat ramrod straight in the chair and was poised as if about to give a news conference or hold a meeting to discuss the city budget. He'd be affable, accommodating, and tell Kate what she wanted to hear. With a man like Littman, it was his arrogance that would do him in.

Ted returned a moment later and Kate confirmed that audio and video were running. He promised Kate that he'd be right there in the room if she needed anything. Ted patted the gun on his hip. "I have no problem taking him out if I need to."

Kate patted her sidearm. "I can handle my own, but I appreciate the backup. It shouldn't get confrontational though. I'd expect if I get anywhere close to confrontational, he'll lawyer up. I'll keep this light."

Kate walked out of the room and closed the door behind her. She sucked in a sharp breath and let it out slowly. She had done interviews like this hundreds of times but her tummy still fluttered right before she walked into an interrogation room. Kate believed any detective that claimed they didn't have nervous anticipation before an interrogation was too arrogant for their own good.

Kate reached for the doorknob and turned it, nudging the door open. "Mayor Littman, I'm so glad you could meet me here today."

Littman stood from his chair as she entered and then sat back down when she did. "I had heard you were injured chasing Peter Lyons. If there is anything I can do, let me know."

Kate inched her slinged-arm forward. "Your hospital fixed me up. I'm sure you're wondering why I wanted to talk to you. I'm sorry about your niece. Unfortunately, she was one of the victims."

Littman brought a hand to his heart and bowed his head slightly. "Thank you, Agent Walsh. It's a hard loss for our family. When her body is released from the medical examiner, we'll hold a proper funeral service. She'll be buried with the honors she deserves."

"Honors?" Kate said, her voice rising a notch.

Littman hesitated and shifted his eyes to the side of the table. His Adam's apple bobbed as he swallowed hard. He offered Kate a smile. "I just meant she'll be buried with the honor our family bestows on all those we have lost. We're a close family and all loved Elise no matter what she chose as her profession."

"I see," Kate said returning the smile. *Strike one.* "You remained close to the Navarros even after the divorce?"

"Very close. The marriage might not have been successful, but I remained a member of the family."

"It's good when it can work out like that." Kate adjusted in her seat. "How did you find out about the murder?"

"The Miami-Dade Police Chief called me directly after Ted informed them it was Elise." Littman leaned back. "We have a terrific working relationship."

"That's good." Kate leaned in ever so slightly. "It must be nice given your other niece is a long-time detective with the force. Have you had a chance to speak to Isa about Elise's death?"

Littman pulled back and broke eye contact. He shook his head slightly. "No. We've not spoken."

"That's surprising. You just said you're close to the family. Given Isa and Elise were twins and your mayoral position, I would have thought calling Isa would have been the first thing to do."

Littman raised both hands off the table in a gesture of conceding. "That probably would have been the right thing to do. I left that to the chief. I figured I'd speak to Isa at a more appropriate time."

"Appropriate time?" Kate asked, stressing the word *appropriate*. "I'm not sure what that means. I can't think of a better time to reach out to a family member than right after a significant death – especially a homicide case that Isa was involved in investigating."

Littman sucked in his stomach and straightened his back. He offered Kate a condescending smile. "I don't always do the right thing it seems. Isa and I don't always see eye to eye so to speak. In truth, I might be the last person she wanted to hear from. Family issues. You know how they can be."

Kate gave him a reassuring look. "It happens in every family."

"Is that why I'm here? You wanted to speak to me about Elise?"

"No," Kate said but didn't offer more.

Littman turned his head toward the door. "Then why am I here?"

"We're speaking with everyone who knew Peter Lyons."

Littman coughed. "I didn't know Peter Lyons."

"I'm sure you did," Kate said, tapping the table and drawing his attention back to her. "Peter was known in Miami Beach. Andre Dale knew Peter quite well. From what I heard you are best friends with Andre. I'm sure your path would have crossed with Peter's at some point."

Littman let out a light chuckle. "Well, of course in that context. I thought you meant knew him well enough to be friends with him. I've met him but didn't know him well."

"So even though a moment ago you said you didn't know him, you have met him and do know him?" Kate asked with an edge in her voice. *Strike two.*

"Yes...I misspoke before," Littman stuttered. He regained his composure and strummed his fingers on the tabletop. "Now that I think about it, I believe I met Peter Lyons a handful of times at Andre's home, usually in a party setting."

"The parties where you'd all pass young women around like party favors," Kate deadpanned and didn't take her eyes off him.

"I don't think that's a fair representation of those parties."

"What is a fair representation then?"

Littman's tongue poked between his thin dry lips as he wet them. "There's nothing wrong with an older man enjoying the company of a younger woman. It happens more than you realize."

"I'm sure as the mayor and even as a private citizen you know paying for sex is illegal."

"No one at Andre's pays for sex."

Kate cracked a smile. "Maybe not directly but you're exchanging money for a good time." She leaned into the table and kept her focus on him. "It is a good time, right? The thousands most of the men pay to these young women, I'd hope they are getting something out of the deal."

"That's not illegal. Men have been dating younger women for millennia and helping to support the women in their lives for just as long."

"That might be an argument if sex wasn't also on the bartering table. The power difference alone between your friends and these young women is enough to raise some eyebrows." Kate leaned back and laughed. "I'm not here to talk about old men who can barely get an erection having to pay for sex though, Mayor Littman. That's a tale as old as time and frankly, it bores me as much as it disgusts me. My question was how well you knew Peter Lyons from Andre's sex parties."

Littman wouldn't make eye contact with Kate. His focus remained on the door. "I've spoken to him a handful of times. He was a quiet guy and didn't say much. From Andre, I knew Peter was a doctor. I knew he had some trouble out in Los Angeles, which is what brought him to Miami Beach." Littman turned his head to face Kate and pounded his finger into the table. "I knew nothing about the murders though,

Agent Walsh. I didn't know Peter was a sick freak like that."

"I never asked if you knew about the murders," Kate said evenly. *Strike three.*

"I assumed that would be your next question," he sputtered. Littman checked his watch. "I really should be going."

"We haven't even gotten to the good part yet, Mayor Littman."

Littman snapped his head up to look at Kate. "What's that supposed to mean?"

"Now that we've established you knew Peter Lyons, why don't you tell me how you knew his mother – Nancy."

CHAPTER 45

Mayor Harvey Littman scooted his chair back and crossed his arms. He stared at Kate across the table. "I don't know what you're talking about. Why would I know Peter's mother?"

Kate noted his defensive posture and the fact that he hadn't come right out and simply said no he didn't know her. She had him on the ropes. "There's no reason to get upset about it. Nancy is local and knows Fanny Fontaine quite well. I assumed since she was in the area that she might be someone that has crossed your path."

Littman's shoulders relaxed but he kept his arms folded. "She isn't someone I've encountered socially."

"That still doesn't answer the question if you've met her or not."

He pinned his gaze on her. "Agent Walsh, I'm the Miami-Beach mayor. I've met a lot of people. It doesn't mean that I remember every one of them. As I said, Peter was quiet and he didn't speak about his mother. I'm sure she was a quiet woman like him so why would I remember her."

Kate waited a beat to see if he caught his own mistake. "You said *was* as in past tense like she's no longer living."

Littman blinked rapidly and fumbled for what to say. "I...I just meant had I met her she was probably that way," he stammered before gaining his composure. "Is there something I'm missing here?"

It wasn't so much that he had used the past tense that told Kate he knew the woman was dead. It was his reaction when she called him out on it. Kate leaned into the table resting her slinged arm on top. "Nancy was murdered. Agent James and I found her body yesterday. Dr. Bruce has already done the autopsy and the crime scene investigators worked hard at gathering evidence."

"That's terrible," he said, looking toward the door. "I'm not sure what that has to do with me. I need to go. There's much to be done at the office."

Kate raised her voice. "You're needed here."

Littman slowly turned his head to face her. "For what?"

"Your fingerprints were found on shell casings found under the bed."

"That's impossible," Littman said, his voice too calm and his affect flat. He showed nearly no emotion at all. It betrayed the words he spoke.

"Why do you think that's impossible?"

He shook his head but didn't say anything. Littman seemed to be still digesting the information. It took him a moment but he straightened up in his chair. With his voice clear and crisp, he said, "There is no way that's accurate. I didn't know Nancy Blackwell and I've never been to her home. You didn't find my DNA. I don't understand what this is about or why you're lying but I'm calling your boss."

"I never said Nancy was shot in her home." Kate watched as the man's face fell. She also never told him the woman's last name. The easy assumption would have been it was Lyons like her son but she had gone back to her maiden name. Kate didn't need to point it out. He knew he'd been caught.

Littman rubbed at his forehead as red crept up his neck and flushed his cheeks. He adjusted the knot in his tie and pulled it down from his neck. "Give me your boss's phone number."

"My boss already knows I've brought you in here. There's not anything for you to discuss with him. He's seen the evidence."

Littman pounded his fist down on the table. "The evidence isn't correct! You're framing me."

Kate narrowed her eyes and shook her head. "We'd have no reason to do that. I need you to explain to me why your fingerprints would be on bullets used to kill Nancy. Who was the woman to you?"

Littman shook his head back and forth so hard Kate worried he might knock something loose. "No. There's no way that's possible. There's no evidence."

"Killers leave evidence behind all the time. It happens more than you think." Kate leaned back in the chair and kept quiet for an uncomfortably long time. She worried Littman might get up or ask for an attorney, but he sat there dumbfounded by the accusation.

Kate pointed her finger marking each point for emphasis. "We know you were there when Nancy was murdered. We know you were in her home. There's evidence to that. I can arrest you right now, but I want to know why. How are you connected to Peter's mother? You can help us if you want to. It will look much better for you with the public."

Kate glanced toward the door and pointed. "We haven't released any of this information. Give me something to tell them. Help me help you. For all I know, it was an accident or a lover's spat that got out of hand."

Littman swallowed hard and his eyes shifted around the room. "It was an accident," he said finally. His voice was hoarse and he coughed. "I need some water."

"We'll get you some." Kate motioned over her shoulder with her hand so Ted would see. "You said it was an accident. Tell me what happened."

Littman took a breath so deep it puffed out his chest. He held his chin high and looked at Kate. "I met Nancy a long time ago through her legal work. She was a reasonable woman, always fighting for the underdog. You can imagine my surprise when I found out she was Peter's mother. Nancy was a quiet person until you got her in the courtroom. Then she was a bulldog for her clients. I suspected from the start that Peter might be involved in these murders."

"You never said anything like that to us. What made you suspect Peter?"

"He's just a weird guy," Littman said with disgust in his voice. "I wasn't sure though. I didn't want to go off halfcocked and accuse someone, but I had a feeling. I went to Nancy to ask her if she knew anything."

Littman rubbed his forehead and then dug his fingers into his eyes. "It got out of hand, Agent Walsh. Nancy screamed at me – asking me how I could possibly accuse her son of something like that. She was a wild woman."

Kate kept her eyes on him. "What happened after that?"

Littman motioned with his hand. "She lunged for me and I shot her. I didn't have a choice. I thought she was going to kill me."

Kate exhaled a brief puff of air. "You just happened to have a gun on your person and accessible to kill her that quickly?" There was doubt in Kate's voice she hoped he picked up.

"I had my gun with me. I didn't know how she'd react or if Peter would be there." Littman lowered his head and remained quiet for a moment. He spoke into his lap. "We might have argued for longer than I'm explaining. At some point, I had my gun in my hand. I had it pointed at her when she became more aggressive. I was just trying to find out what she knew. That's when I shot her."

Things weren't adding up for Kate. "How did you end up in her bedroom? That seems like a strange place to have this discussion."

"I don't remember."

"Sure, you do. Think about it." Kate watched him for several moments and then her voice became angry and mocking. "I don't think it went anything like you're saying. I don't think it was self-defense at all. You're a killer, Littman, and we got you."

Littman pounded his fist down on the table again. "I was doing everything I could to protect our community! The public will understand what I had to do!"

Kate let the moment settle. Calmly, she asked, "Why didn't you call the police after you killed her? Why didn't you call us and explain that you had a hunch and things got out of hand? Even after you went there and killed Nancy, you still didn't tell the cops about Peter. I don't think you went there about Peter at all."

Kate searched his face hoping something would make sense to her. She didn't feel any closer to a reason now than when he admitted it. She was surprised though that he had copped to it. "There's more you're not telling me," she stressed.

"No." Littman shook his head. "I'm telling you everything I know. That's how it happened. There's nothing else."

Kate didn't want him to ask for his attorney just yet and she worried if she pressed him further, that's exactly what he'd do. "Tell me about your relationship with Andre Dale. You even said yourself the two of you were quite close."

Confusion fell over Littman's face. "What do you want to know?"

"Andre seems to be a key player in Miami Beach. You two seem like strange buddies, given his reputation for illegal dealings. Normally, a mayor of a city tries to stay on the up and up."

"We went over this. The parties Andre has and his access to women is not illegal."

"He's been accused of sexual assault," Kate countered.

Littman chuckled. "If I had a nickel for every woman who cried rape after waking up with a little regret..."

"You'd be a very broke man. Women," Kate paused and corrected herself, "people rarely lie about sexual assault contrary to what people like you tell yourselves. Men rarely even report and women often go through a harder time in the criminal justice system after they report than the rapist. It's not something women often fabricate. It's not worth the humiliation they go through in the end."

Littman waved her off. "Everyone's a victim these days. That's what you want to know about? The false allegations? There's nothing to them."

Kate smiled and fixed her eyes on him. She stared at him until he broke eye contact first. "I want to know about the drug operation. I want to know how you and Andre run your operation and how it's connected to these murders and the murder of Nancy Blackwell."

"You're insane." He choked out a laugh. Littman reached for the knot on his tie again and jerked it from his neck. Sweat beaded on his forehead.

Kate knew she had him and she was fairly certain Littman knew it too. An insidious thought crept in. Kate tried to push it aside and ask her next question, but the thought jabbed at her wanting to be explored. She didn't even want to look at him as she asked the question but forced herself to look him in the eyes. "Did you kill Isa because she found out about the drugs? Did you frame Peter Lyons for that murder?"

Kate thought she was swinging into left field with that one, but as the words left her mouth, something felt right. Littman's response confirmed her suspicion.

He looked toward the door again. "I want my lawyer."

It was the worst thing a suspect could say. Kate had pushed too hard. It meant she was done interviewing him. He had invoked his right to counsel and she had to back off.

"Are you sure? Once I leave this room and you call your lawyer, I can't help you anymore."

Just as the words came out of her mouth, the door banged open and they both lurched forward in their chairs. Ted stood in the doorway motioning for Kate to come out of the room. "I need you, Agent Walsh. Right now."

The look on Ted's face was one Kate hadn't seen before. It was a mix of confusion and sheer panic. Kate took one last look at Harvey Littman and then got up from the table. She followed Ted into the hallway. "What's going on? I was going to let him call his attorney."

"It's not that. You were incredible in there."

Kate angled her head to look up at him. "What is it then?"

"Agent James called and needs you right away. Peter Lyons has taken Ava Crawford hostage on a houseboat. Peter said he'd only speak to you." Ted pointed down the hallway. "An officer is waiting for you outside. He'll drive you straight there."

The words banged around in Kate's head and it took her a moment to process it. She pointed to the interrogation room door. "Arrest him and throw him in a cell. I don't want him to have access to Andre Dale for any reason."

With that, Kate took off down the hall walking as fast as she could, hoping to get to Ava before it was too late. The least she could do in this investigation was prevent one death.

CHAPTER 46

Kate thought she'd be taken directly to one of Miami Beach's marinas but instead, the uniformed cop drove her to a home on N. Bay Road situated on Biscayne Bay. She didn't even need to ask the address. There was a crowd of police vehicles in front of the home and throngs of bystanders crowding the street. There was no way anyone would miss it. Kate's driver had to throw on his flashing lights and flip the siren once for the crowd to part and let them through.

As they inched through the crowd, people turned and stared into the car. One woman pointed at Kate and grabbed her friend's arm in excitement. Kate assumed the woman had recognized her from the latest press conference. It was all the confirmation they'd need that it was connected to the Miami Ripper case. The buzz would travel through the crowd and more onlookers would gather, making it harder for the cops standing guard.

The two cops who stood at the base of the driveway caught sight of them and pushed the crowd back as they turned into the driveway. One cop moved a barrier and then motioned for them to pull up to the wrought iron fence that separated the home from the street. Kate glanced to her left and noted the fence went across the entire front of the property with only a small opening for a car to pass through. She didn't know who lived at the home but security had been important to them.

The cop driving hit the brake and flashed his badge to a cop with a clipboard standing on the side of the car. "Agent Walsh is here. She's been requested."

The cop hit the button to open the gate and then leaned into the car. "They are around back. The former homeowner doesn't live here anymore. The house is for sale, but they had a houseboat for guests sitting in the bay. I was told Agent James set up a perimeter and called in the local FBI Hostage Rescue Team. You should be all set back there to do what you do best."

Kate thanked the young cop. She hadn't given any thought to what Declan had already done mostly because she didn't have to. That was one of the things she liked about working with him. He didn't wait to consult with her or ask what needed to be done. He rolled up his sleeves and got to work.

The cop driving pulled up to the home and Kate got out, thanking him for the ride. She flashed her badge to a group of cops standing in the front of the house and asked to be directed to Declan. One of them escorted her around to the back of the home. Kate followed behind the cop as he walked a narrow mosaic pebbled path that had thick vegetation growing on both sides. Every few feet, Kate noticed the remnants of grass shavings like the lawn had been recently cut.

As soon as she rounded the bend in the path, she saw Declan with two other men, one wearing a SWAT vest and the other had HRT across the back. He turned to Kate as if sensing her presence before she even said his name. He left the two men and walked over to meet her.

"What are we dealing with?" Kate asked, pulling her slinged arm closer to her body and adjusting the strap with her other hand.

Declan pointed to the simple two-story houseboat parked at the back dock. It had a wide deck that went around its perimeter, giving the resident some outdoor space. A few chairs were positioned around a small table but, otherwise, the space was empty. "The gardener saw two people on the houseboat. He knows no one is supposed to be back here so he went down to check it out. He only got as far as the dock and Peter came out and pointed a gun. Peter told him he needed to call Agent Walsh with the FBI because he had a hostage. The gardener recognized Peter from the news and rushed to the front of the house where he had parked his truck. He grabbed his cellphone and called 911. Locals called the FBI Miami field office and they called me."

It was all fairly standard so far. "Anyone speak to him yet?"

"The Hostage Rescue Team negotiator tried, but Peter refused to speak with him. He said he has Ava Crawford but there's been no confirmation of her status."

"Have they been in a position to take a shot at him yet?"

"Without knowing Ava's status and Peter wanting to speak with you, no one has tried. SWAT and HRT have only been out here for a few minutes before you arrived." Declan motioned with his hand for her to follow. "Let's get you the phone so you can call him."

Declan walked Kate over and introduced her to the SWAT supervisor and the HRT negotiator.

"You know what to do," the negotiator said and handed Kate a black cellphone.

Even if Kate didn't work directly with a field office, many knew her or at least had heard of her. Kate thanked him and asked him for his impressions of Peter so far.

"On edge and nervous. He demanded to speak to you. He said you'd be the only one who would understand and believe him. I didn't know what he meant and when I tried to press him, he hung up. I called him back and assured him you were on your way. I tried to get proof of life for the hostage, but Peter said he wasn't doing anything until you got here."

Kate exhaled a breath and stared down at the houseboat. Two small windows faced in their direction but both had blinds covering them. "We have no visual in?"

"None." The negotiator pointed toward the water. "We've got a boat out in the water and snipers on the roof of the house and the neighbor's house. We have another lying low in the vegetation but no one has had a visual on them. The way the houseboat is positioned and the closed blinds, we aren't able to see him. We are going to have to breach it or draw him out."

Either option would put Ava Crawford in the line of fire if she was still alive. "Let me see if I can get him to surrender or at least let Ava go."

"Can we take a shot if we get one?"

Kate hated giving the order because she wanted to bring Peter in alive, but Ava was the only person who mattered at the moment. "Of course. If you get a shot without compromising the hostage, by all means, take it."

When he was gone, Kate turned to Declan. "Have you tried speaking with him?"

Declan shook his head. "You know I failed hostage negotiation in the academy."

It was true that Declan didn't have the patience required for the job. "You didn't fail it. You weren't good at it, but you didn't fail it."

Declan pointed down at the phone. "It's the only number logged in there. Give him a call."

Kate held the phone thinking about what she'd say to him. It was one thing to profile a killer but another entirely to have to speak to him when he had a hostage. She pressed the call button and the phone rang twice before Peter answered.

"I told you not to call me! I'm only speaking to Agent Walsh."

Kate cleared her throat. "I'm here, Peter. What did you want to tell me?"

"You're here?" he asked, his voice uncertain.

"I'm here. If you come to the back window, you can see me standing in the yard."

"I'm not stupid, Agent Walsh. I know if I go anywhere near that back window, one of your snipers will take me out."

Kate couldn't argue with him. It was true. "I don't have another way to confirm I'm here. You'll have to trust me then." Kate explained the scenery around them in the hopes she could buy a little of his trust. When she was done and he seemed to believe her, she said, "Peter, you wanted me here. Tell me what's going on."

"Come down to the boat and talk to me. I don't want to do this over the phone."

"They aren't going to let me do that. You have a gun and a hostage already." Kate paused and breathed heavily into the phone. "Speaking of Ava, is she still alive?"

"Yes, she's alive. If you don't get down here though, I'm going to kill her."

Kate motioned for Declan to come closer. She had to think quickly. "That's not going to help you, Peter. Listen, if you send Ava out, I'll trade places with her."

"Absolutely not!" Declan shouted a little too loudly.

Kate didn't have a free hand to motion for him to shut up so she turned her body away from him. "Sorry about that. That was my partner, Agent James. As I said, they aren't going to let me come in there. You have to show us proof that Ava is still alive."

"I'll call you back." The line went dead.

Kate lowered the phone from her ear and turned back to Declan. His face had contorted in anger. "Calm down. He won't talk to me on the phone. If I go in there, at least we save Ava."

Declan raked a hand through his hair and tugged on strands with his fingers in frustration. "He'll kill you, Kate. Even if you weren't injured, there's no way I'd let you go in there. Now, with your arm, you can't even shoot him."

"I can shoot him, Declan. My right hand works just fine. You and I both know that he will take my gun away from me as soon as I go in there. Put a vest on me, hide something in my sling that I can use to protect myself, and let's get on with this. I don't see another way."

As the words left Kate's mouth, the phone rang. She clicked to engage and brought the phone to her ear. "Peter, what did you decide?"

Peter spoke but Kate couldn't hear what was being said. After a moment, a woman was on the phone. She stumbled over her words and sucked back sobs as she spoke. "Agent Walsh, it's me, Ava. He hasn't hurt me, but I'm scared. He said he's going to kill me if he doesn't get what he wants. Please, please...help me."

"You're going to be okay, Ava. Where are you in the houseboat?"

There was rustling on the other end and Ava cried out. "That's enough now," Peter said. "She's alive. I'll send her out as soon as you are in here."

"That's not going to work. You have to send her out first."

Peter screamed into the phone – one deafening screech of anger and frustration. Then his voice went cold. "I'm in control. Got it? Not you, not those dumb cops out there. Not even the snipers with their itchy trigger fingers. I'm in control. You have five minutes to convince them or the only thing coming out of here is two body bags." The call ended.

Kate didn't like this any more than Declan did. Her hand holding the cellphone slumped down to her side as she looked at Declan. She pleaded with her eyes. "We don't have a choice. Get me the SWAT commander and the HRT negotiator. I'm going in."

Declan reached for her. "Katie, please, listen to reason. I know you feel responsible for Isa. I know you feel foolish for not having caught him at the house. Please, don't do this. Don't sacrifice yourself."

Kate locked eyes with him and she could see that Declan's were glassy and wet. He was on the verge of losing it. "I have to do this. He will take her out with him."

"He'll take you, too."

"Let's go make a plan," she said, turning away from him. They had no time to debate it. She was going in with or without his support.

CHAPTER 47

Kate knew she was being reckless. Everyone around her knew the same, but they had figured out quickly they weren't going to change her mind. They had strapped her into a bulletproof vest and gave her three guns. One on her ankle, another on her hip, and the final one in her back waistband. The two obvious ones they assumed Peter would find and take from her. They also wired her for sound.

After everyone got in position, Declan pulled Kate to the side. He pulled her into a hug and rested his chin on the top of her head. "This is so unprofessional and I don't care one bit. I can't lose you. You have to come out of there alive. It's the only outcome I'll accept."

Kate understood because if the situation were flipped, she'd be freaking out completely. "I'm coming out alive. If not, you know where all of my important paperwork is."

Declan cursed. "Don't even say that."

Kate let herself be held like that until the phone rang. She stepped away from Declan's embrace. "Peter," she said, answering. "I'm coming in. When I get to that door, Ava better be standing there to make the switch or I'm not coming in."

"She'll be there. If you try anything, I'll kill you on the spot."

Kate believed him, and the last thing she was going to do was gamble Ava's life. "All I care about is Ava leaving that houseboat safe and alive.

I'm coming down now."

Kate handed Declan the phone and his fingers lingered on hers. When the time came, it was harder than she realized to leave him. Declan was one of the toughest FBI agents she'd ever known, but their bond wasn't one easily replicated.

"I'm going to be fine," she promised as she walked away. Kate didn't turn back to look at him because she was afraid if she did, she wouldn't go through with it. Her legs shook as she walked and she had to focus on putting one foot in front of the other, propelling herself to the dock. Once there, she stepped out onto the dock and steadied herself. The motion from the water lapping at the wooden pillars made Kate think the dock might sway with the motion but it was steady. Steadier than her legs.

Kate walked down the length of the dock and stepped onto the deck of the boat. The door had closed white blinds so she couldn't see inside. Kate reached her hand out to knock and watched as her hand shook. She closed her fingers into a fist and brought it back to her. She swallowed hard and steadied her nerves. When she felt calmer, she knocked once and then louder.

"Peter, I'm here." She was met with silence. Kate called to him again.

A loud splash at the front of the houseboat drew her attention. Kate turned her head but she couldn't see anything. She took a step to move down the deck but turned back as the door creaked opened.

"Get in here now," Peter demanded with the gun pointed at her.

"Where is Ava?" she asked, trying to see past him into the houseboat.

"That was her jumping from the front deck of the boat. I sent her out the front and told her to jump. I didn't trust you." He waved the gun at her. "I held up my end. Now get in here."

"Okay." Kate turned only once to look at Declan where he stood at the top of the incline near the back of the house. She nodded her head at him to let him know she was fine and then focused on Peter.

"What did you want to talk to me about?"

Peter stepped back and let her enter. He pointed with the gun to a middle living room where there was a small loveseat and a chair. "Sit down and we can talk." Kate got a few feet in and he stopped her. "Give me your gun. I know you have one on you."

Kate reached her hand down slowly to the gun on her hip. It wasn't loaded on purpose. There was no way they were going to give Peter more ammunition. She pulled it out of the holster and handed it to him. He wouldn't take it though and motioned for her to set it on the floor near the door.

Peter motioned again for her to sit down. Kate sat on the couch careful not to reveal the gun in her ankle holster. He hadn't asked her about a second weapon and she wasn't going to offer it up. That one was loaded.

Peter kept his gun trained on her until she sat down across from him. Then he rested it in his lap, still pointed at her. "I killed those women as you know."

"Then why take Ava hostage? Why not just turn yourself in?"

"I needed you all here. I needed to tell her, too. Maybe she will tell my story."

"You could have just come to the police station and turned yourself in. I could have spoken to you there and listened to whatever you had to say."

Peter shook his head and looked away. "I'm not turning myself in. This ends here today. I thought I could make it out of Miami Beach and just take a new identity, but that's not going to happen now."

Kate tried to keep her breathing even. She wanted him to focus on something other than killing himself and possibly her with him. "Why did you kill those women, Peter?"

He reached up and rubbed along his brow line. "I've been fighting it for years. Since puberty, I've had an urge to kill. I fought it for years.

There's something wrong with me."

Kate had heard this before from serial killers. The compulsion starts young and they act out in other ways. People think it's cliché when they hear about hurting animals or young children around them. There's fire-starting and late bedwetting, too. The serial killer trifecta is what some scholars call it. Part biological and part psychological. There is usually early trauma in their lives. Not always but sometimes, and they aren't equipped to deal with it like others.

"When was the first time you killed someone, Peter?"

He turned to face her. "Believe it or not but here in Miami Beach. As I said, I fought the urge for a long time. Sometimes just cutting into a patient when they were under was enough for me. I could get the thrill just from that and then I was helping people – saving them sometimes."

Kate didn't want to ask leading questions, but she had a sense of where this was going. "What made you finally stop fighting the urge?"

"I lost my job," he said softly, looking down at his hands. "I lost my girlfriend. I lost everything and there was no reason not to finally allow myself to do what I've been wanting to do for years." Peter shrugged and locked eyes with Kate. "The women I picked deserved it. I didn't hurt anyone innocent."

Kate wasn't here to argue with him only understand. "What does that mean – they deserved it?"

"You've been around here for a few days. I'm sure you've seen how many young women were ripe for the picking. I could have killed far more than I did. They'd do just about anything for the money, but the ones I picked deserved to die. They were the worst. They used men and then discarded them."

"They were paid escorts, Peter. It was their job." Kate took a shot in the dark. "Any chance the first couple of women you killed were chosen because they were connected to Fanny Fontaine?"

Peter didn't break eye contact. He searched her face. "Because she was connected to my mother?"

"It's possible, don't you think?"

"I didn't think of it that way. Fanny always hated me. It was a risk picking her girls. It upped the excitement for me, but then Fanny got too close. She started asking my mother questions about where I was the nights of the murders. My mother assured her I'd never do something like that, and Fanny dropped it after that." Peter rocked his head back and forth. "It was too close for comfort so early on. My mother suspected."

"Is that why you killed her?"

Anger flared in Peter's eyes. "I didn't kill my mother," he said through gritted teeth. "That's why you're here. That's why I had to do what I did. Why I had to get away when you caught me the first time. I had to find evidence."

Kate wasn't sure she understood. "Evidence of what?"

"That they killed my mother." Peter's head shook and he rubbed at his brow, clearly agitated.

Kate relaxed back into the couch. He might kill her, but he wasn't going to do it now. "Tell me about that."

"You won't believe me." Peter turned his head away from her again and looked toward the back of the houseboat.

"I'll believe more than you think." When Peter didn't say anything, Kate urged, "Peter, look at me. I'll believe you."

Peter said it quietly at first and then repeated himself with more confidence. "Mayor Harvey Littman and Andre Dale killed my mother."

Kate wasn't surprised by that admission. "Why would they do that?"

"Because they thought I told her about their secret."

Kate raised her eyebrows. "The drugs?"

"You know?" Peter asked not hiding the surprise in his voice.

"We found out recently. You knew about the drugs and they worried you had told your mother?"

"Yes. I went to her house the other night and found her dead. I couldn't call the police. I knew you'd suspect me. I had to find evidence that they killed her." Peter started to tear up but choked it back. "I had a rough relationship with my mother, but I'd never kill her."

"We have evidence that Harvey killed your mother," Kate said and it was like all the air went out of the room.

Peter deflated in the chair and tears ran down his face. "Is it solid evidence?"

Kate nodded. "I was just at the police station interviewing him before you called me here. We have enough to make an arrest. If that's the only reason you brought me here, we can go now, Peter. Harvey will pay for what he did to your mother. We have the DEA looking into the drug ring, too."

"We can't go," Peter said, dragging out the words. "It's more complicated than that."

"We have time." Kate looked around the room. "You got me here. You might as well tell me what else you want me to know."

Peter sank back into the chair. "Andre figured out I killed those women. He told me he wanted to watch me kill one of them. He had so many questions. I couldn't get rid of him. When I killed those women, it was personal. I wasn't going to let him watch. He got angry, but he backed off because he knew I knew about the drugs."

"I know from your past that you had quite the drug problem. Is that what bothered you about what they were doing?"

Peter looked away again and was quiet for several moments. "My dealer kept me hooked. I don't blame him for my choices, but he didn't help. I tried to get off drugs on my own and that didn't work. He was always there selling me more. When I finally went to rehab to get clean, he even called me while I was there. When I got out, I said no and resisted but he never made it easy. I moved here and found out what Andre and Harvey were doing. I wasn't here two days and Andre offered me cocaine. Then he tried to get me to work with him."

There was something in Peter's voice that told Kate he wasn't telling her the whole story. "Is there something else about Andre that bothered you?"

Peter nodded and said quietly, "He sexually assaulted women. All those women at his parties he kept them drugged. That's why they kept coming back. The money and the drugs – Andre had them at his mercy and he used it against them."

"You seem particularly bothered by the sexual assault. Was the sex you had with women consensual?" There was so much Kate needed to know she wanted to keep him on track.

"Always." Peter stressed the word twice more. "I had consensual sex and then strangled the ones that deserved it. Then I cut out their hearts. They didn't use them anyway and it felt good to be a surgeon again. That old thrill came back." There was excitement in his eyes as he remembered his crimes.

Kate shivered. "How many victims, Peter?"

"No," he said, shaking his head. "They aren't victims."

Kate had to bite her tongue to keep from telling him what she thought of that comment. "How many women did you kill?"

"Eight. The cops found them all."

Kate knew that wasn't true. Isa was the ninth victim.

CHAPTER 48

"There were nine women, Peter. You've miscounted."

Peter smirked. "I didn't kill the cop. You have to set the record straight for me. They will talk about what I did in Miami Beach for years, but I don't want to be accused of killing a cop."

Kate wasn't sure she believed him, although his tone indicated he was serious. "Who killed her then?"

"Andre Dale and Harvey Littman."

"You're sure about that?" Kate asked. She had accused Harvey so it didn't come as a surprise, but she needed to be sure.

Peter nodded. "She doesn't fit my pattern. I only picked women who deserved it and she didn't deserve it. She was good at her job. I liked Elise, too. I would have never hurt her."

Kate kept her eyes on him. "I don't understand. There were similarities between the murders."

Peter sighed, his frustration with her obvious. "I told you, Agent Walsh. Andre knew I was killing those women. He told Harvey and they hatched a plan. What better way to bump off the woman investigating their drug ring than to blame it on the serial killer?"

Kate physically pulled back. It explained why there were differences in the murder scenes and why Isa's heart hadn't been removed – neither Harvey nor Andre were surgeons. It also explained why Peter's DNA wasn't anywhere at the scene. What Kate couldn't make sense of was how it all came about.

"How did you find out they killed Isa?"

"I helped set it up." Before Kate could respond, Peter held his hand up to stop her. "I didn't know I was setting it up. I thought they were going to scare her. That's what they said anyway."

Kate could tell he was lying by the way his eyes shifted as he spoke. "That's not true, Peter."

The corners of his lips turned up in a slight smile. "Okay, maybe not. I'm not responsible for other people's actions though. Long story short, Andre made me set her up. He told me he'd expose me as the killer. I didn't know they'd make the crime scene look like my own. It didn't even occur to me that I'd be a suspect in that."

Kate started to cross her legs and then remembered the gun on her ankle. She awkwardly lowered her foot back to the ground and inched back in the seat. Peter noticed but didn't say a word. "I know that you contacted Elise to meet you. How could they know it would be Isa who showed up?"

"They didn't." Peter shifted the gun in his lap and put his hand around it and traced his finger against the trigger.

It was a subtle move but Kate caught it. *Don't make any false moves. Don't do anything stupid.*

"They had me call Elise and ask for a date. Harvey knew how angry his niece would be that she had been taken off the case. He also knew Isa was at her sister's place that night and would be worried for her. He assumed that Isa might take the date to keep investigating without anyone knowing. When I got Isa in my boat and out onto the water, I asked her some questions only Elise would know. She got the answers wrong. That's how I knew Harvey had been right. It was Isa. I took her to the house where Harvey said to take her and told her to go inside that I'd be in soon. Isa fought me on that, but I told her to go and she went. I left after that. I don't even know what happened in that house."

Kate couldn't tell if he was lying. "What about earlier that night? Agent James saw a boat near a home for sale and then it took off again. We've never been able to find who that was. Was it you?"

Peter lowered his head but raised his eyes to her in a way that was akin to a child about to get in trouble. "Guilty," he snickered. "I figured if I killed a woman that night, you'd know for sure I didn't kill the cop. You caught me and that woman lived. Then I called Elise for our date. That's why I'm sitting here now. We have to set the record straight. I didn't kill a cop or my mother. I won't take the blame for things so heinous."

"What now, Peter?" Kate asked, not sure what to say. She was stumped by his moral complexity. She'd never interviewed a killer like him before.

"Would it be inappropriate if I told you how much I want to be on top of you right now?"

Kate kept her expression neutral while her heart thumped in her chest. "Yes, that would be highly inappropriate and that's not happening."

"Can't blame a guy for trying." He shrugged. "I thought you might want to allow me to have a little fun before I kicked off out of here."

"Where are you going?"

Peter picked up the gun and waved it around. "I'm killing myself, Agent Walsh. I'm not suicidal, but I won't make it in prison. Might as well end it here."

Kate knew that was no justice for the victims or their families. "What about Harvey and Andre? We need you to tie them to Isa's murder. We don't have any evidence."

"I'm not testifying and you're not taking me in." Peter shot up from the chair and placed the gun to his head.

Kate remained calm and looked up at him. "You don't want to do this, Peter. If you're serious that you don't want anyone to think you killed a cop or your mother, you have to turn yourself in."

The gun was pressed to his temple and his finger remained steady on the trigger. There was no fear on his face. "I told you I won't make it in prison."

"We'll compromise," Kate said. "You can kill yourself in your cell. Come in and make a formal statement in front of other FBI agents and the local detective and then you can kill yourself in your cell. I won't even try to stop you."

Peter shook his head like Kate wasn't serious. "That won't happen."

"Why? Lots of people kill themselves in prison. Do your good deed and turn in Harvey and Andre and then kill yourself. There's always tomorrow, Peter. You'll have another chance if you're serious about it. Just see how today goes and then decide."

"You can't be serious?" Peter asked in a mocking tone. "This isn't how you're supposed to talk someone out of killing themselves, Agent Walsh. You're terrible at this."

Kate allowed herself to smile at him. "You'd think I was terrible but sometimes you need to put something off to have a little more perspective. Killing yourself is in your back pocket. It's there if you need it. You don't need it today though."

Peter laughed aloud. "Please, never go into psychiatric practice. Never see patients."

He may have said the words and thought she was wrong, but Peter's hand moved slightly away from his head.

Kate pushed harder. "You'll have a chance to set the record straight, Peter. Both about your mother and Isa. Think about it. We might be able to prove that Harvey was at the crime scene, but he can say he got there as you were killing your mother that's why his DNA was there. You're a serial killer after all and he's a mayor. It's a plausible story."

"That isn't how it happened though."

"You and I know that but who else is going to believe it?" Kate stood and Peter backed up. She reached her hand out in a gesture to take his gun. "Come on, Peter. Set the record straight and then kick off out of here as you planned."

Peter began to sway on his feet. He pressed the gun to his head and closed his eyes and then he backed off again. It was obvious Kate's words had gotten to him. Finally, after the longest minute of Kate's life, he lowered the gun and handed it to her. She couldn't believe that he had given up so easily. Peter turned and walked toward the door.

"Wait there, Peter. If you go out there, the snipers will kill you."

Peter stepped back and turned his eyes to her. "You really need me to make a statement?"

"I do, Peter. You deserve to clear your name." Kate spoke to Declan like he was in the room, hoping it was caught on her mic. "We are coming out to the front deck. The suspect is unarmed and in FBI custody. Stand down and do not shoot."

She looked up to Peter. "You ready?"

He nodded and put his hands behind his back for her to cuff him. He turned his head slightly as she secured the cuffs. "I am sorry about your arm. I don't hurt women who don't deserve it and you gave me a fair shake. I had to get away though."

"All in the line of work. I think you're the first to ever apologize." Kate held onto him with her good arm and navigated him to the front of the boat. Peter stood next to her as she opened the front door and sunlight hit them both square in the face making them squint. Kate didn't have a free hand to shield her eyes so she powered through inching them onto the deck.

Off in the distance, the men on the HRT boat stood down but were ready for action if needed. She and Peter got out to the middle of the front deck and then she called for Declan. After she did that, Kate read Peter his rights since he was now formally under arrest. When she was done, she added, "I appreciate you coming in so easily, Peter."

"I just wanted to clear my n..." Peter never got out the last word because gunfire erupted.

As Kate slammed her body down onto the deck and dragged Peter down with her, she saw the HRT guys turning in every direction looking for a shooter. She landed on her arm and screamed out in pain.

"Stay behind me," Peter said, his voice even and strong. He wriggled his body so he was directly in front of her. "I don't understand why they are shooting."

"It's not the cops!" Kate yelled even though he was right next to her.

Kate remained wedged against the houseboat with Peter in front of her like a human shield. She thought it was done and moved her feet to try to stand, but the volley of shots rang out again and then more. The first shots had missed but the second hit their mark. Peter's body jerked back against her own and he cried out.

Kate squeezed her eyes shut and prayed for reinforcements. The gunfire stopped.

"Kate! Kate!" Declan yelled suddenly standing above her. "Are you hit?"

Kate couldn't even roll onto her back because there wasn't enough room. She was wedged in between Peter and the houseboat. "I'm not hit. Check on Peter."

Declan shook his head. "He's dead, Kate. Come on, let me help you." He reached down and helped her up to her feet. Once she was standing, she looked down at Peter's lifeless body. He had been shot in the head and chest. Blood had pooled all around them. It was only then Kate realized how much of Peter's blood she had on herself. It covered her arm and sling and the front of her clothing.

Kate blinked rapidly trying to make sense of it. "Who shot at us? I told everyone to stand down!"

"It wasn't us. HRT took the guy out as soon as he started firing." Declan pointed out into the bay. The HRT boat idled near a smaller speedboat. Declan radioed in and asked what was going on.

Through Declan's radio, she heard, "One shooter. Came out of nowhere before we could stop him. We are searching for identification now." The radio clicked off and Kate stood there watching them, feeling a mix of emotions she couldn't identify.

Static came through the radio and then a name. "Andre Dale."

Kate gasped and tugged on Declan's arm. "How? How did he know?"

"Ted texted me while you were with Peter. Harvey Littman's attorney dragged him out of there. The chief of police wouldn't let Ted make an arrest. Seemed like Harvey had enough time to tell Andre. I don't understand why he'd shoot Peter or how he knew where we were."

"He was protecting himself. Peter knew too much." Even though Kate assumed Declan had heard what Peter said through the audio, she recounted everything that he had told her including all the details about the murder of Peter's mother and Isa Navarro. There was only one explanation about how Harvey and Andre would know where to find Peter now. She told Declan.

Declan let out a string of curses and then reached his arm around Kate. "Let's get you out of here. You have blood on your face and in your hair. We are going to need to debrief."

Kate let herself be led from the front deck, but she turned her head slightly before they walked up the side of the houseboat. Kate looked down at Peter's body. His crimes were heinous and he deserved whatever justice he got, but Kate had never met a killer who had wanted to protect her. She'd be unpacking the confusing swirl of emotions she felt for a long time.

CHAPTER 49

Kate leaned her head back on the lounge chair to let the sun shine on her face. She dug her bare feet into the sand and smiled. Yesterday, after they left the scene, they had gone back to the hotel so Kate could shower and change her clothes, and then they met Ted back at the police station. He had apologized profusely for letting Harvey go. Kate knew there was nothing he could have done. The order came down from the chief. Their beef was with him.

After meeting with Ted, Kate and Declan met with the chief of police. They had spoken to Spade that morning about everything that had transpired. He promised he'd handle things. Before Kate and Declan even sat down across from the chief's desk, he had taken off his badge and gun and had it on the desk. He resigned right then and there. After that, there wasn't much conversation to be had. He had protected the mayor and Andre for far too long. It was how Andre knew where to find Peter. The chief could have gotten her killed. There might be pending charges against him, but it wasn't for Kate to worry about now.

With Peter and Andre dead, there was only one arrest to be made. Ted arrested Mayor Harvey Littman and then the Miami-Dade PD and the FBI held a joint press conference to inform the public about what had transpired and the charges brought against the mayor. Harvey would be the only one to stand trial. The prosecutor was convinced he could make a solid case.

The work Isa had done was more than enough evidence against her uncle. She had paid for good detective work with her life. Ted assured them that she would be remembered and honored by the police force. Kate had no doubt, but it was still hard to speak about it. She was sure that it would be that way for some time. It was the same with Peter's death.

It was easier for Kate to think about killers as inherently bad or evil. It made her job easier. The good guys against the bad. When she came across a killer who had what she considered redeeming qualities, it made her step back and forced her to reevaluate. But that was the last thing she wanted to do right now with her toes in the sand and the sun on her face.

Before leaving Boston, Declan had convinced her to pack her bathing suit. She had told him they were on a case and not going on vacation. Turns out, they had a little time for sun and fun. Spade encouraged them to take some downtime and to enjoy each other's company.

It was such an odd request that they both shared a look while on the call. It turned out that Spade had assigned them their next case already. This time, they were being sent to Los Angeles undercover to infiltrate a cult that was suspected of all sorts of nefarious activity. They'd pose as a couple. Declan had winked at her while Kate groaned.

The only upside was they had the hotel on the FBI's dime and a few days of peace, sun, and fun in front of them. Soon enough, they'd be wheels up and on to the next case. Not today though.

Declan had on red and blue checkered swim trunks that hugged his muscular thighs. They hadn't been in the sun for more than two hours and already his skin had tanned, which frustrated Kate. All she did was burn and freckle.

"There's Italian someplace on my mother's side," he said glancing over at her and reading her thoughts. "Sexy, right?"

Kate laughed, but she could see how women found him so attractive. His muscles glistened in the sun and his devilish grin would make women fall for him time after time. He never looked like he combed his hair and his wild dark waves framed his head perfectly. He hadn't even started to gray yet but when he did, Kate was sure he'd be even sexier to most women.

"What's that look?" he teased.

"I was just thinking about how you'll be sexy when you're fifty."

He rubbed his abs. "You'll want me then, and I won't let you have me for turning me down all these years." Declan pulled down his sunglasses and homed in on her. "How's the arm? How's your brain?"

Kate sighed. "Arm is fine. You did a good job of covering it so I can go in the water. It stopped hurting already. Brain is as good as it's going to get. This though," she said, pointing at the ocean and beach around them, "is the perfect spot to process." Kate started to ask him about the upcoming case, but he shushed her.

Declan held his beer up and with his other hand pointed to the fruity concoction he had grabbed for her from the hotel bar. "We are not talking about the next case. You are going to drink that and then another and we are going to relax and not think about work for a few days. In a few minutes, you're going into the ocean with me even if I have to pick you up from that chair and throw you over my shoulder. Tonight, we are having a spectacular dinner and then I might even take you dancing. That's all I'm thinking about...and that tiny bikini hugging you perfectly."

Declan took a generous swig of beer and then turned his head to smile at her. "You've always been a tease, Katie."

Kate relaxed back into the chair, kicked her toned legs out in front of her and picked up her drink. She smiled into it as she took a sip.

"I aim to please. Never tease," she giggled. Declan was right, she was just going to enjoy the moment for once and not let her brain plot and plan. He was always just what she needed.

About the Author

Stacy M. Jones was born and raised in Troy, New York, and currently lives in Little Rock, Arkansas. She is a full-time writer and holds masters' degrees in journalism and in forensic psychology. She currently has three series available for readers: paranormal women's fiction/cozy Harper & Hattie Magical Mystery Series, the hard-boiled PI Riley Sullivan Mystery Series and the FBI Agent Kate Walsh Thriller Series. To access Stacy's Mystery Readers Club with three free novellas, one for each series, visit StacyMJones.com.

You can connect with me on:
- http://www.stacymjones.com
- https://twitter.com/SMJonesWriter
- https://www.facebook.com/StacyMJonesWriter
- https://www.bookbub.com/profile/stacy-m-jones
- https://www.goodreads.com/StacyMJonesWriter

Subscribe to my newsletter:

✉ http://www.stacymjones.com

Also by Stacy M. Jones

Watch for FBI Agent Kate Walsh Thriller Series Book #3
   MAD JACK - Early 2022

Access the Free Mystery Readers' Club Starter Library
   Riley Sullivan Mystery Series novella "The 1922 Club Murder"
   FBI Agent Kate Walsh Thriller Series novella "The Curators"
   Harper & Hattie Mystery Series novella "Harper's Folly"

Sign up for the starter library along with launch-day pricing, special behind-the-scenes access, and extra content not available anywhere else. Hit subscribe at
   http://www.stacymjones.com/

Please leave a review for Miami Ripper. Reviews help more readers find my books. Thank you!

Have you read them all?

FBI Agent Kate Walsh Thriller Series
   The Curators
   The Founders

Riley Sullivan Mystery Series
   The 1922 Club Murder
   Deadly Sins
   The Bone Harvest
   Missing Time Murders
   We Last Saw Jane

Boston Underground

Harper & Hattie Magical Mystery Series
Harper's Folly
Saints & Sinners Ball
Secrets to Tell
Rule of Three
The Forever Curse
The Witches Code

Made in the USA
Monee, IL
08 November 2021